BETRAYAL

Martina Cole's 22 bestsellers (so far) – in order of publication. All available from Headline.

Dangerous Lady (1992)
The Ladykiller: DI Kate Burrows 1 (1993)
Goodnight Lady (1994)
The Jump (1995)
The Runaway (1997)
Two Women (1999)
Broken: DI Kate Burrows 2 (2000)
Faceless (2001)*
Maura's Game: Dangerous Lady 2 (2002)*
The Know (2003)*
The Graft (2004)*
The Take (2005)*
Close (2006)*
Faces (2007)*
The Business (2008)*
Hard Girls: DI Kate Burrows 3 (2009)*
The Family (2010)*
The Faithless (2011)*
The Life (2012)*
Revenge (2013)*
The Good Life (2014)*
Get Even (2015)

On Screen:
Dangerous Lady (ITV 1995)
The Jump (ITV 1998)
Martina Cole's Lady Killers (ITV3 documentary 2003)
The Take (Sky 1 2009)
Martina Cole's Girl Gangs (Sky Factual documentary 2009)
The Runaway (Sky 1 2011)

*Martina Cole's No. 1 bestsellers – at time of press she has spent more weeks at No. 1 than any other author

BETRAYAL
MARTINA
COLE

HEADLINE

HEADLINE PUBLISHING GROUP
An Hachette UK Company
Carmelite House
50 Victoria Embankment
London
EC4Y 0DZ

www.headline.co.uk
www.hachette.co.uk

For Freddie Mary and Lewis Clark
Still my kahuna burgers, even all growed up!

And for Debbie in the Karakum shop!
You're a lifesaver!

BETRAYAL

Book One

Behold my mother and my brethren!

Matthew 12:49

When lovely woman stoops to folly
And finds too late that men betray,
What charm can soothe her melancholy,
What art can wash her guilt away?

The Vicar of Wakefield,
Oliver Goldsmith (1728–74)

Chapter One

1981

Reeva O'Hara's voice was loud and harsh as it always was when she had what she considered to be an audience. Even at 8.15 a.m. in her local Co-op, Reeva never failed to entertain. Her saving grace was she could be very funny when the fancy took her.

'So I said, "Go and find your fucking fathers and get some sweet money off *them*!"' She screeched with laughter at her own wit and a few of the other mothers in the busy shop joined in.

Reeva's ever-present cigarette was dangling from her red-stained lips and her distended belly told anyone who cared to look that she was nearly on her time.

Jack Walters, the manager of the Co-op, liked Reeva. She wasn't a bad girl really – she had just been badly used in her time by the many men she seemed to attract. She attracted *him*. She was a good-looking young woman with a warm and generous personality and clearly a healthy attitude towards sex – unlike his wife, Doris, who thought it should take place in the pitch dark and as fast as humanly possible. Jack kept that gem of wisdom to himself though; Doris was as narrow-minded as she was skinny. It was like shagging a skeleton.

3

Doris Walters was looking at Reeva with barely disguised contempt. Reeva was everything she thought was wrong with the modern world.

'Can I help you, Reeva?' Doris's voice said it all and no one was in any doubt that Reeva understood the tone completely.

Reeva smiled a big encompassing smile that completely transformed her face and said loudly, 'Whatever happened to service with a smile? You've got a boatrace on you that could stop a fucking clock!' Reeva leaned forwards as if they were alone before she bellowed, 'Caught him with his cock out again, have you?'

Jack Walters closed his eyes in distress as the shop erupted into gales of good-natured laughter.

'Don't worry, Doris, it happens to the best of us, mate!' someone shouted from the queue behind.

Doris looked at the young woman who she loathed with all her being. Hearing the laughter around her, she turned and walked into the back of the shop, as Reeva screamed out once more, 'I'll take that as a yes, then, shall I!'

She turned to Jack Walters and said kindly, mimicking his wife's voice, 'One will have ten No. 10, my good man!'

The laughter started up again. Jack served her silently, but everyone could see that he was trying hard not to laugh with her.

That was Reeva O'Hara; she was like Marmite – you either loved or hated her.

Chapter Two

Doris Walters felt sick with humiliation. Trust the whore to bring *that* up in front of the other customers.

Her eyes were burning with unshed tears. She had to swallow the urge to go back out front, pick up a piece of wood and fell that painted trollop to the floor. That's exactly what she was with all those bloody kids! All different colours, all with different fathers! Yet Reeva O'Hara walked around like she was *someone*. Hair done, make-up on, attracting attention – Doris saw her own husband looking at her – even though she was ready to drop another bastard on the Welfare State.

But that was it these days: have kids and let everyone else pay for them – honest, hard-working people like herself. They got a council house and furniture provided. It was disgraceful the way these young girls carried on. Whereas people like Doris, who had finished her education, worked, and done it right, were left childless, having to watch as the Reevas of the world dropped chavvies like it was nothing. Which it was to her, obviously. What was this one? Doris screwed up her eyes in concentration for a few seconds. It would be Reeva's fifth child in twelve years. She had had the first one when she was fourteen years old! Brazen as you like, she'd been – belly on display like she had done something good. She had given birth to four handsome sons, one after the other – and even Doris had to admit in her more charitable moments they were always clean and well turned out. They were polite too which was amazing considering what they had to listen to on a daily basis; that girl had a mouth like a city docker.

Doris Walters's jealousy knew no bounds when it came to Reeva O'Hara. She was everything Doris loathed, and Reeva O'Hara had everything Doris wanted: good looks, an open personality, and the ability to produce children even after a one-night stand.

Chapter Three

Aiden O'Hara was watching his mother as she doled out sweets to her boys. She was as mad as a box of frogs but she did her best for them – he knew that better than anyone, and he loved her. She embarrassed him at times with the way she carried on, although he knew that it was her way of coping with the world – with her life, in fact. She was a very loving, caring person and, as Aiden saw it, people took advantage of her because of that. He swore that once he was older he would take proper care of her, and look out for her – especially where men were concerned. As young as he was, he saw a lot more than he let on, but he could only do so much until such time as he grew up. For now, he helped her out in any way he could and he looked out for his brothers too.

He was aware they made a strange-looking family – a mixture of different colours and heritages – but they were still that: a family. His mum made sure of it. Father Hagen had once described her as 'a kind and generous soul' and, even at twelve, Aiden knew exactly what that meant in street parlance!

She seemed to attract wrong 'uns, as his nan would put it, but she had a spark about her that made people want to be near her. Her kids adored her, and a lot of the women on their street admired her – as much for her stance in keeping her numerous children as because she was clean as anything.

He rounded up his brothers and they kissed Reeva before he shepherded them towards school and another day of drudgery.

Reeva watched her three eldest go. Then, taking her youngest son by the hand, she said with a big smile, 'Shall we have a cup of tea and a bun in the café? Be a lovely treat, won't it?'

Porrick grinned happily; he loved being the youngest because he had his mum to himself all day and that was paradise to him.

Chapter Four

Eugene O'Hara, at seven, was already big for his age. His skin was deep black, his eyes were blue and he wore his hair long. He was a quiet lad, but not shy as such.

His teacher, a tall, heavily built woman from Trinidad called Mrs Bonasara, loved him – and she knew that he would have his own crosses to bear as he grew older.

Eugene always sat with Caroline Alba, a tiny, elf-like child with wide, blue eyes and long, blond hair. They were rarely apart but they made for strange bedfellows – not least because Caroline's father was a dyed-in-the-wool skinhead and racist.

Mrs Bonasara could see the two of them talking to Peter Jones, a tall lad who was already overweight, with the makings of a fine bully. From his prominent eyes to his small, mean mouth he looked exactly like what he was – and his teacher had a feeling he would fulfil this early promise by becoming a vicious and uncompromising man if he wasn't curbed soon. None of the other children liked him, and that appeared to suit him down to the ground. Peter was a born loner.

Mrs Bonasara sighed with sadness. If only parents really took an interest in their children now and again, how much hurt and sadness could be avoided. She could see Peter saying things to little Caroline and she quietly made her way round the classroom so she could hear what was being said – whatever it was was obviously distressing the poor child. She sighed heavily once more when she heard a whispered, 'Nigger lover'. No doubt one of Peter's family's favourite expressions, seeing as he used it at every available opportunity, but before she could open her mouth to reprimand the lad, Eugene O'Hara, who had also heard the quip, was already launching himself at the much bigger boy.

The noise was loud and frightening to the majority of the children in the classroom. Mrs Bonasara had to use all her considerable strength to part the two boys and it did not surprise her that the one she really had to keep hold of was Eugene O'Hara. She could see the shock and fear on Peter Jones's face and, against her principles, she felt a small feeling of satisfaction at seeing the bully for once the frightened party.

Mrs Bonasara was holding Eugene against her with great difficulty, so she was relieved beyond measure when Father Hagen burst into the room and took over from her.

Father Hagen was a huge Irishman with a penchant for Irish whiskey and the Bible – in that order. The fact that he was a dedicated teacher saved him from being outed on a regular basis – that and because the children liked him. Without his black clothes and his white collar, he could have passed for a boxer – or a tramp, depending on who was looking at him. But he had a natural affinity with children and he could often get the best out of them.

Mrs Bonasara explained the problem and Peter Jones looked up fearfully at the huge priest who, with a well-timed scowl, could put the fear of Christ up even the older boys.

Father Hagen looked at young Eugene O'Hara and felt a deep sadness. This child had more than his share of burdens and he was a good kid, intelligent and nice natured – it would have taken a lot to make him lose his temper. Although, as with all the O'Hara boys, it was a sight to see when he erupted.

He marched the two offenders from the classroom, aware that it was deathly quiet now. He could feel both boys trembling as he pulled them unceremoniously along to the headmistress's room. One was shaking from anger and the other from fear. And, just like Mrs Bonasara, he thought it would do Peter Jones good to get a taste of his own medicine.

Chapter Five

Peter Jones had experienced one of the worst days of his life. Not only had he been beaten in a fight, but also his mother and father had been called from work and home respectively and told that he was on his last warning. Racist language and violence would not be tolerated and, on top of that, his mother and father had been subjected to a ten-minute screaming match from Reeva O'Hara that had been heard all over the neighbourhood. Reeva, as usual, was the victor – she could whisper and you would hear her in Silvertown.

He was feeling depressed and frightened of what awaited him at home. His dad was a dope dealer who sat in their council flat all day with his cronies, drinking beer and selling drugs. His mum, in contrast, worked in a factory in Romford and, from her daily complaints, it seemed she worked fucking hard. It was a difficult household to relax in, and he hated both his parents for different reasons. That was why he was in no rush to get home.

The pillowcase filled with baked bean tins hit him full in the face and he dropped to the ground. When he looked up and saw Aiden O'Hara, his heart sank right down to his scruffy, unpolished shoes, but it was when he felt the liquid being poured on him that he really began to get frightened. He couldn't move, he was paralysed with fear. And when Aiden lit a match and threw it at him, he felt panic and tears erupt amidst Aiden's laughter.

'It's water, you fucking plank! But next time it will be petrol.'

He was punched hard in the head, and Aiden's voice was serious as he threatened quietly, 'You ever touch my brother again and I *will* fucking harm you, do you hear me?'

Aiden left the big fat lump crying bitter tears and he made his way home happy as a sandboy.

Chapter Six

Reeva was over her upset about Eugene; she was a realist and thought it was best to leave it – it would sort itself out naturally.

She was cooking them a big tea – she liked to cook and her children were always given a decent meal in the evening. Tonight she had made them a family favourite: shepherd's pie with cheesy mash on top and fresh cabbage. The smell was appetising, and she had no doubt they would all want second helpings.

After they had washed their hands and faces, she surveyed her sons as they sat quietly at the table waiting for her to serve them their meal. She felt a sudden rush of love for them – they were so alike yet so different.

The baby kicked and she absent-mindedly rubbed at her belly for a few seconds before she dished up. She watched her Eugene, who was really a sensitive soul, eating his food slowly and quietly. He broke her heart sometimes. Unlike her Patsy – who'd inherited his handsome Jamaican father's looks – her Eugene, bless his heart, looked more African than the Nigerian bastard who had left one morning with her purse and her heart. She had really loved him for some reason, but then she had loved each of their respective fathers in her own way. She had a great capacity for love or – perhaps more to the point – sex.

But she feared that out of all her kids, Eugene would be the one to suffer the most because he wasn't just dark, he was black as night and as handsome as the fucker who had swept her off her feet one winter's night in the Beehive in Brixton. He had looked like an African prince, and tried to bullshit her he was one. He was studying medicine and they had enjoyed that winter together. Then he had disappeared, leaving her with her two kids, another on the way and without a penny to cross herself with. *That* had been what really hurt her.

She shrugged and pulled herself together; she had learned early on in her life that regrets were pointless. They just depressed you and, whatever else she might have regretted, her boys were never included. They were her life's blood and without them she would go mad. As she ate her own food, she looked happily at the pile of ironing she had done that day and, as the smell of the apple pie she had made wafted out of the oven, she smiled in contentment. Whatever else she might want in her life, the mainstay of her existence was in this kitchen with her.

She finished her food and rolled herself a joint; she allowed herself a little puff in the evening – it mellowed her out and relaxed her. And after today she needed it.

Two hours later, the boys were bathed and in their pyjamas, and the kitchen was once more as clean and neat as a new pin.

She put the youngest two to bed and allowed Aiden and Patsy to stay up to watch TV with her for a while, snuggled up on the sofa. That was when her waters broke – and she knew that the latest addition to her family was finally on its way.

She sat up quickly and told Aiden to first get himself next door and let Mrs Obana know that she was on her time, and then run around to his nan's and tell her the same thing. He rushed to do her bidding.

Then, telling Patsy to go up and keep an eye on his younger brothers, she hauled herself up off the sofa and went into the kitchen. She knew that Vera Obana loved her cup of tea, and she smiled as she popped the kettle on.

Vera, a tall, thin woman, with fine, blond hair, was married to a guy from Guyana and they made a lovely couple. Vera had been a midwife by trade, and she was always called in whenever Reeva was on her time. Reeva prided herself on having given birth to all her boys at home with the minimum of fuss.

While she boiled the kettle, she rolled herself another joint; she would need it once the pains really started. Reeva didn't like hospitals – they scared her and she felt that a healthy young woman like herself shouldn't need to go there unless it was absolutely imperative.

Up until now, giving birth had been like shelling peas so she wasn't too perturbed about the coming labour; in fact, she welcomed it. She was dying to have this baby. She hated the last few weeks – they dragged and she always felt tired and fat. She loved babies. They were helpless and they depended on you for everything – it was the only time she ever felt wanted in her life. Each of her children had made her feel important, made her feel she had some kind of purpose. And they made her feel complete – as if she had finally got something right in the chaos that was her life.

She liked Vera and the way she kept so cool and calm. She would always chat to her in a friendly way about nothing and then, before she knew it, the child would be lying on her belly, and that would be that.

Twenty minutes later, her mum had arrived and was taking charge over the household. Reeva finally relaxed. Annie O'Hara's voice was soothing and, as Reeva lay in her large double bed, on a pile of newspapers, she allowed herself a little smile.

'I'll slap the fuck out of you lot if I hear one more word!'

Yes, her mum was here, and she could hear her sons laughing at their grandmother as she scolded them. The trouble with Annie was her bark was always much worse than her bite and the boys knew that, just as Reeva had always known it.

Vera laughed gently and said quietly, 'She's loud, but they know she's all talk.'

Chapter Seven

It was after one in the morning and Aiden was worried. There was an air of tension in the house that he had never experienced before, and that frightened him more than he cared to admit. Even his nan had gone quiet and that was a first in itself.

Vera had phoned for an ambulance, and that meant something was going wrong. He swallowed with difficulty.

He had popped his head around the door and seen his mum lying there white as a sheet, with her eyes closed with exhaustion. He had also seen the blood everywhere that Vera was trying so desperately to stop.

There was a situation here all right and he was getting more and more frightened by the minute. It occurred to him that if anything happened to his mother they were on their own – he knew his nan could not cope with all of them. She had trouble finding her way to Bingo; she would never manage four boisterous lads. For the first time in his life he was experiencing real terror. He didn't like the feeling one bit. He wanted to cry, but he knew he couldn't, otherwise it would alert his little brothers to the seriousness of the situation. He had to be strong for all of them.

When the ambulance finally arrived, he breathed a sigh of relief and, despite the protests from the adults, he insisted on going to the hospital with his mum. He was scared to leave her side, in case something happened when he wasn't there. He sat in the ambulance with her, holding her hand and willing her to regain consciousness. She looked so white and so vulnerable lying there with that huge belly and the black rings under her eyes, he had to swallow down the tears once more.

Suddenly all hell let loose, and he was pushed out of the way roughly as the ambulance men rushed to perform CPR. He found himself praying as he watched his mother finally open her eyes and look into his. She smiled at him, and he threw himself at her, holding on to her tightly, the tears flowing now and the fear subsiding in his chest.

Ten minutes later, his little sister came into the world in all her brutal glory and he watched, fascinated, as she was cleaned up and placed in his mother's arms. His mum was crying with happiness. That was the secret strength of women – even at his young age he knew a man, no matter how hard he might be, could not give birth and then smile like nothing had happened.

His mum motioned for him to come over to her and he sat beside her, looking in awe at the new baby she had produced amidst so much drama.

The ambulance man ruffled his hair and said kindly, 'Little sister for you, mate. You make sure you look after her – you're the big brother, don't forget.' Then he said to Reeva jovially, 'Picked her time, all right! Thought we lost you there for a minute!'

Reeva smiled tiredly as she answered him, 'Take a bit more than having a baby to finish me off! Tough as old boots, me.'

'Bleeding has subsided anyway, but my guess is you will need a blood transfusion before they let you go home. You'll need a few stitches as well. But, all in all, I think you had a result.'

Reeva looked down at her new daughter and said gently, 'Oh, Aiden, my son, might have known it was a girl, eh? All that fucking drama!'

'Takes after you, Mum!'

Even the ambulance men laughed at that quip.

'Do you want to choose a name, son?'

He nodded, suddenly shy. Then, looking down at the wrinkled red face of his new sister, he said seriously, 'She looks like Sister Agnes at school! All screwed up and miserable.'

Reeva laughed gaily and said, 'Agnes is it then! Agnes Marianne O'Hara. That's got a ring to it, I reckon.'

She placed his sister into his arms, laid back and closed her eyes; this was the first time she had experienced problems while giving birth and she had to admit it had scared her. She made up her mind there and then that this little lady would be her last one. She had five kids and she was still only twenty-six years old – even she knew when enough was enough. No matter what her neighbours might think about her, she wasn't as silly as they believed.

She watched as her eldest son nursed his new sister and she felt content. Whatever happened in her life from now on, she had her kids and that was all she really cared about at the end of the day. They were the real constant in her life, and she was sensible enough to know that they were the only people who would ever really love her.

And Reeva needed love so very much.

Chapter Eight

Aiden looked down at the tiny scrap of humanity that was his sister, and he felt a surge of love so strong that it frightened him. He loved his family, especially his mum, but this new sister – his only sister – had affected him like none of the others. She was beautiful for a start, with dark silky eyelashes and piercing blue eyes. But he felt she was also like his own child in so many ways.

She would depend on him, like his mother did, and she was his blood. That was so important to him – though he couldn't put it into words, of course. This little girl was without anyone to really take care of her properly. His mum was a flake; she did her best but God Himself knew she was liable to just give up at any given moment and follow her own star.

The arrival of little Agnes had affected him deeply, and he vowed to make sure she had the best that life could offer. He knew that as a female she would not get her due, but he would make sure she got whatever she needed, no matter what. Family was everything and, as the head of the O'Haras, Aiden was going to make it his life's work to see them all right.

Reeva watched as her eldest son kissed his sister. She felt happy but at the same time uneasy. Aiden sometimes took his responsibilities a bit too seriously but, as her mum was always pointing out, it was a good job someone did.

Oh, her mum knew her so fucking well.

Chapter Nine

1984

'For fuck's sake, Mum! He is a piece of shit!'

Reeva sighed dramatically as she listened to her eldest son rant about her latest lover. He was such a fucking prude in so many ways.

'But, Aiden, he is *my* piece of shit and I love him.'

And that she did. She loved him very much. She just couldn't see herself from her son's point of view, see how the situation looked to the outside world, and especially to her children.

'He treats you like a cunt, Mum.'

Her son might be telling the truth, but Reeva could not give up her new man. Tony Brown was everything she had ever wanted. He was big and black and he was handsome, and he told her he loved her – something she needed to hear. He fucked her properly and that was everything to her. She was a very sensual woman who mistook sex for love – she always had. Reeva was the fuck of the century but, other than that, she meant nothing to her paramours. They knew it even if she didn't.

Her eldest son had sussed that out many years before and he knew exactly what was on the cards for her. He had lived it all his young life.

It was three o'clock in the morning and Tony Brown was trying to kick their front door in. It was the kind of drama Reeva revelled in, determined to cause a big upset because the man she thought she loved was not giving her what she wanted. Aiden had been here with her time and time again.

They both heard the splintering of the wooden architrave as the door was finally kicked into the small hallway. Rolling his eyes in annoyance, Aiden walked out into the hallway to try and head Tony off at the pass, though he didn't hold out much hope.

'Do you know what she's fucking gone and done, Ade? The fucking vicious whore!'

Aiden stood stoically in the irate man's path to try and deflect his anger. Reeva was half-drunk and, on top of the Valium she popped like sweets, she could not see for the life of her how inappropriate this entire scene was. The only thing on her mind was that she wanted Tony but he didn't want *her* any more. In Reeva's world that meant you fought back with any ammunition you had: in this case going around to Tony's home and spilling the beans to his wife of ten years.

Aiden stood his ground and Tony Brown, drunk and stoned as he was, realised that, whatever Reeva might have done, her kids should not be witnessing this scene. He looked at the children standing on the stairs, especially the little girl, her eyes wide like flying saucers in her head. She was visibly trembling. Feeling the anger leave him, he said to Aiden quietly, 'I'm sorry about this, Aiden, mate. But your mother caused me untold fucking aggravation today . . .'

Aiden had it in his heart to try and understand the man's reaction. When his mother was hurt, she lashed out. And when she lashed out she went for it, big time, no half measures for her.

23

Agnes ran to her mother and grabbed at her legs, clearly frightened by the tension in the house. Reeva picked her up and then said loudly, 'Go on then. Fuck off back to your ugly wife and kids! You were a useless shag, anyway. My Eugene's got a bigger one than you . . .'

Aiden closed his eyes in distress as he knew that a man like Tony Brown was not going to take *that* lying down. The whole street was aware of the altercation and was listening to what was commonly called the 'O'Hara Cabaret'. This was not a one-off – this was how all Reeva's relationships ended. That's if the man in question didn't just disappear into the night, of course. The more cowardly ones tended to do that when Reeva got too hot to handle.

'Coming from someone who's had more men than she can fucking count, it's a wonder you can feel anything down there. It's like the Blackwall Tunnel!'

Aiden sensed this was on the verge of deteriorating once more into a slanging match so he walked purposefully towards Tony Brown and nudged him over to the broken doorway.

Tony looked down at the boy and felt shame envelop him. Aiden was a good kid and he didn't deserve the shit Reeva seemed to revel in. He held his hands out in a gesture of supplication and said sadly, 'I'll get the door sorted in the morning, OK?'

Aiden smiled ruefully. 'Appreciate it, Tony. Now, you get yourself off. This lot have got school tomorrow.'

Tony made his walk of shame past the neighbours, who were all trying to get a glimpse of the action, and cursed himself for his escapade. But that woman could make a saint swear! Now he had to go home and face his wife – and try and repair the damage as best he could.

Reeva watched him go, holding her daughter tightly to her and crying into the girl's thick hair. The action made Agnes start to whimper. After attempting to put the front door back as best he could, Aiden took his sister and, giving her to Patsy, he walked his mum into the kitchen. Then, settling her on a chair, he lit her a cigarette and poured her out a large vodka and Coke.

Reeva watched her son as he ministered to her and she felt the tears come faster. *This* was the only man she had ever been able to depend on – her Aiden. Her boys were all so good to her. Patsy, bless him, had put the others back to bed and now there was a semblance of normality in the household once more.

Lighting himself a cigarette, Aiden put the kettle on to make tea. 'This has got to stop, you know, Mum. You frightened Agnes tonight and, as big a bastard as Tony Brown is, you shouldn't have grassed him up to his old woman.'

Reeva wiped her eyes with the back of her hands and said sadly, 'Why does this always happen to me, Ade?'

He was pouring out the tea as she spoke and he felt a constriction around his heart at the utter despair in her voice. She knew the answer to that question as well as he did, but he answered her anyway. Bringing the teas to the table he sat down beside her and, grabbing her hand in his, he said truthfully, 'You always go for the wrong ones, Mum. You meet them and they move in within days. Then the fighting starts. You should have a rest from blokes for a while and wait for one who is right for you.'

Reeva smiled through her tears at her earnest son who was genuinely trying to give her advice. There were only fourteen years between the two of them, and that was never more evident than when they sat chatting like this. He was always trying to pick up the pieces of her life.

'I tell you something, Mum. When I get married it will be to the right person, I know that much.'

Reeva smiled to herself. Even at fifteen he sounded so wise. Much wiser than her.

Hearing Agnes begin to cry her head off, Aiden picked up his tea, kissed his mum on the cheek and hugged her for a few seconds. 'I'll bring her in with me and Patsy tonight, tell her a story.' As he walked into the hallway he said over his shoulder, 'And don't you go out anywhere, OK? Get yourself off to bed and forget about that bastard.'

Reeva didn't bother to answer him.

Chapter Ten

Frank James liked Aiden O'Hara. In fact, he liked all the O'Hara children, even though they were the bane of his life. He even liked the mother, Reeva, although he despaired at her lifestyle. But Aiden was a clever lad and he deserved the opportunity to go on to better things in life.

As he approached the O'Hara household, Frank was not even remotely surprised to see a workman reattaching the front door and repairing the architrave around it. It wasn't the first time. He walked into the house, calling out Reeva's name, and he heard a scrambling in the bedroom – and whispering. In the kitchen, young Agnes was in a lobster-pot playpen watching him with huge solemn eyes. She was another beautiful child; Reeva did have exceptionally handsome children, he'd give her that.

Reeva came down the stairs in a short dressing gown that showed a lot of her long, slender legs, the ever-present cigarette in her hand.

'Oh, Mr James! I wasn't expecting you.'

She was smiling happily at him as she put the kettle on. Frank was quite happy to enjoy the view. She was a very good-looking woman and he appreciated beauty. He noticed that, other than the destroyed doorway, the rest of the house was, as usual, spotlessly clean.

'I just thought I would pop around about Aiden.' He sat down at the kitchen table before saying calmly, 'As we've discussed before, he's a very intelligent boy and I really think he could do well in higher education. University is certainly on the cards if he applies himself.'

Reeva puffed up with pride at the man's words and she smiled at him in a friendly manner.

'He is clever all right, Mr James. Must have inherited the brains from his old man because I'm as thick as shit, as you know.'

Frank closed his eyes. The one thing he would never get used to was the casual use of bad language by the children and the parents.

'But you know my boy – all my boys, in fact. They will go their own roads. I mean, I encourage them. But that's all I can do really.'

He took the proffered mug of tea and thanked her, unable to keep his eyes from her breasts that were still surprisingly firm considering she had given birth to five children. His own wife's had mysteriously disappeared after their one and only daughter – not that there had been much there to start with.

Reeva sat down and crossed her legs in a very dignified manner and Frank felt hot under the collar. She really was a disconcerting woman. She smelled faintly of sex. Sex and freedom – that was the only way he could describe it. She was a sensual being, it was in her DNA. It was who Reeva was. He had noticed that even when she had been at school, and he smiled wryly as he remembered how much trouble she seemed to attract.

'I was wondering, Reeva, if I might talk to him alone and go through some options with him? I would hate for him to fall through the cracks.' He sighed. 'Aiden's fifteen now and he is already becoming hard to handle. He needs to be taken in hand soon. Otherwise it will be too late.'

Reeva could see that the man was deadly earnest and that he had her son's welfare at heart. But she was nothing if not a realist. If her Aiden didn't want to work then no one or nothing would make him.

'Oi, Reeva! The door's finished.'

Reeva stood up and left the kitchen. Frank heard a door open and saw a man clump down the stairs wearing nothing but his boxer shorts, and pay the workman cash in hand. He felt especially embarrassed when Tony Brown walked into the kitchen as if he owned the place and poured himself a cup of tea.

Reeva lit another cigarette as she came back in and made the introductions, finishing with, 'Mr James thinks that Aiden could go far. University, even.'

Tony leaned against the sink and sipped his tea before saying, 'Don't surprise me a bit, Reeva. He's a good lad, bright as a button. Good with numbers, I know that.'

Frank was surprised to find an ally and he leaped on it, saying seriously, 'All Aiden needs is a stable influence, Reeva. He really has the makings of a fine scholar. And his reading is exceptional. He's flown through Hermann Hesse!'

Reeva smiled with pride. 'Well, he is doing the Second World War. In history, like. But wasn't he a war criminal?'

Frank ignored her and ploughed on. 'I've spoken to your social worker and she agrees with me that Aiden needs some extra help. Now, there is a chance – only a chance, I admit – that he can go away to a private school that caters for children like him. Who would offer him a balanced environment and the chance to study without . . .' He looked around him and was suddenly lost for words. He also felt a sudden hostility surround him like electricity. Reeva wasn't smiling any more; she was staring at him with open hatred.

'What? You mean leave me? Leave this house?'

Frank tried to sound jovial as he said, 'Only during term time, Reeva. It's a wonderful opportunity for him, really.'

Reeva lit yet another cigarette and, blowing the smoke into Frank's face, she said harshly, 'Out.'

Frank was nonplussed for a few seconds. That one word had sounded like a declaration of war, which it was to Reeva. The thought of her Aiden being taken away from her was anathema and she said as much. 'You can tell that fucking social worker I will put her through the fucking wall before they take my boy off me. I swear that. Now, come on. *Out.*'

Tony Brown held up his hand and said sternly, 'Hang on a minute, Reeva. I think this would be a good thing for Aiden. And, like Frank said, he will be home for the holidays. It's a good opportunity, especially if it ain't costing you a fucking penny.'

Reeva turned on him. 'Tony, this is fuck-all to do with you, OK? My Aiden ain't going fucking nowhere. No. Fucking. Where. And that is the end of it. Now, if you don't mind, Mr James, I want to get back to bed with my boyfriend before either his wife turns up or the boys get back from school. So, goodbye and no thanks.'

Tony shook his head at Frank sadly, as if to say 'I tried'.

Reeva saw the man out and slammed the door resoundingly behind him. Agnes had watched it all without a murmur. She just stared at them with her big eyes that looked like those of an ancient.

'You're out of order, Reeva. This is a wonderful opportunity for that lad – and he is clever. You should have bitten the man's hand off.'

Reeva shook her head and held back the tears. She knew that Tony was right, but she couldn't cope without Aiden. He paid the bills and sorted the money, he helped her get from one day to the next. He was the brains of the family outfit and without him she would sink without a trace. But how could she explain that to Mr James? How could she justify refusing her son's education because without him, as young as he was, she couldn't even get through a day?

'He is going nowhere, Tony. I couldn't be without any of my kids.'

Tony walked over to her and held her tightly. He had come back last night with his tail between his legs because his wife would not give him houseroom. He knew Reeva would have him. 'You're a good mum, Reeva. But that geezer was offering Aiden a chance to get out of all this.' He gestured around him.

Reeva knew he was absolutely right. But she could not let her boy go.

Chapter Eleven

Aiden looked at his headmaster calmly. He knew only too well what Mr James had witnessed at his home the day before and he was past being embarrassed about it. But, as he listened to Mr James talking of the wonderful opportunity he was being presented with, he almost allowed himself the luxury of getting excited about it. But he knew that he couldn't. The social worker, Marjory Smith, was a nice woman. True, she was scatty as a bag of bollocks, as his mother described it, but her heart was in the right place. He would have loved this chance, but he couldn't take it. Reeva would not last five minutes without him. She blundered from one disaster to the next – it was what she did. She didn't mean to, but in many ways it was as if she was still the kid.

So he shook his head vehemently. 'Why would I want to go somewhere like that? Away from my mum and my brothers and sister?'

Marjory Smith looked at the handsome boy with the high IQ and a mother who, though she loved her children, had no moral compass whatsoever, and she could have cried for the waste of a young life. She guessed that Aiden was frightened to leave his mother to her own devices. Marjory admired him for that but it grieved her to see him give up such an opportunity because his mother couldn't control her sexual urges. Because that is all it amounted to at the end of the day: Reeva O'Hara and her next sexual conquest. They were frequent, they were passionate and they always ended in tears.

'Look, just think it over, Aiden, OK? Here's everything you need to know. Just look it over this weekend and if you change your mind you can call me. But we need to know soon – these places are very few and far between.'

Aiden took the proffered folder and left Mr James and Marjory together, knowing they were despairing of him and his refusal. But what choice did he have? He placed the folder in the nearest bin and went to round up his brothers. Tony Brown looked like he might be on the scene for a while and he wanted to warn them. Fucking Reeva, sometimes she did get on his tits.

Chapter Twelve

Tony had asked Aiden to pop out with him, saying there was a couple of quid in it for him. Aiden agreed to go willingly – he was always up for getting an extra bit of cash. He knew that with Tony it wasn't going to be legal work but that didn't bother him either. He was fifteen and he knew his way around a fucking corner.

As they drove into Essex, Aiden looked out at the passing countryside, enjoying seeing the nice houses and the large gardens. 'I'll have a drum like these one day, Tony.'

Tony laughed. 'I reckon you will, Ade. I assume you know about the school they wanted to send you to?'

Aiden shrugged as if it meant nothing. 'I told them it was bollocks. I couldn't leave Reeva. She needs me.'

Tony Brown felt a terrible urge to stop the car and hug the deeply decent lad sitting next to him. But, of course, he didn't.

'It would have been a good opportunity though. I told your mum to run with it. But she said no.'

Aiden was grateful that Tony had tried on his behalf. It said a lot about the man. Sighing heavily, he said seriously, 'She ain't bad with money, but only if I explain it all to her first, you know? I work out what she needs to pay and what we need for the kids. She's a blinding cook and we eat well. No processed shit in our house. She looks after us like that. But you and I know, Tony, that she is not a woman who should ever be left to her own devices. Without me, the drink and drugs would spiral out of control and she would eventually lose the other kids. But, saying that, I love her and she loves us. We look out for her and for each other.'

Tony Brown had never liked Aiden more. He had been forced to grow up at a young age and he didn't resent Reeva for that, he loved her for keeping them together. Tony hoped to God that Reeva knew how lucky she was – his kids were like fucking leeches in comparison.

'Do me a favour, Tony, will you? Don't break her heart too much. Every bloke that leaves destroys her a little bit more. She ain't a bad person. She's just a girl who needs a lot of love, that's all.'

Tony grinned and said sadly, 'I'll try, mate, but you know what she can be like.'

Aiden laughed. 'You're preaching to the converted, Tony!'

As they pulled into a farmhouse, Aiden looked in awe at the beautiful property that was reached through electronic gates. From the mullion windows to the pristine blue of the pool the house said 'class'.

Tony stopped outside the front door and shut the engine off. 'This is the home of Eric Palmer. He is the biggest drug dealer in the South East and he's looking for a few lads to distribute around London using the train services. There's a good few quid in this if you do it right, and I have a feeling that you'll be shrewd enough to play this opportunity for all its worth. Now, you sure you are up for it?'

Aiden O'Hara smiled gamely. 'Is the Pope a Catholic?'

They laughed together and went into the beautiful house.

Chapter Thirteen

Eric Palmer was a small man with a big voice. He was self-made and a legend in East and South London with the reputation for being a good businessman – fair but hard – and outrageously ruthless. You only ever fucked up once and that was it.

He looked Aiden over and smiled disarmingly, displaying very expensive teeth as he said jovially, 'You're a big lad for fifteen. How's Reeva these days?'

Aiden shook hands with him and said with careful nonchalance, 'She's my mother and she is doing well, thank you.'

The warning was clear and, instead of being insulted at the boy's words, Eric Palmer immediately took a shine to the kid. He had heart and loyalty. Loyalty to his mother showed fucking true grit as far as Eric was concerned. Most men would have disowned that whore sooner rather than later.

'Good on you, son. Remember, wives come and go but you only get one mum.'

Aiden smiled that handsome smile he had and Eric Palmer decided that he liked him. He had something about him – something he could use to his advantage. He offered Aiden a cold bottle of beer and then he took them out to the patio around his swimming pool. As they sat down, Eric could see the boy looking around him in wonderment. He also saw the glint in his eye; this kid could be a grafter. A serious grafter. According to Tony, who wasn't the sharpest knife in the drawer, Aiden was a mathematical genius. And the younger you got them, the better, as far as Eric was concerned. You could mould them into what you needed for different jobs and, if they had the nous, they then went on to bigger and better things. If they couldn't hack it, they were taken out of the game in the early stages of play. That was the way of the world they inhabited.

'So, Aiden, I need a lad to recruit for me a series of other lads who are too young to be nicked for serious crimes. I need product moved all over the Smoke and by public transport. The Filth never really take kids into the equation. I need you to be as silent as a fucking mute and, if by some extraordinary chance you *do* get a capture, you keep your trap shut no matter what the Filth might threaten you with. Because what they threaten you with will be nothing compared with what I will fucking do to you, OK?'

Aiden shrugged and said intently, 'I'll keep my mouth shut, Mr Palmer, as long as you make sure my mum gets a decent wedge every week.'

Eric looked at Tony and the two men began to laugh their heads off. 'Oh, Tony, I think this kid will do.'

Aiden took a pull on his beer and then joined in the laughter. He was going to university all right, the University of Life. He wondered where this would take him and he hoped it would be somewhere he wanted to be.

In the car on the way back into London, Tony said seriously, 'You did well there, kid. You could really bring in a good wedge, you know.'

Aiden nodded and said quietly, 'Don't worry, I intend to.'

Chapter Fourteen

1988

'For fuck's sake, Mum, why do you get this drunk?'

Aiden was annoyed. He had a lot going on tonight and the last thing he needed was to have to sort her out and any problems that she might have incurred during a whole day on the piss. At least Reeva was maudlin – that always was a good sign. It meant that she was on the verge of sleeping it off.

Patsy O'Hara rolled his eyes to the ceiling. Personally, he had had her up to the back teeth seeing as how he was the one who'd had to remove her from the working men's club. 'Honestly, Ade, you should have heard her! Fucking right embarrassing it was.'

Aiden felt for his brother but he still couldn't allow him to be disrespectful to their mother. 'Well, she's had a lot on lately and you know she can't cope with aggravation.'

Patsy sighed in annoyance. 'Pity she has to keep causing it then, ain't it?'

Aiden didn't bother to answer him. They had all felt it at some point – it was what Reeva did to people. They loved and loathed her at the same time. But Aiden, being the eldest, felt he had a duty to take care not only of his mother but his entire family, especially his little sister.

Reeva was trying catch the drift of the conversation but it was beyond her. She had been drinking since 10 a.m. and everything and everyone had fled from her mind. She knew she was in the wrong, but she wasn't exactly sure why. As she fell sideways on the sofa, and started to snore softly, little Agnes lay beside her and attempted to cuddle her.

'What did the Old Bill say?' Aiden asked as he put a blanket over them.

Patsy snorted in derision. 'What they always say, Ade. "Just take her home." You know she clumped Big Pete's wife, don't you? Nicest woman you could ever meet.'

Aiden sighed again. 'I will sort out Big Pete and his fucking fat wife. Luckily he has a soft spot for Mum.'

Patsy laughed and said snidely, 'Yeah. And the trouble is, she has a soft spot for everyone else, does our mum.'

The blow knocked Patsy off his chair and on to the floor. He looked up into Aiden's angry countenance and shook his head in disbelief.

'Why do you always stick up for her?'

Aiden looked fit to be tied and Patsy felt a glimmer of fear. 'She is our mother and, no matter what anyone else thinks, she is the only parent in our lives. Yes, she goes off the rails occasionally but she is the only constant we are ever going to have, and the fact that she is our mother demands – fucking *demands* – our loyalty no matter what. I can't believe you sometimes! For all her faults she would die for each and every one of us. She is a victim. Don't you ever forget that.'

Aiden looked at his two youngest brothers and said gently, 'Eugene, you take Agnes and try and amuse her. And you, Porrick, get Mum's quilt and cover her up properly. I don't think she could quite manage the stairs tonight.'

Both boys rushed to do his bidding as they always did. Aiden was the king of the household and they knew he was the provider in more ways than one.

Aiden took a twenty-pound note out of his wallet and said to Patsy quietly, 'I have a bit of business tonight. Get this lot fish and chips and keep your eye on them, OK? I don't know when I will be back.'

Patsy took the money and nodded at his brother. As he went to walk from the room, Aiden pulled him back and hugged him tightly.

'I know how you feel, believe me, Patsy. But, seriously, she really can't help it. You know her. She'll be Mother of the Year tomorrow.'

Patsy shrugged and said honestly, 'She forgot about Agnes again. We'll end up with social services all over us like a rash if she don't sort herself out.'

Aiden hugged him again, crooning gently, 'I know, mate. I know. I will sort it, don't worry.'

Patsy shrugged his brother off saying, 'I hope so, mate, because she's getting out of hand.'

Aiden watched his brother walk out of the room and he felt the urge to cry. He had a lot on and the last thing he needed was Reeva playing up.

Chapter Fifteen

Eric Palmer was a happy man. He had just got off with the biggest capture this side of the Thames, and that was because of one person. As Aiden walked into Eric's offices in Green Lanes a cheer went up and Aiden, rosy red with embarrassment, laughed and accepted a glass of champagne.

'You fucking Brahma, boy. How did you do it?'

Aiden shrugged. 'Let's just say I have a persuasiveness about me.'

Eric admired the lad. He should have known Aiden would not tell anyone anything with a room full of witnesses. That was the fucking beauty of this kid. He wouldn't have a shit lest he thought it out and planned it down to the last detail. He was a natural-born villain.

'Come through, son, and we'll have a chat.'

Aiden followed the man happily. He liked Eric Palmer and he admired him. But, more than anything, he wanted to *be* him.

In the back office Eric poured them both a large brandy and, giving it to the boy, he said seriously, 'This is thirty years old and far better than that champagne shite. Now, tell me how you did it.'

Aiden sipped the brandy and coughed as the strength of it hit the back of his throat. He liked the burn as it slipped down into his gut. He held the glass up in a toast and said genuinely, 'I could get used to this, Mr Palmer.'

Eric loved the way Aiden was so respectful – he still gave him his title which spoke volumes as far as he was concerned. He was a tall, handsome lad and looked a lot older than his nineteen years.

Aiden sat in the chair opposite Eric's and said in the usual quiet voice he used when discussing business, 'Young Jimmy Croft's dad got a big capture and he's in for a lump, no getting away from it. So I told him to tell his dad that if he held his hands up there would be a oner a week for the family in it, and a guaranteed job when he came out. I also said his debts would be paid off. It's ten grand but it's cheap at that price, really. We both know Johnny Brooke would hassle him, even in the clink, would fuck up the family to get his money. Treacherous cunt, Johnny is. I mean, who goes after someone's wife and kids? Wanker. So, that's the score.'

Eric was over the moon. Aiden had got them out of deep shit for a lousy ten grand. It was fucking amazing.

'All the statements have been done. I told the lad the main shit and he passed it on. I didn't say anything until I thought it was all in hand, like. Plus some of that lot –' he pointed with his thumb to the closed door –'might have felt the urge to add their five bob's worth and that would have defeated the object. This needed silence and solitude, if you get my drift. Now he's going down happily, knowing his debts are paid and his family has a decent drink. I also guaranteed him an easy time in the clink. His own cell, et cetera. It was the least we could do, really, considering.'

Eric Palmer felt the urge to kiss Aiden. He had single-handedly sorted out a serious bit of large, and he had done it quietly and without fanfare. This kid was a natural problem-solver who saw what needed to be done and then went for it without the fuss of muscle, threats or fucking violence – unless absolutely necessary, that is.

'He will get that and more, my son. He has taken me out of a big fucking hole. And as for Dennis Harper . . .'

Aiden held up a hand and said seriously, 'That's the other thing. Dennis unfortunately died yesterday – heroin overdose in the Scrubbs. Drugs, eh? Such a problem in the prison system these days.' He sipped at his brandy before saying, 'That cost me five hundred bar. A mate owed me a favour.'

Eric Palmer was, for the first time in his life, speechless. Dennis Harper was a huge bugbear and Eric had not been able to get near him. That this kid had managed it put him in a whole other league.

Aiden basked in Eric's abject admiration, which was just what he had expected and planned for. He was going places, and he was determined to do it on his own terms.

Eric Palmer jumped out of his seat and shook his hand roughly. Aiden could see the man's gratitude in his eyes, in his stance, in everything about him.

'You, my son, are a fucking diamond! I can't believe you managed it.'

Aiden, who always played things down until he was sure of it working out, said quietly, 'Well, let's wait and see. I never count my chickens!'

'Oh, it's worked, my son. My brief was on earlier – we just couldn't work out why I was out of the frame.'

Aiden shrugged nonchalantly. 'Glad to be of help.'

Eric was thrilled and he said generously, 'You are going places, and you are going those places with me.'

Aiden smiled that handsome smile of his that looked to all the world like he was as trustworthy as the Holy Father himself. And Eric Palmer fell for it hook, line and sinker.

'Come on, let's get back to the party. You, my son, deserve to have the night of your life tonight.'

Aiden O'Hara didn't expect anything less. He had pulled off the seemingly impossible and, in many ways, it had been a lucky fluke. He had met the right people in the right places at the right time. But he wasn't about to say that to anyone, least of all Eric Palmer.

Chapter Sixteen

Aiden came home at 2 a.m. to hear Tony Brown and his mother fighting. He was drunk and not in the mood for any more of their histrionics. He felt sorry for Tony in some ways because he knew that, despite his mother's best antics, Tony did genuinely care about her these days. He'd stuck around anyway. But she was hard work for all concerned.

'Oh, for fuck's sake!' The voice was loud and aggressive. As Aiden walked into the front room he saw his mother, awake now and up for a row, and Tony bending over her. But it was seeing Tony's fear as he walked in that really affected Ai It told him just how much his reputation had been this night. It also saddened him, because T nearest thing to a real father Aiden had ever kn also introduced him to Eric Palmer *and* he had put up with Reeva longer than anyone else had – indeed had apparently left his wife for her. That in itself was a miraculous fucking achievement.

'Look, Aiden, I wasn't going to clump her or anything . . .'

Aiden looked at the man in horror. ''Course you weren't! Fucking hell, Tony. It's me, Aiden. I know what a mare this one can be.' He smiled at his mum. 'Sober again, are we? Up for another row?'

Reeva was wrong-footed now. The fight left her as quickly as it had arrived. 'You all right, Aiden, my son?'

Tony breathed a quiet sigh of relief. Aiden had that effect on people, and especially on Reeva. They adored each other. Strangely that didn't bother Tony because he knew that, without her eldest boy, Reeva would have gone off the rails years ago.

'I'm all right, Mum, unlike you, of course. You do realise that you forgot about Agnes again today, don't you? While you were pissed and clumping Big Pete's wife, your daughter was left to her own devices.' Aiden smiled at Tony as he said in a friendly manner, 'Put the kettle on, Tone, would you? I need to talk to Mother of the fucking Year here. Put her wise to a few of her failings.'

Tony was only too pleased to oblige. He could hear them talking from the kitchen anyway so he left the room quietly, pleased to see the contrite look on Reeva's lovely, if infuriating, face. She really was the most aggravating female he had ever ⬛cross. Yet, like Aiden, he almost understood her. Aiden ⬛ined to him once that his mum was so sure whoever ⬛leave her that she instinctively drove them ⬛ something to do with her father walking out on her and her mother when she was a little girl, apparently. It was all a bit deep for him, if he was honest. But even the school had admitted that Aiden was a bit of a boffin so he assumed the boy knew what he was banging on about. He made the tea.

Reeva was contrite as always when she sobered up and she listened to her son with a suitably tragic face. That trick had not worked since he was nine but now was not the time to point that out to her!

46

'Look, Mum, you forgot Aggie again today and that really ain't good, is it? Not only could she be hurt or kidnapped, but it could bring social services breathing down our necks again. And that is the last thing we need now.'

He was talking to her in a quiet, reasonable voice and she appreciated that. Her head was hammering and her mouth was drier than a buzzard's crutch. She knew she was in the wrong big time and now all she wanted was a fag, a cup of tea and her bed – in that order.

'Where is Agnes?'

Aiden stifled a smile. 'She is in bed, like the others. But I mean it, Mum. Our Patsy has got the right hump with you and he has every right.'

Reeva closed her eyes and nodded. Then she lit herself a cigarette and was grateful when Tony brought in the teas. Tony winked at her and she felt the urge to cry. He had lasted a lot longer than any of the others and, even though she had a sneaky feeling that was because of her Aiden and his business acumen, she did believe that there was a part of Tony Brown that genuinely cared for her. Though, like everyone else, she couldn't think what that could be. The tea revived her and she sat up straighter. The thing with Reeva was, even after all the kids, all the drink and all the drugs, she was still a beautiful woman.

'I promise you, Aiden. I will be good in future. But I had a shit day. That old bag in the Co-op was on my case again this morning. I weren't in the mood for it. I mean, what the fuck have I ever done to her? She is like the wronged wife every time I go in there. Sniffing and looking down at me.' Aiden laughed and said, 'You had taken five Dexedrine, Mum. I slapped Billy Marshall today and told him if he ever sold you anything but puff in future I would kill him. So save the stories for Agnes at bedtime, eh?'

Despite her annoyance, Reeva laughed with him. She knew when she was caught out. And Tony marvelled at this family who could fight one minute and laugh the next.

Chapter Seventeen

Agnes was sitting on Aiden's lap and he was holding her tightly to him. Eric Palmer was impressed to see the lad take care of his family like a father. As Aiden picked up a cream cake and gave it to his sister, Eric felt the urge to cry, and wondered if he was going soft in his old age. His own kids were spoiled brats who were only interested in themselves. This boy was single-handedly keeping his family together and, with Reeva as a mother, that had to be a full-time job.

'I like cake, Ade.'

Aiden laughed at Agnes and said gently, 'Everyone likes cake, darling. God invented cake so you could celebrate things like birthdays, and to comfort you at other times when you are sad. Nothing like a cake to cheer you up, eh?'

She laughed delightedly with him. Eric noticed she was a beautiful child; she looked like she had a bit of Arab or Turk in her, with huge blue eyes and jet-black hair. Aiden would be chasing the men off with a shotgun if she got her mother's build.

Eric remembered the young Reeva. God, she could bring a grown man to his knees with a smile. Trouble was, she was liable to be the one on her knees. She was a girl all right. He had had her himself – before she had so many kids, of course.

Now he was sitting in a café on the Roman Road having a business meeting and this lad had brought his youngest sister because, as he had explained, his mother was indisposed. Eric assumed she had the hangover from hell.

'The thing is, Aiden, I think it's time I introduced you around to my other business partners. They all know about you, and I think you would do well to get a handle on the different businesses I have.'

This was music to Aiden's ears. It meant Eric was grooming him to take over eventually, providing he proved himself fitting. Which he would – this was what he had been aiming for. This was what it was all about. He smiled, and there was genuine pleasure in it. Eric Palmer liked to be appreciated. It showed a man's mettle if he was big enough to acknowledge when someone was doing them a great kindness.

A man walked into the café and Aiden immediately stiffened. When the man approached the table he instinctively tightened his hold on Agnes, who was immediately aware of the change in atmosphere. Her huge eyes were troubled now and she snuggled into her brother. The man was big and sweaty-looking, with a bald head and dead eyes.

Eric Palmer smiled and said casually, 'Aiden O'Hara, let me introduce Detective Chief Superintendent Smith. Bent Filth and all-round prize cunt. But he's my prize cunt so he's harmless. Smith, this is my protégé, Aiden.'

Aiden was amazed at the way the Old Bill didn't react to the insults. He just stuck out his hand and Aiden shook it, bewildered now. Then Eric and Smith both laughed together, like the old friends they were.

'You bastard, Palmer!'

Then Smith looked at Agnes and said seriously, 'What a

beautiful child. Mind you, son, your mum's a good looker, no doubt about that, eh?'

Aiden felt that he had walked into a nightmare. This man was hated, and not just by criminals. Yet here he was, in broad daylight, having a cup of tea with them and acting like he was welcome. Which, from Eric Palmer's point of view, he was.

'You are now under Smith's protection, son. So, play nicely!'

The two older men laughed again and Smith said seriously, 'Remember, son – things are often not what you first think. Most of life is smoke and mirrors. Now, I'm going to have a cup of tea and get myself off to the station. Got murders going on at the moment and I mean that literally. Two men shot in Mile End last night. Fucking Jamaicans, always bring their feuds into the street. Much easier all round if the bodies just disappear. But what can you do? They like to make examples. Logic there, I suppose.'

Aiden listened to the two men talking and realised that for all his so-called intelligence he had a fucking lot to learn. He guessed this was what this meeting was about. Eric was bringing him into a world that needed to be negotiated very carefully if you wanted to survive in it. And Eric Palmer had survived a lot longer than his contemporaries. Not only was he still alive, but he wasn't banged up for thirty years either.

Agnes had now taken quite a liking to the big, bald man and Aiden was amazed when Smith took her on his lap, happily chatting away to her as if this was a normal event. Just a normal day.

Chapter Eighteen

Reeva walked into the Co-op to get her cigarettes. She was still fragile after the events of the day before and she had to be on her best behaviour – Aiden had made that plain this morning at breakfast. She would pick up her fags and then she would go to the butcher's to get something lovely in for dinner. And she'd make some cakes. She was once more on the maternal wavelength, happy to be looking after her family. Agnes had gone with Aiden for a few hours so Reeva had time to sort herself out. The house already looked spotless, and she had even washed her nets.

Now, as she waited to be served, she saw Big Pete's wife, Carol, looking at her in the window and, with her usual front, Reeva smiled and waved at her as if nothing untoward had happened between them. Carol smiled back and walked into the shop. She was an imposing woman with a beautiful face and an easy-going personality. The latter was a requisite if you were married to a man like her husband.

'All right, Reeva.'

This was a form of address, not a question, and Reeva smiled engagingly as she answered her. 'Yeah, mate. I'm good. About yesterday . . .'

Carol flapped her hand in dismissal. 'We have all done it, love! Too much to drink too early in the day.'

They laughed liked drains, and the incident was over and done with. Then they started the serious gossiping and stood together for a good ten minutes, either slaughtering mutual friends or sympathising with them, depending. Reeva was in her element.

Jack watched the women, relieved, and ignored his wife, Doris, as she scowled at them with disapproval.

Suddenly the door was smashed open and two young men in balaclavas came inside brandishing a shotgun and a small handgun.

Jack couldn't believe his eyes. He knew that robbery was on the increase but he never dreamed that he would be on the receiving end of it. He heard Doris cry out in fear and moved towards her to protect her. That was when one of the firearms went off. It shot by his shoulder, grazing the skin, and he didn't know who was the more surprised – himself, or the lad who had inadvertently fired his gun.

Reeva stepped forward quickly, shouting angrily, 'What the fuck do you think you're doing, you dozy pair of fucking twits? Fucking out on the rob in this weather?'

The boy with the shotgun was terrified, Reeva could see it in his eyes. The other lad was shaking after the gunshot had frightened him with its noise.

Then she heard one of them say sharply, 'Oh, fuck! It's Aiden's fucking mother!'

The two lads ran from the shop into the harsh sunshine and Reeva and the other occupants were left staring at each other in shock.

Then Jack Walters seemed to realise he had been shot at and he collapsed on to the floor. There was pandemonium.

Chapter Nineteen

Aiden O'Hara was like the Antichrist. That someone had robbed his local shop while his mother was on the premises was basically unbelievable. He could not comprehend such outrageousness, such stupidity. It did not take him long to find out the names of the culprits and apprehend them. After giving them a serious hammering, he made clear to all and sundry that anyone even *thinking* of robbing on his manor would be dealt with harshly. This was backed up by Eric Palmer and so was now like the eleventh commandment, written in stone and never to be forgotten.

Doris Walters, despite herself, had to show her gratitude and, in a strange way, she *was* grateful because it could all have been so much worse. Reeva was suddenly made aware of just how much of a reputation her boy was garnering for himself. It was a real eye-opener. That Doris Walters now served her with something approaching politeness spoke volumes in itself! And Reeva was not about to let something like this pass her by without making the most of it. No, Reeva O'Hara was the new Violet Kray as far as she was concerned. And she was determined to milk it for all it was worth.

Chapter Twenty

The deeper Aiden went into Eric's world, the more it amazed him. He had suspected that Eric Palmer was into all sorts – he had just not realised how far the man's arm could reach. No wonder Eric was always watching his back – he walked a fine line every day of his life because a lot of the stuff he was involved in was not to everyone's taste.

Today Aiden was in a private house in Kensington, where *very* young girls and boys were used by much older men. He concealed his shock easily – looking like he wasn't bothered was his natural demeanour. But inside he was disgusted. These were little more than kids for all their make-up and sexy clothes. Even in the big, bad world of Faces there were many who would view this kind of set up with scandal and abhorrence. Prostitution was always there but the management of kids was frowned on by more than a few hard men.

The man he was accompanying was called Rufus Martin and he was a big Rastafarian with gold teeth and a serious paunch. He smoked dope continuously and smelled like an ashtray.

'Bit young, ain't they?'

Rufus shrugged, saying quietly, 'This is where the money is, boy. This is what the men who come here want.'

Aiden kept his own counsel. There was no way he would ever be heard saying anything even remotely detrimental about anything Eric controlled. He already knew how to play the game and his natural reticence was working for him. That didn't mean he had to like it, but he reasoned that everyone had to do things they didn't particularly like or agree with. That was part and parcel of life, no matter who you were.

He followed Rufus through to the so-called offices. In this case they were in the basement of the house and were surprisingly smart, considering. Behind a large mahogany desk sat a blonde with pale green eyes and an alluring smile. Aiden felt her looking him over as if he was on sale and he returned the look as best he could. But he was bowled over. The woman was stunning, and it seemed she knew it as well as he did.

'And *you* are?'

Her voice was well modulated but there was still a cockney twang there and that helped with Aiden's unaccustomed nervousness.

Rufus laughed loudly. 'Put the boy down with those green eyes of yours. This is young Aiden, Eric's protégé!'

The woman sat back in the chair and appraised Aiden once more and he felt the heat of her gaze wash over him. Only this time she wasn't taking the piss.

She waved a well-manicured hand at Rufus and said dismissively, 'Bye, Rufus.' The big man left without a murmur.

'Sit yourself down and let's get acquainted, shall we?'

Aiden did as he was told. Never in his life before had he felt like this. He was aware that this woman liked the effect she was having on him. He had a feeling she had the same effect on most of the male population.

She stood up and held her hand out elegantly for him to shake it, saying seductively, 'I'm Jade Dixon and this is my house.'

Chapter Twenty-One

Reeva and the other kids were watching *Knight Rider* repeats when Aiden finally arrived home. Reeva jumped up immediately and put the kettle on. She was once more on the up and up and, as a consequence, everything she did was with vigour and a smile.

Aiden could tell she had had a few drinks but nothing catastrophic, so he was happy enough. Agnes ran to him and he picked her up and kissed her, asking the boys what they had been up to and what had constituted their various days. He was, for all intents and purposes, the man of the house.

Tony came into the room and smiled widely on seeing Aiden. The two men shook hands. 'How's madam been?'

Tony and Aiden laughed as she shouted from the kitchen, 'Oi, I fucking heard that!'

The kids were happy, Reeva was happy and Aiden was over the fucking moon. He had somehow fallen in love in the space of a few hours, and that was not something he would ever have envisioned. Especially not with a woman who peddled other women and children for a living and was a fair bit older than him. But he felt so good he was willing to run with it.

Reeva brought in the teas and they all started to chat. This was what Aiden loved; this family life when everyone was acting normally and they could at least pretend for a while that it was not an illusion based around his mother's moods and her capacity to imbibe huge quantities of drink and drugs. Mainly she let down her children, who lived in constant terror of what she would do next; she was a fucking flake at times. She disappointed Aiden because he felt she should *always* put them first. But the drink and the drugs were her escape. She would get out of bed, all sweetness and light, and then she would go on a bender, and those benders were legendary. Why she did it was a mystery but, as Aiden reasoned, their whole faith was based on one mystery after another – one more wouldn't do any harm. Reeva's life was a constant stream of chaotic events followed by weeks, occasionally even months, of absolute perfection where she cooked, cleaned and gave her kids the attention they needed. And, in fairness, even when she was on a bender they never disputed that she loved them dearly.

Aiden understood she was still young and that she felt the need to get out and away from her responsibilities. She craved drama and the knowledge that she was still attractive. When things got rocky with Tony and he took off for a bit, she got lonely and, when the loneliness got too much, she sought out company and excitement to recapture her youth. With that belief she still had hope; hope of a real partner, a real man who would be there for her always. Aiden didn't share that hope, but he admired his mother's optimism. And she was the eternal optimist, even though the men she gravitated towards were about as much use to her as a fucking pork chop in a mosque. He made allowances for her, providing she didn't start too much trouble, because whatever people might say about her, he knew that she did the best she could. She pretended that what people said about her didn't bother her, but it did. Nevertheless she had fronted out each of her pregnancies and she had loved every one of her babies – for that he would always love her in return.

But Aiden was well aware that his feelings for Jade would not be welcomed by this woman who he adored and hated in equal measure because his mum couldn't cope without him orchestrating her every move and she'd see him moving away from her. He had started protecting her at a very young age and now she depended on him far more than was healthy for either of them. But he was a man now, in his own right. And he was in love, really in love, and he couldn't think of anything else.

Chapter Twenty-Two

Jade Dixon was thirty-four years old and looked a lot younger, but then that had always been in her favour. Jade had started her life in a mother and baby home, before being adopted by a *nice*, wealthy, Christian couple. The mother she had inherited had been a manic-depressive and the father had a penchant for young girls. Very young girls, the younger the better, so Jade's life had been blighted pretty much from the get-go. Privilege had come at a big price and she had finally escaped aged thirteen with a man she had met at a fair. He was the first in a long line of men who had seen her, wanted her, had her and ultimately used her in more ways than one. By fifteen she was selling herself and she had learned a valuable lesson: men were to *be* used, not the other way around.

Since that lightning-bolt revelation she believed she had done quite well for herself and, in the grand scheme of things, in the world she inhabited, she actually had. For a start she was rich; she had her own home close to work and a smart car. She was also practically devoid of anything even remotely resembling empathy or love. The nearest she had come to love was for her dog and when she'd died having puppies Jade had washed her hands of even that. She was like a very beautiful doll that was smashed inside but outwardly looked perfect. She knew how to make the best of her startling good looks and she took pride and pleasure in her appearance. It was, after all, her stock-in-trade. Not that she flogged her arse any more, of course, but it gave the girls she had working for her something to aspire to.

If she could work her way up, why couldn't they? That was the message she always conveyed, and they believed it. Jade manipulated everyone in her orbit, and she was hero-worshipped by the girls she handled. She made sure of that much.

Now she had been sent a fucking child to train in the ways of the world and, though she would do as she was told, there was an anger inside her about it. But she knew better than to cross Eric Palmer. For all his good-natured banter, he would skin her alive and not even break out in a sweat. Oh, she knew all about Eric and his little foibles.

The new boy, Aiden, seemed to have a good head on his shoulders, and he was easy on the eye. He looked much older than his nineteen years, had a good physique and, in fairness, he had been very well mannered and polite, which was always a plus in her game. So many of the men looked down on the working girls – and that was another thing that angered her. And, as everyone knew, it did not do to get Jade angry. Jade Dixon angry was not a pretty sight and it always ended in tears for whoever had irritated her.

But Aiden intrigued her. He talked about his mother like she was the second coming, and he had looked at her as she had *wanted* him to look at her. It was always good to have people in your corner, another thing she had learned at a very early age.

So, she dressed carefully for the second meeting with him. She wanted to look her absolute best. She was going to bowl him over.

Chapter Twenty-Three

'Where you off to, Aiden? You smell like a poke of devils!'

Patsy was holding his nose and laughing. Aiden punched him lightly on the shoulder.

'I'm off out to learn a new trade, my son. How's it going with you?'

Patsy smiled, looking pleased with himself. 'Yeah, good. I'm earning so much money but, like you told me, I am not flashing the cash and bringing any interest down on me.'

Aiden nodded in approval and Patsy preened at the praise.

'Remember that, mate. People get jealous when you are earning, and they ain't. The Old Bill might be cunts but they ain't stupid. So, just save your money somewhere that ain't a fucking bank, all right? Eric is well pleased with you. Before you know it you will be out there with me.'

Patsy grinned. That was his ultimate goal.

'So, what's it like, this new place you're working, Ade?'

Aiden sighed. 'To be honest with you, Patsy, I wasn't too enamoured at first. But once I got me head around it I was all right. It's interesting, and a bit of an eye-opener, if I am being truthful with you. But it's a big money-spinner and Eric has got it all sewn up there.'

Aiden smiled, bent down and kissed Agnes and then, walking

out to the kitchen, he hugged his mum tightly, saying quietly, 'Don't know when I will be back. You all right for a few quid?'

Reeva grinned and said quickly, 'Well, I could do with a couple of bob, son.'

Pinching her cheek hard, he said jovially, 'Then ask Tony. I left it with him. Can't have you going on a bender, can we!'

Reeva was annoyed and it showed – but she laughed anyway. 'You're a right wanker at times, do you know that?'

He grinned once more and kissed her on the cheek, saying, 'I had a good teacher, didn't I?'

She chased him out of the house, hitting him with a tea towel, making the other kids laugh at their antics. But deep inside Reeva was hurting. There were jokes, and there were jokes. She knew that he didn't mean any real harm – it still hurt, though.

Chapter Twenty-Four

Jade Dixon was watching her new protégé with experienced eyes, and she had to admit he was a clever one. He took everything in without endless explanations on her part or questions on his. Now, though, she saw his eyes widen and she stifled the urge to laugh.

'Yes, Aiden. That is who you think it is. He is not the only one either. We get all sorts here, from MPs right down the scale to TV stars and family entertainers. That is why it's so expensive. It's our guarantee of privacy that they pay for, plus we don't act as if we are judging them. Though that bloke over there with his cock out is actually a judge!'

They laughed together and Aiden looked around him in amazement. There were more than a few household names here and for some reason that disgusted him further. One man he remembered from a kids' programme when he was younger. Somehow that made it all the more sinister.

Jade pulled him through to the offices and poured a couple of large Scotches. As they sipped them she said gently, 'Look, Aiden, someone is going to provide for people like these. Have done since the dawn of fucking time, I should imagine. As Eric so rightly points out, it might as well be us on the earn as someone else. Plus the girls are treated well here. It's much better than a lot of places – believe me, I know that for a fact.'

Aiden downed the Scotch in one burning gulp and tried to shrug. Despite herself, Jade was pleased at his revulsion. It showed her that he still had some kind of moral code. Not that he would keep it for long – you couldn't in this game. Whether you were the seller or the sold, it broke everyone eventually.

She poured him another stiff drink and said calmly, 'Get that down your Gregory and we will go out and mingle with our perverted, fucking well-paying guests and we will smile and act like this is all normal. Take my advice, mate. That is the only way to stay sane.'

He was shocked to hear the rough cockney come out of her perfectly shaped mouth and, despite himself, he laughed at the incongruity of it. He didn't know what to think, if he was honest.

She held her hand out and he took it, and together they went out and he learned how to play this particular game. But all the time his eyes were on her and they both knew it. Somehow, with her there, he didn't notice what was really going on around him – the old men with the young girls and boys, the debauched look of them and the way they acted like what they were doing was perfectly natural. He saw a couple of the men look at him speculatively and he felt the anger rising inside him, even as he let them down gently. There were thousands of pounds passing through this place on a nightly basis and, as Jade had pointed out to him, it was a job. Someone was going to do it so it might as well be them. Aiden was a realist and he could see the sense in what she said.

Chapter Twenty-Five

Reeva opened the door to her old friend and neighbour, Francis Mullaney, and she smiled widely in genuine pleasure as she ushered him into her home. Francis was a small man; it was rumoured that in Ireland he had been an aspiring jockey but he had caught the gambling bug. Now he worked at Fords and spent his weekends in the pub like most of the men in their neighbourhood. He had three daughters, if she remembered rightly, and an English wife with badly dyed hair and an under-bite.

'Can I get you a cup of tea?'

He shook his head and also declined the seat she offered him. She saw him looking around in wonder and, instead of her usual pride in her home, she felt a faint uneasiness.

'So, what can I do you for?' She was smiling but it didn't reach her eyes.

Francis shrugged and took a deep breath. 'Look, Reeva, I need to talk to you about your Patsy.'

Reeva nodded, not offering a word about her son.

'My eldest, Siobhan, is on drugs and tonight the police brought her home. She had been missing since yesterday morning. When they left I hammered the fecking bejasus out of her. She told me who her dealer was and I went and hammered the bejasus out of that bastard too. The bottom line, Reeva, is it's your Patsy who's supplying him, and plenty more besides, according to him.' Francis stood there expectantly, waiting for her to react.

'Have you told the Old Bill any of this?'

He looked insulted. 'Of course not, Reeva. I'm not fecking stupid. Give me some credit, woman.'

'You can see yourself out. I will sort this, OK?'

Francis left, taking her at her word. Once he was gone she picked up the phone and dialled the pub. Tony needed to get his arse home and get it home now. Then she went upstairs and systematically pulled her two eldest sons' room apart until she found what she was looking for. Such was her anger it didn't cross her mind that Aiden might not appreciate her looking through his private stuff. But she was too far gone to think about that.

Chapter Twenty-Six

Patsy O'Hara was amazed to see Tony Brown. He had been talking to a girl called Lisa Gordon at a party inside a tower block in East Ham when Tony came in. He left the party immediately, a worried look on his handsome face. The music was far too loud, and it wasn't until they were in the lift descending to the ground floor that he finally understood what Tony was telling him. He felt his stomach turn to ice water as he realised the consequences of what was being said. It didn't help that he was half-drunk and very stoned.

Tony bundled him into his car, a Mark I Cortina, and started driving back to the house while Patsy lamented his actions and questioned exactly how he was going to justify his stupidity to his older brother. Tony listened to him with half an ear; he knew exactly how this was going to end and, if Patsy had half a brain and dropped the drugs, he should know that too.

Patsy was sweating and the fear sobered him up in double-quick time.

Reeva he could handle – he knew she was on his side no matter what – but with Aiden and his new persona, he wasn't sure about him at all. And it seemed that Tony Brown was feeling exactly the same way.

Chapter Twenty-Seven

Jade Dixon had set out to ensnare Aiden, and he was not averse to her actions. In actual fact he could not believe his fucking luck! She had taken him into an empty bedroom in the house that he soon realised was exclusively for her use. There was make-up, clothes and even jewellery there. The room had the particular smell that seemed to emanate from her: expensive perfume and Sobranie cigarettes. And, as she kissed him, he felt as if he was going to explode.

He'd had his share of girls, but this was his first real woman, and it was heady stuff. She even kissed differently, slower, exploring his mouth with her tongue. He could feel the energy pulsing from her and he hoped against hope that he wouldn't embarrass himself by finishing before he had even started. Pushing him back gently on to the bed, she stripped him and caressed him, and she made him feel like no one ever had before or would ever again. She was good at her job, and he never realised for one second that it was all an act on her part. She did what she always did with men: she used them to her advantage and that always started by her fucking their brains out. Once she had him in her thrall, she knew she would have the advantage over him.

Aiden O'Hara was quite happy to let her use him – in fact,

he had never wanted anything or anyone so much in his life before. When she finally let him come, he knew what nirvana felt like and he was eager as fuck to feel it again and again and again. As they lay together afterwards, smoking and drinking Rémy Martin, he felt as if he had finally arrived.

A discreet knock at the door broke the bubble; it seemed he had a private visitor waiting for him downstairs. Jade lay back as he quickly dressed, and she stretched herself out and waited calmly for him to return to her. She was eager to get on to round two. She could see herself in the huge mirrors on the walls, and she eyed herself dispassionately. She knew she was beautiful and she knew exactly how to make the best of herself so the man involved got the best views. It was her life's work, after all.

She stood up and poured herself another brandy, all the while admiring her reflection. When she finally realised he wasn't coming back she didn't know whether to laugh or cry. For the first time in years a man had fucked *her* and left *her*. Not even a man – a *boy*. She finally got dressed and went back to the so-called party. If he had achieved nothing else, he had certainly piqued her interest.

Chapter Twenty-Eight

Agnes was crying, and her elder brothers were trying to calm her down. But Patsy's cries and Aiden's anger were permeating the whole house.

Aiden had never felt such an urge to smack his brother as he did at this moment. How could he be so fucking stupid? Had he taught him nothing?

Patsy was terrified and, as he looked at his older brother, he felt the terrible force of the man's personality. He was a big lump, was Aiden, but it was more than that. There was an edge to him that told anyone with half a brain that he was capable of killing you without a second thought.

'You are selling locally? After *all* I told you about keeping a low profile, after everything I fucking said? Now we have that cunt Mullaney coming round here calling us fucking drug dealers! What are you fucking on?'

Patsy looked at his mother for help, but she just sat there calmly smoking a joint and watching the proceedings without expressing a word. She had served him up, but would she let Aiden really harm him? He feared that she would.

'I have sent for your little fucking muckers, especially the bastard who grassed you up to that silly whore's father. Francis might have used a baseball bat on him, but that will seem like heaven after I have finished with him, you useless stupid piece of shit.'

Patsy knew that when his brother was like this the best way to deal with him was to keep quiet – extremely quiet.

Reeva watched her sons dispassionately. This was something that needed to be said, something that needed to be sorted. They could have got their collars felt thanks to this useless lump. But at least now Patsy would heed the warning and listen to his brother's advice in the future. Her Aiden was going places and he would take them with him, of that much she was sure. And there wasn't anyone – not even her own flesh and blood – who was going to stop that happening, not on her watch anyway. She knew when to keep her trap shut, what was admissible and what fucking well wasn't. Dealing to your friends, who then went on to deal to your neighbours, was the height of foolishness and folly. Patsy might just as well have handed himself in to the Filth and been done with it. But then her lad was still young and, as everyone knew, the young were lazy. The only good thing was that the young were still able enough to learn from their mistakes. At least, she hoped so where her Patsy was concerned. He needed a fucking wake-up call, all right.

As Aiden's fist connected with Patsy's head, Reeva watched the ensuing beating without a reaction. She was with Aiden on this one.

It was only when the other kids ran downstairs and intervened that Aiden seemed to calm down. Reeva watched him as he pacified them, picking up Agnes and hugging her, talking to them calmly as he sent them back to bed reassuring them that everything was going to be OK and that he would make them pancakes for breakfast.

Patsy lay on the floor, bloodied and bleeding while this was going on, and Reeva left him where he was. He needed a lesson. She felt a moment's irritation when Tony came into the room with a bucket of ice and started to administer aid to her errant son. But that was Tony all over these days, as soft as shit. It was part of why she cared for him. But, unlike her, he couldn't see the big picture. She knew her Aiden had deliberately kept his work away from his home, and the fact that Patsy had not understood the importance of that left a lot to be desired where she was concerned. Aiden had pulled them up out of the shit and given them all a good life and that was an achievement in itself.

When Aiden came back in and gently started to help his brother she was happy to do the same. But the message was loud and clear to Patsy and Tony: Aiden called the shots.

Patsy understood then that, as much as his mum loved her children, she would not stand between any of them and her oldest son. He was heartbroken that she could stand by and not intervene as he was beaten. But it was also a learning curve, because he knew now that he had to look out for himself. Patsy needed to man up and prove himself as someone to be trusted in every way.

Chapter Twenty-Nine

Eric Palmer was waiting patiently for Aiden to come and explain the situation to him, confident that the boy would have it in hand. He was disappointed that young Patsy didn't have the nous to know right from wrong but he made allowances because he was Aiden's brother.

When a contrite Aiden finally arrived, Eric listened to the boy and let him know, in a nice way, that it was deeds such as this that could bring them down. Little acorns and all that, but he was sure that Aiden had sorted the situation out to everyone's satisfaction. His bloodied knuckles were proof of that.

But Aiden was not appeased. His brother had nearly brought disaster on the family and that would not be easily forgotten, or indeed forgiven. One thing that most people never realised was, like Eric Palmer, Aiden O'Hara held grudges. And he never forgot anything that he felt had in any way cast him in a bad light. He talked his way back into Eric's good books and left him to go back to the brothel in Kensington. But by the time he got there, Jade Dixon had long gone. Aiden O'Hara was not happy.

Book Two

A man's character is his fate.

Heraclitus (c. 540–480 BC)

Am I my brother's keeper?

Genesis 4:9

Chapter Thirty

1990

'What on earth is Agnes on about, Aiden?'

Reeva was annoyed and it showed. Tony had disappeared again which wasn't, in itself, a big blow. The bugbear was he had not come back for three days and now Reeva was getting worried.

Aiden shook his head in despair and said patiently, 'Your young daughter, your "baby" as I believe you refer to her in your more friendly moments, needs money for a school trip to, of all places, Westminster Abbey.' He pulled his sister on to his lap and hugged her close saying, 'Don't worry, sweetheart, I will sort you out.'

Agnes was squirming to get away from him as he kissed her over and over again, his stubble scraping against her skin. Even Reeva laughed at the scene and she didn't think she had a laugh in her. Aiden slipped his sister twenty quid and she ran from the room to get ready for school. He looked at his youngest brothers and, sighing, gave them both twenty quid too.

Patsy, who was ironing his shirt, said jokily, 'Costs a fucking fortune, keeping this lot sweet, Ade.'

'Can't give to one without the others, can you?' Aiden smiled at Porrick and Eugene as he spoke and they grinned back, well pleased with this outcome. He poured himself another cup of tea and, as he sipped it, he said in a mock-tragic voice, 'Don't worry, Mum. He'll be back when he's hungry.'

Patsy chimed in then with a snide, 'Or when he's skint!'

The boys laughed and Reeva felt her simmering anger begin to boil. Yet she knew deep down they all liked Tony. The two-faced bastard that he was – he was still *her* Tony.

Eugene, who was the joker of the family, said, completely deadpan, 'He must be fucking starving by now. He's been gone nearly four days!'

They all started laughing again and Reeva willed herself not to react. It wasn't often her Aiden was home in the mornings. He usually spent most of his nights with his fancy woman; so she didn't want to spoil the mood.

Agnes came into the kitchen in her school uniform and Aiden looked at her with pride. From her blue eyes to her thick, dark hair and tanned skin, she was absolutely stunning, even at nine.

Patsy was a typical half-caste. You could see his West Indian heritage and he was a good-looking fucker – he turned a few heads when he hit the town. Then there was Eugene, with his African blackness, handsome in an aloof kind of way, and very, very funny. He was also the bookworm of the family; he would read anything from a takeaway menu to *The Times* newspaper. He had made the entire family join the library so he could get out more books in their names. Aiden had a feeling he would go far in life. Eugene had something about him, he had a stillness, an aura that made people listen to him. Then there was Porrick, with his red hair and milk-bottle white skin. He was quiet, but he could stand up for himself. He wasn't tall like the other boys, but what he lacked in height he made up for in ferociousness, as Eugene had found out on more than one occasion. Porrick would fight to the death; he wouldn't give up or admit defeat. He had a Napoleon complex in that he would fight the biggest fucker to prove his worthiness and show that he was not to be fucked with in any way. Aiden, like the others, admired Porrick for that.

It wasn't easy, being born into a family like theirs; they were a motley crew, each with different fathers, all different colours – and so completely different to the people around them. They were a world apart in many respects, but they worked as a family unit and that was what mattered. Aiden adored his brothers and his sister, and he would never let anyone fucking mug them off.

He watched as the kids sorted themselves out, getting extra slices of toast and drinking the last of their teas.

'Jade is picking me up in an hour, Mum.'

Reeva took a deep puff on her cigarette and said sarcastically, 'She's good at that, ain't she? Picking up men!'

Aiden closed his eyes and took a deep breath. The atmosphere in the kitchen was suddenly charged and the younger kids went quiet. Aiden started to laugh, a jovial laugh that made them breathe a sigh of relief. Then, straight-faced he said with quiet vehemence, 'You do make me fucking laugh at times, Mother. You have been round the block a few times yourself, in case you'd forgotten. You fucking old hypocrite.'

Reeva laughed scornfully as she retorted, 'I'm fucking younger than her!'

Aiden closed his eyes and then he said nastily, 'Yeah, but you would never know that, would you? Be fair, Mum, though. She looks ten years younger . . .'

When Reeva launched herself across the table the children scattered out into the hallway. Of all the things they had witnessed in their young lives, Reeva attacking Aiden was not one of them. Agnes was screaming in abject fear as Patsy tried to separate his mother from his brother.

Aiden was holding Reeva by her wrists and, unable to scratch or punch him, she was trying to kick him. With the help of Patsy, Aiden forced her back on to the kitchen table and held her as she screamed profanities and tried to escape until she ran out of strength.

When, finally, she was crying loudly and shuddering with distress they let her go. Aiden bundled her into his arms and held her until she calmed down. Patsy went to Agnes and tried to do the same for her but she was inconsolable with fear and terror. Picking her up, he brought her into the kitchen where Aiden sat his mother on a chair and took his little sister into his arms. Aiden held her and soothed her until she calmed down, but he was feeling an anger that he knew was well founded and liable to explode at any second. He looked at his mother and he knew she saw the turmoil he was experiencing and, for once, she had the grace to look away. This is what Reeva did best – upset everyone and then acted the victim. But this time they knew she had gone too far.

When Jade Dixon came in a few minutes later she took one look at the scene around her and said pointedly, 'Been playing happy families again, Reeva?'

Chapter Thirty-One

Annie O'Hara loved her daughter with a fierce passion but she despaired of her at times. For everything Reeva was, Annie knew that deep inside she loved her family with all her considerable heart. The trouble with Reeva was that she had what Annie always thought of as 'a screw loose somewhere'. She could go weeks being as good as gold and then the devil seemed to take over and she was impossible in more ways than one.

Today seemed to be one of those long and pointless days. The kids had filled her in on the morning's events, and Annie accepted she would have to forego her Bingo this day to keep an eye on her daughter, and make sure she didn't get into too much trouble. Aiden had asked her specifically to stop Reeva from ruining everything in that particular way she had when she was on a roll. Annie knew that he was absolutely right. Her daughter needed policing. To make matters worse, Aiden's relationship with Jade Dixon was like a red rag to the proverbial bull to Reeva, who thought it was all wrong. Annie could see that it wasn't really the age difference – it was just plain old jealousy on Reeva's part. Reeva would have been the same with any girl that Aiden took up with. In many ways she treated her eldest son as the husband she had never had, and she didn't like the thought of him putting another woman before her. In her more rational moments, she acknowledged that what she felt was wrong, outrageously wrong. But then the jealousy would overwhelm her and she would lash out. She wound up regretting her anger eventually. But by then the damage had been done.

Annie poured them both more tea and Reeva sipped hers disconsolately.

'You know, Reeva, there's a good side to Jade. She's had a tough life in her own way.'

Reeva sighed heavily and lit a cigarette. Taking a deep pull on it, she said sarcastically, 'Oh well, that's sorted then. Shall I invite her round for dinner? Or how about Sunday tea? She's a fucking infection, that's what she is. And she has infected my son.'

Annie simply smiled and shook her head calmly and Reeva felt the shame that always accompanied her mum's reasoning. Because, although she hated to admit it, her mum was *always* right in the long run. And that rankled.

Annie gently grasped her daughter's hand in hers. 'You know your trouble, Reeva? You can't stand him wanting anyone but you. He's your son, not your husband, and if you don't sort yourself out soon you will end up losing him for good.'

Her mother was giving her sound advice, but for the life of her Reeva would never acknowledge that. How could she? Reeva had always been economical with the truth, especially when it pertained to her own actions and feelings.

'Oh, Mum.'

Annie pulled her daughter into her arms and held her tightly as she talked her down, and tried to make her see reason in the chaos that was her world.

'I can't let him leave me. I need him to sort me out, and sort the kids out . . .'

Annie held her and listened with half an ear; she had heard it all so many times before.

'He would never leave you, Reeva, or the kids. But I warn you now, if you push him this time and force him to make a choice between you and her, you could lose him. Oh, he would still be there for you, but he will have to take a big step back. Jade is a sensible woman, and she is a good person in many ways. You have to find some kind of common ground with her, because she is not his usual squeeze – she is someone he respects, as well as loves. And that's a dangerous combination. Take it from me, love, I know what I'm talking about. If only I'd done things differently with your dad . . .' She trailed off, seeing the pain flare in her daughter's eyes as she reminded her of the first man to leave her.

Reeva didn't want to listen, even though she knew her mother was right. She couldn't bring herself to admit the truth of the situation. She saw her son as wholly hers, and that was that.

Chapter Thirty-Two

Aiden was immediately aware that there was some kind of crisis. This was one of the premises used for what was termed 'special requests'. What that actually meant was that the merchandise here was younger than any of them dared admit out loud, even to one another.

As they let themselves in, a tall woman with a hooked nose and expensively styled hair closed her eyes in obvious distress saying, 'Thank fuck you're here. I think she's dead.'

Jade immediately took control and, grabbing the woman's arm roughly, she said, in a calm voice, 'Relax, Rita, and show me where she is.'

Relieved that she could now pass the buck on to someone else, Rita Shaw nodded and led them up the small staircase to the room where a young girl, no more than twelve, lay on a double bed covered in blood.

'Jesus Christ. What the fuck happened here?'

Aiden's voice was quiet and Jade could see that he was in danger of losing his temper. Turning to him she looked straight into his eyes. He saw the warning there, and he took it on board.

Jade waited a couple of seconds to make sure he had regained his composure before she said assertively, 'I can deal with this.

You go and find out what happened, calm the situation down, eh?'

Her rationality communicated itself to him and, taking a deep breath, he nodded once before leaving the room with Rita Shaw in tow.

In the kitchen he saw three of the younger girls and a boy of about thirteen sitting forlornly around the table. A huge man with sad eyes, sparse blond hair and a crumpled suit was sitting watching over them and, as he caught Aiden's eye, there was a deep sadness there which was not actually mirrored in his own. But by now he knew how to play the game.

Unlike this man, Aiden was acting a part. Over the past few years he had begun to feel less and less empathy for the people he supplied or dealt with on a daily basis. This was just another part of the business, and that was how it had to be. He was shocked at the girl's demise and at her youth. But he was, at the end of the day, a realist. Not that he felt the person responsible should get away with it. This was, after all, beyond the pale in his world. But he had become hardened to the world of nonces and he was sensible enough to know that he had to act like he was outraged, even to Jade, who, despite her upbringing, still harboured a lingering care for the youths under her protection. Aiden had guessed some time ago that to admit that he no longer had much of a conscience was not conducive to good work relations, and this bloke here was a prime example.

Joe Redpath was a strong lad, but he was also a softie where certain things were concerned. He had told Eric time and again not to give him the younger merchandise to look after – he was too chicken-hearted for the task. Yet Eric seemed to find that amusing and often put him on duty in these more 'select' establishments, as they were referred to in the trade. Joe hated

it with all his being but he did what was asked of him nevertheless. He was paid to do a job and he more than fulfilled his
duties – that was a matter of pride with him. It didn't mean he
had to like it, as he pointed out at every available opportunity,
even though his complaints seemed to fall on deaf ears.

'Janey!'

Aiden's call reverberated around the two-storey flat and, within
seconds, a girl of about nineteen with long, red, waist-length
hair and a noticeable squint rushed into the room saying breath-
lessly, 'Sorry, Aiden, I was calming the twins down.'

He nodded and said in a low voice, 'Take this lot and keep
them quiet. Has Rita rung the doctor?'

She nodded and gathered the children together, taking them
out of the room with her, grateful to get away from the man
who terrified her.

Joe Redpath looked at Aiden with as much contempt as he
thought he could get away with and said quietly, 'I've got the
fire going in the main front room to burn the sheets and stuff
and I have already briefed the kids that it was a terrible accident
– though they don't believe it, no more than I would. I've also
put the man responsible in the back bedroom. I've locked him
in, more for his benefit than anyone else's. If I go near him I'll
break his fucking neck. I have roughed him up a bit, I admit
that. He's a cunt, and that is the long and the short of it. I
won't be fucking buying his records no more, put it that way.'
Joe shook his head sadly and said with finality, 'I am sorry, Ade,
but I ain't working this shit no more. If Eric don't like it I will
go elsewhere.'

Aiden nodded. 'I will sort it, Joe, don't worry. You let the
doctor in, mate, OK? And I will take care of Twinkle Toes up
in the back bedroom. Fucking nonce.'

Joe nodded and Aiden left him, walking heavily up the stair-case to deal with the man concerned. He was a big popstar with a huge following and a reputation as a ladies' man. The truth was he couldn't get it up with a real woman; he liked them young and flat-chested. He was a fucking animal, but he paid well. Well, he would have to, wouldn't he, given the nature of his fantasies and his public persona?

It never failed to amaze Aiden the people they dealt with. Household names some of them, from all walks of life, and backgrounds and environments. The only thing they had in common – other than their penchant for young kids – was the fact they were fucking loaded, seriously wedged up, and well able to pay to indulge in their peculiar tastes. Although he didn't feel the same shock as he had at first, Aiden still looked down on this particular clientele because they lived a lie in one way or another. But then wasn't everyone guilty of that to some extent?

He sighed deeply as he opened the bedroom door and looked at the handsome man sitting miserably on the edge of the bed. He looked like what he was to Aiden – a big, debauched bully. It was well known that he was spiteful with the girls and, as such, he paid extra for that privilege.

Plastering a neutral expression on his face, Aiden said softly, 'I'll get you a brandy. I am sure you could do with one.'

The man nodded and said in a surprisingly deep voice, 'I don't know what went wrong. We have played that game before. If she had only kept still none of this would have happened . . .'

His voice trailed off and, while Aiden poured him a large Courvoisier, he controlled the urge to slam the bottle into the man's face. He left the man sipping his brandy; he had heard the doctor arrive and he wanted to know the state of play.

The doctor was a middle-aged man with a balding head, and

a bad case of psoriasis. He also had a hygiene problem that included halitosis. He was arrogant and badly dressed and no one on the job liked him, especially not the boys he requested. The girls too loathed him and so did Aiden. He was disgusting in every way. He was useful, though, in that he would sedate the more nervous newbies and, of course, he would prescribe drugs for the clientele's satisfaction, if requested. He had a big practice in Hampstead and he was known for his willingness to give out slimming pills without any questions. And he had a seemingly never-ending supply of like-minded contacts who had money and status and, significantly, influence – the latter, of course, being the most important.

The doctor had a very big celebrity clientele because of his generosity with narcotics and this was what inflated his already high opinion of himself. Apparently he was a good doctor in other ways and was often called in by the police to carry out autopsies on some of their more outrageous murder victims. This might have been to do with the fact that the Chief Superintendent was also a regular visitor to this particular establishment, although he liked girls of about fifteen so he didn't see himself in quite the same way as he did the other clients. He saw *his* girls as almost grown up, and he liked them to pretend that he was doing them the favour of a lifetime. People's hypocrisy would never cease to amaze Aiden O'Hara. But it was what made him a serious wedge so he was quite willing to overlook a lot of things.

Doctor Flint was washing his hands in the small en-suite bathroom as Aiden entered the room. Aiden noticed that Jade was white-faced and looked as if she was going to be sick – that was a definite first for her, as far as Aiden knew. That she was kind to what she always referred to as 'the merchandise' didn't exactly hide the fact that she had a decent streak running through her somewhere, and he knew she argued with Eric about customers like the quivering popstar who had caused this latest fucking debacle.

'What happened?'

She was shaking her head, her huge eyes actually glistening with tears, and he instinctively put an arm around her. At least the doctor had had the grace to cover the poor child up.

Flint's booming voice came out of the tiny bathroom as he wiped his hands. 'Shoved something up inside her a good few hours ago, I would say. Peritonitis is my guess. Ripped her open inside.'

His voice was matter-of-fact and that was not lost on Aiden or Jade. Just another fucking day to this bloke. Aiden was gritting his teeth in suppressed anger.

'What? What did he use?'

Flint shrugged. 'I won't know that until I remove it but, if it is what I think it is, you don't want to know, laddie.'

He walked into the room and said to Jade, 'Get her sent to mine. I'll do what's required. Talk to the Chief, he will smooth it over. We'll have her sorted in a few days and cremated without a fuss. I deal with a lot of street kids in my volunteer capacity. This will be all forgotten about in no time.'

He touched her arm gently and Jade moved away from him. Flint was aware of the move and Aiden saw the anger in the man's eyes. He was acting the hero and not getting the thanks he expected.

'How's our singing star? Does he need a sedative?'

Jade nodded and then, seeming to pull herself together, she said in a quiet voice that was full of forced humility, 'They all love their chemicals, don't they? Thank you for coming so promptly, Doctor.'

Flint grinned. This was better, this was what he liked.

Aiden waved him out saying, 'He's in the top bedroom. I'm sure he will be delighted to see you. Give him one up the arse for me!'

The doctor actually laughed at what he perceived as a good joke and left the room.

When they were alone Aiden pulled her into his arms and, holding her to him, he said gently, 'Come on, Jade. This happens, we both know that. It's part of the game.' He drew her closer and kissed her gently on her cheek. Then he was all businesslike as he said, 'Has she any family? Is there anyone who could cause us trouble?'

Jade gave a sad, disgusted shake of her head before she said, 'We bought her two years ago for an ounce of heroin. She was only supposed to stay a month. Her mother had been pimping her out since she was a toddler by the sounds of it. The heroin was too good for the silly bitch and she overdosed that night. We have had her ever since. You know Eric, he loves a fucking bargain, bastard that he is!'

She placed a hand on the girl's hair, which was thick and abundant – and the only thing visible now she had been covered up with the blood-stained sheet.

'She never had a fucking chance.'

Aiden really didn't know what to say, so he kept silent. Jade walked from the room, and a few minutes later he followed her.

The girl's body and every piece of furniture in the room was gone within the hour and, by the time Eric was made aware that anything had gone awry, the room had been scrubbed with bleach, repainted and refurnished. This was what he paid them for. And Eric paid them very well.

Chapter Thirty-Three

Jade was lying in Aiden's arms. Neither of them was in the mood for sex and instead they held each other tightly. The day's events had thrown them both.

Aiden was Eric's blue-eyed boy, the clever lad, the problem-solver. That should have made him feel good, but this time it didn't. He had erased from the world a child who had never known a day's happiness. It was as if she had never existed. That bothered him for once, because it had hit home that, without him, the same thing could have happened to his brothers or sister. It was a small step for some kids: they ran from one situation only to find that they were in another one, far scarier than that they had left behind.

'You all right, Jade?'

He felt her move away from him and, as she lit them both cigarettes, he watched her in the lamplight. She was looking older today, and even though he knew she was still a beautiful woman – especially to him – she was nearer forty than thirty and that was something she was very aware of. He noticed the lines around her eyes and her mouth but they didn't bother him one bit. He loved her – not just her body or the sex they had, but *her*. His Jade.

He took the cigarette from her and pulled on it deeply.

'I don't know, Aiden. Poor little mare.' She smiled slightly as she said, in a jokey voice, 'Must be going soft in my old age!'

He laughed with her and, sitting up in the bed, he kissed her shoulder gently. 'Cost that piece of scum a hundred grand to keep it quiet. Imagine the papers if this came out? Let alone the fucking judicial system, eh?'

Jade snorted angrily and stabbed her cigarette out. Then, immediately lighting another, she said bitterly, 'He would see the advantage though, wouldn't he? Always about fucking money for Eric.'

There was a bitterness in her voice that Aiden had never heard before. Where was the hard bitch he had first met? Was she actually going soft like she said? He wondered at her showing such emotion; it just wasn't like her. He pulled her into his arms and was disconcerted when he realised she was crying. He had never seen her cry.

'Hey, come on, Jade. You know there was nothing anyone could have done . . .'

But she cried harder. He was nonplussed at what to do; this was something he would never have expected in a million years. He kissed her gently and tried to pull her face up to his, but she just buried her head in his chest.

Jade Dixon had fallen for this young man. Against her better judgement there was something about him that attracted her. For the first time in her life she actually enjoyed sex with a man and, even though she didn't feel this way every time they coupled, it was often enough to make her see that he meant a lot more to her than she would have ever thought possible. They worked well together, even with the age gap, and she believed that he genuinely cared for her. He made her feel wonderful when he was with her and he respected her for the right reasons. Now, though, she had fucked it up and she had to tell him.

She pushed him away from her, and saw the concern in his eyes as he looked into her ravaged face. But this was not the time to be thinking of how old she looked – even she knew that.

'What the fuck is wrong, Jade?'

She looked at this lad, because that was what he was for all his size and his intelligence, and she said heavily, 'I'm fucking *pregnant*.'

She saw the mixture of emotions that crossed his face and was surprised to find the first one was happiness. Surely he couldn't expect her to have a child? Have his child at her age?

Aiden smiled widely. 'Really? You are having a baby? My baby?'

She nodded and, even though she had cried off her expertly applied make-up and she looked every day of her thirty-six years, Aiden knew he had never loved her more.

'This is the best news ever, Jade. I know it wasn't planned but what a baby we will make, eh?'

She couldn't answer him, because she quite honestly didn't know what to say. He was holding her tightly to him, and talking nineteen to the dozen, and suddenly she wondered if this might be a good thing. She knew that this was probably her last chance of motherhood even though she had never wanted a child before in her life, and wasn't that sure she wanted one now. But now she knew that if she *did* have this child, Aiden would be there for it and for her. He was already a father to his younger siblings and he took family seriously – really seriously, because anyone who could put up with Reeva had to be family-minded. Whereas she had no familial loyalty because she had no family to speak of. None that she wanted in her life anyway. But this child she was carrying would be her family, wouldn't it?

'But I will be so old when it's born, Aiden . . .'

He laughed at her and said jovially, 'Stop it, you dozy bitch. You're beautiful and you're clever and you are mine. This baby will be like a fucking superchild: with your looks, my brains and our nous, it will rule the fucking world!'

Despite her reservations she was picking up on his excitement and, when he kissed her long and hard on her lips, she responded.

'This is a gift from God, Jade. A child is a blessing, you know? And after that poor girl today think of how lucky our child will be. Boy or girl, I don't care. It will be a part of us, won't it? You and me can live on together in this baby!'

Then he started to really laugh and Jade laughed with him. It was such abandoned laughter, and it felt good to be laughing. But Aiden's laughter was much longer and harder than hers.

'Come on, Aiden! Tell me what we are laughing at?'

He was wiping his eyes with glee as he said loudly, 'Reeva, me mother. She will be a granny! I bet that won't go down too fucking well!'

He was laughing once more. But Jade wasn't joining in now. She didn't find that funny at all.

Chapter Thirty-Four

'Look at him! He's fucking terrified, Aiden.'

Aiden laughed at the awe in his brother's voice. 'So he fucking should be. Wanker.'

Patsy O'Hara loved working like this with his brother; he had had a lot of making up to do and had learned a lot in the past two years. They were in a small lock-up in Basildon – a row of abandoned garages that Aiden, in his wisdom, had purchased for the company recently. It was the perfect place for jobs like this. They were quiet and the people who lived nearby had no intention of getting involved with anything. Why would they? This was an area where anyone with half a brain kept their noses out of other people's business.

Patsy poured out a generous measure of Scotch and passed the glass to his brother who sipped it nonchalantly as he studied his prey. Larry Brookmeyer was a big man in every way: wide of girth and loud of voice. It was said mouth that had landed him in his latest bout of trouble. That, and the fact he had had his hands in Aiden's pockets. Never a good idea at any time, but less so when he had informed his esteemed colleagues that he wasn't scared of 'that little runt'.

Aiden was fuming, with what Larry had said about Jade. Jade, who was near her time, was feeling very vulnerable what with her age and everything else. Larry had said he had always wondered what it was like to fuck a pensioner. That was a very unfortunate turn of phrase to use. Some people really should not go near drugs of any kind, especially cocaine. It was cocaine that had signed Larry Brookmeyer's death warrant.

Aiden could almost have overlooked the insult if it had been Larry's only crime. If only he'd kept his mouth shut about Gloria – Aiden's latest bit on the side. Young and lovely Gloria, with her pert breasts and her long legs. And a snatch that could grab you like a vice! Gloria who, thanks to this idiot, had come to the attention of Jade. Not that Jade had mentioned her, of course – she had too much fucking class. But Aiden was sure she knew – there was nothing that went on in the Smoke that Jade didn't know about. Oh, the once delectable Gloria was next on his list of things to take care of! Mouthy fucking mare didn't know when to keep her trap shut either.

He sighed in annoyance. Yes, he had fucked Gloria, but that hardly counted as an engagement. And he had *expressly* told her to keep it on the down-low. Instead, the stupid whore had broadcast it to the nation and for that she would pay and pay big time. He was going to ensure that she never fucked with anyone again – she would always remember that she had fucked him – in more ways than one.

But first things first – Larry was about to be taught a lesson. Aiden rubbed his hands together with relish as if he was the presenter of a Saturday-night programme, delivering the prize to be won to the audience.

'Now, Larry. I want to revisit a few of the things you have said recently. Namely the "fucking a pensioner" barb. Were you on the fucking Bostik, you dozy shit?' He sighed theatrically. 'That was bad enough! But also mouthing on about me and a certain little bird who shall remain nameless, and who should have stayed fucking nameless, especially to my better half, the lovely Jade.'

Larry was in serious trouble, but he was sensible enough to realise that he had to take any punishment coming to him. Aiden possessed a very low threshold for aggravation; he was not a man to cross.

'Look, Aiden. I can't apologise enough, mate. It was the drink and the drugs. I've promised my wife I would sort myself out, and this lot now has been the wake-up call I needed . . .'

He was stuttering in fright and Patsy found that amusing. 'Oh, you will be waking up, all right. Only not in the way you think, mate. You will be waking up in intensive care, methinks. That's if you ever fucking wake up, of course.'

'Give me the petrol, bruv.'

Larry's eyes were like flying saucers as he saw Patsy O'Hara pick up the petrol can and hand it to his brother. The lid was already off and the fumes were suddenly overpowering him. As Aiden poured the liquid all over Larry's head he started screaming in fear. Aiden belted him across the face with the empty can, and knocked him senseless. He had no empathy for him. He wanted the fucker gone, once and for all.

Finishing his drink, he calmly lit a match and tossed it on to the sodden man. The flames engulfed him in seconds, and the screams were loud, like an animal.

The chair he was tied to was metal and, as it heated up, it added to the man's pain and terror. The garage door was open and Aiden and Patsy stood together, smoking cigarettes, and watched.

Patsy nudged his brother gently and pointed at the fire extinguisher. But Aiden pointedly ignored him, shrugging him off aggressively.

When the man's eyes melted, Patsy brought up his lunch and Aiden was laughing so hard as his brother spewed his guts up that a group of young lads riding by stopped to watch the spectacle. When they saw the burning effigy in the garage, however, they quickly went on their way.

Rubbing his brother's back gently, Aiden finally said, 'Come on, mate. Let's go and get you a nice cold drink of water, shall we?'

Aiden was smiling as he picked up the fire extinguisher and put the man out. He then locked up the garage and, turning to his brother, he said jovially, 'I need a pint. Thirsty work, burning rubbish.'

Chapter Thirty-Five

Jade was nearly on her time. Apart from a small, neat bump, she looked no different from usual. She had watched what she ate, had stopped smoking, except for two in the evenings, and rarely touched alcohol. Aiden had been insistent, saying he had read an article in *Woman's Realm* about pregnancy and now thought he was a fucking expert on it. Why and where he had read the magazine, he couldn't recall. But it seemed he had remembered every word of the article.

Jade was tired, and she would be glad when this baby was out of her and breathing for itself. She did not like this housing of another human being, and wondered at women like Reeva who were prepared to do it over and over.

She had found out about Aiden's paramour – a stripper who was half her age and who could talk the hind leg off a table by all accounts. A complete airhead of a girl – that was the worst thing. Larry might have opened his big trap but Jade had known about Gloria almost from the off. Gloria had bragged about her conquest to all and sundry.

She squeezed her eyes shut in distress. She had still not said a dicky bird to Aiden, and that was how she was going to play it. She would keep her dignity, but having this child inside her only seemed to add to her humiliation. In a strange way she

understood his logic: he still wanted her but he seemed frightened that if they had sex it would somehow harm the child.
When they did have sex, he was gentle and almost courteous
– not their usual way of fucking each other's brains out. She
knew that he saw her now as a mother, and that was what had
changed him.

But she didn't want to be a mother if it meant he didn't want
her as he always had. Her whole life had been coloured by the
sex act, and now she had found a man who could actually make
her feel something she was not about to let him go. She felt
the sting of tears. Aiden was already crazy about this baby, but
what did that count for if he changed towards her? He was too
young for her, and she was too old for him, but finally she felt
something akin to love and she was loath to lose that.

The baby kicked and she put her hands on her tiny belly and,
for a few seconds, she wished the child dead. She couldn't let
anything or anyone come between her and Aiden. She just knew
it would destroy her.

Since they had found out about the baby and moved in
together, Jade's feelings had only intensified. She loved being
with Aiden every day. Jade Dixon was in love for the first time
in her life and that fact frightened her. She saw love as a weakness, and weakness of any kind was anathema to her. She was
also experiencing jealousy for the first time in her life and she
hated herself for it. She had always prided herself on her even
mindedness where men were concerned – she had used them
and that was that. She had never had a female friend of any
kind, just acquaintances and, again, that had suited her fine. So
why did she now crave another woman to talk to about what
was happening to her? She could only blame this child, and the
hormones, or whatever it was that made her feel suddenly so

alone and so vulnerable. Either way, she didn't like this way of living and she knew that she had to get a grip on herself and her emotions before they spilled over and she said things she would regret for the rest of her days.

But one thing she knew for sure: she would never let Aiden know just how much he had hurt her. She had always seen emotions as a weakness, and now she knew she had been right all those years. They left you exposed, they left you in a state of flux, unable to control your thoughts. She didn't like it one bit.

She wasn't cut out for this childbearing malarkey, that much was obvious. She forced herself to concentrate on the ledger in front of her; the books were not going to balance themselves.

But all she could see in her mind's eye was Gloria, with her girlish breasts and her wide, open smile. All she could see was Gloria's youth and, with the baby inside her and the dragging feeling she'd had in her back all day, she felt tired and old. She blinked back the sting of tears. If someone witnessed her crying she would lose her hard-won credibility overnight.

Chapter Thirty-Six

Gloria was admiring herself in her bedroom mirror. She was a good-looking girl and she knew that she had to make the most of it while she could. Her mother had been a looker too, but she had saddled herself with three kids by the time she was twenty-two and she didn't want Gloria to waste her opportunities. It was a refrain that Gloria had heard over and over again; she listened to her mother carefully and acknowledged the wisdom of her advice. There was no way she was going to live like her mum, on social security, robbing Peter to pay Paul, and putting up with men who were beneath her to try and get a few extra quid into the house so she could live a little better.

She had decided before her fourteenth birthday that she wanted a lot more than her mother, and she would go all out to get it. Not being an academic, she had known her only chance lay in marrying money. 'Lay' being the operative word!

Now she had hooked the big prize in Aiden O'Hara and she was determined to have him on a permanent basis. She had it all planned: she already had him in bed – eventually she would produce a child and her life would be settled. He would look after her, she was depending on that. Aiden would *have* to look after her, if she was producing his next heir. If she was going to all the trouble of having a baby, it would be one with a father who could enhance her life – not fucking stunt it like it had her mum's.

The plus side was, of course, that he was very good-looking, and that made her job just that little bit easier. And the change in people's attitudes when they found out that he was her boyfriend was amazing. The respect was evident – heady stuff to a girl who had grown up with nothing of value, not even a good family name. Gloria craved recognition and, through her relationship with Aiden, she felt she was finally getting it. She daydreamed of them together, maybe even married, in a beautiful home where they had all the latest appliances, and where they lived in harmony and nothing was denied her.

As she admired herself, she could hear her mother arguing with her latest beau, a hard-drinking Scotsman with a serious amphetamine habit. She closed her ears to the noise, something she had taught herself to do at a young age. She loved her mum, but her taste in men was somewhat questionable. Christ Himself knew she had had to fend off enough of them over the years, and they had tried their best, the fuckers. 'Helping with her homework' was a favourite expression, but she had sussed them out from the off. Her mum, for some obscure reason, had always been willing to give them the benefit of the doubt. But, again, she knew the score, even with all that old fucking fanny her mum spouted. Gems like, 'You got the wrong impression' and, 'Why do you always think everything's about *you*?' It was a hard road. She actually felt sorrow for her mum and her determination to hang on to a man, no matter what. Her mum had to do what she could to survive – she knew that she would most probably do the same.

But she actually believed that her Aiden really loved her and, as she had said on numerous occasions, that Jade Dixon, as

105

pretty as she might be, was an old lady in comparison. And Gloria saw herself as a fair person, who would give anyone their due, even a woman who, as she pointed out at every available opportunity, was actually old enough to be Ade's mother! There was really no competition with that fucking fright. After all, *she* was young and gorgeous; so, in reality, what more could Aiden want?

Her friend Tamara had pointed out that Aiden had been with Jade for a long time; she was pregnant by him already and, as far as she knew, they were tight. But Gloria had overlooked that shit. How could he want Jade over her? It just wasn't possible. She had youth on her side. What did Jade Dixon have?

The fighting between her mother and her paramour seemed to be getting louder and no one was more shocked than her when her bedroom door was kicked open and she saw Aiden and his brother Patsy standing before her like avenging angels. Aiden was shaking his head slowly, as if unable to believe what he was about to say.

'Oh, Gloria. You have seriously fucked me off, lady.'

She looked into Aiden's eyes and knew immediately that he was not a happy bunny.

He smiled at her as he said seriously, 'How could you even think that I would put you over my Jade? Are you on fucking drugs?'

She was terrified and knew instinctively to keep quiet and to not answer back. He looked manic, frightening. Murderous.

'I told you to keep your fucking trap shut, didn't I?'

He looked at his brother Patsy as if to verify his statement. Patsy nodded in agreement.

'But this fucking mouthy whore couldn't keep her fucking trap shut.'

Aiden sighed theatrically, looking around at the bedroom. Somewhere in his mind he was sorry for her; he actually understood her actions. He should know what it was like to want to get on, get away from your life. But this dozy mare had crossed the line, and she had given his Jade cause to doubt him. That could not, and would not, be overlooked.

He smiled at her, that charming smile that had made her drop her drawers in double-quick time. Then he said almost sorrowfully, 'I fucked you, darling. And now I am in what is called a quandary. See, you have caused me untold aggravation with your fucking opinions and your discussions with people I would cross the road to avoid. And, thanks to you, they now know my business. My private fucking business! So I have to shut you down sooner rather than later. You do see my dilemma, I'm sure?'

Gloria was devastated because she had really believed she had hit the jackpot with Aiden.

'You are fucking gone, lady. Your big trap has made you talk yourself into some serious aggravation. My heart goes out to you. But anyone who upsets my Jade can only be on a death wish. I will leave you with that thought, you useless fucking cunt. Like anyone would really want you!'

Aiden looked at his brother and nodded. Gloria saw all her hopes and dreams fading before her eyes.

'But, Ade . . .'

Aiden looked at her as if he had never seen her before and she saw in his eyes the disdain that he actually had for her.

'Shut the fuck up! I will leave you in the capable hands of my brother Patsy.'

He turned away from her and then, as he reached the top of the stairs, he turned back to face her and he said seriously, 'If you ever mention my name again, I will hunt you down like the fucking dog you are. Do you understand me?'

Her beautiful eyes were filled with tears and she nodded her agreement and, for a split second, Aiden felt a small sliver of sorrow. After all, she had been a good little fuck, bless her.

He heard the beating that Patsy was administering as he walked down into the cluttered hallway. He smiled benevolently at the people standing in the doorway of the front room, and tossed a wad of money on to the floor.

'Make sure she is on a train out of here sooner rather than later. Don't make me come back and finish this once and for all.'

He heard them scrabbling around for the money he had thrown and sighed inside. There was some serious scum in this world, and he was lucky enough to understand exactly how best to take advantage of them. It was a knack he had.

Chapter Thirty-Seven

Eric Palmer was thrilled with his protégé – he had found himself a worthy successor in every way. He saw himself in Aiden – the want and the need that he had once felt in abundance. It was a yearning that only a few people understood and acted upon at the right time in their life. He knew many an old Face that could have gone far but they had not had that fucking burning need, and it was that which drove you on to bigger and better things.

For as long as he remembered, chasing the dollar had been all he had cared about. He had embraced the earn from a very young age and he had been quite happy to do whatever was necessary to keep said earn. He had been a vicious and violent bastard, but that was expected – you didn't enter the world he had with kind fucking words and a knitting pattern. You went in with the knowledge that you were more than willing to cause serious harm should the need arise. You went in knowing that you were going to make enemies and you had to be sure in yourself that you could happily obliterate those enemies along with your new counterparts. It was all about having the front to put your money where your mouth was. Luckily for him, he had had that front. He had made a point of proving himself to everyone who mattered and also to the people who didn't matter. It was about getting a powerful reputation for oneself far and wide, and he had managed that quite quickly.

Then, once you had proved your worth, you had to be willing to embrace those people who were wary of you and what you were capable of, and bring them into your businesses. Unless they were troublesome, of course – then you had no choice but to take the fuckers out. Some people just asked for it; all mouth and no trousers, as his mum used to say. Plenty of talk but a bit shy when it came to doing the actual deed required. It was a lot harder than people realised to deliberately bring harm to strangers when it came down to it. It was one thing talking a good fight, but it was a completely different thing when you were asked to violently hurt someone who had never done anything to you personally, who you might even have socialised with, gone to their wedding or drunk with in the local pub – who you might even be related to either by blood or marriage.

But it was what separated the men from the boys, and brought the next generation of Faces to the attention of the powers-that-be. It was how you proved your worth, and how you moved up the ladder of success. There were more than enough fucking strong arms in the world; what set you apart was if you were capable of anything, if you were without conscience. Couple that with a quick brain and a natural aptitude for an earn and you were guaranteed your place in the hierarchy.

In reality, in the world they lived in, there could only ever be a few men who were capable of achieving such importance. That stood to reason. There was only so far most men were willing to go. That was fine with Eric; that was their prerogative. But *he* had been willing to fight his way to the top, and he had never once regretted any of it. Furthermore, he had ensured that he stayed there. He had understood the need to surround himself with people who could guarantee him a good wage. That was the key – to work with people you knew would want the earn as much as you did.

Once you found them, your job was to bring them onside and give them the respect they deserved and keep them close – so close that they couldn't shit without you knowing about it. You had to know what they did, why they did it and, of course, who was with them at the time when they perpetrated their ghastly deeds. That was how close you kept the people you delegated to. At the end of the day, a man in Eric's position had to be wary of trusting anyone. If you trusted someone too much, or gave them too much responsibility without keeping a close eye on them, you were basically making a cunt of yourself. That would be tantamount to suicide in his world. There was always some fucker waiting in the wings to try and take what you had worked for. He should know, because that is exactly what he had done many moons ago as a young man.

Eric had watched and he had waited and, eventually, he had fucked over the man who had given him his first chance. He had never felt any guilt over what he had done – as far as he was concerned the man deserved everything he had got.

But while you might never completely trust anyone, you did need to find people who you could mould and who you could depend on. They were the people you nurtured, who you kept close, who you gave your blessing to and who you allowed to work their magic in your name. That was the secret of success; how you could extend not only your businesses, but also your empire. Other people were suddenly in the frame if it all fell out of bed. You, as the boss, learned early on that to keep yourself safe you needed to surround yourself with the best of the best.

He had done all of that, and he demanded loyalty from his chosen few to guarantee that, no matter what happened, he would never see the inside of a prison cell. No one could fucking usurp him, and that was because he knew enough about his world to make sure that he groomed his workers from a young age.

But with Aiden O'Hara, Eric was breaking his own rules. He thought of the lad as family. He couldn't help it – Aiden was the son he wished he had. As unpredictable as he could be, Aiden was old school. These days, youngsters thought they were fucking Al Capone because they could provide drugs but they would never put their money where their great big mouths were. They believed they were gangsters because they dealt a few drugs, and yet not one of them had ever proved themselves in any way, shape or form. The closest they had ever got to villainy was listening to American rappers. They were middle-class tossers who couldn't broker a real fucking deal unless someone like Aiden did it for them. These new customers were quite happy living on the edges of the criminal world because they couldn't even work out that they were being royally mugged off. It was laughable.

As he waited for Aiden to arrive, he felt a sense of complete and utter contentment. He was at the very top of his game, he had more money than he could shake a fucking stick at, and he had a young man who he had moulded in his own image to step into his shoes when the time was right. He trusted Aiden O'Hara more than he trusted his own flesh and blood; he believed that Aiden had an inherent sense of loyalty that was rare in this day and age. The sixties were long gone, and the big prison sentences handed down had made the new generation of Faces willing to serve up anyone for a sentence they could not, in reality, cope with.

But Eric believed in his gut that Aiden would rather do the time than be seen to betray the people around him. He saw him as a decent lad, a grafter and a family man in every way – especially now he was about to become a father. He had no doubt that Aiden would go all out for this child, as he had for his brothers and sister. Eric felt that he could finally begin to take a well-earned step back and enjoy the fruits of his labour. He would have a big decision to make in the near future but he believed that that future had Aiden in it – as long as he toed the line, of course. That went without saying, as far as Eric was concerned. He might love Aiden like a son but he would never let him forget why he had his power and who had allowed him to have it. That was Eric Palmer's modus operandi and nothing or no one could or would ever change that.

The phone rang and Eric answered it, before he slammed it down and, calling out to his driver, Dessy Marks, he said happily, 'Jade's having the baby so the meeting's cancelled.'

He was actually pleased for her. He liked Jade; she had been his many years ago and she was a complete user, but it seemed that young Aiden had actually tamed her. Jade was a legend in her own lunchtime – she'd been through more men than the YMCA – but they appeared to be happy. Well, time would tell. He wished the best for them. They were both grafters, and that would always be what mattered most to him.

Chapter Thirty-Eight

Jade delivered the baby without any drama and in record time. There had been no complications and she felt wonderful as she cradled her brand-new son in her arms. The force of her feelings had startled her, especially when he had been placed on her belly. She had looked at this new person, this child that she had created, and the sheer rush of love had been as unexpected as it had been wonderful. She suddenly understood the power of procreation and, for the first time in her life, she had a blood relative. The enormity wasn't lost on her; she had never felt this kind of connection with another human being until now.

She was holding the baby to her breast when Aiden arrived, and she smiled widely at him, high on adrenaline and hormones. Seeing Aiden with his serious and worried countenance she felt a terrible urge to cry, not because she was sad but because, for the first time in her life, she felt an absolute happiness.

She looked into his eyes and said gently, 'We have a son, Aiden. A beautiful son.' Aiden looked down at the child and beamed from ear to ear. Then, kissing Jade tenderly on the lips, he took the baby from her. He was clearly comfortable with holding a child. But, then, he would be, with Reeva as his mother – he was the nearest thing to a father his siblings had ever known.

'He's beautiful, Jade, like you. He is fucking perfect.'

Jade laughed. 'He's over nine pounds! Big lad.'

They laughed together, and Aiden knew that he had never loved anyone like he loved this child and his mother. Jade looked tired and rough, but she had never seemed more lovely to him than she did at this moment. She had given him a son, a beautiful, handsome son.

'I love you, Jade. You know that, don't you, darling?'

She smiled and nodded her head. She was aware that he was apologising for his jaunt with Gloria and she accepted it. She believed that he meant it, that he was sorry, but she also knew he would do it again; it was the nature of this particular beast. He was too young for her. But she would hold on to him as long as she could because she genuinely loved him, and sometimes she didn't understand why that was. But, today, looking at their son, she felt complete for the first time in her whole life and that was a good feeling. She would not ruin this moment with her fears for the future; the future would happen no matter what. Today she just wanted to enjoy the birth of her son.

'I was on me way, and when I got here and realised you had had him, I was fucking dumbfounded! Quick and easy according to the doctor.'

Jade laughed again. 'You know me, Aiden. I never turn a drama into a crisis! Honestly, it was over in a few hours! And I feel all right, really – a bit tired, but other than that I feel great.'

He kissed her again and, sitting on the bed, they admired their new son together. Aiden looked at Jade with such love and gratitude she felt the sting of tears. She really loved this man, and she wished that they were of an age. He was a good man, he was the man she wanted – the only man she had ever wanted. But today the fifteen years between them seemed to be enormous and it frightened her.

The baby started to cry and Aiden passed him to Jade, saying happily, 'Aiden Junior is a bit of a stroppy fucker when the fancy takes him!'

Jade settled him as best she could, aware that Aiden was watching her every move.

'He's his father's son then, ain't he?'

Chapter Thirty-Nine

Reeva walked into the room, all cheap perfume and camaraderie, determined to be nice and not to cause any aggro. She was on what she liked to call 'best behaviour'; the prospect of meeting her first grandchild was heady stuff to her.

She looked down at the tiny bundle that Jade was holding out to her. For that gesture alone, she was grateful to Jade. Picking him up, Reeva held him close to her chest and, as she looked down into his little red face, she felt a tug of love that was almost tangible. This was her first grandchild, her Aiden's child. The love came easily.

Reeva had always loved babies – the way they depended on her, needed her. And this little chap was no different. With all hers she had always tried to waive the drink and the hard drugs until they were at least six months old. Then her usual needs had surfaced and she had suited herself.

She looked at Jade, a woman who had just given birth, and she saw the tiredness and the vulnerability in her. She also saw the hope in Jade's eyes that Reeva would accept the child and not cause any undue aggravation. For the first time ever, she actually liked the woman who had ensnared her son.

Reeva smiled crookedly and said seriously, 'He's beautiful, Jade. Looks just like his dad when he was born.'

Unconsciously they all breathed a silent sigh of relief.

Chapter Forty

1994

Reeva was happy that her grandchild, Aiden Junior, was a big part of her life. After all, he was her baby's baby. She had struck up a truce with Jade these days. They were not exactly bosom buddies, but they tolerated each other. In truth, Reeva had come to quite like her. Love her or loathe her, Jade was a woman after her own heart in many ways. She didn't suffer fools gladly and she knew how to take care of herself. She was a survivor and Reeva got that. Despite her initial feelings for Jade, she had come around to seeing that she was a strong-minded woman. And that was an essential attribute if she was going to be with Aiden.

Her Aiden loved Jade but he was not a man who could be depended on to be faithful. He treated her shamefully in many respects and because of that Reeva could find it in her to feel bad for the woman and understand Jade's wariness where he was concerned. At the end of the day, Aiden was her son, her boy, and Reeva would always stand by him even though, as the years went by, that was getting harder and harder.

Jade had always given her her due, treated her with respect, and Reeva could not fault her as a mother or as a family member. And she was thrilled that Jade was happy for her to look after her grandson.

At four, Aiden Junior was as bright as a button – something that did not escape his doting grandmother. She saw this as proof of her own children's strength and intelligence rather than something that he might have inherited from Jade or her side. Whether Reeva liked Jade or not, she was devoid of anything even resembling family – that was just a fact.

Now this was Reeva's happiest time of day, when she had him to herself and his parents were at work. She was dreading him starting school, even though it would only be part-time at first. They would miss him. Tony loved the little fella too, and all her kids were mad on him – especially Agnes. She was like a proper little mum to him.

At thirteen, Agnes was developing fast and, with her blue eyes, she was a dark-haired version of Reeva. But that was where the similarity ended. How it had happened Reeva could only guess, but her daughter was a real Holy Joe, never out of the fucking church. Her bedroom was like a shrine to the Virgin Mary, and she had enough sets of rosaries to start her own market stall. Even her nan was worried about her – and Annie was the one who had always forced religion on them. And, as for their priest, Father Hagen! Well, talk about encouraging her. She went to six o'clock Mass every morning *and* evening prayers. She spent more time in that church than she spent at home. Still, Reeva was convinced that once she discovered boys that would change. And the change couldn't come quick enough as far as she was concerned.

As she played with her grandson she sighed with happiness. Aiden was making a good life for their family, and that was all that mattered to her. That and this young lad, who for some reason she treated better than she had ever treated her own kids. She had been on far fewer benders since her little prince had been in her care – only the odd weekend – and, if she was honest, she felt better for it. Tony took the piss out of her and she knew he had a point – she was a better parent to this boy than to all her other kids put together. She loved being a granny, but unlike with her own kids, she could give this fucker back as and when it suited her. That was the best thing of all.

Chapter Forty-One

Jade was not happy. She was being rowed out of Aiden's latest gig. He was up to all sorts of skulduggery and the fact that she was not a part of it bothered her.

Throughout their whole time together he had listened to her advice, had asked her opinion and respected her thoughts on any of his deals. In reality, she had not just been his sounding board, she'd also been the person who had made sure that his plans came to fruition. He was a clever bugger with a natural fucking knack for the dark side. He could always find a con or a way of making any deal that bit sweeter. But he had always relied on her to be the voice of reason, especially when she was teaching him the different businesses. She had taught him well and they were a fucking good team. Her expertise and his willingness to create new earns was their strength and was what gave them the edge.

This time, however, he was deliberately going out on his own, making sure that she did not have any idea what he was dealing with. That hurt, especially as she made a point of discussing *everything* she was involved in with him, and she made it clear that he understood just how much she respected his advice. His ego was bigger than Cheops's fucking Pyramid, but she had always made a point of never treating him like the boy he was, even when she had felt like it. Because for all his fucking so-called nous, without her at his side, showing him the ropes from every angle – not just Eric Palmer's – he would have been hard pushed to learn everything as quickly and as thoroughly as he had.

Aiden's problem was that he was an arrogant fuck, and she had the knack of heading him off at the pass, so to speak. She was his voice of reason, even if he would never admit it. He was still a young man, but he looked and acted a lot older – her relationship with him was what kept *her* at the top these days. That hurt. It really smarted, because she was a serious earner, and she kept the day-to-day shite running smoothly because Aiden could never be bothered with the nitty-gritty. He couldn't sustain enough of the long-term interest needed to keep all these bright ideas of his going. He left that to everyone else – mainly Jade, as she knew better than anyone else. He couldn't see that businesses needed nurturing, needed to be looked after and watched over. He was often bored within weeks and then he went on to the next thing that caught his imagination. She would then bring in the right people in the right positions to ensure that everything ran smoothly, so he could swan around like the dog's fucking gonads looking for his next earn. Without her, everything would fall apart, and she had a feeling that Eric Palmer was as aware of that as Aiden was. But Eric's attitude was 'you don't have a fucking guard dog and bark your fucking self'. The fact that Aiden was now branching out on his own not only offended her, but it also worried her. Without a guiding hand, he wouldn't look at the fine detail of his latest venture – and then it would be too late. Even more worrying was her suspicion that if he didn't want her to know about it then it was obvious he did not think she would approve. She had a feeling that Eric Palmer was on board and that he and Aiden were up to something dangerous, something they knew she would not want to be part of. Her fear was that Eric Palmer would more or less hang Aiden out to dry if it all went pear-shaped, and that was something she would not fucking countenance.

Chapter Forty-Two

Aiden was absolutely thrilled with his latest business venture. Eric Palmer was, as he told Aiden at every available opportunity, as happy as the proverbial pig in shit. It was a departure for both of them, new territory, and the whole concept was just full of opportunities that would make them all a really serious earn.

When Aiden had explained his idea initially, Eric had been very wary. But, once he had thought it through, he had seen the cleverness of Aiden's proposition. The boy had a knack for seeing the potential in a scam and this latest one was fucking perfection. Now, as long as they used their brains and made sure that no one could pinpoint them as the instigators, they were home and fucking dry. It was a piece of piss, which was how Aiden had so picturesquely described it. Eric believed that Aiden was right about using front men to do the deals, and that had all been arranged and agreed upon.

Now they were enjoying the celebration of a deal well done, and an earn beyond their wildest dreams. If Eric had a few misgivings, they were damped down by his greed; he chose not to dwell on them because, when all was said and done, this was Aiden's fucking baby. If it fell out of bed he could feign inno-cence – which was Eric's fallback position with everyone he worked with. He made sure nothing could ever come back to him.

Also, they were now playing with some seriously big boys, and if it did go wrong, the only person in the frame would be Aiden. On the other hand, if it came out on top he would have an in with the men who controlled the international markets. It was a win–win for Eric, but it was a serious gamble for Aiden. And they both knew that.

Chapter Forty-Three

Agnes O'Hara hated being herself. It was not easy being the only girl in a family of boys, especially when her older brother was someone like Aiden. Everyone was scared of him – even some of the teachers at her school. Except the nuns and the priests; they were not impressed by anyone and Agnes liked that. Not that they didn't try and screw him for every penny they could, and Aiden was quite happy to let them squeeze him for contributions – he relished being in a position where he could give them the readies they needed. Playing the big man proved that he'd been right to follow his own road and not take up the chance of university down the line.

But that was Aiden all over – it was important to him to look and act the big man. And, of course, he loved the opportunity to lord it over everyone in his orbit, playing the rich, benevolent benefactor. Her mum and her brothers ate that all up.

She could hear her mum calling her for her dinner and sighed. She had begun to hate living in this environment, pandering to her eldest brother's every whim. Her mum thought the sun shone out of his arse; if he told her that black was white she would agree with him. Her mum treated him like visiting royalty, even though he left his son here for days on end, because he and Jade 'worked' so hard. They bankrolled this place and that was all her mum seemed to care about. Along with young Aiden Mark Two, of course. Though Agnes loved that little boy with all her heart; he was like another brother to her. Aiden loved that his son was adored and treated so well by everyone – he saw it as a validation of himself and his place in the community. That was important to Aiden – people giving him his due, and her mum loved it as well. That wasn't hard to understand; after all, Reeva needed that approbation, given she had five kids without a father in sight. Her mum was as good a mum as she knew how to be, and for Agnes, at least, Tony had been a father of sorts – he cared about them all in his haphazard way. And unlike her brothers, he didn't act as if Aiden was the Messiah coming to visit his followers. Not that her mum or her brothers could see that. They saw Aiden as the answer to their prayers. And Aiden fed on their adoration, because that was what he needed from everyone around him.

Reeva popped her head round her bedroom door, saying gaily, 'Hello, lady. Your dinner is getting cold!'

Agnes followed her downstairs because it was easier than starting an argument. As she walked into the kitchen Aiden Junior piped up, 'Aggie, Aggie, tell me the story of Daniel in the lion's den again. My favourite one, that is.'

Reeva rolled her eyes to the ceiling, saying sarcastically, 'A right fucking riveting yarn, that is, Aggs.'

Agnes ignored her mother and, smiling widely, she said to her nephew, 'I always loved that story too. I will tell you it again later, OK?'

Reeva dished up her homemade lasagne and placed a mixed salad on the table. Then, sitting down with them, she lit a cigarette and poured herself a glass of wine.

'So, Aggs, how was school?'

Agnes shrugged and said nonchalantly, 'Good, Mum. It's always good, you know that.'

Reeva smoked her cigarette and nodded her head, but she had no more interest in her daughter's studies than she had in learning fucking plumbing. Agnes knew she only asked about her because she thought she should. Reeva just went through the motions. It made Agnes's life easier because the less Reeva knew, the better for everyone.

Agnes ate her food and she enjoyed it. Whatever else her mum might be, she was a fantastic cook. Agnes loved her mum very much, but they didn't understand one another. Agnes's life was so far removed from her mum's idea of happiness that it was like she inhabited another planet.

'You off to Mass tonight, then?'

Agnes sighed heavily as she answered her. 'Of course. I go every evening. You know that, Mum.'

Reeva smiled and Agnes knew exactly what was coming next, but she didn't react – that would be a waste of time.

'Well, how about me and you go out tonight instead? Have a girlie night together. There's a big do on at the pub. We could do a bit of karaoke, have a laugh, you know?'

Agnes laughed then, a genuine laugh. 'You ask me this all the time, Mum, and you know I won't go. It really isn't my thing.'

Reeva laughed too but said seriously, 'How do you know if you don't even give it a go?'

Agnes couldn't answer her because she didn't know how to answer her mother without insulting her.

Reeva sighed gently and rolled her eyes in annoyance. 'One fucking night, Aggs. Just give it a go.' She grabbed her daughter's hand across the table and squeezed it tightly. 'Just once, darling. Just give it a fucking chance. If you hate it I will never ask you again.'

Agnes knew that her agreeing would make her mother happy so she said lightly, 'All right, then. But if I don't like it, promise me you will not ask me again?'

Reeva grinned happily. She was convinced that if only her daughter got into the swing of things, she would find out what she was missing. All her girl needed was an invite into the real world, and the knowledge that going to Mass was not the be all and the end all. She was nearly fourteen years old and she was like Granny Grump. She was a beautiful girl and the world was passing her by. Reeva felt that it was her job to remind her daughter of that.

Chapter Forty-Four

Aiden was irritated and he made no bones about making sure everyone around him knew it. Jade was acting like he was a fucking inconvenience, and he could not get a certain Gerry Murphy on the phone. Gerry Murphy was the stepping stone he needed to complete this deal of a lifetime. Without him, it would all fall apart.

Gerry Murphy had brought this fucking deal to his table and promised him the fucking earth on a plate.

And now the bastard was suddenly not to be found.

Aiden was absolutely steaming with anger and humiliation. He had promised Eric the deal of the century, and now it seemed that it had completely fallen apart. No one fucked about with Aiden O'Hara and lived to tell the tale.

Patsy was frightened of his brother's colossal temper, which was getting worse by the hour. He could see it in his stance, in his brother's eyes and in the way he was stalking around the room like a man demented. Patsy wasn't the Brain of Britain, but he could garner enough about his brother's dealings without having a government White Paper on it. But Patsy would never let Aiden know that he understood everything that was going on – that was his safety net. His brother trusted him because he believed that he was not capable of working out the economics of their day-to-day dealings. In short, Aiden thought he was a fucking moron, and that suited Patsy, especially at times like this. He loved Aiden but he was sensible enough to understand that Aiden would not like it if he thought his brother knew the score. Patsy believed it was safer to play the fool.

He had no interest in making his brother see him as a threat. He had already had his card marked once, and wasn't about to make that mistake again. He had a good earn himself these days, and his affiliation with Aiden was kudos enough. But he had cottoned on early as to how his brother's brain actually worked. He watched his brother stalking around the plush office that he was so proud of, and made a point not to say a fucking dicky bird. He only hoped that Gerry Murphy was dead because, if he wasn't, he soon would be and it wouldn't be pretty. Murphy had committed the cardinal sin: he had fucked Aiden O'Hara off big time, and that didn't augur well for anybody.

Chapter Forty-Five

Jade was cross that she was having to pick her son up from the pub, but she knew there wasn't a lot she could say to Reeva. She had explained to her on more than one occasion that she didn't like her little boy being in a public house – especially the ones that Reeva frequented. The principle of the fact that Reeva spent more time with her child than she did rankled, but Jade was honest enough to admit that she wasn't really the maternal type. God Himself knew she loved her son, but she could not for the life of her imagine endless days in his company. That would be torture to her – she was climbing the walls after the first hour with him if they were alone. And looking after Aiden took up most of her time anyway. She had to be grateful that Reeva was much more suited to that than she would ever be and more than willing to take her son off her hands. She didn't want to rock that boat. So she gritted her teeth and walked into the pub as if she was thrilled to be there.

Reeva was all smiles and friendliness as she waved her over to join them.

'Hello, Jade, darling. You sit down and I'll get you a drink, mate. I'm celebrating! My Agnes has deigned to join me for a night out!'

Jade smiled back and took a seat. Aiden Junior was wide awake and clearly thrilled to be in such an exciting environment. She pulled him on to her lap and, smiling genuinely now, she said to Agnes, 'Finally wore you down, did she, Aggs?'

Agnes grinned. 'I am thirteen and my mum thinks I should be out clubbing every night! The fact I do my homework is beyond her comprehension! She thinks I am a boring bastard and I have a feeling that she might be right.'

Jade didn't laugh at her words, she just shook her head in despair. 'You know what she's like – if a man doesn't fancy her she thinks she's failed. She's still stuck in the seventies. I mean, come on, Aggs. Look at her hair!'

They laughed together then.

'When I think that she was pregnant at my age! I wish she wouldn't try and turn me into her, you know.'

Jade hugged her son to her, and when she saw the thick make-up and the revealing clothes that Agnes was wearing thanks to her mother's interference she felt a heaviness upon her. The girl looked much older than she was, and she also looked like a trollop. Reeva had dressed her in what she thought of as fashionable clothes but on Agnes they looked so wrong. The girl had so much going for her, if only Reeva could see that far ahead. Agnes was still a girl – a beautiful girl – but she was not trying to grow up before her time and Reeva seemed to take that as a personal insult. Agnes was developing by the day but, unlike other girls, she wasn't interested in her body or her looks. As a girl who had been forced to grow up long before she was ready, Jade respected Agnes for that.

'We are going to sing "Grease" together in a minute, Jade! Me and my mum. I wish I could come home with you.'

Jade laughed again. 'She means well, Aggs, even though she doesn't realise how crass she can be.'

Agnes sighed and nodded in agreement. 'I love the bones of her, but I know that I disappoint her.'

Jade embraced her affectionately. 'Look, she doesn't *get* you, Aggs. You and her are like chalk and fucking cheese.'

Agnes nodded once more. 'I know, Jade.'

Reeva came back to the table with a tray of drinks. 'I got us all doubles, girls, and a round of shots.'

Agnes looked at Jade and rolled her eyes.

Reeva necked her vodka shot and, pretending to shiver, she shouted loudly, 'Let's get this fucking party started!'

Chapter Forty-Six

Aiden was stripping off in the bedroom, and Jade was lying in their bed watching him. She loved his body; she felt that it was perfect in every way, because it *was* perfect for her. They suited one another, and when they came together it was amazing, every time. She still felt that they were meant to be together.

'Only your mum would think that it's perfectly normal to get her thirteen-year-old daughter drunk. For fuck's sake, Aiden, you need to talk to her. She seems to think that poor Aggs needs to not just get drunk but, I am assuming, fucking laid! It's a disgrace.'

As Aiden looked at Jade she realised that he had been drinking and that he was not being too responsive to what she was saying.

'Come on, Aiden, you know I'm right. Agnes does not want, or indeed feel the need, to drink alcohol. It's a good job that one of them has a sense of what's right and wrong.'

Aiden took a deep breath and then, smiling nastily, he said, 'Look, Jade, I know you and my mum will never ever be bosom fucking buddies, but I'm warning you now. Stop slagging her off to me. Every chance you get you fucking slaughter her. Well, do you know what? She looks after my boy just as she looked after all of us, lady. You should thank her on your knees because we both know you are not exactly fucking maternal, are you?

She might not be Mother of the fucking Year, but you knew that and you still let her look after Aiden Junior. So, darling, you fucking tell me if she's good enough for you!'

Jade looked at the man she adored, and whose life she had tried to make easy, who she had educated in every way she knew how and for whom she had stepped back to give the chance to make something of himself, even though she knew that he wasn't ready, didn't have the nous yet that was needed to live and survive long-term in their world. She saw the anger in his face, the complete disregard for her and her feelings. She saw then that he believed that he had overtaken her, that he was her superior, that everything she had done for him, taught him, was forgotten. He was to all intents and purposes his own man.

Well, she wished him all the best with that fucking stupidness and foolishness. She had no choice but to fight her corner, because she was not a woman who would allow herself to be treated so badly.

She turned on him and said ferociously, 'You do not dare speak to me like that, Aiden. Do I look like I have "cunt" written on my fucking forehead?'

Aiden heard the hurt and the anger in her voice, and he saw that he had gone too far. He had known all along that he was being unfair, but he was on edge over the Gerry Murphy dealing, spoiling for a fight and feeling guilty for leaving Jade in the dark. He had wanted to prove to her and to himself that he could do whatever was needed on his own. Plus he knew that she would have warned him off this venture, so he had not asked her opinion. She would have run a fucking mile. And she would have been right. He had been royally mugged off.

Gerry had decided to have him over, and that was something he could not swallow. Now Gerry was a fucking dead man walking. But Aiden was in too deep to walk away without a serious comeback. Suddenly the enormity of what he was embroiled in had hit him like a sack of shit. He wanted Jade on his side, wanted her input, needed her sensible head. He relied on her more than he wanted to admit.

'Well, fucking answer me, Aiden, because none of us will sleep tonight otherwise, I can guarantee you that much.'

He shrugged in dismissal, well aware that it would send her off her head. She was a lot of things but stupid had never been one of them.

Jade came out of the bed, all teeth and nails. She had been quiet for too long. And now she needed to remind him that the man who could put her down had not been born yet.

Chapter Forty-Seven

Aiden felt like he had gone ten rounds with Joe Bugner. Jade could have a fight, and fight like a fucking man at that. Last night she had come at him with everything she had and – he held his hands up – she was within her rights. He had still not been able to tell her the truth of the situation though, and that was what was really bothering him.

He opened his eyes and wondered what the day would bring. For the first time in years he woke without knowing what to expect. He didn't like the feeling one bit. He ached all over, and he deserved it. He had treated Jade like a fucking nobody, had spoken to her like she meant nothing to him, and now he was awake, sober and remembering the drama of the night before, he knew that he had a lot of making up to do. And on top of that, he had to explain to Eric that his latest scheme had fallen apart.

He had invested a lot of money in Gerry Murphy's fucking bullshit. He had trusted him enough to lay out a fucking small fortune. Serious bunce, as the saying went, and it had been for nothing. Gerry had taken it all. And the fact that he had also talked Eric into investing in it as well . . . That was what he would not, indeed *could* not, forgive. No one made a fool out of him, and Gerry Murphy was going to find that out to his detriment. There were some things that could never be forgiven and this was one.

He could hear Jade talking to Aiden Junior, and he wished more than anything that he could take back his stupidity of the night before. Jade came into the bedroom with his son, and he glanced at her with trepidation. She looked good, but Jade was a woman who made a point of always looking the business. Make-up perfect, hair immaculate and her clothes were the envy of most of the women around her. She was a beautiful woman, and he could never deny that. She held an attraction for him that was beyond age, beyond everything. He loved her still and he always would, no matter what.

'Bye, Daddy. Uncle Patsy is taking me to Nanny's.'

Aiden kissed his son and felt the force of the child's love for him. He couldn't look at Jade, though, and he watched as his son bounced out of the room, unaware that there was anything wrong. But both Jade and Aiden knew that there was a divide between them, and it was because of him and his need to always make himself the main man, even though they both knew their strength came from working together. It was part of what drew them to one another, the way they could think along the same lines, could understand what each other expected, wanted or indeed needed. Now, because he had deliberately chosen to ignore that, he had been bitten on the arse.

Jade stood in the doorway and, looking directly at him, she said quietly, 'Get your arse out of that bed, and let's try and salvage something from this mess, shall we?'

He didn't have the guts to look her in the eyes, and they were both aware of that fact.

Jade laughed sarcastically. 'Fucking gun-running? You couldn't run a ladder in my tights, you fucking imbecile. And you think

I didn't know about it? *Really?* Have you no respect for me at all, Aiden? Did you honestly think I didn't know what was going on after I introduced you in the first place?'

She shook her head in abject disappointment and he realised that he should have known better, that he should have understood that, unlike him, Jade Dixon would always be aware of everything that was going on in her orbit. She was far too shrewd for anything else.

'Then you wonder why I won't fucking marry you. If you don't fucking start using your brain, boy, I will be *burying* you. Now, thanks to you and your lack of fucking brainpower we are all going to have to deal with the IRA *and*, I might add, Eric fucking Palmer who, I know from old, will not be impressed with this latest debacle. Think about it, Aiden. They were *my* contacts. Eric has made a point of *never* dealing with the Irish. Now you have involved him in the worst possible way in a deal gone south.'

The slamming of the front door reverberated through the whole house and, against his will, Aiden found himself flinching at the sound.

Chapter Forty-Eight

Agnes was tired out after last night's shenanigans and she wondered at her mum who thought that the answer to her daughter's teenage angst was make-up and boys. She hoped that her mum would not start giving out yards as usual. Her mum believed that girls were only put on this planet to make men happy, that they were far below men in the grand scheme of things. It really galled her, even though she could never argue that with her mother. Reeva saw everything in her life as pertaining to the male sex; she believed that without a man, she had failed. Agnes would never point out that, if that was the case, her mum had failed over and over again because every man Reeva had snared had left her with a belly full of arms and legs. None of them knew anything about their fathers except their names.

Agnes wanted a bit more than a drunken tale of a stranger who Reeva had taken up with, and who had eventually been the reason for her kid's existence. All her mum ever said was that her dad was really handsome, kind and gentle. It wasn't enough. And anyway, Reeva had said exactly the same thing to Eugene when he'd once asked about his father. Agnes wanted to know *where* she came from. She guessed she was either Turkish or Arabic; her face told her that much. But, unlike her brothers, it bothered her that she had no knowledge of her heritage. As her brother Patsy had so succinctly put it, 'Who gives a fuck, Aggs? Mum has always been there for us. She is more sinned against than sinning. Remember that. She kept us and she loved us.' Then he had smiled as he said, 'Especially when she had you. She had really wanted a daughter after us lot, and you were her last one. You are her baby.'

Agnes had accepted then that she could never make her feelings known – like her brothers, she had to let it go. She couldn't ask her mum about her background – anyway, knowing Reeva, she had probably never asked. Agnes appreciated the fact that her mum had kept the children her bad decisions had created. For all her mum's lunacy, Agnes respected her because she had not once thought of aborting any of her children. Reeva had kept them all without fear or favour, even though she had been looked down on and dragged through the mud where public opinion was concerned. She had loved them with a ferocity that people outside their family could never understand.

Nevertheless Reeva's lifestyle had impacted on her children's lives. They had each been aware of that from a very young age. As well as being different colours, they were all different personalities. Whether that was because of their parentage Agnes didn't know. But what she did know was that a family of both black and white siblings – and everything in between – marked them out as 'different' to the average person in their orbit. Coupled with the fact that Reeva had spent her whole life fighting that prejudice, this had probably made them the people they were. It had made her mum the woman she was, because she had never had it easy. How could she? Reeva had stepped outside of everything that was deemed acceptable. Worst of all was that Agnes perceived that her mum's pretence at not caring about other people's opinions had been an act from start to finish – it had been how she coped with the consensus of public opinion. Reeva had fronted it out but there had to have been times when that was more than a young woman could bear.

Agnes could not imagine having a baby at fourteen like her mum, and then producing more and more at regular intervals by so many different men. But she understood now that after Aiden, her firstborn at fourteen years of age, her mum's life had been well and truly over. Until Tony, the only men who would go near her mother were not exactly reliable, were not looking at Reeva as a prospective wife. They were men who saw her as a good time, who had never seen her as viable marriage material, who, as soon as she fell pregnant again, couldn't wait to run out on her, even though they had left her with their flesh and blood. Her nan had told her that her mum's trouble was she believed what she wanted to believe in the moment, and that she had never understood the difference between sex and love. What she really wanted was love and that she got from her children when men let her down over and over again.

Agnes had no doubt that each of those different men, who had never even stayed around long enough to see their child born, had what they saw as 'real children' with the women they had married. That really galled her, because they had used her mum, her house and her mum's body without even wondering about the kids they had produced, and left without a backward glance. Agnes hated the men for that, hated that they were able to get away with leaving their children, and no one vilified *them*. But her mum, who had been used and who had never once thought of destroying her children, had been left to face the music alone. That Reeva had kept them together as a family was something that Agnes would always respect her for, even though her mum did her head in on a daily basis – even though the family circumstances made them second-class citizens in most people's eyes.

A girl at school had called her mum a whore and Agnes had found herself beating her up in the toilets at break time. She had held in her anger and hatred until she could put her in her place in private. And she had done just that, battering the fuck out of her, and making sure that the girl in question was well aware of her feelings. She had explained in graphic detail what would happen to her should they *ever* have a similar disagreement in the future.

The news had soon done the rounds at school and she had the satisfaction of seeing that no one would ever say anything detrimental about her mum again. She had not even known she had so much rage inside her until then, but it had proved to her that she could defend herself if she needed to and, thanks to Reeva, she would spend her life defending her mother's choices, living down her mother's lifestyle. It had been a big learning curve for her. The realisation that, no matter what she achieved or how well she might get on in her life, Reeva O'Hara was the yardstick she would be measured by depressed her because she was the antithesis of her mum in every way. She was, by her very nature, a good girl, and she was determined to prove people wrong. She was going to get an education, and she was going to make something of her life. That was what she strived for every day.

Chapter Forty-Nine

Gerry Murphy woke up with a blinding headache and a thirst of biblical proportions. He sat up warily, knowing that with the amount he had drunk he could expect the worst. It wasn't the first time: he drank on a daily basis – it was an occupational hazard. He was a free spirit and he loved nothing more than an Out. Especially an 'Out Out', a wonderful cockney term for 'I will get home at some point in the future'. Gerry loved the whole concept of that. His weakness was always going to be the Out: once he had a few drinks, everything else went to the wall. Well, he didn't give a flying fuck. And why should he?

Gerry was a handsome man with a fine head of black hair. The drink didn't seem to affect him too much and he put that down to his ancestors – all good IRA men with what the Irish called a good stomach. They could all take a drink, and then take another drink – and another. They were men to be reckoned with, men who banged their own fucking drums.

God knew, he felt like shit today though. He'd had a great fucking night but now, as he looked around him, he wondered how the hell he had ended up here. It was a shithole – dark, dank, and the bed he was lying on didn't even have a fucking pair of sheets. It was like a fucking cheap man's kip! Gerry laughed to himself, wondering what high jinks he had got up to. He must have been drunk as a skunk to have come back somewhere like this. He could only hope that the woman he had pulled was built like a fucking porn queen because nothing less would explain this dive. He had shagged some dogs in his time, but they were good-looking dogs. In fairness, no matter how drunk he got, he had never woken up with a fucking serious fright. He prided himself on having a built-in shit detector, and it had never failed him yet. But this place was fucking rancid.

He stood up, stretched and, yawning loudly, he walked towards the door. He needed a piss, a cigarette and a coffee in that order. As he approached the door it opened and, smiling widely, he said happily, 'All right, darling? I'm pleased to finally meet you.'

But instead of his usual squeeze coming through the door, he saw Aiden O'Hara.

'Well, Gerry, this is a real fucking treat.'

The glint in Aiden's eye told Gerry Murphy that he was in deep shit. He was a man known to be well able to look after himself but he wasn't going to talk his way easily out of this situation. He had dropped the bollock of a lifetime because he should have taken the money and run. Instead, he had called in to see an old mate in Kilburn and one thing had led to another. As the details of the night before came back to him he wondered at how he could have been such a fool as to think this fucker wouldn't have tracked him down.

'Come on now, Aiden. I will hold me hands up. I made a big mistake. But there's still plenty of room to manoeuvre.'

Aiden grinned snidely. He had him bang to rights and they both knew it.

'The only room you have now is what I choose to allow you. I trusted you, Gerry, and you took my money under false pretences. That was not wise, mate. That's what's called in London, having a fucking death wish. As far as I am concerned, all you need is a last fag and a fucking blindfold. But Kevin Barry you fucking well ain't.'

Gerry Murphy could not remember how he got to this place but he shrewdly realised that he had been served up by his so-called old mate in Kilburn. That meant that he might not have the backing he usually relied on, which told him that his latest stunt had been frowned upon by the people who mattered. He was suddenly aware that he had been left in the wind, that he was most probably on his own – and the people he dealt with were interested in working with Aiden O'Hara.

Gerry was just collateral damage now. He had pushed his luck on more than one occasion, and he had been warned about his actions and the need he had to con people out of their hard-earned money using his credentials and reputation without fear or favour. He had been made aware as to how that could undermine the cause and now he was paying the price. It was fucking annoying. He had been a crucial part of the cause since he was a lad and, for all his fuckery, he still believed in it whole-heartedly. It rankled that he was being cut loose for the likes of Aiden O'Hara. 'Look, Aiden, you know this was never personal. Is there any way I can resolve this situation?'

'Always the fucking same thing with you. "Nothing personal". Well, Gerry, this *is* fucking personal to me. I trusted you. I thought you were a diamond geezer. It's not even the money. It's the fucking piss-take I'm taking umbrage to. It's the knowing you believed you could treat me like a complete cunt.'

Gerry Murphy looked truly frightened now, and that went some way to making Aiden feel better.

'You made the mistake of a lifetime. You, Gerry, my old

mucker, are going to tell me everything I need to know. I want the ins and outs of the cat's arse, and you will tell me, boy. Because now I am dealing *directly* with your fucking organisation. That means that I need to be not only forewarned but also fucking forearmed. I want to know everything you know.'

Gerry Murphy laughed then. 'You can't even imagine what you are dealing with, Aiden. Believe me.'

The arrogance had returned. Gerry still believed in the cause, no matter what might have happened.

Aiden laughed himself. Shaking his head sadly, he said quietly but with venom, 'You stupid cunt. You *will* tell me what I want to know.'

Then the beating started. In fairness to Gerry Murphy, as Aiden told anyone who asked, he kept his trap shut until the pliers were brought out. Aiden always gave credit where credit was due. He could not help but admire bravery in all its forms. He had liked Gerry Murphy and it grieved him that the man had seen fit to try and have him over. That was an unforgivable sin.

Gerry Murphy had lost all his fingernails and toenails before Aiden finally gave in to his temper and threatened to remove his eyelids. Then, and only then, did Gerry Murphy realise he was going to have to swallow his knob and tell Aiden everything.

Chapter Fifty

Jade was tired and she looked it. As she wiped off her make-up she stared at herself in the mirror. She had to admit that, although she was ageing well, the bottom line was she was still getting older. But she had a lot going for her, not least her ability to clear up Aiden's mistakes. When he had told her the full facts of his Gerry Murphy story, she had done what she did best – she had used everyone in her orbit to find the fucker and bring him to heel. Only she could summon that much clout, and she was gratified that Aiden seemed to appreciate that fact. It was *her* contacts who had found Gerry Murphy in Kilburn, and *her* contacts who had made sure he was served up without too much trouble. For all his clout, Aiden still didn't understand that the world they inhabited did not suffer fools gladly. He might have made his mark – she knew that he was well respected, his phenomenal temper was legendary and his violence was something that was capable of instilling fear into the hardest of hearts – but he was still a youngster. Luckily, he had Eric Palmer backing him up, and his reputation on his side. Aiden was over the moon with her for stepping in and delivering Gerry Murphy to him on a plate. He could not thank her more – but they both knew that the damage had been done. It hurt her to know that Aiden had been willing to go into business with people *she* had introduced him to without including her. That he could be so fucking snide had made her have a complete rethink about their relationship. He was clever in so many ways, but his weakness was that he really believed that he could control everything and everyone around him with his good looks and his ability to turn on the charm if necessary, combined with his temper and penchant for violence.

Now, to save his face, she had ensured that this business with the Irish would go ahead anyway. It had to, because Aiden would not have the sense to see the big picture – all he was focused on was punishing Gerry Murphy for trying to have him over. She had no choice but to make the deal to save his face and stop him being ridiculed. In spite of everything she could not bear to see him brought low, even though she knew in her heart that it would have been the best thing for him. Because if ever a man needed a reality check, it was Aiden O'Hara.

Chapter Fifty-One

Gerry Murphy knew when he was beaten, and he had been royally beaten by Aiden. In a way, he couldn't blame the man for his ire. He had had every intention of carrying out their plan, which would have been very lucrative for them both. Unfortunately, Aiden had certain rules and guidelines he wanted followed, and Gerry had ignored them. His complete disregard for Aiden had been his downfall. And now he had no choice but to deliver.

Never before had anyone outside the cause had the guts to pull him up, give him a tug. His affiliation had guaranteed him a swerve and he had believed that his unreliability had been all right because he was part of something so much bigger. He had been served up by his own this time, though, and he could never forget that. They were telling him that he had gone too far. Now, lying on a concrete floor in a cellar somewhere, he was much more inclined to agree with Aiden's way of thinking. One eye was closed, he knew a few ribs were broken and the teeth that had been extracted were all telling him he had fucked up big time. He had lost his fingernails and his toenails and, even though they would eventually grow back, he knew that it was pain that most people couldn't endure. But he was alive and that alone was enough for him at this moment in time.

It was obvious that he had underestimated Aiden. Now he had to convince him that he had every intention of following through on their deal. But Aiden was not in the mood for chit-chat. In fact, he would lay money on Aiden O'Hara being so fucking aggravated that he was not going to be approachable any time in the near future.

He was absolutely right. Aiden was practically spitting feathers. It was bad enough that this cunt had made a fool out of him, but the fact that Jade had been the one to sort it was like a red rag to a bull. Aiden had trusted him, had known him for years. He had weighed out serious amounts of bunce, and this prick had taken it with a cheeky smile and a cheery wave.

'Where's my fucking money? You better have my fucking dough!'

Gerry sighed heavily. 'I told you before, your money is as safe as houses. I might have gone on the trot for a few days, but that's me. It's what I do. I always see my business partners all right. I know you think differently and, Aiden, I get it. But you can't last as long as me in this business without producing the goods.'

He shrugged painfully, trying to act like he was back on track, that the previous few hours meant nothing to him. 'I like a fucking Out Out. Where is the harm?' He could see that Aiden was not in the mood to listen so he took another tack. 'Look, Ade, I can guarantee you a serious return on your investment. I will arrange for you to meet with the supplier. But you have to believe me when I tell you that your money is as safe as houses.'

Gerry Murphy prided himself on his gift of the gab but he was cutting no ice with Aiden O'Hara. For the first time ever he was feeling nervous. If he didn't watch himself Aiden would finish him without a second thought. This was about pride and, knowing that he had finally pushed his Irish colleagues too far, he had to broker a deal that would suit everyone, especially Aiden. He was lying on a concrete floor minus his nails and nursing broken ribs; it was the wake-up call he needed. It was obvious that the people he worked for wanted Aiden on board, and that he had told Aiden more than was good for either of them frightened him. His mum always said to him and his brothers, 'People only know what you tell them.' Until now he had never understood the power of that statement.

Chapter Fifty-Two

Reeva had sensed there was something not right between her son and Jade, but she didn't feel confident enough to ask him about it. There was a definite coolness between them. She had a feeling that whatever had gone wrong was her Aiden's doing; for all Jade's faults, there had never been a hint of scandal where she was concerned.

Oh, she knew that Aiden had taken a few fliers over the years and, as long as the girls concerned had not brought any trouble to the family door, she had swallowed. Although, as a woman who had been used by men all her life, she had not been too impressed with his antics. As she had got older, she found that she didn't have the temperament to allow such shenanigans in her own family.

She admired Jade: without her, Aiden would be adrift. Meeting Jade was the best thing that could ever have happened to him – not that she would ever say that out loud, of course. In spite of their fractious beginning, Jade had somehow inveigled herself into Reeva's heart. She was a fucking diamond. For all his reputation and his friendship with Eric Palmer, Reeva knew that without Jade Aiden would have fucked everything up for himself a long time ago. And he had nearly lost everything thanks to his foolishness. Tony had told her enough to make her see that her Aiden had dropped the bollock of a lifetime.

He was lucky that Eric Palmer adored him and he was grooming him to be his successor. But her lad was still only twenty-five. He was going to have a long wait until Eric finally let go of the reins. And Aiden was going to have to watch himself because *he* was being watched by all and sundry – people only too happy to see him fall off his pedestal. He was of the opinion that he was beyond reproach and, until now, that had been the case. He had been given plenty of rope by Eric Palmer only to go and virtually hang himself. Thanks to Jade, though, he was basically home and dry.

Reeva knew her son; he would not suffer this shit without swearing that he would get his own back at some point. Her eldest son was the love of her life in many respects and she worshipped him. He had just never understood that not everyone in his orbit felt the same way about him as *she* did. He had always been the main man in their home, but out in the real world he was still seen as up-and-coming. Because there, Eric Palmer was the main man. And if Aiden carried on this way he was going to be a fucking liability. He was so arrogant, acting like he was so much better than everyone else. He needed to be brought down a few pegs by Eric and Jade, for his own good.

Plus, his treatment of Patsy bothered her. He was his brother, but Aiden talked to him like he was a fucking mug or a fucking romancer. Patsy would follow him into the bowels of hell without a second thought. He loved his brother and he worked for him happily. He trusted him to look out for him, to take care of him. But Aiden treated him like dirt, and that was starting to irritate her. Aiden was of the opinion that without him they were worth nothing, acting like they were dragging him down. He was even short with *her* at times.

It was only the thought that she could lose her grandson that had stopped her giving him a piece of her mind. In her heart she knew that Aiden was more than capable of taking the boy away from her. He could be very petty-minded and very vindictive if thwarted. That she even thought that her son was capable of such actions told her everything. Suddenly, she didn't trust him any more.

She especially didn't like the thought of Jade and Aiden at loggerheads. It worried her. The fact that Jade refused to marry Aiden had once pleased her; now their marriage was something she craved. It would cement her place in Aiden Junior's life. Jade Dixon loved that she was looking after their boy – she had never once tried to keep Reeva and her grandson apart. Even though Jade wasn't exactly motherly, Reeva knew that she loved that boy with all her heart. And it meant the world to Reeva that Jade trusted her with her precious son, and appreciated her for everything she did for him.

She sighed as she took a large steak and kidney pie out of the oven. She had the whole family for dinner tonight, and she was looking forward to it. They were all growing up and growing away from her, but that was real life.

Tony let himself in the front door. He had picked Aiden Junior up from school and, as the boy ran to her and grabbed her legs in a tight grip, she felt her usual happiness at having the child around her.

'Hello, my little darling.'

She picked him up into her arms and hugged him tightly to her, loving that he hugged her back.

'Hello, Nanny. Granddad Tony said he was going to take me to the park.'

Reeva grinned happily. Her Tony, who she had never thought

would have stayed so long with her, loved this child as much as she did. She had been surprised to realise that she actually loved Tony too. Really loved him. Not just because they had amazing sex, but because she had finally understood that, against the odds, they had become genuine partners who cared for each other.

Tony poured himself a cup of tea from the teapot that was constantly on the cooker. 'Go and get changed, champ. Let me drink me tea and then we will hit that park.'

Aiden Junior ran upstairs to get changed and, going to Tony, Reeva put her arms around him. Kissing him gently on the lips, she said quietly, 'He loves you, Tony. You're a good man.'

Tony laughed and, grabbing Reeva's arse, he pulled her to him tight. 'Come on, Reeve, after all these years! Of course I love him! Like I love you, girl.'

She knew he meant what he was saying and she laughed with happiness. 'Who would have thought it, eh? Me and you, Tony.'

'Listen, Reeve. You always rang my bells, girl. Stop selling yourself short. You're a good woman.'

Aiden Junior came back into the kitchen shouting, 'Come on, Granddad Tony. You promised me the park!'

Tony rolled his eyes with mock annoyance. 'Oh, all right then, mate. Off we go.'

Reeva watched them leave and felt the urge to cry. Tony had stayed with her longer than any other man and had also been the only one to ever make her feel even a modicum of safety. He was also the only man ever to make her feel that life was about more than her kids. All those years when she had been alone with yet another baby, that had been her mantra: I don't need a man, I only need my kids. But it had been a load of old bollocks. Every time she had been left holding the proverbial baby it had broken her heart. Every time she had hoped that the father of her latest child would stand by her. None of them had.

Finally, in His own way, God had been good to her. He had given her Tony. He had given her a man who accepted her no matter what, and He had given her kids someone to rely on. She had come out on top. After every disappointment, after every time she had given birth alone and had been forced to pretend that none of it mattered, Tony had made her see, finally, that life could be good. That she could be loved; that she could be needed.

Chapter Fifty-Three

Jade was exhausted. She had been having trouble sleeping since the aggravation with Aiden. There was a terrible void between them. She was partly to blame but, for once, Aiden had to understand that without her he just wasn't in such a position of power. At least, not the kind of power that he imagined was his. He had his creds but that was because of Eric Palmer, and because *she* had always made sure that he had all the back-up he needed. Now he had been made aware of those facts, his pride was killing him. But she was not about to assuage his ego; this time he would have to acknowledge that she had as much clout as he did in certain areas. More, if she was being honest. There were a lot of Faces out there who, even though they might give him his due and respect him for what he had achieved, had been in the game longer than he had, and they were still active earners. Aiden needed to understand that a lot of their business was about dealing with other people with creds. And it was about keeping the fucking peace and working alongside them. Just because you might be the main earner didn't give you the right to throw your weight about and demand what you wanted. The latest debacle had brought this home to Aiden. Even he couldn't pretend that he didn't understand it.

Jade had allowed him to do whatever he wanted because of

their age difference and that was what really fucking burned. Standing back and letting him have his head had landed them all in a situation that no one in their right mind would be in if they had even half a brain. She was annoyed with herself for pandering to his ego for so long.

Right now, she was meeting with Eric Palmer. She wished she had never agreed to this latest deal to save Aiden's skin. Eric trusted her and respected her decisions, but that didn't mean he wouldn't try and blame her if it didn't go to plan. People like Aiden and Eric Palmer spread blame around like fucking jam. There was no way any of this was ever going to be their fault. People in their world were only as good as their last earn. It was wrong but it was the way it worked. She knew that better than anyone, and it was why she had stayed at the top for so long. She had always fucking earned her keep, she'd made sure of that.

Chapter Fifty-Four

Eric Palmer thought the world of Jade, he always had. He appreciated her business acumen and, more to the point, her loyalty. Jade was a one-off really– she was a Tom who'd had the nous to take herself that one step further. She was a grafter in every sense of the word. She had proved herself worthy of his interest and he had never regretted that. He admired her and he trusted her, which was something he would never admit to anyone.

It had been a bonus to find she'd taken Aiden under her wing. Because, as clever as that fucker was, Eric Palmer depended on Jade to keep him on the straight and narrow. Aiden was an earner, but Eric had begun to see that, without this woman beside him, he would never reach his full potential. The boy had earned his creds and no one could deny that he had a brain full of ideas. But his youth still made him a liability, as had been proven recently.

It was a shame that Jade had not been born a man, because she had the nuts to make it in the world they lived in. She had gone further than most women would have been allowed to – and that was because of him. She had gone further than most men, if he was being really honest. Jade Dixon was the anomaly that only turned up every so often: a woman with the mentality needed to succeed in their world.

Eric had taken Jade to his bed when she was far younger than he had thought and she had shown a natural aptitude for the work early on. She had wanted to make something of herself, and she had. He still felt guilty about their short relationship. He had never believed that she was so young; she had been *so* experienced. She had used him and he had accepted that eventually, but it still gave him sleepless nights. He had never really been a chancer – he had seen Jade and he had wanted her. Now, of course, he knew that she had wanted him for her own reasons. She had known, even then, how to manipulate the people around her. He had been used, and that was something that had never left him. He still admired her resolve: she went after what she wanted and she tended to get it, no matter what the price.

Thanks to Eric, and his knack of finding people who were capable of living in the world he created and who he could trust, no matter what happened, Jade Dixon had found her niche. He had given her the opportunity to ply her trade, and she had proven her worth to him on more than one occasion. He had never regretted bringing her on board. In fact, she was one of the best earners he had. She was also the voice of reason and that was one of her main attributes. Aiden O'Hara and Jade were a real good combination and now they had a child together. Aiden, for all his nous, needed a guiding hand – a hand that she was more than qualified to give him, even as she was wondering if it was going to be worth her time and trouble. Oh, he could read Jade like a book!

Watching her, he felt terrible because he really didn't want to have to do this. Sighing heavily and theatrically, he said quietly, 'You can talk to me, Jade. I've already worked out that you were the one who made sure our Aiden didn't make a fool of himself.' He tried to look like the good guy, like the friend he thought he was.

Jade laughed then, a real laugh. It sounded wrong in Eric Palmer's posh new offices, the offices that Aiden had insisted on.

'Eric, Aiden is a shrewd fucker. You know that as well as I do. But he doesn't think some things through. There are too many people offering him deals, more people every day pandering to him because he has so much power. In time he will understand all that old fanny. But for now he still doesn't get that certain deals need to be watched and that his reputation isn't enough. I do the day-to-day shit while he swans off and looks for more lucrative deals, looks for more excitement. So don't fucking try and pretend you never knew this was on the cards.'

Eric smiled. 'I do know that, Jade. You are absolutely right. We gave him too much too soon. But, in all my years on the street, I have never met anyone who can think up an earn like him. Your influence is noted and I can't deny that you can rein him in. But give him the time to learn and no one will be able to touch him.'

Jade raised her eyebrows. 'So, you are happy with him gun-running. *Really?* When he was just dealing with Gerry Murphy, I wasn't too bothered. But now he's involved with some serious fucking people.'

Eric Palmer nodded. 'True, but it's a good earn, and we just provide the guns on the streets. As Aiden pointed out, this way we can monitor who has got what. The main money comes from sending them overseas, of course, but he has that covered too. He has the savvy that we need, Jade. All you need to do is keep an eye on him.'

Jade shook her head sadly. 'So, basically, I have another fucking business to look after. I don't trust the Irish, Eric. Not this fucking lot, anyway. They see themselves as above us. They don't really think we are credible. They are funding a war, we are on the rob – two completely different fucking things.'

Eric Palmer knew Jade spoke the truth but he also believed that Aiden was right. He had pointed out that if they didn't deal with the Irish, someone else would and, whoever that might be, they would then have the backing needed to take anyone down if necessary, and he said as much to Jade.

'We need the Irish onside. That, Jade, is simple economics.'

She could see the logic, but she wasn't happy about any of it. 'I still don't trust them. Plus, once we are involved with them, we are not just looking at the regular Filth, who we can control, coming after us with everything they have got, but we will have to swerve the agencies who are geared up to look for anything pertaining to terrorism. It's a whole different ball game. And all the people that we have on our books will run a mile once the IRA are mentioned. You know, Eric, you never did understand that, while we might have evidence of them fucking little kids – the evidence against those nonces – if the balloon ever went up, and we were accused of dealing with *terrorists*, the people we have onside now would run a fucking mile. Our so-called power would be null and void overnight. Those fuckers protect their own – it's been proven to us time and time again. Look at last year with that MP, the one after boys so young even *we* wouldn't go there. He walked away from it all because the bloke who accused him disappeared into the system. What I'm saying, Eric, is sometimes it's better to do one deal with these fuckers and then drop it. Personally, I don't think it's worth the aggro.'

Eric Palmer could hear the fear and worry in her voice and

that bothered him because Jade Dixon was game for literally anything. If she was not interested then maybe he should have a rethink.

Seeing the uncertainty on Eric's face, Jade took the chance to drive her point home. 'Honestly, Eric, I have a bad feeling about this. People are always afraid of terrorism. Open the papers. People clear a bus or train if they hear an Irish accent. It's ten years too late. But they are still *bombing* people. If you get us involved in this we can't get away from it, no matter how much money we throw about. We are basically fucked.' She opened her arms in a gesture of supplication. 'Aiden is like you, he just sees the bottom line. *I* see that we would be allying ourselves with people who attempt murder indiscriminately. We are not part of their cause, Eric. We would be vilified by our own people eventually. It's why you've never got involved with this before – so why start now? And I certainly don't want to have anything to do with it now. I think we should get a quick stash of firearms and then fuck them off.'

She made a good argument. She was talking sense. Eric trusted her to know more about what was going on out there than he did these days. He relied on people like Jade and, more so, on men like Aiden to be his window to the world. They were the people who gave him the day-to-day information that allowed him to ply his trade. He didn't want to immerse himself in it any more. He was taking a step back and that was what he paid people for – and he paid fucking well. But now in taking his eye off the fucking ball he had allowed Aiden to walk them all into this latest fucking aggravation. Listening to her, Eric believed that Jade knew what she was talking about. He trusted that Aiden had a good head for earns. This time, unfortunately, he had gone a bit too far. Once he understood the economics,

Aiden would understand that it was not in any of their interests to pursue the relationship. He would tell Aiden that they would only bankroll one buy; after that, they could not justify the expense. It was up to Aiden now to extricate them from this deal.

Jade sighed heavily. 'Do you know something, Eric?' She was shaking her head in despair. 'I have already brokered the deal. We bring in *one* shipment, and then we walk away. Honestly, I wonder at times what the fuck you lot would do without me. I explained that we couldn't guarantee the safety of their product. That, with hindsight, we were not in a position to overlook our other businesses to concentrate on them and that we were already bringing guns in from Belgium, et cetera.'

Eric laughed then. 'What fucking guns from Belgium?'

'The guns we are now bringing in on a much smaller basis, mainly handguns. Nothing too outrageous. We can offload them immediately because I have already talked to Jimmy Ortega. He's a good Brixton boy, as you know. He's over the fucking moon. After the second shipment I will explain that we are in line for a capture. So he will swallow his big, huge knob – and I am speaking from experience here, he is a big lad! Then we disappear into the woodwork and pretend this never happened. You know and I know, Eric, that any guns found nowadays are somehow all brought back to the IRA. Gerry Murphy will do this one-time deal and that's it as far as we are concerned. There is no comeback for any of us from his Irish colleagues because they understand that Gerry fucked himself over.'

Eric Palmer was more than impressed. 'You sorted all that out today, Jade?'

She smiled. Her first real smile. 'Of course, Eric. I wouldn't say it if it wasn't true.'

'You are one fucking clever bird. I always knew that about you.'

Jade laughed again, but it was a sneer more than a laugh. 'Oh, well fuck me sideways. I'm so impressed. I have been working your biggest scams for years, Eric. I have earned you fortunes! Not that I haven't earned a good wedge myself. But did it never once cross your mind that I could only ply my trade because I made a point of befriending people who could further my cause? The Filth, for example? I made it my mission to get them onside. The same with the Irish. I gave them whatever they wanted because I knew that it would be the only leverage we had if everything should ever fall out of bed. Which it has. And I realise that you never *once* gave me the fucking benefit of all that. You never once understood just how much I watched your back. No matter what happened I always sorted it, like I have tonight with Aiden. Now I have to ask myself honestly if you ever once appreciated just how fucking loyal I have actually been?'

Eric Palmer was shocked at the vitriol in her voice, and he was also shamed because he had never given credit to just how much power she had. He wondered how he had have never realised this woman's acumen. Tonight she had, with a few phone calls, talked them out of something that would have eventually destroyed them. She had single-handedly given him exactly what he wanted, without asking anything in return, or trying to do a deal with him beforehand. He was actually humbled by her loyalty and her decency.

'I can't argue this with you, Jade. I can only say that I never really appreciated you fully until now. I always had the highest regard for you and I always knew that you were a brilliant businesswoman. Tonight, though, you have made me see that I have in you, Jade, a real fucking diamond. I can't explain to you just how much I underestimated you. But I can assure you now, that will never happen again.'

Jade believed he meant every word he said, but she was well aware that Eric would never refer to any of this again. So, shrugging nonchalantly, she said quietly, 'I'm not trying to blow my own trumpet. But you need to see the people around you that are there for you. Aiden, especially. He adores you. He spends his life trying to prove himself to you.'

Eric Palmer looked into her eyes. 'I never doubted that for a minute, darling.'

Chapter Fifty-Five

'Look, Aiden, you have to get past this. You made a big fuck-up, but it's sorted now and that's it. We've all been guilty of it.'

Aiden didn't answer Jade. Instead he walked out of their bedroom on to the landing and made a big performance of knotting his tie. He was angry – angry and humiliated.

Jade followed him out and tried to hold him in her arms but he shrugged her away.

'Turn around. I always do your tie for you.'

He looked at her in the mirror and turned towards her slowly. Jade knotted his tie expertly. When she was finished she grabbed the tie and pulled him towards her, kissing him violently on his lips.

Letting him go, she said saucily, 'I've missed that, Aiden. I've missed kissing you, darling.'

Taking her in his arms, Aiden pulled her into his body and, holding her tightly, he said angrily, 'You know that I'm still annoyed, Jade. You fucking made an idiot out of me.'

Jade knew better than to argue with him; there was nothing she could say to minimise his hurt. She even understood exactly how he was feeling. But she couldn't tell him that. In her bed he was a man, but outside the bed he was a boy in so many respects. A boy who couldn't see that she had pulled his arse out of a fire! A fire that he could never have saved himself from. It had been three weeks since the aggravation with Gerry Murphy and his behaviour was really wearing her down. Although she and Eric had explained the situation from their point of view, Aiden couldn't accept that he had done a wrong one, that he wasn't anything less than perfect. Oh no, that would be too easy. But the fact that he could have jeopardised everything else they were involved with was to Aiden like a giraffe's fart. It went right over his head.

He was still standing on his dignity, acting like they had ganged up on him and were deliberately ruining his future. It was fucking scary just how close they had come to ruination because of him. But Aiden just couldn't see it. Or, more to the point, he *refused* to see it, and that was really starting to bother her. Jade was finally losing patience not just with this latest stupidity, but with her life in general. Aiden treated her like a cunt and now that was beginning to smart. She had taken him into her world – there was nothing that he could ever offer *her*. She believed that the time had come for her to remind him of that fact.

'Why don't you just fuck off, Aiden.' She held up her hands and waved him away from her. 'Who the *fuck* do you think you are?' Her anger had got the better of her now and she shoved him away from her, pushing him towards the stairs.

He laughed at her. 'You sure, Jade? Because if I go, I go for good.'

She shrugged, all the fight leaving her suddenly.

'Do you know what? I can't do this any more, Aiden.'

Aiden turned to her and she saw the arrogance and the anger in his handsome face. She saw him for what he was – what he really was – not what she had chosen to believe he was. She saw how little he really thought of her, how juvenile he was when he didn't get what he wanted and he thought he had been crossed.

'Listen to me, Aiden. You do *not* look down your fucking nose at me. I have been *fucking* good. I have put up with your stupidity for over three weeks. Well, guess what? My patience is running out. Grow the fuck up, Aiden. What are you? Fucking twelve?'

Despite her anger, she could not help looking at him and admiring how handsome he was. What it was about him she didn't know, but he rang all her bells – even now, when she could quite happily punch his fucking lights out.

'You can fucking *act* as good as you like, Jade. But I know the truth, never forget that.'

Jade looked into his eyes and the anger inside her, the fury at his snide remarks and his complete disregard for and her feelings, bubbled once again to the surface. She knew he couldn't wait to leave her, that he needed the validation of some little tart he would pick up. He couldn't wait to get away from her and the truth of what he had started – and she had finished for him. And she wasn't going to take that lying down.

'If you walk out now, Aiden, you ain't fucking coming back in this house. I'm not a fucking silly little girl, playing fucking silly little games. You walk out of here tonight and I swear on my boy's life, you will never darken this fucking door again.'

She walked away from him and, as she made her way down the stairs, she felt a calmness wash over her. For once she had the upper hand with him. She knew that if he did walk out she would not ever let him back in her life. It would hurt her, but she would be better off without him. She couldn't play this game any more, pretending that everything he did was OK. She had no intention of spending any more of her time making him feel good about himself when that meant she had to put herself down. It was ludicrous! What the fuck had happened to her? When had she decided that her life would be about making him feel better about himself? When had her life meant that she forgot about herself?

In the kitchen she opened one of the cupboards and took out a bottle of whisky. She grabbed a glass from the draining board and poured herself out a stiff drink. She had not felt this angry with anyone for years. But over the last few weeks Aiden had pushed her to the limit.

She downed the Scotch quickly, savouring the burn in her throat. Then she poured herself another large glass. As she turned around to take her drink into the sitting room, she walked straight into Aiden. He took the glass from her and he swallowed the drink down. Coughing at its strength, he said seriously, 'You are the only person I know who can drink raw Scotch, lady.'

She smiled and, taking the glass from him, she poured him another. Then, going to the sink, she picked up a second glass and, pouring herself another measure, she said lightly, 'I meant what I said you know, Aiden. I refuse to do this shit any more. I have done nothing fucking wrong, as you well know.'

She leaned against the sink, sipping her drink and wondering where this conversation was going. She still couldn't trust him, and it occurred to her suddenly that, if she was honest with herself, she never had trusted him really. Never trusted him to stand by her. The knowledge hurt her.

Across the kitchen Aiden studied her. She was looking her age in many ways. She was still a beautiful woman, though. He loved her with every part of his being, and he could never imagine being with anyone else, not like he was with her, anyway.

She was the mother of his son, and she was the only woman he truly respected. That he often took a flier with another girl he didn't see as a problem. After all, Jade had his son; she was the important one as far as he was concerned. And, in his mind, that should be enough for her. He knew she wasn't a fool; she had to know about his extracurricular activities, so to speak – that was a fucking given. But she chose to ignore them, which suited them both.

As angry as he felt about the Gerry Murphy situation, he knew that Jade meant every word she said. That was one of the things he loved about her: what you saw was exactly what you got. She didn't suffer fools gladly and she didn't ever make threats unless she meant them. Her words had finally penetrated his psyche – that she was willing to fuck him off told him all he needed to know. He couldn't live without her, which he saw as his Achilles heel. He was aware that she had given him the biggest swerve in recorded history and he should be grateful.

So why did he still feel that, between Jade and Eric Palmer, they had cunted him off? Because that was *exactly* how he was feeling. Right or wrong, he resented the way they had treated him, and it was not something he would forget in a hurry. But he couldn't be without her. He went to her and hugged her to him, enjoying the smell of her skin, the feel of her body against his. He loved her, he always would. But, at this moment in time, he didn't like her. He didn't like her at all.

He would swallow his knob because there was nothing else he could do, but that didn't mean he would ever forget this insult. Because an insult it was. Whatever Jade and Eric tried to tell him, they had between them treated him like a fucking no one, a fucking nothing. The humiliation burned within him. They had proven to him that he couldn't trust the people closest to him, that he needed to be wary in the future and look out for his own ends. As much as he loved Jade Dixon, he could never truly trust her again and Eric Palmer was someone he needed to keep a close eye on. This was a learning curve for him, all right. He might be a lot of things, but he wasn't a fucking idiot. In his mind, this was tantamount to a declaration of war. This had told him that he needed to watch his back and he would do just that in the future.

Aiden O'Hara understood that, in many respects, he was now on his own. This was how he was going to live his life, the only way he could go forward. He had no intention of walking away from Jade and his son. The thought of being without them was anathema to him. But something inside him was broken now. He knew he could never trust any of the people around him again. After this betrayal, how could he? *Why* would he?

Chapter Fifty-Six

Agnes was laughing with her mum when she heard her brothers arguing outside the front door. She sighed heavily and, as usual, went to try and calm the situation. This felt like her main job in life at times – being the voice of reason, talking everyone down. It was wearing because she loved them, and she hated to see them arguing and fighting. She opened the door to see Patsy and Aiden at each other's throats. Well, Aiden was at poor Patsy's throat. No change there.

Patsy had always been Aiden's scapegoat – they all knew that, even if they never actually said it out loud. It wouldn't be worth the hassle. Aiden could do no wrong, of course.

'Calm the fuck down, Ade. Everyone on the estate can hear you shouting and hollering!'

Aiden, she could see immediately, was *very* drunk, and so was Patsy.

She brought them both into the house, saying sadly, 'Really! Arguing again? You're my brothers and I hate seeing you carry on like this.'

Normally that would bring any of her brothers to their knees. They adored Agnes and saw her as too fragile to be hurt or upset in any way, which always worked in her favour. And why she used it when necessary. She played the female card at every opportunity. Surrounded as she was by so many men, she had learned early on in life how to use her innocence to her own advantage – none of the boys had ever worked it out.

But Aiden wasn't having any of it tonight. 'Shut the fuck up and get yourself to bed, lady. I'm surrounded by mouthy women and I'm really not in the fucking mood tonight.'

Reeva stepped between her eldest son and his two siblings, motioning to both of them to go to bed, which they did without a word. There was something going on with her first-born and she could see that he was up for a fight. When he was like this the best thing was to not give him reasons to start aggravation. But, by the same token, she would not take any of his shit. Tonight *she* was not in the mood – she'd been on the rainbow too. So, fuck him. She was not going to let him put *her* on a fucking downer.

'Excuse me, Aiden. This is my house and you can't come round here reading the fucking riot act to all and sundry.'

One thing Reeva knew was that no matter what might occur her eldest boy would never start anything of importance with her personally. His brothers were fair game but never her. He was far better than that.

Aiden came into the house tamely and she shut the door behind him. She followed him into the kitchen, wondering what the upshot would be and how best she could talk him down. She knew all about the latest aggravation, but she was not going to let on. Her son was hurting – his pride had been damaged and, being the man he was, he would not let that go lightly. Tonight he was drunk and he was wound up, she could see that straight off. But she stood her ground.

'*Your* house is it, Mum? I do believe I bankroll this fucking drum and I have for years. I bankroll your fucking boyfriend and all, even though he's a useless prick. But then, you know that better than anyone, don't you, Mum?'

He laughed nastily. Lighting up a cigarette, Reeva watched him warily, unsure now how to deal with him. It seemed that he wasn't just drunk or on a bit of coke. He looked to her like a demon. His eyes were like slits and his whole body was tensed ready to fight.

For the first time ever, Reeva felt frightened of her own child. There was something different about him. There was a hatred in his voice, in his stance, in everything about him, that she had never experienced before. He seemed like he was out of control. He looked at her with such venom and she didn't know how she was supposed to react. She was seeing a man who had scores to settle, who was looking for a fight, looking to cause harm.

She was not going to fight him, no matter what. In fact, she had no intention of letting him win this fucking silent argument. That was exactly what he wanted and something in the back of her head was telling her that she must not let him get the better of her. She had to talk him down, and make sure that they didn't have any conflict. He wanted that too badly, and he was so far gone he would fight her if she wasn't careful.

He laughed sarcastically as he said, 'Oh come on, Mum. What's the matter, eh? Not like you to put your latest fuck over your own kids, is it? I mean, think about it: *you* put everyone and anyone over us lot. Like the fucking race relations board, ain't we? One thing I could always say about you, Mum. You never discriminated, did you? As long as they were a piece of fucking shit you were straight in there, legs wide open, come on down, boys! Then, when they left you, *we* picked up the pieces. Well, actually, *I* picked up the fucking pieces. It was *me* who fucking kept this family afloat. It was *me* who always made sure that we were OK. It was *me* who always tried to look out for us all. Remember Eugene's dad, Mum? Big black bastard. Knocked me about, as well as you. And poor Patsy! He hated Patsy more than he did me. He bullied him every chance he got. And then how about Porrick's dad? That was a nice change for us. A vicious Irishman this time. Oh, Mum, you certainly knew how to look after your kids, didn't you? You can't even *imagine* what your fucking choices did to your family, to your kids who you always say mean *more* to you than anything. You think that we never sussed you out? That we never wondered why not one of our dads stayed around long enough to see us brought into the world?'

Reeva listened to her son and her heart broke because there was a lot of truth in what he said. But she didn't deserve hearing him say all that without telling him a few home truths in return. Her anger got the better of her now and she faced her eldest son and, forgetting her fear of him, she screeched, 'You're right, Aiden! I was *never* going to be Mother of the fucking Year, was I? But I *kept* you all. And, as for you, you fucking wanker, I was *fourteen* years old when I had you. I might not have been Snow fucking White but I've never pretended to be. So you can criticise me all you want if it makes you feel better about yourself, but I did the best I could for you. I made more than my fair share of mistakes, but at least I fucking kept you all! And each time it was harder and harder to hold my head up. But I did it. I never regretted any of you, Aiden. Remember that. I didn't turn my back on you, on any of you, even when I felt like it.'

Aiden looked at his mum, who he had always defended, who he had always loved no matter what, and he saw how much he had hurt her feelings. As drunk as he was, he knew that he had been so out of order. He had deliberately set out to hurt this woman who he knew would give up her life for him, or for his siblings. Through the drink and the cocaine he had taken that night he still had the grace to feel ashamed and embarrassed that he was capable of expressing such vitriol towards the woman who had always been by his side, no matter what. Reeva had always been his biggest advocate, he knew she would lie for him if he needed it. He knew that he had brutally taken out on his mother not only his own anger, but also his own frustration. That he had achieved so much in his life and then been brought so low was something he could not come to terms with. Now he had taken his anger out on his mother, on the only person he knew he could always rely on. He was sobering up by the second.

He glanced around the room where he had grown up and into the man he now was. Seeing the fear and the uncertainty on his mum's face he felt the shame overwhelming him. How could he have ever thought that he could denigrate her like that?

Reeva walked out to the kitchen, afraid to say anything more. If she wasn't careful, her eldest child would say something that neither of them could ever forgive. It had gone much too far already. She poured herself a very large vodka and knocked it back in one gulp. Aiden followed her and watched as she did what she had always done since he could remember: she self-medicated. But what could he say? He pulled her round to face him and he saw the fear in her eyes, and wondered at how they had ever been reduced to this.

'Mum, I'm sorry. Really, I didn't mean any of it. I could fucking kick meself . . .'

Reeva pulled away from him. She wasn't at all impressed with what he had said to her, and she wasn't about to let him get away with it. She was so incensed with him and the way he thought he could treat everyone around him. For the first time ever, she wasn't on his side. His words had hit her deeply. She had realised that what he had said were his real feelings. It broke her heart that he saw her as so fucking low on his radar.

'I don't want to hear it, Aiden. You have no right to talk to me like that. I tried to do the best that I could by you all.'

Aiden knew that he had really offended his mum, a woman who he had always thought was unable to be offended. She had always acted like everything said about her was no more than water off the proverbial duck's back. Now he knew that his words had really got under her skin, that *he* had really got under her skin. He had touched a nerve and now he didn't know how to make it right, how to tell her he didn't mean a word of it. That he was hurting and he wanted someone else to hurt as well.

Agnes came into the kitchen then and, pushing past her brother, she said, 'Come on, Mum. Let me take you to bed.'

Reeva smiled sadly and allowed herself to be removed from her son's presence. She couldn't wait to get away from him. She couldn't argue with him tonight; his words had broken her heart.

Agnes looked over her shoulder and said quietly, 'You're a fucking bully, Aiden. Just go home. Don't you think you've done enough tonight?'

Aiden stood in the kitchen where he had spent the majority of his life and, for the first time in years, he actually cried. He couldn't stop himself. The anger and the frustration of the last few weeks seemed to overwhelm him. He had suffered the humiliation of Jade and Eric's interference in a deal that he *still* believed would have brought them untold riches – because he could have kept everyone on board and, more to the point, he could have used the Irish contacts in his favour. He just couldn't see the problem. He still believed that if he had been given the chance he could have run it all without any problems whatsoever. He could have worked it out in such a way no one could have ever touched them. After all, that was what he did best. That was what Eric Palmer paid him to do. That deal could have earned more money in a few months than they were now earning in a year. And they were fucking earning money hand over fist already. Instead he had been completely bypassed by Eric Palmer. That was bad enough, but knowing that his Jade had worked alongside Eric to put a stop on him was something he could not get his head around. Everything he had achieved had been wiped out overnight by the two people he had trusted the most. He sobbed like a baby.

Patsy came into the kitchen and, taking him into his arms, he said softly, 'Let it out, bruv. Let it go, mate.'

And he did. For the first time in his life, Aiden O'Hara allowed his feelings to be shown in public. He was absolutely devastated by the disloyalty shown to him by the two people he cared about most. But he was also crying because, deep inside, he knew that he had fucked up and that they had been right to put a stop to his gallop. That was something, of course, that he would never admit. He had not admitted it to himself until now. He would always argue that he could have handled the Irish and anyone else if necessary. He could not back down.

All his brothers came to him now. Porrick and Eugene were

both nearly in tears themselves, shocked at seeing their big brother brought so low; he was always the strong one. They hugged him tightly because he was like a father to them and they loved him even as they feared him. Seeing him crying and vulnerable scared them even while they marvelled that, for the first time ever in their lives, Aiden actually needed them. Until now they had always needed him.

Chapter Fifty-Seven

Reeva and Agnes sat in Reeva's bedroom, listening to the commotion going on downstairs. Reeva got up quickly but Agnes pushed her back down on to her bed.

'No, you don't, Mum. Let him hang as he grows. The boys are with him. He spoke to you like shit. Don't let him get away with it. He *always* gets away with everything. He's an arsehole. Who the fuck does he think he is?'

Reeva looked at her daughter and saw the determination in her eyes. She understood then that this girl of hers was much stronger than she had ever believed. And she also realised that her Agnes didn't actually *like* her brother Aiden. She watched her daughter as she picked up the phone to ring Jade to tell her that Aiden was drunk. And Reeva was relieved when Jade finally arrived and took Aiden home. A little bit of Reeva was sad because she knew that Aiden adored his little sister. He would move heaven and earth for her.

Book Three

Lousy but loyal.

Anon. East End slogan, George V Jubilee, 1935

He that is not with me is against me.

Matthew 12:30

Chapter Fifty-Eight

1998

'Fuck off, Eugene. You're having me on, ain't you!'

Agnes was belly laughing at her brother's antics. And Eugene, the natural jester that he was, was playing to the gallery. He had a real knack for making people laugh, with his lust for life and sunny disposition.

Eugene, who had been such a quiet child, had developed into a young man with a big personality, liked by everyone who came into contact with him. The girls loved him and he, in turn, loved them. He was already over six feet and he was built, as his mother told anyone who listened to her worries about him all those years ago, like the proverbial brick shithouse. With his father's dark-chocolate skin and high cheekbones, and his mother's full lips and blue eyes, he was like catnip to every female in a five-mile radius.

'Seriously, Aggs. I kid you not. I was fucking nearly captured! But I extricated myself before her dad got anywhere near!'

Agnes was still laughing. She loved her brother Eugene; he was the closest to her really. Unlike the others, he didn't see it as his daily mission to watch her like a hawk – he was more easy-going. As a result, they had a real connection as siblings and, more to the point, as friends, even though he spent his every waking moment trying to chat up every female in his world, and she was what their mum referred to as a Holy Joe.

Agnes still spent all her spare time at the church. She received Holy Communion every morning at the six o'clock Mass, and she also helped out there most evenings with everything from feeding the homeless to helping the kids who were getting ready to receive their first Holy Communion. She would patiently help them learn the catechism and then she would help them to understand what it actually meant. Agnes was a daughter that most parents would pray to God for. She was a genuinely good girl, who had never once given her family any reason to worry about her. She had no interest in anything except her religion.

At seventeen, she was doing very well at school and was determined to make something of herself. As Reeva complained to anyone who would listen, her only daughter was her absolute polar opposite! And, even though she bemoaned her daughter's lifestyle, there was a small part of her that was proud that her only daughter was without any kind of stain. That her girl, her beautiful girl, could hold her head up despite her mother's reputation, and that she had such a nice nature, such a capacity for love. Reeva had to admit defeat. Although she had wanted a best mate, a girl she could put on make-up with, a girl she could go shopping with and who she could go out with drinking and clubbing, she had finally had to accept that she had a daughter who was not the outgoing type. Agnes was not interested in having a good time, and she wasn't going to use her good looks for her own end.

Reeva had struggled to understand her for a long time. But as the years passed she had swallowed her dismay and she had finally seen the advantage in her daughter's behaviour. Unlike

Reeva, her girl wasn't eager to grow up and experience life at a very young age; her Agnes wasn't afraid that life would somehow pass her by.

That had always been Reeva's worry as a girl, that she was missing out on everything when, truth be told, she had missed out on so much because she had given birth to her first child at fourteen. She had never really given herself a chance. Her daughter wanted to wait until she was ready before she went out into the world. She wanted to finish her education and make something of her life. Her Agnes had her fucking head screwed on!

Now, as Eugene and Agnes walked into the kitchen, Reeva, who had only had a couple of drinks because Aiden Junior was coming over for tea, said loudly, 'What were you two laughing at? I could hear you coming up the road.'

Eugene grabbed his mum and hugged her tightly to him, kissing her on her forehead. 'Never you mind. What's for dinner? I'm starving.'

Agnes was already putting the kettle on to make them all tea. She loved it when it was like this, when everyone was happy and there wasn't any conflict.

'I made a chicken and mushroom pie, and for afters we have a lemon cheesecake. All you lot ever bleeding think about is your stomachs.'

Agnes laughed happily. 'That's your own fault, Mum. You fed these boys too well. God knows how their wives will cope!'

Reeva was thrilled at hearing her daughter say out loud what she secretly believed was the truth. She knew that, food-wise, she would be a hard act to follow. It didn't occur to her that Agnes might just be telling her what she wanted to hear.

'Aiden is dropping the little man off soon and, once he's

settled, I will be dishing up. Patsy is working late and Porrick is with him. I don't know, it's like a fucking transport café here these days.'

'Is Tony here for dinner, Mum?'

Reeva shrugged. 'He's got a bit of work today. Shouldn't be too long. Pour that tea out, Aggs, it will be stronger than a docker's piss if you leave it much longer.'

Eugene rolled his eyes with disgust. 'Oh, Mum, you silver-tongued bastard.'

Reeva laughed with her son and didn't comment when her only daughter picked up her tea and made her way upstairs to her bedroom. It hurt Reeva that her girl didn't seem to want to spend too much time in her company; she knew that it was because she had had a few drinks. Agnes didn't like her drinking during the day and, even though she never said as much, the fact that she escaped to her room at the earliest opportunity hurt Reeva's feelings. She felt that she had somehow failed her daughter and, even though she had no intention of ever changing her lifestyle, her disapproval still bothered her. Eugene was sitting at the table and, picking up his mug of tea, he sipped it loudly before saying seriously, 'You know what she's like, Mum. Miss Goody Two-Shoes. But, seriously, she has a point. You do look a bit pissed, and our Aiden will be here soon with the son and heir. And you know him, he never holds back on an opinion, does he?'

Reeva didn't answer. All her boys were Aiden's acolytes and accepted him as the main man in their lives. Generally that was something she was pleased about. Yet as much as she loved Aiden it irritated her that he was treated like the dog's gonads every time he graced them with his presence.

She knew she was being unfair, because she was already half

pissed. That was why they rarely took any notice of what she said; they knew that she would rather have a drink than bring attention to herself. But it didn't mean she didn't love them all. Because she did.

Chapter Fifty-Nine

Jade was not in the best of moods. She had experienced what she would call an absolutely shit day. First of all, she had been expected to clear up a mess in one of the houses. A very wealthy punter had got as drunk as a skunk and decided he wanted a fight with one of the security guys. Unfortunately, he had picked the fight with a large and very aggressive Jamaican who had no intention of letting anyone mug him off. Especially not a fucking Hooray Henry who thought he was the dog's danglers.

Those were the Jamaican's words, not hers.

The man in question had eventually been given the hammering of a lifetime, but only after he had pushed and pushed for a fight. He had not been protected, so he had been the recipient of a seriously good fucking hiding. Without fear or favour he had been smashed into the ground. Fists and feet had been used without a thought. For the first time in his life he had learned that sometimes a big trap could really get you in trouble, could get a body hurt.

The Jamaican in question was new to the job, and he had not been told that, when a situation like that occurred, he was expected to just defuse the situation and walk away – under no circumstances was he to raise a fist. The people they dealt with paid so much money they were basically given a free pass, no matter what happened. Obviously that had not been explained properly. Unfortunately, the man who had sought out the fight had a history of throwing punches while spouting racist shite. So he had finally been given exactly what he had inadvertently asked for and never expected in a million years. The bully had been given a hiding. He had been on the end of a fist that he had never believed would ever come his way. The man had a history of picking fights with the security staff and, until now, he had been allowed to get away with it. The men he abused had walked away quite happily, knowing they would be well compensated. Plus they were sensible enough to know that, in the environment they worked in, a lot of the men were liable to act the big man, to try and make themselves look like they were macho men. They wished, the complete fucking wankers!

Jade believed it was because they had to pay for the women they slept with and, because of that, they felt the urge to make themselves look masculine in front of the women that they were paying good money for. But this time it had backfired and the man who had always been given a swerve was now in hospital and looking at serious money to replace his missing teeth plus plastic surgery to put his eye back in its original position.

In all honesty, Jade was glad he had been given his come-uppance – he was a fucking pain in the arse who thought that his name and his money gave him the right to treat everyone around him like shit. The girls he paid for were not big fans of him either. That told her everything she needed to know. There were punters you might not find attractive but they treated you well. These were the punters you liked, who you could have fun with. These were nice men, really – men you trusted because you knew there were no ulterior motives. Normally she would have given the man in question a real talking-to, explained that although his huge fee allowed for this kind of abuse that still didn't mean it was right. That maybe he should have a quick rethink about the girls he requested. But today she really couldn't be arsed. She was glad the moron had finally been taken down a few pegs.

They disgusted her, the men like him who really believed they had some kind of God-given fucking right to treat everyone around them like shit because they had a few quid. Truth be told, she could buy and sell the majority of the fuckers these days. They were only countenanced because of who they were related to, and because of how much money they spent. They were only really useful to her when things started to fall out of bed. Then they were worth her time.

Jade sighed in frustration. She had the hump.

Today had been a particularly trying day in her calendar, for more than one reason. She had been contacted by another trollop who thought that all she needed to do to get what she wanted out of life was tell her about how Aiden spent all his time with her. It was bad enough that the girl worked for them in one of the strip clubs, but that she actually believed she could ring Jade's personal number was what really angered her. That a trollop, who *she* had paid wages to, had the nerve to think that she could actually contact her personally was beyond the fucking pale! Jade knew that Aiden was never going to be a wilting virgin, but the fact that he seemed to pick his paramours from their workforce really did bother her. He had no fucking imagination, apparently.

He loved her and always would – of that she had no doubt. But that he would fuck a hole in a fence was something she was also more than aware of. It was why she still refused to marry him. She resented him when he put her in this kind of position. It humiliated her, and she deserved much better. But when Aiden was chasing his cock, his sensible head was not in attendance. That the girl had seen him enough times to think she had some kind of claim on him told her all she needed to know. Why did he feel the need to romance them? She already knew that the girl in question, Destiny, was a beautiful young girl. They always were. But she had rung Jade and told her that she was in love with Aiden, and he was in love with her – that was something Jade could not shrug off. It was the certainty in the girl's voice that had really communicated itself to her. It was obvious that Aiden had been romancing her. And the silly bitch believed him.

She wasn't sure she could do it any more. She didn't want to go through all this again. It hurt her far more than she would ever allow herself to admit. But this time she had to step in because, if she didn't, who knew what the fuck would happen? That was the real fear for her. She couldn't ever trust Aiden when he was caught out, not just by her but by the whore he was shagging.

She cried in her anger and pain.

Chapter Sixty

'Jade, come on. You know that my Aiden absolutely adores you.'

Jade laughed half-heartedly. She wasn't in the mood for any real discussions, especially not with Reeva. If one of her kids murdered every one of her neighbours she would still argue the toss, say they were in the right, that they had been goaded!

'Tell Destiny that, Reeva, will you? I can't be arsed any more. It's too much like hard fucking work.'

Reeva felt genuinely upset because, over the years, she had realised that this woman was the best thing that could ever have happened to her son. It wasn't only about her grandson, because she believed that Jade would never stop her seeing him. She knew that Jade actually did like her. They had bonded over the years, and she was as angry as Jade was at Aiden's latest stupidity. She knew that Jade was not jealous – she didn't lose any sleep over her son's bits on the side. Reeva admired Jade because she didn't turn a drama into a fucking crisis, but she could understand why Jade saw his behaviour as insulting. She saw it that way herself. Aiden was her son, and God knew she loved him, but if she was Jade she would have taken him out a long time ago. 'I know what you are feeling, Jade. But he has too much of me in him, I think. I could never be faithful in my younger days . . .'

Jade hugged the woman who could aggravate the life out of her with a few words, but who she could not help growing to love as the years had gone on. 'Look, Reeva, you were a great mum, in your own way. Don't you dare fucking try and make excuses for him. Just do me a big favour, please? Let me leave Aiden Junior here for a few days while I sort everything out? Can you do that for me?'

Reeva found herself nodding in agreement even though it was the last thing she wanted to do. She felt like she could tear her eldest son a new one without a second thought.

'You have fucked off much better-looking girls than this whore, Jade.'

'I know, Reeva. But this girl worked for me – she's someone I have had to deal with. That is far too fucking close this time. I've swallowed my pride more than once. But I think that this girl is the end of it for me, this time.'

Reeva could see the hurt and the humiliation and she could really understand how Jade must be feeling. She knew that Jade wouldn't accept being treated so badly and so publicly. This time Aiden had really queered his fucking pitch. Jade was at the end of her patience where Aiden was concerned.

'I know the girls talk. But they have to respect me, Reeva. If they don't then I ain't doing my job. He is undermining me! This whore of his actually had the fucking nerve to ring me, Reeva, to lay down the law! That tells me that she thinks she has some kind of hold over him. Better I walk away now with my dignity because I have told him time and time again, do what you like but don't rub my face in it.'

Reeva felt like crying. Jade was a very proud woman and, no matter what she might have done in the past, there had never been even a hint of impropriety where Jade was concerned since she had been with her boy. Reeva had been on the woman's case since day one. She had investigated her like a fucking Old Bill. She had made a point of enquiring of anyone and everyone about Jade's life, made it her mission to find out all she could. And she couldn't fault her.

But she couldn't say the same about Aiden, fucker that he was. Why did he have to always pick those girls who thought they were in with a chance? Like he would ever put one of them over his Jade! She would give him an earful when she saw him, she was determined about that much. Who the fuck did he think he was?

When Jade left the house, Reeva poured herself another large drink, telling herself it was because she was so upset about her son's behaviour. But she knew that she would have poured the drink anyway, because that was what she liked to do. She liked a drink. Why was that such a big fucking deal? It wasn't like they didn't know her, was it? That they didn't know that she enjoyed an alcoholic beverage on a regular basis. That she had enjoyed drinking since she had been a young girl. If she had not liked drinking so much, the chances were, none of her kids would have seen the light of day. When Tony got in he listened to her going on incoherently about how Aiden had finally fucked up and, as always, he agreed with her and poured her into bed. He guessed there was something occurring, but he would keep his counsel until he knew exactly what was what.

When he checked on Agnes he saw that Aiden Junior was beside her in the bed and he sussed out what had probably been the cause of Reeva's drunken ramblings. After all, it wasn't a big secret any more. Destiny Smith, stupid whore that she was, had made sure about that. Did these females never learn? The best they could hope for was an old Face with a few quid and a chequered past, and giving these men kids younger than their grandchildren. The girls should be sensible enough to know that, if they used their loaves and sat it out, they would be left with a house and a few quid. They weren't the first wife; they weren't really seen as deserving of anything. These girls were the man in question's last fucking hurrah. They were the ones who were willing to sell themselves that short. They deserved all they got.

Chapter Sixty-One

Aiden O'Hara was feeling good about himself. He believed the time was at hand when Eric Palmer would step away from the businesses and pass the reins over to him and Jade. It was what he had been waiting for – patiently waiting for – because he had always thought the world of Eric Palmer.

Aiden had made it his mission in the past four years to get himself back on track to be Eric's successor after his monumental fuck-up with the IRA. It still haunted him. But he was more determined than ever to show he had what it took. So he'd looked for his next money-making scam like the fucking calculator he was. Aiden had seen the potential of the earn in the drug trade. He had even weighed out forty grand for a pill press so they could make the merchandise themselves. They now had presses and chemists all over the UK so that they could control certain areas. Eric was over the moon. He thought Aiden was just like him in his heyday. Aiden kept his ear to the ground and he made sure that he was told everything that was occurring in their world, whether it was in the clubs, or on the pavements. Knowledge was power, as Aiden was so fond of saying. He was very careful to never act without Eric's express say-so, to never try to do anything without his knowledge, giving him the respect he was due. But Aiden could see Eric was losing the edge.

Putting his legitimate money to work had become his main interest thanks to Aiden's persuasion. It was common knowledge that legal businesses were the golden ticket in his game. And now, if the Filth ever came knocking, he would always be in a position to explain how he paid his bills and bought his properties. Or, in his case, loads of fucking properties.

Aiden's mantra was easy and sensible: *always* be able to explain how you manage to drive your prestige car, pay for your big fucking house, and fund every part of your lifestyle. You needed to pay all the taxes you are required to, because the taxman – or, more to the point, the VAT man – is the only cunt who can enter your home without a fucking search warrant. Rape and murder kids, and the Filth still have to make sure they have a good reason to come into your home – a rapist has fucking rights. But owe a bit of tax and those fuckers could be in your drum without a by-your-leave. It was absolutely disgraceful. Rapists and paedophiles were never seen as being as important as tax evaders – that was what really annoyed villains.

It was a different world, and Aiden had explained all that to Eric. How it was important to be able to tell the taxman to take a flying fuck, but also to ensure that every shit he had ever passed could be proved in triplicate. That was Aiden's forte. He had explained the importance of being seen as legitimate, how only a complete mug would be stupid enough to take on the tax people. He had finally convinced Eric of his opinion, and Eric had been impressed by his acumen. He had finally realised just how important it was to look as if you were as honest as the proverbial day was long. Aiden felt he had proven his worth to Eric over and over again.

Now everything he had ever wanted was within his grasp and he couldn't be happier. As he sipped a large brandy at his desk, he looked around him with satisfaction. This is what he had been working towards, this was what he deserved.

Patsy crashed into the room with his usual aplomb, and Aiden started laughing. He loved his brother but Patsy was about as subtle as a fucking twelve-gauge shotgun.

'All right, Patsy.' It was a form of address.

Patsy sighed heavily as he said, 'I'm all right, but you ain't, bruv.'

Aiden stopped short. Opening his arms out in a gesture of supplication, he said seriously, 'Explain yourself?'

'You are such a fucking mug, Ade. Do you even know that?'

Aiden looked at his brother in surprise. Today had been the day they had been waiting for. He had told Patsy earlier that, from now on, they were on a fucking roll. They were so close. Now his brother had burst into his office calling him a mug.

'You fucking talking to me, Pats? Are you on a death wish or what?'

Patsy O'Hara looked at his brother with absolute disgust. 'You know what, Aiden? You really are a grade-A cunt.' Patsy knew his brother better than anyone. He knew everything about him – the good as well as the downright fucking snidey. 'You spoken to your Jade yet? I'm assuming that's a fucking negative. Only I think you might have finally fucked it up with her.'

Suddenly Aiden wasn't smiling any more. He had been trying to get her on the phone but he had not been able to. Until now, it had not occurred to him that she might be avoiding him. 'What the fuck are you on about?'

Patsy loved his brother, but he wished that Aiden could see himself as others saw him at times. He was so fucking disloyal to the people who really mattered and that bothered Patsy because he believed that if you could completely disregard the mother of your child, you could not be trusted by anyone else. Patsy liked and respected Jade Dixon. Without her his big brother could not run everything as well as it was run now. 'What am I on about? Fucking *Destiny*, of course! Once more you have picked a fucking slag bag. And another mouthy one at that. She is telling all and sundry that you love her! That you are going to marry her. Will you ever fucking learn, Aiden?'

Aiden felt sick. This was why he couldn't get his Jade on the phone, why his mum was swerving him. Today of all fucking days. If Eric Palmer got wind of this he would be like the Antichrist. Everything they were being given was because Eric trusted Jade to run it as she always had. He knew that Eric didn't believe that he was capable of running the day-to-day business because he didn't have any interest in that shit. It bored him. And that was the one thing that Eric Palmer had always been wary about. Without Jade onside, Eric believed that Aiden would lose the edge, that he would not bother to chase things up and keep on top of it all.

Aiden turned on his brother angrily. 'Well, she's talking out of her arse. Jade ain't stupid. She knows that's a load of old fucking fanny.'

Patsy shook his head in absolute disbelief. It aggravated him that his brother could kid himself as and when it suited him. It was at times like this when he really could smack him one. Aiden was so arrogant, and so sure that he could worm his way out of anything. Which of course, where Jade was concerned, he usually could.

'You were always the clever bastard, Aiden. We knew that and accepted it. But for someone with so much fucking so-called intelligence, I don't get how you can pick up with an idiot like Destiny. She rang Jade today, telling her everything about you and her. She has Jade's number and she rang Mum's place as well. But, as luck would have it, Tony answered and then he called me. You are a car crash, Aiden. You know when you can see it about to happen but you can't stop it? That is *you*. Jade is the best thing you ever fucking had. You're a great team. She has your son and, more to the point, Jade is the only person who can run the businesses on a day-to-day basis. Because you fucking couldn't organise anything without her standing beside you. You need her for more reasons than you could ever realise. You know that as well as I do.'

Aiden was angry at his brother's words, at his accusations. He wasn't a man who could ever accept criticism. Especially when he knew it was the truth.

He was aware that Destiny was waiting for him in a flat he owned in Manor Park. She was twenty years old, pretty as a picture, and she had the body of a porn star – his usual fucking outside squeeze. He had never given her any reason to think she was that special in any way. In fact, he had told her from day one that he could never offer her anything other than his time, and obviously he had made sure that she didn't lose out financially by being with him, even though he knew that she would use the relationship to further her career in some way. They all did the same and, if he was honest, that appealed to him. He liked that he was seen as a man's man. He liked that he was known to have other women on the side. He saw it as part of his persona. He was a scallywag, a womaniser. But he also made sure that people knew that it didn't take away from his love and respect for Jade. Most of his outside girls were just happy to be noticed by him. Why did people like Destiny think they could fucking force him into wanting them? Why did they think they were in with a chance?

Patsy could see that he had really annoyed his brother and he was glad. He said as much. 'Did you really think that putting that girl up in a flat and giving her a wage wouldn't make her think that she might actually be in with a chance? She believes you are going to marry her.'

Aiden looked at his brother for a long moment. He knew that what Patsy was saying was absolutely right, but that didn't mean he wanted to listen to him. He was irritated. Today should have been his fucking triumph. He had felt today that Eric Palmer was ready to give him what he wanted. That he was finally willing to walk away. Now he had his brother on his case – and it looked like Jade was going on the trot. It was his own fault: he pushed things to the hilt, especially Jade. She accepted him taking fliers but when he kept the girls in his life for a while, he knew that it really vexed her. And that was partly the reason he did it – he wanted to see how far she would let him go.

He also knew that there was a viciousness in him that made him feel the need to prove to her that he didn't need her. Even though he really *did* need her. There was a nasty streak in him where women were concerned. But he loved his Jade. She was his girl. He felt that when they had found each other it had been written in the stars. Together they were a force to be reckoned with. They complemented each other in every way that mattered; not just sexually – they worked together beautifully. She understood him, and she had taught him everything of relevance that he had needed to know. That was something he could not, and would not, ever forget. Even today, he knew that, without Jade, Eric Palmer would not walk away with such ease. Eric saw them as the perfect partnership. And it was. He couldn't imagine his life without her. She was the mother of his son, and she was the only woman he would ever love. But his brother's criticism had hit a nerve. He didn't have to take anything off anyone any more.

'Listen, Patsy. I know you love all this fucking drama . . .'

Patsy held his hands up in defeat. He was tired and he couldn't be bothered to argue any more. His anger suddenly left him; he was wasting his time – Aiden didn't give a shit either way. But it grieved him seeing Jade brought so fucking low. He liked her, respected her – they all did. Even his mother had changed her tune. Yet his older brother treated her like dirt.

'I'm done, Aiden. I am only trying to help you. You can sort your own shit out this time, because I ain't threatening Destiny, all right? You're on your own, mate. But be warned. Mum is backing Jade to the hilt.'

Aiden sat in his chair after his brother walked out on him and he looked around his office. He usually loved the feeling of being here, being in control of everything and everyone around him. But right now all he felt was a great anger towards Patsy. He would never forget that he had spoken to him with such disrespect, even allowing for his brother's insistence that he was only helping him and trying to make him see the error of his ways.

Aiden could never allow that kind of disrespect to go by without some kind of punishment. He swallowed down a large brandy and then, when he felt calm enough, he left the office determined to sort out his household arrangements once and for all. But he was shaking with anger, and that never augured well for anyone.

Chapter Sixty-Two

Destiny Smith was feeling nervous but, thanks to a few vodkas and a couple of lines of cocaine, she had convinced herself that she had done the right thing. She loved this flat; it was large, spacious and really well furnished. It was her home now – thanks to her Aiden, who footed the bills. He had told her that it was hers and she had been so thrilled. She had liked him from the first time she had met him and now she believed that she loved him. Her big worry was that he had never allowed her to bring up anything to do with that Jade – every time she mentioned her he batted her off and changed the subject.

She sighed in annoyance. Jade was as old as the hills! Of course he would rather be with her – she was young and gorgeous. The problem was that Aiden had a child with Jade. She had ensnared him when he was a young lad – it was common knowledge.

So, today, Destiny had finally decided that she had to take matters into her own hands. Like her mum always said, you had to take what you wanted from life – no one was going to give it to you.

She studied herself in the mirror, and the reflection made her smile. She was really lovely. Aiden O'Hara came to her regularly and she knew that he enjoyed her. She didn't exactly *enjoy* him as such, but she believed that would come in time. The fact that he had set her up here told her everything she needed to know.

The other girls at the club had been bitchy, telling her that he would never leave Jade, that she should get what she could out of him. That had *really* offended her – they were just jealous.

Nevertheless she was beginning to worry because he had not been in contact since she dropped the bombshell on Jade. She could only think that it was going to be harder than she had thought for him to extricate himself from the relationship; after all, they did have a kid together. But she could do that as well – she was younger, years younger, and she could produce a whole family for Aiden if needed. She hoped that wouldn't be the case, though – two kids max was her limit.

She reapplied her make-up, and brushed out her long, blond hair. She was wearing nothing but lacy black knickers and a lacy black push-up bra. She knew exactly what he wanted from her and she made a point of providing exactly that. What was between her legs was the real interest for him. And she knew enough about men to know that, for the majority of them, that would be more than enough.

She heard a key in the door and smiled contentedly. She had known he would come; she couldn't believe that she had doubted him.

Chapter Sixty-Three

Eugene was worried, but he followed his brother Patsy without a word. Patsy was clearly annoyed but he knew better than to question him. Patsy was a lot more like Aiden than he realised – both of them were determined to do what they wanted when they were angry enough. Tonight Patsy was angrier than Eugene had ever seen him before.

Patsy looked the typical Jamaican; he had the Bob Marley look going for him. Eugene, though, had a unique look that women loved. He was the darkest of them all – with his mother's startling blue eyes. He could be hard when necessary but, unlike Aiden and Patsy, he didn't see his life as just a series of violent acts. He always joked that he was more a lover than a fighter, even though, when pushed, he could hold his own with the best of them. He always made a point of sorting out his own shit, instead of going to his brother. He had his own reputation – he just didn't see the need to *look* for trouble. 'Look, Patsy, what is going on tonight? Where the fuck are we going and why?'

Eugene had been having the time of his life in one of the clubs they owned, and he wasn't impressed with being dragged out without any kind of explanation.

Patsy stopped the car, a brand-new BMW that Aiden had

given him for his birthday. The irony wasn't lost on him. Like everyone around him, he had Aiden to thank for his good fortune.

'Have you really not heard anything today?'

Eugene shrugged. 'Such as, Patsy?'

Patsy closed his eyes in annoyance. 'About Aiden and that fucking thing he's been shagging, Destiny?'

Eugene laughed. 'It's hardly a fucking secret, is it?'

Patrick looked at his brother with disgust. 'Well, Jade knows. Destiny rang her today and gave her the full fucking bifta.'

Eugene still didn't understand what was going on; he honestly didn't really care. 'And that matters because?'

Patrick grabbed his brother by his shirt and, pulling him towards him roughly, he said angrily, 'That matters, Eugene, because Aiden will kill her. Jade wants us there and so that is where we are going, OK?'

Chapter Sixty-Four

Jade smiled gently as she saw the shock on Destiny's face. All her instincts were telling her to smack this stupid girl from one end of this flat to the other. But she knew that would be a pointless exercise.

Instead she said kindly, 'Destiny, sweetheart, my advice to you is to get yourself dressed as quickly as possible.'

The girl was young and very beautiful. Jade had known that already, but it didn't stop it hurting.

Destiny recovered faster than Jade would have given her credit for. 'I'm going nowhere, Jade. I'm waiting for Aiden. I'm sorry if you feel hurt but I love him, and he loves me.'

As she spoke she was dragging on her dressing gown; she had never felt so exposed in her life. Jade in the flesh was not as old-looking as she had let herself believe. In truth, she looked fucking amazing and, even in her shock and horror, Destiny had the nous to see that this was a woman who had a presence.

Jade shook her head sadly. 'Listen to me, sweetheart. Aiden doesn't give a flying fuck about you. Take it from me, darling, I am here to *help* you. Believe me, if I was here to teach you a lesson you would be spark out on the floor now. So go and get yourself fucking dressed.'

Destiny stood in front of her nemesis. She was so stunned

that she didn't know how to react. But the woman's voice was very serious, and it sounded very honest.

Then Jade bellowed, '*Now!* He will be here soon and, take it from me, he won't be as fucking easy-going as I am. You fucked up, lady, you committed the cardinal sin: you made him feel bad about himself. The minute you made yourself known to me you became his mortal enemy. Now, get moving.'

Something in Jade's voice, in her demeanour, told Destiny Smith that she was telling her the truth. She could hear the underlying fear in Jade's voice, and she knew then that it was all over for her. She did as she was told.

Five minutes later they left the flat and Jade walked her quickly to her car. Jade found it in her heart to feel sorry for this young girl who, unlike her, had not found out yet that the men in the world they inhabited were not worth the proverbial wank, that tonight was the first heartbreak in a long line of heartbreaks and this girl would never understand that until it was too late. She would give her a few grand, and hope that she made some kind of life for herself in Spain. She had a few addresses for her, and a few contacts. Because Destiny couldn't stay here after tonight's debacle. Her Aiden, who she thought loved her so very much, would not let her walk away from this night's fucking aggravation. He would harm her. He would cheerfully wound this girl because he would think she had crossed a line and caused him problems.

Chapter Sixty-Five

Aiden arrived home as the dawn was breaking. Jade was sitting in the kitchen waiting for him patiently, and when he saw her she could see the fear on his face.

'I assume you saw Patsy and Eugene.'

He nodded calmly. She looked so beautiful to him. Sitting there, she was ladylike and perfectly groomed, as always. She was everything he could ever want in a woman. If only she knew how much he adored her, how much he loved her.

'I took Destiny away, Aiden. She was just a lovely girl who you wanted, like you have always wanted these girls. But I am warning you now, once and for all: you had better not ever humiliate me again. I don't give a shit about you fucking the staff. But the next time I hear you have singled one out I will make it my fucking goal in life to destroy you. I am the mother of your child and I think that I am pretty easy-going. But this is the last time you *ever* make me involve myself in your fucking mess.'

Aiden sighed deeply, looking for all the world like he was the wronged party in this debacle. 'I was going to make her understand that tonight. I don't know why she thought she could cause so much upset. I could never love her, Jade, you know that.'

Jade closed her eyes. She was so tired, so fed up with him and his antics. 'This is the last time, Aiden. You can fuck who you like, I really don't care. But if you ever bring this kind of trouble to my door again, I will drop you like a fucking hot cake. Do you understand me?'

He wiped his hand across his face, and that told her just how bothered he was about her and about what she had done this night. That he would have harmed that girl without a thought bothered her more than she would ever admit – it told her what she had always known and tried to resist. The fact he had put Destiny up in one of their properties, and allowed her to believe that he loved her, was something Jade couldn't get her head around.

But that she loved him, Jade couldn't deny. Even knowing what he was capable of, that he was completely without any kind of moral compass, didn't make her love him any less. That was how broken and warped she was.

Aiden knelt in front of her and, taking her hands in his, he said sincerely and with tears in his eyes, 'Honestly, Jade, I can't fucking tell you how bad I feel. You know I love you, darling. You are everything to me. I would fucking kill myself if that would prove to you how much you mean to me.'

Jade had heard it before, so many times. She knew that he meant every word he said, but the intelligent thing to do would be to walk away for her own peace of mind. Because Aiden was a complete headcase and he would never change. But, even knowing that, she still couldn't bring herself to leave. As bad as he was, they had a connection that was as toxic as it was necessary for them both.

'I love you too, Aiden. I never loved anyone until I met you. Now we have our boy, and we have a life together – a *good* life together. Eric wants us to take over from him, he trusts us as a partnership because we work so well.'

Aiden could feel his heart rate slowing down at last. The fear that Jade would walk away was gone. He knew she was capable of walking away from him. That she was the stronger of the two. There were times when he hated her – when he wanted to punish her for what he saw as her disloyalty in going to Eric behind his back. Those were the times when he wanted to rub her face in the fact he could have any bird he wanted. But, deep down, his biggest fear was losing her; losing not just the partnership built on real love, but also losing her as his voice of reason. Losing the only person who could tell him he was in the wrong, and who he would listen to. She had introduced him to the world they now controlled. She had shown him how to take advantage of opportunities, and how to use those opportunities to the best advantage. He knew that, without her by his side, he could never have achieved as much as he had. Jade was the person who put all his plans into action; she was the woman who made him feel invincible, who would always have his back. She had proven that even if it rankled. He depended on her much more than he would ever admit.

As he pulled her into his arms and kissed her deeply, he felt her melting into him. No matter what happened between them they could never resist each other physically.

Chapter Sixty-Six

'For the love of my life.'

Jade forced a smile as Aiden bowled in with a huge bunch of flowers. This was his usual way of saying sorry to her for his fucking outrageous disloyalty. For treating her like she was nothing in the grand scheme of things.

Since the upset with Destiny Smith he had made a point of proving to her that he was some kind of a changed man.

She took them from him, saying breezily, 'You keep spoiling me, Aiden! I could get used to this.'

It was what he wanted to hear, she knew. It was like a game but one she didn't like playing any more, even though she had no choice if she wanted to keep him by her side. The sex was still amazing – that would never change. They had some kind of animal fucking lust that somehow transcended everything else. But day-to-day they were both aware that they were trying too hard – or, more to the point, Aiden was trying too hard.

Aiden was watching her intently and she felt as if she was on display. She didn't know how to react to this new Aiden – they were both on their best behaviour, and it felt wrong, as though they didn't really understand one another any more, when that had always been their strength. She was pussyfooting round him, spending a lot of her time making him feel good about himself. It was a shame he didn't return the favour; after all, she was the one who was always left feeling angry and humiliated.

She made them coffee and as she sat down to drink hers she said brightly, 'We're meeting with the Clarks at Treacys in Barking later. It's close by for all of us and we can talk in peace – I asked Michael to make sure no one sits nearby. More to the point, if it does get a bit aggressive we are surrounded by friends. But I think I can talk them into a good deal, Aiden.'

Aiden grinned happily, 'OK, then. I will meet you there, but I think *I* could talk them into anything that I wanted if the need arose.'

Jade didn't answer him; she knew it was pointless.

He kissed her on the lips. 'I'm going into the offices in Canary Wharf this morning. I need to sort out the clubs. Patsy is meeting me there, so he will probably be coming to Treacys too.'

Jade nodded. She had expected as much. 'That's fine. I have a few bits to do this morning with Eric. See you later.'

She waited till he had left the house and then she sat back heavily. She was nervous as fuck; the Clarks were not going to be as amenable as Aiden expected. But it was a deal already brokered by Eric Palmer and, no matter what Aiden might think, it was basically set in stone. Eric Palmer might be taking a step back, but he would not appreciate his word being overlooked. This was his last hurrah, and it would make sure they earned for a long time. Eric Palmer was shrewd enough to know that this was one deal Aiden couldn't be allowed to broker. Aiden wouldn't see the long-term benefits. Actually, Aiden wouldn't see any of the benefits because he didn't like the Clarks. His biggest fault was he could never see further than his own fucking nose. Eric Palmer had already given them his word so the meeting today was nothing more than lip service. Eric wanted this, and Jade knew she had to ensure that it all went off without a fucking hitch of any kind. Eric's word was his bond – it had to be, that was the only way they could conduct any kind of real fucking business.

Although her Aiden's reputation as a shrewd businessman had grown, his unpredictability, coupled with his knack of finding a slight where there wasn't one, and his insistence on bringing trouble to people's doors on a whim, had caused him to lose a lot of his credibility. His violent nature would always cause people to think twice about crossing him, but it also made other people chary of dealing with him – that was what he could never get through his thick fucking skull. Too much, too soon really. He had been given everything by Eric Palmer at such a young age, rather than coming through the ranks like everyone else. He just couldn't get that the people in the world they lived in had to sometimes swallow their knobs and deal with men and women they would avoid if given the opportunity. That the golden ticket was about getting on with the people you were dealing with.

Aiden was capable of so much more than anybody realised. He had such a bad attitude that he made himself unpopular, but he could sniff out a deal in seconds and broker it so everyone felt they had gained something. He was as sharp as a fucking tack where money was concerned. But then somewhere along the line, he would nause it all up through abject stupidity. He would suddenly turn away from the guaranteed earn, arguing that he believed there was something untoward occurring when the deal was being done. That he believed there was skulduggery afoot in some way. That he felt slighted and thought he should mention it. He would upset everyone on a whim.

Jade was expected to straighten all that out, which she would do, of course, making sure that everyone involved was made to feel like they were the only important person. She had a knack for that. Then, when Aiden came down off the drink and the drugs, he would act like a Vestal Virgin.

Without her interference, Aiden O'Hara would not have the creds he had. Eric Palmer counted on her to keep him on the straight and narrow. Eric Palmer knew that, without her on board, Aiden O'Hara would just destroy everything they had achieved overnight. *She* was the person that Eric Palmer trusted to keep his earns on an even keel. *She* was the person who made sure that nothing went wrong. In reality, she made sure that Aiden didn't fuck up. She did just that because Aiden listened to her. He trusted her.

But the real problem was, she wasn't sure that she trusted him any more. That was the fucker of it all. For all the flowers and attention, he was treating her like shit, and she wasn't a woman who suffered fools gladly. Aiden was flying a bit too close to the wind for her liking. He had fucked her off to such an extent that she could happily stab him, with a large smile on her face. That she had been reduced to helping out his latest paramour so that he didn't get the chance to violently harm the girl really made her angry. She knew that she was wrong to forgive him every time that he hurt her. If she wasn't so damaged, she would have had the sense to walk away from him a long time ago. But she couldn't do that because, no matter what he did, she still loved him.

Now they were to meet the Clarks and, without her beside him, Aiden would not have the patience required to bring the meeting to the conclusion expected. Eric Palmer really under-stood the long-term benefits that the Clarks could bring to the table. Aiden would only see that he didn't like them, because they were like him – all about the front. Like Aiden, they were forever on their dignity, looking for a slight, angling for a row with anyone they thought wasn't giving them their due. Well, they didn't need to be friends. This was business and Jade understood that they could earn a lot of money together. Like Eric Palmer, she was more interested in the earn than in personalities. That was how you garnered money and power. You worked with the people who could best serve your purpose. It was a lesson that Aiden could never understand.

Well, he would have to rethink all that now, because the Clark brothers were exactly what they needed at this particular time, and they were willing to take the big risk this deal entailed. She only hoped that Aiden had the sense to see that. Because if he didn't she was more than willing to point it out to him. And not in a good way either.

Chapter Sixty-Seven

Eric Palmer was happy with his decision. He had a great crew working for him, and, even though he was taking a big step back, he made sure that everyone who mattered knew that he would be straight back on board should the need arise. He might not be hands on any more, but he was willing to forego all that if he felt in the least mugged off.

As he sat in Treacys restaurant he wondered how Aiden could be so foolish as to let someone like Destiny Smith bring him so much grief. He had told him as much and he could tell Aiden hadn't liked that. Eric knew he took criticism badly. For such a clever bastard where work was concerned, Aiden had no sense when it came to women. That was his big weakness, like many a man before him. He didn't see that women could be the downfall of even the strongest of men, that they were far more dangerous than they appeared. Those women had a different mind-set and were willing to throw caution to the wind when they wanted something bad enough. Aiden was a dangerous fuck, but that didn't mean he wouldn't one day meet his nemesis and find himself on the receiving end of a situation that he could not control; Eric had seen it so many times in the past. Eventually, everyone came up against a will greater than their own. It was the way of the world.

Eric stood up smiling easily as Colin and Timmy Clark came into the restaurant.

They were both imposing, powerful men, who always made an entrance, not just because of their size, but because they were both very loud and very jovial. They were also very good-looking, with thick blond hair, dark blue eyes and fantastic bone structure they had inherited from their mother – a Swedish beauty who had married a huge Irishman, as handsome as he was feckless.

'Good to see you, lads.'

The Clark boys shook hands with Eric and he was reminded of just how physically strong they were. They might not be the brains of Britain but they were still men you wouldn't cross without a fucking good reason. They had their creds; if they didn't, he wouldn't be dealing with them now.

'You're looking well for a man about to retire!' Colin Clark was smiling happily as he sat down at the table.

'Not so much retiring as taking a step back, lads. I will still have an interest in the businesses, of course.'

Timmy Clark, the younger brother, laughed loudly. 'Yeah, heard that before. But good on you, mate. As long as you are still our main point of contact we are happy little bunnies!'

Eric heard the threat and, as he had expected as such, he smiled lazily. He knew that Aiden wasn't a man you took on lightly, though he had to wonder if the fucker had done his homework.

'As long as you only get in touch with me in emergencies, I'm happy enough, guys.'

Eric knew that he had told them what they wanted to hear. He could understand that they were not too enamoured of Aiden, though they both liked and respected Jade. But Aiden

O'Hara, for all his fucking faults, and they were legion, was still the person who he saw as the only *man* to take over his position. As long as he had Jade by his side, there was nothing he couldn't achieve. That was the truth. If these bastards wanted a step up then they had to understand that. He had a feeling that they did, but he wasn't holding his breath.

The waiter brought over a very expensive bottle of red wine and they chatted amiably as he poured them a large glass each.

'This is the life, eh? Good wine and the knowledge that we are going to make a fucking big profit. But I warn you, Eric, you have to keep your young puppy in order.'

Colin was laughing as he spoke but they were aware of the seriousness of his words. It was a warning, and not a very veiled one.

Eric Palmer was a man with more creds than these cunts could ever hope for. The fact that he was even talking to them at all was a fucking big deal. That Colin thought he could start a conversation with a fucking threat was a joke. Eric wasn't laughing now. Not even smiling. The Clark brothers were suddenly reminded of why Eric Palmer was at the top of his game, why he had been there for so long.

Leaning forward in his chair, Eric said nastily, 'With all fucking respect, *boys*, you two will be working for *me*. And I would advise you both to keep that in the forefront of your fucking little minds. I don't like feeling that I'm being mugged off, or that I'm being threatened by people who I could wipe out on a whim if the fancy took me. Do you two get my fucking drift?'

The Clark brothers were both immediately apologetic, especially when they saw that the restaurant was empty other than people who clearly worked for Eric.

'Listen, Eric, there was no insult intended. But you have to see our point of view, mate.'

Eric took a large swallow of his wine before he answered seriously, 'That puppy you mentioned is my boy. He is who you will be dealing with on a daily basis. He is the man I trust with not only my life, but with *all* my businesses. A man who I know would eat you two for breakfast, and fart you out two hours later. If you two can't hack that then you have come to the wrong fucking place.'

The Clark brothers knew when they were being put in their place. And they also knew that Aiden O'Hara was going to be who they had to deal with. That was their biggest fear, if they were honest. It wasn't an ideal situation, but they were sensible enough to know that they had tried to push their point of view over, and Eric Palmer had basically told them that they could go and fuck themselves.

Colin Clark knew when he was beaten. He was a realist, if nothing else. 'Of course, Eric. If that is your wish then we are obliged to go along with it. No insult intended. We just needed to know the score.'

Eric grinned. 'As long as you understand the situation, I'm a happy camper.'

The lines had been drawn and Eric Palmer had got his point across. He might be stepping back, but he had shown them that he wasn't about to be treated like a fool. He was stepping back in name only. What could they say to that? The Clark brothers were shrewd enough to know when they should retreat. They had believed that Eric Palmer was taking a big step back and, after what they knew about Aiden and his penchant for a bit of strange, they had thought that they could push for a better deal. It had not worked out for them. They were gutted but they weren't about to lose any sleep over it. They had tried it on, that was expected. Eric Palmer had put them in their place, and made a point of telling them that he was still a figurehead.

All in all, Eric Palmer felt that he had paved the way for Jade and Aiden. He trusted them to do the job. Whatever happened between them, they were a good working partnership. He had arranged to meet the Clark brothers an hour early so that he could get all the shit out of the way. He had been right to do that. Now the Clarks would think twice before they tried any funny business. Especially as Aiden would not be in the mood for anything that was even remotely irritating.

Chapter Sixty-Eight

Colin Clark was not a nice person. He would actually be the first man to admit that. He was more than aware of his limitations. He had a problem with most people around him. He just wasn't what was called a 'people person'. He was an antisocial fuck, as the prison psychiatrist had so colourfully explained to anyone who would listen to him. Especially when Colin had nutted him during the course of one of their weekly sessions, something which Colin insisted had just been his natural reaction to their lively banter.

Colin took that description as a massive compliment and mentioned it whenever he could slip it into a conversation. The psychiatrist had also mentioned that Colin was as cunning as they came, and was the proud possessor of an above-average intelligence. He had also refused to ever see the man again, something else that Colin took as a compliment to his status as a nutbag.

Colin was a hard fuck to understand, let alone work with. He believed that everyone around him was a complete cunt until they proved themselves otherwise. He was willing to work with anyone, for the simple reason he believed that he could sort out *anyone* at any time, if the fancy or indeed the need took him. That was his strength in many respects; it helped enormously with the world he lived in and was what had got him as far as he had. He had a reputation for not suffering fools gladly, but he also had a reputation for making sure that anyone who worked alongside him *earned*. He knew how important that was. People didn't have to like you – they just needed to trust you. If they fucked up then that was it as far as he was concerned. As long as they didn't dare to fuck him over, they were in. You didn't ask people to invest in a business that wasn't worthy. That was a given. More so because he knew that, without investors, he had no fucking business, anyway.

That wasn't to say that he didn't sometimes cook the books in his favour, obviously, and offered less than he knew he would actually provide. In fact, he was known as a man who could not be trusted one hundred per cent. Not that it bothered him. As far as he was concerned, he provided a decent wage and that was enough for him, and the people he dealt with got a good earn, and it was a fucking good earn. Especially as they were people who he was willing to take a chance on, who he introduced to the world of fucking villainy. Without him they were basically fucked. After all, he wasn't fucking Woolworths. Everyone he dealt with was on the fucking rob in one way or another.

He saw his job as giving certain people the opportunity to utilise their individuality. He was always open to new grafts, to good earns. He was willing to listen to anyone who might have a genuinely interesting and workable idea. The fact that he would steal the idea was neither here nor there. He was the one who gave them the chance to put their ideas into practice. He was willing to take a chance on them. Colin was an entrepreneur. Without him, they would earn sweet fuck-all.

Basically he knew that he was earning off other people's ideas, off other people's hard work. But that was exactly what any business worth its salt did, surely? He showcased and bankrolled these people's ideas. He gave them the opportunity to shine.

He believed that he was entitled to everything he got, after all, these people had come to him. They sought him out, not the other way around. Without his interest the ideas that were given to him were worthless. He could not for the life of him see that, without the people who were shrewd enough in their own ways to work out these brilliant ideas, he was bereft of anything even remotely interesting. He could take someone else's brainchild and run with it. Once he understood what the actual economics were he could, and did, make sure that he was the main earner. Then, if it had legs, he would insist on purchasing what he referred to as his 'rights'. If they argued for more of a piece, he took serious offence and acted like he was absolutely without any idea what their problem might be. Then he would lose his fucking rag. That meant basically that he just threatened the people concerned, and took whatever they had offered him as his own.

He couldn't think of an original idea if his life depended on it.

Colin took other people's intelligence and he made it his mission to give those ideas a new edge. That was how business worked in his world. He had always depended on other people and ideas that he could utilise to his own ends, and made them far too frightened to give him a tug when they finally under- stood that he had mugged them off. He knew that he was seen as a fucking leech to a lot of the men he dealt with, but those same men didn't give a flying fuck when he was good enough to pay them off.

His brother, Timmy, however, was a completely different

entity. Timmy Clark was basically the opposite of his brother; consequently, he was often overlooked. He didn't have much to say for himself, and he was happy being in the background. Though anyone in the know realised very quickly that it was Timmy who really had the nous. That it was actually Timmy who kept everything going when Colin Clark lost all interest, which he did on a regular basis. Colin had a very short attention span; he also didn't really interest himself in the day-to-day of the businesses. He depended on other people to carry out what he saw as the boring part of his growing empire. In short, Colin was the Aiden to Timmy's Jade.

Now, as they all prepared to meet up, each camp was wondering what the outcome was going to be. They had heard about each other, had listened to the gossip about each other, had both decided early on what they were supposed to think.

It was the personal aspect that fucked up so many criminals in the past. Personal feelings were of no good to any of them. It was pride that put most people away, when they forgot that the earn was the important thing. It was not the sixties any more; vendettas were a thing of the past. There was enough for everyone if they used their fucking brains. Eric Palmer was hoping that it didn't all fall out of fucking bed within seconds, and he had basically told Aiden that he wanted this, no matter what. If Aiden used his loaf for once there was a serious earn on the cards. What more could any of them want? But Eric feared deep inside that Aiden would do exactly what *he* wanted regardless of anything or anyone. Threats meant nothing to Aiden. He welcomed conflict; he saw it as a necessary part of the criminal life. He enjoyed it because he loved nothing more than what he referred to as a challenge. It was a very nerve-racking time for everyone concerned.

Except for Aiden and Colin, of course. They were looking forward to the meet. They didn't think twenty minutes ahead let alone five years. Both of them were incapable of thinking anything through; they were both lucky enough to have Number Twos who were the real brains behind the outfits.

Eric Palmer believed that, together, these two could probably make a really good devil's contract. That was what he was depending on. They were what were known as kindred spirits, and he only hoped that they would see that together. Together they were capable of great things. If they were enemies, though, he would only be able to stand back and watch the explosion.

Chapter Sixty-Nine

Agnes was worried. Her mum had the hump with her because they had argued over Aiden Junior, and her mum drinking when she was supposed to be looking after him. Drunk usually meant aggressive with Reeva, and that was what annoyed Agnes. She was fed up with being the fucking designated adult, when her mum was supposed to be the responsible one here. True, she did the job required, ninety-odd per cent of the time, but everyone assumed that when Reeva went on a bender, Agnes would be there to sort it out. That meant, of course, that she always had to be on the lookout to make sure that Aiden Junior, who was growing up fast, was taken care of.

Even though she was the youngest, her brothers thought that she should do what was expected of her. It didn't matter that she might want some kind of a life of her own. That would never even occur to them.

Jade understood, but she also preferred that Agnes was on hand to look after her son, because Reeva couldn't be depended on for any length of time. And it wasn't just Aiden Junior Agnes had to look after. When her mum was completely out of her brains and off her fucking tree, her brothers just assumed that Agnes would take care of her no matter how paranoid Reeva might be or how aggressive she might become. And this wasn't

231

something that occurred just occasionally – it was a constant threat.

With or without drugs Reeva could cause a fight in an empty house if the fancy took her. Though, on the drugs, she was obviously far worse than usual – that was when the Old Bill would be required to attend. Reeva fought with anyone at the drop of a hat; she loved the drama of it all.

Take today, for example. Agnes was trying to talk her mum out of fighting Mrs Connelly from up the road because she believed that the woman – who was seventy if she was a day – had reported her mother to the police. Mrs Connelly was a bit like Reeva, in that she was no wilting violet. In fact, she was still known to have a physical fight should the need arise. She had three sons – one doing life for murder, two banged up for bank robbery.

Now, as Agnes stood in Mrs Connelly's garden, trying to talk her mother down, she attempted to bring some kind of sense to the situation. Not that either of the women concerned was interested, of course. They were both drama queens who loved nothing more than an audience. All she could hear was cursing and threats. Neither of them was listening to her – they never did, especially not her old mum, who treated her with complete indifference.

She had finally tracked down Tony. Bless him, he was a good man. He understood her predicament and was on his way in a black cab.

Reeva had just got into her stride, as everyone within a five-mile radius probably knew. She wasn't exactly quiet when she went off on one.

'Out here now, you old bitch! You would phone the Filth about my lads?'

Mrs Connelly would no more phone the police than she would shag the parish priest. Everyone knew that, it was a complete joke. She was a lot of things but a grass wasn't one of them.

Agnes grabbed her mum's arm and pulled her round to face her. She was so angry that she didn't care about the onlookers any more. She wasn't interested in trying to keep this on the down-low. It was well past that now – this was about damage limitation.

Slapping her mother hard across the face, she shouted angrily, 'For fuck's sake, Mum! Listen to yourself, will you? You sound like a complete moron. You both do. You're like a pair of fucking idiots.'

Somewhere in Reeva's brain she knew that she should be listening to her girl, that she was talking sense, that she was so out of it she couldn't trust herself. But that didn't mean she had to put up with her daughter treating her like a mug in public and so she said as much.

'Hang on a minute, lady. Are you going against the family for a fucking stranger? For this fucking old bitch!'

Agnes sighed; she felt like crying. She hated all this, she hated when her mum was so out of it she caused murders. Then, when she woke up the next day, she would demand to know why no one had seen fit to stop her, why everyone had allowed it to go as far as it had and why her daughter had not just taken her home as any normal person would have done. Reeva would argue until black was blue that her kids, who she would fight to the death for, should keep a lookout for her, especially when she was drunk. Reeva really convinced herself that her kids should make sure that these kinds of situations should never have been allowed to evolve. Her attitude was that she would always look out for them and they should do the same for her, especially when she was completely off her nut and needed them to look after her the most. She would reason that there was nothing that any of her kids could do – no matter how bad – that she would not make sure that they had an alibi. And, credit where it was due, that was the truth.

But that didn't mean much to her daughter. It was her daughter – who had never been in trouble with the police or anyone for that matter – who was expected to sort out her shit on a regular basis. Worst of all, Reeva actually convinced herself that she was the one in the right.

'You know what I'm like, for fuck's sake. And you never thought to stick up for me? I have been maligned, I have been insulted.'

The list would go on and on, even though they knew she was just drunk and looking for a row. It could never be her fault, of course. God forbid that she should ever take responsibility for any of her actions.

Agnes smiled gently, saying kindly, 'Mum, just shut up, please, and let me take you home.'

Agnes sounded calm and reasonable. She was used to pretending – it wasn't the first time she had been expected to talk her mum down. Reeva was so out of it she couldn't even see her daughter properly.

Drawing herself upright, Reeva said, with as much dignity as she could manage, 'Get this fucking lunatic out of my way, please!'

Agnes looked at Mrs Connelly, saying nicely, 'You are really not helping the situation. You do understand that?'

Mrs Connelly, who had a face like a serious car accident and was as lairy and as unpredictable as Reeva, said viciously, 'I am only defending myself, young lady. Ask anyone. Your mother was the fucking aggressor here.'

Agnes looked at the old woman who was just like her mother. She lived in her council house, and depended on her son's reputation to give her the means to give vent to all her frustrations. Like her mum she drank far too much than was good for her, and looked for trouble at every turn. She measured her useless life on her son's criminal enterprises. It was so sad and so unnecessary. It was a waste of everything that God had given them. Agnes had finally had enough of them both.

'OK, Mrs Connelly, I get what you're saying. So should I get *my* brothers here, then? Is that what you want? My brother Aiden, and the others, going after your sons, who are all banged up and are basically sitting targets? I mean, you let me know what you want out of this. Because I just want to go home. I don't want this in my life. I can't be arsed to listen to this shit. So you tell me what I am supposed to do for the best and, believe me, I will do it.'

Mrs Connelly, as drunk as she was, heard the unspoken threat to her boys. She knew that she should just retreat and lose face, but it was hard for her. Her sons were away for the duration, and they were all she had. Yet if she wasn't careful she could bring a lot of trouble to their doors and they had enough to contend with. They had broken her heart – she had nothing, no grandchildren, no sons. All she had to look forward to was the monotony of visiting them for a few hours every month.

When she saw Eugene and Porrick arrive, Agnes felt herself finally relax. As drunk as Mrs Connelly might be, Agnes saw the fear that her words had instilled in this old, argumentative cow. Like Reeva, Mrs Connelly thought that she had every right to insult and pick a fight with anyone within her orbit but, when she was reminded that her sons might be in danger, she saw when to take a big step back. She had wanted to front up Reeva, and now it had gone wrong for her.

Agnes was so sick of this world they lived in, where this kind of occurrence was seen as the norm. Where a lonely old lady like Mrs Connelly had nothing left except her sons' reputations. It was a disgrace; grown women fighting each other as if that held some kind of importance. Trying to prove something to people they didn't even really know, let alone care about, who didn't give a fuck about *them*.

Eugene and Porrick soon salvaged the situation and the police left, grateful to be able to leave it in someone else's hands. Mrs Connelly was escorted back into her property, and Reeva left the scene as though she was the victor. Everyone knew where their loyalties lay.

Eugene hugged his sister to him as they returned home, but Agnes shrugged him away. Reeva was still mouthing off, shouting the odds without a thought for anyone else around her. Then Patsy strolled in like the conquering hero, ready to sort it out.

'Come on, Mum. Relax, it's over.'

Patsy was pulling her into his arms, trying to calm her down. But Reeva wasn't having any of it. 'Fucking relax? Are you serious? Did you hear what that old bag said to me?'

'Come on, Mum. Forget it. Just relax, eh?'

That was when Agnes finally lost her temper. '"Fucking relax, Mum!" Is that it, Patsy? She caused a big fight in the street. I had to leave Aiden Junior to sort it out, and none of you think that she has done anything *wrong*? You all expect *me* to pick up the pieces, look after Aiden, and, of course, keep my eye on Mum – the biggest kid of them all. Well, I am fucking sick of it. She *disgusts* me. When I see her like this, I fucking *hate* her, and I hate you lot for dumping her on me.'

Eugene understood where she was coming from; he had always known that, where Agnes was concerned, it was unfair. Aiden left her to her own devices with Reeva because they trusted her and because they saw it as her job. She looked out for her nephew and she looked out for their mum – that was what family was expected to do.

And Patsy felt that, as she was a female, it was expected of her. 'Come on, Agnes, think about it, girl. Mum needs someone to keep their eye on her. You are the only girl, that means it is your job. It's not like you earn a living like the rest of us, is it?'

Agnes looked at her brothers and, shaking her head in despair, she said honestly, 'Do you know what, Patsy? Fuck you now.'

She left them to put Reeva to bed, and she slipped into her own bed where her nephew was sleeping peacefully. She was finished with them, and she had to make sure that they understood that. Tonight was the last straw.

It was time to save her own life, because she was determined that this was not going to be her future, no matter what her brothers might say. And if they thought they could just put Reeva to bed, they had another think coming. She wasn't going to bed without her usual fucking antics.

Chapter Seventy

Aiden was looking forward to meeting Colin Clark. They had heard of one another, of course, but they had never actually crossed paths in any meaningful way. They both wondered about the other, especially as they seemed of a kind. Everyone that Aiden had spoken to said the same thing: they were like two peas in a pod. That didn't please him, because he had also heard that Colin Clark could be a bit of a cunt, so he assumed – rightly as it turned out – that people thought the same about him. Food for thought.

Aiden wanted to believe that the people he dealt with had a high opinion of him, even though he knew that wasn't likely. He had a reputation as a good boss, but not as a good bet. He didn't care about being liked but he did want to be respected. Knowing that Jade was the one that everyone apparently listened to, he needed to prove himself once and for all with this new partnership. The fact that he had once destroyed his creds overnight was something he still found difficult to digest, but it showed how precarious his position was. He had fucked up and, in doing so, he wiped out years of good work. He'd been playing catch-up ever since – that was what was so hard to accept.

Eric Palmer had forgiven him, he knew that. Eric was willing to let bygones be bygones because Eric still saw him as his natural successor. The problem was, though, that he could never forgive Eric Palmer or Jade. He loved them both but his belief that they had systematically tucked him up ate him inside.

He would always resent the fact that Eric Palmer had given Jade the power that should have been his. It was why he continued to do the dirty on her even though he wasn't exactly proud of it. Between Jade and Eric they had fucking humiliated him, and they had tried to pretend that they were only trying to look out for him.

Now, however hard he worked to redeem himself, the damage had been done. And, as much as he loved Jade, there was a part of him that couldn't really ever trust her any more. Even after all these years he still felt that he was being judged and that, without Jade at his side, Eric Palmer would never have trusted him again.

Everyone else had forgotten it – it was so long ago! But his fuck-up was something that he remembered every day of his life, and the fact that he continually felt that he wasn't truly trusted was becoming his Achilles heel. He was desperate to prove himself – nothing he did felt enough. He tried to bring in more money than had been expected, taking on everything required without a word, finding new ways to earn an extra crust out of it. It was obvious to everyone that he was determined to prove himself. Now his foolishness with Destiny had set him back again – Eric Palmer had made his disappointment clear.

Aiden O'Hara was a complete one-off; he would never forgive, let alone forget that he had fucked up and, his personality being such as it was, he would always blame those closest to him for it.

Chapter Seventy-One

Agnes had been dragged out of bed because Reeva had caused fucking murders, as she had predicted. She left them all to it; Tony had tried to calm her down but Reeva was having none of it. She was so out of her head that she had finally reduced them all nearly to tears. She was right up on her highest horse fighting and arguing with everyone and none of the boys knew what to do with her. Well, welcome to Agnes's world.

They had no choice but to bring in the big guns; Aiden had been summoned and he was not impressed in the least. 'So let me get this fucking straight: I'm supposed to care about Mum having a fight with a fucking neighbour? Are you taking the piss, Aggs?'

The boys were nervous; they knew that Aiden had had to put off a big meeting to come here and calm their mother down. Aiden could not understand why the sister he adored was creating so much trouble for him. Everyone knew she could cope with Reeva better than anyone else. Now she had threatened to walk out on Aiden Junior unless she had some sort of assurance that this kind of trouble would never happen again. It was beyond him. What the fuck was he supposed to do? Agnes was right in what she was saying: they left her to sort out Reeva and her fucking usual crap on a regular basis because she was the only other female in the house. Clearly that was the right thing; after all, women understood women. Agnes was basically the only really sensible head in the house when their mum went on the piss, so she should be the one to rein Reeva in. And yes, she was expected to look after Aiden Junior and make sure that everything went along smoothly because she was the *sister*; she had to pull her weight. It wasn't that hard, surely? He said as much.

'Hang on, Aiden. Tonight not *one* of this lot could fucking cope with her. I went to bed, and look at the upshot. You have had to come to try and sort it. I rest my case!'

Aiden looked at his mother. She was slumped in a chair, and Helen Keller would have known that she was completely out of the game.

'I'm sorry, Aiden, but when Mum goes off on one, I don't think Agnes should have to fucking sort it. Or sort your son out.' Eugene smiled his apology at Jade as he continued seriously, 'Aggs has taken the brunt of Mum's fucking lunacy for years. I think she has a point, Aiden. And tonight was not exactly a one-off, was it? Tony tries to keep her in line, and we know that she can be good for ages. But when she does go off, it's like the fucking atomic bomb. If Aiden Junior wasn't here no one would give a flying fuck, would they? I think that Agnes should be given her say. You know as well as I do that Mum can't be trusted without her in the house to keep that child safe.'

Aiden was looking at his brother with hatred, because he never could listen to the honest truth – most people didn't have the nerve to tell him the truth outright, but Eugene was willing to say his piece.

Porrick stepped forward then. He was smaller than his

brothers, but he was a true O'Hara in that he could have a fucking row if called upon. 'He's right. Mum is lovely, but when she goes on the piss, none of us can fucking stand her, let alone control her. It is left to our Aggs to sort out your fucking son, because let's face it, Aiden, that is the most important thing at the end of the day. He's always here. When Mum's on a good one, that's marvellous. But when she decides to go on a serious fucking bender, we leave it to Agnes. I'm with Eugene – this needs to be fucking sorted once and for all. Why should Aggs be expected to sort everything out? He is your fucking kid.'

Aiden was looking around him at his brothers and his sister as if he had never seen any of them before. That he was annoyed was a given, but the fact that they were in the right was what he had a problem with right now. Tonight of all fucking nights; they had to choose this night to make a fucking point. Patsy stepped forward then and, shrugging, he said quietly, 'Sorry, Ade. I agree with them. I've always thought it was OK to leave this to Aggs, but they have a point. Aiden Junior is *your* son, and when Mum is on a good week he is more than welcome. But when she goes off the rails, why should our Agnes be expected to sort it all? She ain't like us. She shouldn't have to look after Mum, let alone your fucking kid. He is a big lad now, Aiden, but he still climbs into her bed and sleeps with her because he knows it's the safest place to be.'

Porrick added, 'Mum was off her head and the Old Bill was called and, in fairness to Agnes, she always defuses the situation. You know she's the one who looks after little Aiden, especially when Mum goes on a drugs bender, or on the fucking piss . . . She's quiet now, but Mum threatened to pull a knife on us earlier. Aiden, she was fucking dangerous. She's a fucking liability in more ways than one.'

Agnes could have kissed him. She really had not expected them all to support her. After all, this was her life now. Reeva had been on spectacular form tonight, but now she was slumped on the sofa she didn't look in the least bit worrying. That was the problem – by the time the boys got home she was over her tantrums. It was Agnes who had to put up with it all day. She looked at Jade who winked at her surreptitiously. Agnes knew better than to drag her into any of this. Jade was always on her side. She loved Jade even though there was a big piece of her that wanted to question why her son was here so fucking often and not in his own house. But she knew the answer to that as well as anyone else in this family.

Jade spent her life policing Aiden, not just because of the women – Jade was too intelligent to care about them. She policed him because he couldn't be trusted. He had a lot of Reeva in him; when he decided to go his own way no one could stop him. As a result, Aiden Junior was at the house a lot more than was good for any of them – especially Aiden Junior himself. He was old enough now to question why he was not at home with his parents. Why was he always at his nanny's? There was clearly a reason, and it wasn't a good one.

Aiden was fuming that he had been forced to cancel his meeting with the Clarks to try and sort out a load of fucking old fanny. What had possessed his sister, Agnes, to pick today of all days to cause fucking murders? He opened his arms out in a gesture of supplication, and they could see the anger in his face.

'Are you taking the fucking piss? Have I missed something here?'

Agnes could see that he was about to go off on one of his usual tangents and, before he could say another word, she shouted, 'Have you not listened to a fucking word, Aiden? It is always about *you*! Everything in our lives has always been about *you*. Well, I'm not doing this any more. Tonight was the last time I will ever stand between Mum and her latest enemy, acting like a fucking referee. How Tony puts up with it, I don't know. But I refuse to let you lot leave me in sole charge of her. And that means I'm not going to look after your son either. I am sick of it. I'm a big girl and I'm not prepared to spend my life cleaning up other people's messes.'

Aiden looked at his little sister. She was a good girl, and he loved that about her. She understood the importance of keeping herself decent. He could sense that Jade was watching him closely, expecting him to provide a solution. And, as angry as he was, he knew that this was his territory – that as the eldest they looked to him to sort everything out. If he was honest with himself, he should have made sure that it had never come to this. He had looked after them since day one, and that was why they revered him. He had to listen to them now, he understood that, but it didn't mean he had to like it.

This was the first time ever that they had confronted him, even criticised him. This was a big thing for his siblings and he had to do something constructive, show willing. Seeing his brothers stand together against him for Agnes wasn't something he was happy about. One half of him was impressed by the fact they were so loyal to the little sister they loved. But the other told him that he could never really trust them. That was a learning curve in itself and it hit a sore spot.

Jade could tell exactly what Aiden was thinking; she knew him better than he knew himself. She understood just how fucking badly he would choose to take this; he would see this as a personal insult, a betrayal. He would never in a million years understand that his brothers were not being personal – that they were just trying to look out for Agnes. Unfortunately, everything in Aiden's world could only ever be about him.

Jade shrugged, as if there was nothing Aiden couldn't sort out if he wanted to. 'I think the boys have a point, Aiden, you know? We all love Reeva and she can be a fucking star for ages. But we know that it's just a matter of time until she goes off on one again, and there will be another night just like this.' She pulled Agnes into her arms, hugging her tightly. Agnes hugged her back; she knew how to play the game.

Aiden sighed heavily; clearly he was on his own and that everyone had made their minds up.

'Well, be fair, Jade. You are the one who always dumps Aiden Junior here, darling.' He smiled easily.

Jade nodded slowly; she wouldn't lose her temper. 'Absolutely, Aiden. I know how much he loves your mum. But you're right. Will you tell him that he can't come here any more?'

Aiden looked into her eyes, and he could see that he had really upset her, that she had not appreciated him trying to place all the blame on her. He had hurt her deeply with a cheap shot. This was a fucking nightmare; his brothers were fronting him up, and now his Jade, to whom he knew he owed a fucking big sorry, was also trying to put him on the spot.

'I know that she adores him, and he adores her. But when she goes off the grid like this, Aiden, we can't expect Agnes to pick up the pieces. The drink we can cope with – it's the amphetamines or the cocaine that really cause the trouble.'

Eugene was watching Patsy's reaction because, of all Reeva's boys, Patsy was the one who could pre-empt Aiden. In truth, they all expected Aiden to turn on Jade. But he didn't.

Instead, Patsy said honestly, 'Ball's in your court, Aiden. What do you suggest we do?'

Everyone in the room was quiet, holding their breath because, in reality, tonight had been like a declaration of fucking war. It was a criticism of Aiden – even though it was done in a placid and nice way. That was not something their brother would swallow without taking some sort of umbrage.

Aiden was furious and it was only because Jade was looking at him so intently that he thought that maybe he should box a bit clever. This was, without a doubt, of significance to his siblings. That his mother was in a drunken and drugged stupor really wasn't helping either. This was important to everyone here, except him. His reaction to this night would be of enormous importance to all of them in the future.

Aiden was a lot of things, but he wasn't stupid. He knew when it was necessary to play the part required. He knew that and he had to deal with this in a reasonable and competent manner even if he couldn't care less about this shit. He took a deep breath and, letting it out slowly as he found a smile, he said seriously, 'You are right, of course. Tonight was a fucking disgrace. But we all know what Reeva is capable of.'

He looked at his siblings one after the other, finally allowing his gaze to settle on Agnes.

'We should never have left you with so much responsibility, Aggs. And I will make sure that this never happens again, darling. You have my word on that.'

Agnes grinned. This was exactly what she wanted to hear, even though she didn't believe any of it. But she had witnesses and that was all that she really cared about.

'Look, Aiden, I love having your boy here, you know that. But when Mum goes off, I need you lot to back me up. Fucking hell, we were nearly nicked tonight.'

Aiden snorted angrily. 'Like that would ever happen, for fuck's sake. Like the local plod would fucking dare!'

Agnes had no intention of making this easy for her brother. 'Hang on a minute, you. *I* was the one dragged into it, not you, Aiden. *I* am the one who has always had to sort out her shit. I have been doing it since I can remember. I'm the girl, so you all leave me to sort Mum out. I'm sick to death of it. I want a life too, you know.'

Aiden sighed heavily; it was taking all his willpower not to lose his shit.

'Well, what exactly do you want, Aggs? I'm not a fucking mind reader.'

She felt she had won at last.

'What I want is a wage. A *decent* wage. You know I had to leave school to look after her but I need a life too. So, money and help with Mum when she goes off the rails. That's all. I deserve that and more, Aiden.'

He was more annoyed than he thought possible – was she taking the fucking piss? She didn't need to cause this fucking aggravation to get what she wanted – all she had had to do was ask.

'I want a guarantee that if Mum even looks like she is going on the rampage one of you lot will come as soon as I call.'

Aiden shrugged in agreement.

Tony felt like kissing Agnes; this was what he had wanted for years. They all knew that one day Reeva would go too far – that it had not happened already was a miracle. And Jade knew that Agnes had needed to bring her brothers' attention to the fact that she was left in sole charge of Reeva. When Reeva went on one it wasn't exactly an easy fucking ride, and it was something that they avoided like the plague. Jade was as bad as the boys in some respects; after all, she left her son in this house five nights out of seven – more if she could get away with it. But that wasn't because she didn't love her boy, it was because she needed to keep her eye on Aiden. He had a chip on his shoulder these days, and there was nothing she could do to change the situation. Eric Palmer knew it too, and that was the real concern.

Aiden looked over each person in the room closely. They were each in no doubt that he felt that he had done what was expected – and that he wasn't happy about how it had gone down tonight.

Agnes felt a moment's sorrow for him, but she quickly swallowed it. This was her only chance to make them see what was actually going on in her life, how shit it was that she was expected to shoulder her mother's lunacy on a regular basis. She didn't regret a second of it. For the first time ever, she had made her brothers stop what they were doing and admit that she had the rough end of the stick. She deserved not just their affection, which she knew she had always had, but also their time, and more importantly, their interest – that was something she had not had from any of them for years. That was why she had needed to cause so much aggravation this night. If she wasn't careful, she would get lost in her mother's world of violence and alcohol and she was determined that was *not* going to happen to her. She did what everyone expected from her and what she knew was the right thing to do, but she was fucked if she was going to carry on doing it without any of her brothers recognising just how difficult it was for her.

248

Chapter Seventy-Two

Jade got into the passenger seat next to Aiden, and, as she put on her seat belt she said airily, 'That was a turn-up for the books.'

Aiden pulled away from the kerb with a screech of tyres; he was not amused at all. 'Oh, I don't know, I think you might have had a hand in that fucking nonsense, Jade. You and Agnes are as thick as thieves.'

Jade didn't say anything for a while. Aiden was more than aware of his shortcomings; she didn't need to remind him. They drove through the night together in silence. Jade knew when to keep quiet and when to press home a point.

'She looks after our boy, Jade, you know that as well as I do. I wonder if it's good for him, you know, being around my mum so much.'

Jade sighed gently. She had known he would say that to her and now it was her job to placate him, make him feel good about himself. She had just had to wait for him to start the conversation – she knew that he would talk to her first. That was how she coped with him on a daily basis; it was like an intricate puzzle that she played twenty-four hours a day.

'Look, Aiden. I pick him up and take him to school, and it's not like he is at the local fucking comprehensive, is it? We both work long hours, and that's the truth. We just dropped the ball for a while. Agnes is a star and she's the reason we let our lad stay there, because of her sensible head. I know she picked a bad time to put forward her case. But fucking hell, your mum was so out of it tonight she couldn't even defend herself.'

Aiden knew that she was not just telling him the truth, but that she was saying it in the way that he wanted it. Jade was absolving him of any kind of wrongdoing. She knew what he needed.

'I fucking hate her at times, you know? All my life I have had to fucking either live her down, or sort out her fucking antics. But she is me mum. She loves us, and she adores our lad. If she could just stop going off on one of her massive benders . . .'

Jade didn't say a word; neither of them was ever going to say what they really thought. It grieved her that she had to play a game with this man of hers. She always had to swallow her pride and temper her natural reactions because she could not stand it if she lost him. Without her beside him, he would completely fuck up everything they had worked for. Eric Palmer depended on her to keep Aiden on the right track, but she understood how hard that was for a man like Aiden.

'Listen, Eric's ensconced the Clarks in the club. It's not too late. We can meet them there. And, think about it, Aiden, it wouldn't do any harm for them to think that they weren't our priority, would it?'

That was exactly what Aiden wanted to hear; it appealed to his ego as Jade had known it would. It saddened her how low she was willing to go to keep this man and his ego onside.

Chapter Seventy-Three

Patsy, Eugene and Porrick were following Aiden and Jade to the club. They were aware that they had been the cause of serious annoyance where Aiden was concerned, but they were sure that they had done the right thing. They felt bad about Agnes. She was a good girl, and she had never been any trouble to them. She had never even had a boyfriend, really. Plenty of boys had shown an interest in her, and their mum had done everything in her power to get Aggs to go out with them. Reeva thought her daughter was unnatural because she didn't think that drinking, clubbing and looking for a man was the highlight of life.

Eugene lit a joint and, taking a deep toke, he held it in his lungs for a good while before letting out the smoke. Then, passing it to Patsy, who was driving, he said seriously, 'Fuck Aiden. Who does he think he is? And Jade for that matter. They dump that boy there for days on end. They know that Mum can't be trusted for any length of time.'

Patsy laughed and passed the joint to Porrick in the back seat. 'Remember when she went after your teacher, Porrick! Coked out of her head when the school rung up saying you had been suspended for fighting.'

They were laughing now, as they remembered one of Reeva's more spectacular moments.

'Fucking hell, when Mum burst into the classroom I nearly fainted. Poor old Mr Thomas, he shit himself. Then when she started rowing him out . . . ! I know she was a pain but, in fairness, she always had our backs.'

'Thing is, though, she's a complete nutbag. Look at tonight – she has been a fucking diamond for months, and then she just decided to go on one of her fucking mad half-hours. She was on the coke again. And when I find out who supplied her they won't fucking be stupid enough to do that again, I know that much. Poor Agnes is really treated badly by us. No, we did the right thing tonight. Our little sister needed to make her point.'

Porrick was nodding in agreement, and, laughing once more, he said nastily, 'Our Aiden needs a fucking reality check. I mean, I know he is good to us, I would never deny that. But be honest, guys, I don't know if I trust him. He never seems to me like he is on the same planet as everyone else. I think he sees himself as above everyone, including us.'

Patsy pulled the car to a halt; it was like an emergency stop on a driving test.

Then, turning around in his seat, he grabbed his little brother by the throat and, pulling him viciously towards him, he said threateningly, 'You fucking stop there, mate. Aiden is our brother, and he is also the reason we earn a fucking good wage, and why we can live a charmed fucking life. Don't you ever criticise him to me again. Do you hear me, Porrick?'

Eugene pulled them apart and, seeing the fear on Porrick's face and the disappointment on Patsy's, he wondered how long it would be before real trouble would begin.

As much as he loved his brothers, Aiden included, in his heart of hearts he agreed with Porrick one hundred per cent. He didn't trust Aiden either. The difference was, he had the sense to keep his opinions to himself.

'Come on, you two. It's been a fucking poxy night. Let's get to the club and have a few drinks, for fuck's sake.'

Patsy started up the car again, and they carried on to the club, but no one was talking. They didn't know what to say.

Chapter Seventy-Four

Colin Clark had not been impressed to have the meeting cancelled at such short notice.

Being the type of man he was, he looked for an insult and convinced himself that there was some kind of skulduggery afoot. Not that he had expected anything less, of course. Aiden O'Hara was a cunt of the first water as far as he was concerned. It was only the fact that Eric Palmer was the main broker of the deal that had really piqued his interest. Eric Palmer was a man you would be a fool to refuse if he saw fit to offer you an earn. He had his creds, and he had them in spades. As big a fucker as he could be, Colin Clark knew that if Eric Palmer wanted to offer him a deal, he would bite his fucking hand off, and kiss his boots if that was what was needed. Who was he kidding? He would happily kiss the fucker's arse.

This deal was what he had dreamed of, what he had been waiting for. He needed an in when it came to the big money, and if he could achieve that, then he would feel that he had done his fucking job. This was a golden opportunity – and even his brother didn't need to drum it into his thick head. This was a different level of villainy, and that he had something Eric Palmer wanted pleased him no end.

The only fly in the ointment was Aiden O'Hara. He didn't

like him on principle. Aiden O'Hara was his nemesis in many ways. He was a hard fucker, that was a given, but then so was Colin and a lot of others. That Aiden had been fortunate enough to come to the attention of Eric Palmer was just how the world worked. Colin Clark knew better than anybody that the majority of people who achieved in the world of criminals were often only there because they were in the right place at the right fucking time. He accepted that, even though it galled him if he thought about it too much.

Colin had earned himself a good reputation and, because of that, he had always believed that it was only a matter of time before he would be noticed and brought into the inner circles that he craved so desperately. But, as his brother, Timmy, had reiterated over and over, he had to find a way to work with men like Aiden because, if he didn't, Eric Palmer would abandon them without a second fucking thought. Aiden O'Hara had Eric Palmer's ear, and to the outside world, he had proved himself worthy. Although, if all the gossip was to be believed, Aiden had fucked up more than once because of his massive fucking ego. Knowing that could only work in Colin's favour – if he used his loaf. His brother might be the brains of the outfit, but Colin had the cunning required to get on in their chosen profession. He could sniff out an earn, as well as a snide – that was his contribution to the partnership. Timmy always respected his reaction to any deals offered because, although Timmy might have a brain like a calculator, it was Colin who had the nous to suss everything out. That was what had got them as far as they had.

Aiden O'Hara was Eric's blue-eyed boy, and he held him, and that old woman of his, Jade, in high regard. He trusted them with everything he had, and that was a very impressive shout-out to anyone who had to deal with them. It was something that Colin Clark could not dispute and had the utmost respect for. In short, whatever people might say about Aiden O'Hara, Colin understood that he was not a man to underestimate in any way.

Now, as he stood at the top bar in the new club that Aiden had recently opened, Colin could not help but wonder what the next step would have to be, how they were all going to merge as a single unit where the deals were concerned. Tonight could be either the making or the breaking of him and his brother; this was what people would refer to as a watershed moment. If it all went fucking pear-shaped there would more than likely be ambulances arriving.

Colin gestured to the barmaid for another drink. Timmy was chatting up a right fucking horror with dyed black hair and an unconvincing breast job – she was just his cup of tea. Timmy always went for the obvious, the girls who would flash their clouts for a few drinks and the promise of a bit of coke. He argued that it suited him because they knew what the score was – especially him!

Colin could see his point, but personally he avoided those fucking slags like the plague. They tended to gravitate to wherever you were and act like they were family or something. They believed because you fucked them once, it gave them some kind of reason to come into your real life. As if you would be seen in daylight with them! What did these girls expect? They weren't exactly fucking virgins who were all big eyes and turn the lights off. They fucked like porn stars – nothing was off the menu. Like that would encourage some kind of love job! He would cross the road to avoid them. Why didn't they suss that for themselves? He wasn't looking for the love of his life, but he wasn't willing to trump some old sort who had been with everyone within a ten-mile radius like his brother. No, Colin liked to romance a nicer class of woman. He was quite happy to take them out a few times, spend a few quid on them. They had to be a cut above the usual, and they had to be decent girls. No bad language, no dirty jokes, and definitely no interest in drugs – that was a complete no-no as far as he was concerned. He had his standards, unlike his brother – though, in fairness, Timmy loved them and left them without a backward glance, and the girls were quite happy for him to do just that. Colin, though, liked to work for it – he liked to earn his reward. It was all the sweeter when he finally slipped them a portion, knowing that they weren't giving out to anyone with a nice car and a few bob.

As he ordered yet another drink, he saw his brother step away from his latest horror and, turning towards him, he realised that Aiden O'Hara had just walked into the bar with his brothers. One thing about his brother, Timmy, was nothing, absolutely fuck-all, ever got past him. Colin stood stock still and watched as Timmy stepped out to shake hands with Aiden O'Hara. He looked him over greedily, interested in this man who he would have to work with on a daily basis.

'Great to see you, Aiden. We understand you had a situation tonight. This is my brother, Colin, as you know.'

Colin held out his hand and, as he gripped Aiden's outstretched hand, he was amazed to see that Aiden was just a bit taller than him, although they were similar in every other way. Both were muscular, well dressed and they were both far too interested in the other. They stood there hands clasped for a good thirty seconds, and then, laughing, they hugged like long-lost relatives.

Timmy Clark watched them with apprehension; he felt instinctively that these two men should never be allowed to form any kind of alliance. They were volatile, flakes in many respects, and neither of them would ever see a deal through to the end. That was what Timmy Clark and Jade were for. But, apart from all that, these were men who were dangerous enough alone, the last thing they needed was a kindred fucking spirit. But the damage was done. Despite everything they had decided about the other, once they had met properly they were on a fucking love job. Talk about two peas in a pod! They genuinely really liked each other.

Aiden grinned roguishly, but said seriously, 'Oi, where the fuck did you purchase that fucking suit?'

Colin laughed out loud; he couldn't believe his luck. 'Bespoke, Aiden, of course. And cheap as fucking chips, and look at this . . . !' He opened his jacket and showed Aiden his name hand-embroidered on the inside pocket.

Aiden was well impressed, and it showed. 'Do you know what, I want you to introduce me to your fucking tailor, mister.'

Patsy and Timmy were amazed to witness these two men who until now had never really formed any kind of relationship outside their families, treating each other like visiting royalty. They were only too aware of their brothers' lethal similarities. What should have been a good thing was potentially a catastrophe of Olympian standards. These fuckers were both complete lunatics; loners who were only able to be persuaded to do the right thing by the people they trusted. No one had predicted them striking up a friendship immediately; both were renowned because they didn't exactly encourage friendships. Now, though, they were like a pair of long-lost brothers, drinking whisky together and asking each other questions – not in the usual confrontational way they grilled people, but with genuine interest in each other's answers.

'Fuck off, Colin! *Casino*? Fabulous film. Joe Pesci as Nicky. Brilliant portrayal of the character. I was gutted when they fucking took him out.'

Colin Clark laughed with delight. 'I said exactly the same thing. He was fucking brilliant. When they killed his brother in front of him, I don't mind admitting, I had tears – actual fucking tears – in my eyes. He was my favourite character too.'

Timmy Clark and Patsy O'Hara looked at each other in amazement. Nothing was actually said, but they understood the enormity of what had just occurred. As Eugene and Porrick chatted up the birds and drank, Patsy felt the urge to smash the pair of them because they really didn't get what was going on. When Aiden called them over and introduced them, they were as happy as fucking larks because they liked Colin Clark as well. Who wouldn't? He was a handsome, jovial man, full of smiles, full of jokes, willing to laugh at himself. But Colin was a blond Aiden – he was a fucking psychopath in a handmade suit who had just met his black-haired counterpart.

Patsy would have laid out good money that these two men would not have ever liked one another. They would have worked together only under observation, and because Eric Palmer desired it. But now they were drinking heavily together, and acting like they had known each other all their lives. Which, in a funny way, they probably had.

Timmy Clark handed Patsy a large vodka and tonic and, shrugging, he said, 'Eric already explained that it will be me and you doing the donkey work, but I pretty much worked that one out for myself. I'm sure you know the score as well as I do. So let's take a leaf out of their book and decide how we are going to work this so it's in everyone's interest.'

Patsy took a large swallow of his drink before saying genuinely, 'I hear you, but tonight I think just a few drinks are in order. Let's see how these two develop over the next few days before we plan any kind of strategy.'

Timmy nodded; there was a logic there that he could not overlook. Chances were they would be fighting the fuck out of each other at a whim, or over a sudden slight if the fancy took either of them. Neither was known for their willingness to make friends. In fact, they were both known for the complete opposite.

Both were antisocial fuckers, who nobody approached unless they had to. But as the night went on the two men seemed to get on like the proverbial house on fire.

Chapter Seventy-Five

Jade listened to Eric Palmer with her usual quiet demeanour. She could listen intently and, unlike most of the women Eric had known, she didn't interrupt at every available opportunity. Jade had the mind of a man – not that he would ever say that, of course, but it was one of the things he admired about her.

Like everyone else, Eric was interested in how the meeting between Aiden and Colin had gone. Unlike everyone else he thought it was a good thing that they were so friendly with each other. Eric Palmer recognised that there would be friction – that was par for the course in the world they inhabited – but, by the same token, you didn't have to like the people you did your business with. If that was a requirement, no one would ever earn a fucking shilling. If you genuinely liked the person you were dealing with then that was a bonus, but realistically no one gave a flying fuck. It was about finding the right person to do your business with and, regardless of personal opinion, you just kept them on an even keel. It wasn't fucking rocket science; most of the people you were forced to deal with in the criminal world any normal person would cross the road to avoid. You weren't going to fucking marry the cunt – it was just business.

It annoyed Eric that he had to explain this to an old hand

like Jade. She knew better than anyone the need to deal with people you couldn't fucking stand, but you made sure your personal feelings were kept private.

'Look, Jade, the bottom line is it's a good thing if they get on. Fucking hell, you were more worried that they would hate one another. Now they are like fucking bosom buddies you are still not happy. Is it because you think they will be out on the hunt, darling? Colin has a reputation, I know.'

Jade sighed heavily; she was offended that Eric could think she was that shallow. 'Are you finished, Eric?'

He nodded, unsure of where this was going. As far as he was concerned this was a winning situation for him. He couldn't get what the problem was.

'Listen to me, OK? Aiden wouldn't know a friend if they fell out of a tree and landed on his fucking head. He has acquaint-ances, and he has me and you, who he loves and respects. You because you are what he wanted to be all his life, and me because I am the woman he saw as his mentor. I am the only person who can tell him what he doesn't want to hear. He knows that I would never put him wrong, that I will always have his back. He loves our boy because he sees him as a part of him. Aiden Junior is his flesh and blood, and that has an importance for him because of Reeva. She might not have done much in the way of parenting but she made sure that her kids understood the importance of family. Now, I know you think we are worrying about nothing, but I am telling you now, Eric, that Colin Clark and Aiden is not a healthy relationship. They are both fucking two paving slabs short of a patio. They are too mentally unre-liable to become a team. They already egg each other on, dare each other to do things that are not just fucking stupid but make no fucking sense. I don't know where it will end.'

Eric sat quietly as she spoke and the fact that he was questioning her told her everything she needed to know. Well, he didn't give a fuck; he was retiring, and he was just bankrolling everyone.

'Last night they caused murders in a private gambling hole in Barking. They turned up drunk as fuck, and pulled a gun on old Tommy Brewer because he asked them to keep the noise down. It's a big money game as you know, because it's our game. We own that fucking club. Aiden took advantage of that and I am not going to let that slide, Eric. He needs to be put in his place, sooner rather than later. He knows that he has not fulfilled his early promise, and I blame you for that. Too much too soon, and he fucked up. Now he is putting everything he can lay his hands on up his nose, and drinking like a fucking fish, and that is not good for any of us.'

Eric Palmer listened. She was right – she always was. 'I know what you are saying, Jade, and I agree, but that's Aiden. He has fucked up, yes, but, by the same token, he has flashes of brilliance. And he has a reputation as my main man. When it comes down to it there isn't a man on the pavement willing to take him on. That is just plain fact. I *know* that you are his fucking dream – he adores you – and he knows deep down in his boots that you are the real brains of the outfit. Oh, God! He had such fucking promise, and he still has the mental capacity to find a way out of any eventuality. My advice is to put him on the right track. You are the only person he listens to.'

'Eric, darling, listen to me, please. Aiden and Colin Clark are not a good partnership. Remember that I warned you about them.' Standing up, she stretched with tiredness. 'I'm going to pick up my boy, and I'm going to spend a rare evening with him. Because, for once, your businesses can run themselves. I need a break, Eric.'

He smiled at her. He genuinely cared about Jade.

As she slipped on her coat, she said quietly, 'Seriously, Eric, even Reeva is not impressed and that alone speaks volumes.'

After she left, Eric Palmer poured himself a large brandy and, as he sat behind his desk, admiring his expensive offices, he sighed heavily. He truly believed that Aiden and Colin were a good fit; the fact they got on so well could only be to everyone's advantage. He had taken on board what Jade had said; he trusted her with his life. But he also knew that she had her own reasons to keep Aiden beside her and not want him out on the fucking town with Colin Clark. They were getting a reputation together, and that suited Eric Palmer. The truth was, he genuinely saw their friendship as bringing nothing but good to the table. Both were well known for their aptitudes for extreme violence, and for the fact that they would not suffer fools in their circle. They were men of honour in their own way; they believed that you should never bite the hand that fed you. He trusted Aiden to keep Colin in line because, when all was said and done, it was Aiden who would be calling the shots. Eric had made perfectly clear that he expected that from Aiden. Aiden had appreciated his input, because it took the onus off him. Aiden could always remind Colin that it was Eric who ran the show and, even though he was retiring from the front line, he would still be running everything for a good while yet.

Chapter Seventy-Six

Reeva was not really sure about Colin Clark, but she had to admit he did make her smile at times – he could be very funny. As she dished up one of her legendary dinners, she could not help laughing as he said to Aiden, in mock annoyance, 'Hang on a minute, you, Aiden O'-fucking-Hara. I still think that *Scarface* pissed all over *Goodfellas*.' He looked around the table at all the brothers and they were laughing as he said jovially, '"Say hello to my little friend!" Hilarious and clever dialogue from Oliver Stone. The man is a fucking legend.'

Aiden was laughing along with everyone else. 'No way. You can't beat *Goodfellas* when they did the robbery at the airport. That was fucking class. Especially when that cunt turned up with his old woman in a fur coat. I loved the truth of that. He had told them all, don't spend any money, do not draw attention to yourselves. It stands to reason.'

Colin grinned and, taking a large mouthful of Reeva's perfectly cooked roast beef, he said truthfully, 'Yeah, I give you that one. Very astute. But when they went after his wife, I didn't like it. That's why I fucking loved Tony in *Scarface*. He wouldn't harm a woman or kids. He shot the fuck before he could blow the car up.'

Porrick was rolling up, he loved this banter – they were like a fucking comedy duo. 'Look, *The Godfather* is the ultimate. It had everything.'

They all turned to look at him in shock; he wasn't normally one to throw out an opinion.

Eugene shrugged as he poured out the wine. 'I agree with him, though for me it was *The Long Good Friday*. Stunning fucking film, and British.'

There were nods of agreement. Reeva loved dinners like this; her boys around her, feeding them good food and watching them enjoy it.

Eugene put his fork out to grab another roast potato when Colin said jokingly, 'You are really black, Eugene. Blacker than him.' He gestured to Patsy.

Tony looked straight at Reeva, wondering how she would react, while the others looked at Aiden.

'I mean it in a good way, mate. But Patsy is much lighter than you, ain't he?'

Patsy didn't find the conversation funny at all, and that was clear when he said dangerously, 'Why would you give a fucking fuck?'

Aiden looked around the table for long moments before saying to Colin, 'My brother, the *brown* one, not the really *black* one, has a point, Colin. Why would you fucking care?'

Colin Clark sensed immediately that he had just made a major fuck-up. The tension around the table was palpable. Suddenly, laughing uproariously, Aiden said, 'Are you trying to say he is not as black as he's painted?'

Colin started to laugh then too. 'Fucking Spike Milligan, talking about Gandhi!'

The others smiled in relief though there was something going on that none of them could understand. Reeva felt dread deep inside and it frightened her.

Just then Agnes came in from Mass. Aiden pulled out a seat for her and she sat down quietly, looking around the table at her family and, smiling shyly at Colin, she said, 'What have I missed?'

Aiden hugged her tightly saying happily, 'Nothing really. How was Mass?'

Agnes sighed. 'Really nice. I like the new priest, he is young and he isn't as serious, you know?'

Aiden was busy piling her plate with food. 'I know. I think he will do well. Aiden Junior likes him, and he is usually a good judge of character.'

Colin Clark was watching Agnes surreptitiously; she was a good-looking girl and decent too – she was a fucking Brahma. Bit too religious for his liking but he respected her for her beliefs. The chattering had started once more around the table and the awkwardness passed, but Colin Clark had learned a big lesson. Thanks to Aiden he had dodged a bullet. Aiden had chosen to overlook his faux pas, but Colin was quiet for the rest of the meal, and that did not go unnoticed. There had been a subtle shift in the dynamics somehow, and everyone around the table was aware of that. Colin Clark was amazed to find that it had worried him when he had believed that Aiden had taken offence. Not just because it had made him a bit nervous but because he actually did like him.

Book Four

Lord, how oft shall my brother sin against me and I forgive him? Till seven times?

Matthew 18:21

Because I don't trust him, we are friends.

Mother Courage and Her Children,
Bertolt Brecht (1898–1956)

Chapter Seventy-Seven

2002

Joshua Dyke, known affectionately as Joshie D, was a DJ, a drug dealer and an all-round nice guy. The product of a Scottish mother and a Jamaican father, Joshie had inherited both his parents' excitable personalities, along with his father's thick dreads. Like the O'Hara boys, he had blue eyes and that gave his already good looks the edge where the ladies were concerned. Also the men. Joshie was bisexual, as happy with a male partner as he was with a female. His long-term girlfriend had had his twin sons, and she didn't seem in the least bit bothered about his sexuality. Although it was a real bugbear as far as a lot of his contemporaries were concerned – they were not sure how to react to him. His lifestyle was so far out of their remit. These were men who were brought up to be men – real men. The fact that Joshie D was a bit suspect, but could still hold his own if needed, seemed bizarre to them. His saving grace was he could fight like fuck, as had been proved on more than one occasion.

Joshie embraced his lifestyle with exuberance and extravagance. He dressed like a male model and he could command an audience wherever he appeared. He was working on music with other artists, and making a name for himself in the real world. He could also work out a deal down to the last penny. His cousin was a big man in Jamaica and Joshie had a house in Kingston, where he spent a lot of time – not just DJing but arranging deals too. He was on his way, getting a reputation in the club world and in the world of criminality. Nothing was out of reach for anyone who had the nous to go for it these days and Joshie had everything to play for.

Aiden O'Hara had deliberately nurtured Joshie because he recognised that he could be a viable part of the organisation. Aiden found that Joshie's sexuality didn't bother him as much as it did everyone else. He wasn't that interested in other people's sex lives. As long as they earned, that was enough for him. But it went deeper than that with Aiden; he was surprised to find that he liked Joshie and he wasn't alone. Patsy thought he was a diamond and Eugene, who was working with him, thought he was the dog's knob. He bothered Porrick, but then, everything bothered Porrick. He was turning into a very particular bloke; he had a fucking opinion about everything. Now, as Aiden waited for Colin and Joshie to arrive, he poured himself a large brandy. He had a feeling he was going to need it. Patsy was quiet, and he poured his brother a drink without asking him. As he passed it to him, Patsy said tiredly, 'We're going to need this – Colin has been pretty vocal about his opinion on Josh.'

Aiden shrugged. 'I know, bruv, but I must be honest. I really don't get his fucking anti-gay shit. Why would he let that bother him?'

Patsy grinned. 'You never cease to amaze me, Aiden. In all honesty I thought you would have been more bothered than him.'

Aiden knocked his brandy back and poured another large glass. 'I'm offended by that, Patsy. Why would I care?'

Patsy closed his eyes in annoyance, because whenever Aiden

felt he was being judged in any way he always resorted to acting like he had been deeply offended. Maybe he was; Patsy didn't give a shit either way.

'Come on! We know that Porrick is as gay as a Mexican tablecloth, but none of us mention it, do we?'

Aiden shook his head. 'You might not have, but I've discussed it with him. Difference is, I don't give a fuck. I remember him as a kid. He was always a bit of a fucking drama queen, quiet as he was. How many times did he watch fucking *Dirty Dancing* with Mum and Aggs? I mean, think about it, Patsy.'

Patsy started laughing. It was infectious and the two brothers were roaring together, holding on to each other, both caught up in absolute mirth.

'Remember Mum, when she caught him in his room with that mate of his, the really effeminate one? What was his name?'

Patsy was nearly on the floor now. He was almost crying with laughter. 'That Nigel bloke. The one with the blond highlights. Even our Agnes sussed that one, and she's as green as the proverbial grass.'

They were still cracking up when Eugene and Porrick entered the room, and that just made them worse.

'Well, what's the big joke then?' Porrick said nastily.

Patsy just shook his head saying, 'Believe me, you don't want to know.'

Aiden stopped laughing. 'You know what, Porrick? You have a bad fucking attitude. Sometimes, as I have told you on more than one occasion, it can be fucking annoying.'

Porrick didn't answer. He was as red as his hair, and that was never a good look. He was clearly angry – much angrier than was good for any of them. His fists were clenched, always a sign he was spoiling for a fight.

Eugene tried to keep the peace saying, 'Look, let's all calm down here. We are brothers, for fuck's sake.'

'Really? You are reminding me, the eldest brother, that we are related? I'm the one who makes sure we are on a fucking earn, you all work for me, remember? You having a fucking tin bath, Eugene?'

Eugene sighed; Aiden had a point. There were times when Porrick could conjure an almighty row out of a mere look.

'All I'm saying is, we don't need to be at odds now, do we?'

Aiden and Patsy looked at each other with disbelief. Then, shaking their heads together, they both stared at Eugene as if he had just dropped through the ceiling.

'What I'm telling you, mate, is that I'm sick of having to apologise for my two youngest brothers. So you either take Porrick in hand, or you two can piss in the wind and get yourselves another fucking wage packet.'

Patsy shrugged and poured them more drinks. It was to everyone's benefit if they just let the matter drop, but Aiden had been getting annoyed with Porrick over what he called his antisocial behaviour for a while. There was a kink in Porrick that was beginning to worry him. He was a young man who did not seem to have a cut-off point – he would push and push even when it really wasn't sensible.

As they took their drinks, Aiden looked at his youngest brother and he said seriously, 'I mean it, Porrick. You keep causing ructions for no good reason and I am not going to go on saving your arse every time you upset someone. If you weren't my brother you would have had the shit kicked out of you by now. You got to start reining in your natural fucking bastardy.

Because you are starting to piss me off now! And that is *never* a good idea. Remember that in future.'

Porrick was offended by his brother's reaction. After all, this was rich coming from Aiden O'Hara, a man who lived on a different planet to everyone else.

Chapter Seventy-Eight

'If Aiden finds out he'll go ballistic, Agnes. You know that as well as I do.'

Agnes was frightened but she was not going to back down. She was entitled to her own life, and that was something she was not going to forget.

Jade and Reeva looked at each other in shock. This was Agnes, she was like a nun in waiting. How could she be telling them this, especially now? Not that Reeva understood the real problem here, but Jade was well aware that Aiden was about to do the biggest deal of his life and Agnes could fuck it up in seconds with her news. For the first time in years, Jade was actually sweating with nerves. Reeva on the other hand wasn't as bothered as she made out; if she was honest she was secretly pleased. Finally she and her daughter had something in common! Reeva wasn't stupid, she knew that people had questioned how on earth did someone like her raise such a good girl. It grieved Reeva that she had been born when she had – these days no one would have batted an eye at her lifestyle. It amazed her when she bumped into her mother's cronies and they told her how their granddaughters were having babies and saving up to get married. When she remembered what she had been forced to endure from them it did sometimes make her angry.

Hypocrites, the lot of them. A part of Reeva was pleased at how the times had changed, but it still rankled. Still, she was proud of how she had fought to keep her kids and, whatever people might think of her, she loved them more than anything else in the world.

'Actually, Reeva, it's not *if* Aiden finds out, is it? It is *when.*'

Reeva pulled her daughter into her arms then, looking at Jade, she said honestly, 'I do get it, Jade. But life happens. You should know that better than any of us.'

Jade could see the logic of what Reeva was saying, but she also wondered at how this woman could not see that her daughter's predicament just might cause a teeny bit of upset.

Tony was sitting at the kitchen table, drinking a beer and smoking a joint, and, getting up, he pulled Reeva and Agnes into his embrace. 'I think Reeva has a point for once. Agnes is not a child any more. She doesn't have to answer to Aiden or anyone.'

Jade lit a cigarette and, smiling tightly, she didn't answer him. Sometimes she could not help but wonder what planet this family actually lived on. She closed her eyes and wondered, not for the first time, why she cared so much.

Agnes pulled away from her mother and, sitting at the kitchen table, she said seriously, 'It's my life, and the sooner you all understand that, the better.'

Jade looked at this beautiful young girl, who really believed that she had some kind of say over her own life, and she said flatly, 'Well, good for you, Aggs. I hope it keeps fine for you, I really do.'

Then she left the house; she was expected at the big meeting, and she was late.

As she pulled away from the kerb she wondered at where this

was going to go, where it was going to leave them. She didn't hold out much hope for an amicable solution, though stranger things had most probably happened at sea, as Reeva was always trying to convince them.

Chapter Seventy-Nine

Joshie D liked Aiden O'Hara a lot, mainly because he had understood from their first meeting that, unlike most of the people he dealt with, Aiden couldn't give a fuck about his 'exotic' lifestyle. He had heard that expression and he had liked it – he felt that it really did encompass his way of living. As he entered the building that Aiden owned in Mayfair, he felt a rush of respect for the man. Aiden O'Hara had come a long way, and that was something he could really appreciate.

As the ugly goon in the cheap suit ushered him into the lift, he smiled magnanimously. After all, who was he to look down on a fellow brother? The man was big, black and, without doubt, good for nothing more than being a fucking heavy. But at least the man did his job with a certain respect, so he had that going for him. That was another thing he liked about Aiden O'Hara: his workforce was taught the usefulness of being polite and unobtrusive. There were more than a few complete fucking morons in the game who still didn't quite understand the new wave of characters or the new businesses that they were creating. They were destined to die out like the dinosaurs they were. The days of open threats and taking people out in public were long gone. The older men were given their due – after all, they had earned it – and the ones with a bit of nous had embraced the new generation. They'd ensured that their sons had been educated so they were well able to join the new world order. If they were not able to keep up, they were just rowed out, simple as that.

Joshie had turned up alone, but he didn't need an entourage; he liked to do certain deals with the minimum of fuss. He was also aware that showing up alone not only made him look good, but it also conveyed the message to the people involved that he trusted them enough to not feel the need for any kind of backup. The fact that he had a car with his own people outside was neither here nor there – his arriving at the actual meeting alone was enough. He wasn't a fool; he knew that his cousins in Jamaica and Brixton would guarantee his safety. But it looked good and it was part of his reputation now.

As he walked into the main office, he smiled easily. He was a powerful-looking man – big and fit as a butcher's dog. But then, so were the four O'Hara brothers – even the short red-haired one who it was rumoured was also a follower of Dorothy.

Aiden smiled widely and held out his hand. As they shook, Joshie noticed that Patsy, who he had always really liked, was pouring him a glass of Cockspur rum. It was the little things that really mattered sometimes. He took the glass and sipped his drink slowly; they had all the time in the world.

The offices were everything he expected them to be, from the black leather sofas to the huge antique desk that Aiden O'Hara was leaning against so nonchalantly. The windows faced the road and he could see the traffic and the pedestrians as they went about their busy little lives.

Joshie D sat on the sofa opposite Aiden and, grinning, he sipped his drink and said amiably, 'My cousin Marvin, as you know, can provide as much product as you require from our connections in Colombia. The coke is pure – believe me, it can be cut as many times as necessary. It's not the usual shit. It's in keys as always, but it will be delivered in bulk and, once it arrives in the UK, it's up to us to move the product wherever it's required, OK? That is Marvin's only stipulation. When it gets here it will be lodged in one of his safe houses. He will take the responsibility of delivering to the UK as part of his end. But, the truth is, he knows that the majority of gear gets captured because the people involved don't do their homework. The Filth are on it from the off and that's because too many people are involved. There is one thing that we all know: the main trouble with the UK is the same people are involved over and over again, and everyone knows who they are, including the Filth. So Marvin has set up a network of people and places to ensure that not just his product, but also his partners and the people who work for him, are protected. That means that he will bring the product into the UK and will make sure it is delivered to a safe haven before you have anything to do with it. He has seen the abortions that certain people have caused over the years – we all know what I am talking about, don't we?'

Aiden and Patsy were smiling; they knew exactly what he was referring to. The biggest worry was getting the stuff from its initial point of contact – whether that was the docks or from a private airfield or from a fucking lorry driver. The more people were involved, the harder it was to keep things on the down-low.

'That sounds perfectly logical to me, Joshie. For my end the money is in place and, once we know where the product can be accessed, we will guarantee that it will be removed with the minimum of fuss.'

Joshie D held his glass out for a refill. 'I know that, Aiden, it is what I have guaranteed Marvin. He is OG you know – he's been in this game for years. Not just here but the USA too. You will get on well with him, he is a straight arrow. But – and please don't take this the wrong way, Aiden – he is what Jamaicans call a "bad man". A bad man in Jamaica is completely different to a bad man here. It's a different world in the Caribbean.'

Aiden nodded his agreement even though he thought it was a load of old fanny.

He knew and respected a lot of the Jamaicans, but he wondered how long they would last in London. Kingston was like a village in comparison, but he knew better than to say that. He wanted Joshie to feel that he trusted him, because he did. Plus, it was Joshie who he would be dealing with on a regular basis anyway and it never hurt to encourage good relations – Jade always preached that. He wondered briefly where she could have got to.

'That is much appreciated, Aiden. By the way, how is Eric Palmer? I hear he's not well.'

Aiden and Patsy deliberately didn't make eye contact. 'Oh, he's all right. Hard old fucker, he is. I think we will have to shoot him!'

They all laughed.

'Good to hear, Aiden. He is a nice old boy.'

Aiden overlooked the smugness in Joshie's voice; he knew that old-timers like Eric were seen as also-rans and as old-style Moustache Petes. But, the truth was, Eric was still on board for all his pretence at retiring. And, in honesty, Aiden was glad of that because Eric Palmer had never once steered him wrong.

'Where is Colin Clark? I assumed he would be here.'

'Oh, don't you worry, you will see him soon enough. Let's just say I wanted to deal with this by myself. This is entirely my deal. Colin will only be involved when I begin moving the product to its final destinations.'

Aiden saw the pleasure on Joshie's face and knew that he had boxed clever.

Colin Clark was his mate, but it suited Aiden that Colin didn't feel comfortable around Joshie D because he could do what he wanted without having to explain himself. Colin Clark had made his opinion of Joshie perfectly clear, and Aiden had never once tried to contradict him. That was his fucking look-out, and it worked for everyone concerned, especially for Aiden, and that was all that really interested him.

Chapter Eighty

Jade was waiting for Aiden at the club on Charing Cross Road, in the small office she kept on the top floor of the building. She had had to talk him into purchasing this whole building; he had not wanted to at the time, but now he could see the sense in her reasoning. She lay back in the chair and relaxed her body. She had poured herself a rare Jack Daniel's and Diet Coke – she needed a serious drink before she saw Aiden.

She glanced at the CCTV and saw that the club was filling up quickly. She noticed Aiden's latest squeeze – a tall, blonde girl with natural breasts and long slim legs. The girl was pretty rather than beautiful, but she had something about her. She actually seemed nice – she wasn't pushing herself forward. In fact, Jade felt sorry for her. She just hung around hoping that Aiden would turn up and notice her. It was depressing really.

She saw Aiden and his brothers as they came through the doors downstairs and she braced herself for what she knew she had to do. She waited patiently for him to come upstairs, and she felt a small sense of triumph as she saw Aiden walk past the pretty blonde without a second glance. She also saw the tragic look on the girl's face and she could not help feeling a moment's sorrow for her. Not because Aiden had blanked her, but because she didn't *get* that she was worth so much more than him.

As the boys came into the room, Jade was smiling, as always; none of them would ever know what she really thought.

'Sorry, Aiden, I got completely held up at your mum's. *Big* drama. You all know the score, guys. Anyway it's done. How did the meeting with Joshie go?'

Aiden shrugged. 'Perfect.'

Jade smiled and Aiden felt the pull of her. She was beautiful, and he never once forgot that. As big a fucker as he could be, he knew that he would never love anyone like he did Jade.

'No Colin?' She said it very gently, but with a sarcasm that wasn't lost on any of the men in the room.

Aiden opened his arms out as if in wonderment and said seriously, 'No. No Colin. Why?'

Jade took a deep gulp of her drink before saying, 'Agnes is pregnant, Aiden, and it seems that Colin is the fucking culprit.'

All four of the brothers seemed to suddenly stand to attention; they were looking at her as if she had just stabbed a new-born baby to death, they were that shocked at her words.

'*Our* Agnes is pregnant?'

She looked at Eugene and nodded her head. Aiden was looking at her as if he had never seen her before; his whole demeanour was that of a man unable to comprehend what he was hearing.

'It's been going on for quite a while and, according to Agnes, they are in love, and getting married.'

Jade was watching Aiden and she was getting more and more frightened by the minute.

'That snidey bastard! Sniffing round her and none of us had a clue!' Porrick was red-faced once again, and his words seemed to spur the others into action.

'He is fucking dead! Never once did he ever ask to take her out on a date . . .' Eugene, like Porrick, was incensed with the sheer enormity of what they had been told.

Patsy was watching Aiden. He knew that, whatever happened, he could not let Aiden loose without good cause. Aiden looked at Jade, and she could see the anger and the disappointment in his eyes. Agnes was his baby sister. He adored her because she was everything that he classed as good. She was a good girl, a good Catholic. She was the one female he'd believed was without stain.

Jade stood up and, going to Aiden, she held his hands in hers. Looking to Patsy for help, she said quietly, 'She's adamant she loves him, and that he loves her, Aiden.'

All the boys were looking at Aiden, waiting for him to decide what they were supposed to do.

'I understand that you might be angry with them but, in all honesty, Aiden, you wouldn't have given them your blessing, would you? Agnes isn't a little girl any more, she is a grown woman. And I tell you now, she will fight for him, Aiden. I saw that myself tonight.'

Aiden was nodding his head in agreement, but they could see that he was trying his hardest to keep his temper.

'Think about it, Aiden. You and Colin are good mates. He knew that you wouldn't have countenanced him taking Aggs out. But, in fairness to him, he wants to marry her. He loves her and she loves him. And, whatever you lot might think, she is of an age to do what the fuck she likes. She doesn't need anyone's fucking permission. She can marry him if that is what she wants.'

Porrick pushed her away from his brother shouting, 'He fucking snuck around her under our fucking noses! He knew what he was doing, Jade. He knew that it was out of fucking order, otherwise he would have courted her fair and square.'

Jade sighed heavily, aware that she needed to calm everyone down, especially Aiden. 'Oh, really? Grow up, Porrick. So, you think if he had asked to take Agnes out, you lot would have been amenable? Agnes couldn't go out with *anyone*! You lot made sure of that. Well, I'm sorry, but even though this was done underhanded, let's be honest – it's not like she had any fucking choice, is it? No more than Colin Clark did. On the upside, the marriage can only be a good thing.'

Aiden breathed in deeply, and he held the breath inside him for a long moment. Then he exhaled it slowly. They knew he was attempting to calm himself down, that he was trying to make sense of what Jade was saying to him.

'Listen, Aiden. If you kick off, Agnes will go to him without a backward glance. They have made a child. And you know how powerful that can be.'

Aiden looked into her eyes and she could see him struggling to keep a lid on his emotions. Eventually he said calmly, 'You are right, darling. These things happen.'

Patsy was looking at his two younger brothers with a warning that they were both aware of. Aiden was like a man demented inside, but he knew that Jade was right. He needed to box clever. He needed to calm down.

Chapter Eighty-One

Colin Clark was worried, but he was convinced that he could talk Aiden round. He had not intended to get Agnes pregnant – he had taken the necessary precautions. But he knew that he had no choice but to do the right thing. He wasn't about to tell Aiden O'Hara or his brothers that he was not going to stand by their little sister. He wasn't on a fucking death wish.

In all honesty, it wasn't going to be that much of a hardship. Agnes was a beautiful-looking girl, and she was a good girl – that had been the attraction, coupled with the knowledge that she was Aiden's little sister. She was the real forbidden fruit, and he had not been able to resist the temptation. It wasn't like she had been an easy nut to crack either. She was a decent girl – something that was hard to find in these times when girls could basically live like a man and often fucking did.

Now, as he sat with his brother, Timmy, he understood the enormity of what he had actually done. He had never envisioned anything like this in a million years. Fucking hell, the days of unplanned pregnancies were well and truly over, or so he had believed, anyway. Now he was like a fucking teenager caught with his cock out, and he didn't like this feeling one bit.

'You have pulled some fucking stunts in your time, Colin, but this one takes the fucking biscuit. You have no choice but to marry that girl, and do you know what? I feel sorry for her, because she is worth fifty of you.'

Colin didn't answer because his brother was right. He didn't deserve Agnes, and Christ Himself knew she did *not* deserve to be tied to him. It would be a church do – a big Catholic marriage, he imagined. They all went to Mass, even fucking Aiden. They were practising Catholics; that didn't mean anything to him, but Agnes would take it as seriously as she took everything else in her religion. All he could do now was make the best of a bad situation. The one good thing was that he did genuinely care about Agnes.

She'd been a virgin and he had taken his time to romance her but it had been more than worth the time and effort required of him. He had really pursued her, and he had done it with a vengeance – there was no way he wasn't going to bust her cherry. Making sure that her brothers wouldn't find out had only added to the excitement. They had sneaked around like fucking criminals, as Agnes had said on more than one occasion, to which he had answered, 'Well, I am a criminal' and they had both laughed. That had been the key – eventually he had laughed her into bed, along with a few wines. Just to relax her, of course. A bonus was that she had really liked it from the off. Sex with her was a revelation. She had taken to it immediately. Her mother's daughter, he supposed. Everyone knew that Reeva was a connoisseur of the one-eyed snake! But he couldn't deny Agnes had really gotten under his skin, something that he had not expected.

'Come on, get your arse in gear. I told Aiden and his brothers that we would meet them at Reeva's.'

Colin Clark followed Timmy without a word. True, he had really fucked up, but if he used his loaf he could smooth this over. The one thing that he kept reminding himself was, once he married Agnes, he would be related to Aiden. They were close friends, but this situation could really drive a wedge between them unless he could convince Aiden that this was actually a good thing.

He needed to make this work because his friendship with Aiden had given him a new life – he had actually enjoyed the relationship between the two of them more than he could ever have believed. He really did care about him.

Nevertheless Aiden scared him too. As mad as he could be – and he could really lose the plot – Aiden O'Hara was far ahead of him, mainly because Aiden didn't even know how fucking crazy he really was. That had been a learning curve for Colin. He had always planned his next move with care and worked out just how he could create another little bit of his public persona so that people remembered him. Aiden, on the other hand, took no such care. There was no thought beforehand, no planning to make the big impression; Aiden just did whatever he wanted without fear or favour. Colin had learned to respect him for that over the years.

Now, because he had not been able to resist Agnes, everything was in jeopardy. Timmy Clark drove them to Reeva's house with hate in his heart. Not for the O'Haras but for his own brother, who should have known better. Who should have thought about what he was doing, and how his stupidity was going to impact on the life they had worked so hard to achieve.

Chapter Eighty-Two

Reeva had cooked all morning – a nice beef casserole with mashed potatoes and roasted vegetables. She knew that there were going to be upsets; she had been there, fucking done that. The trouble with girls like her Agnes was that no one ever expected them to get in trouble, and when they did, it hit everybody concerned like a sack of shit.

She watched her boys as they waited for the Clarks to arrive. It amused her that her Porrick, her youngest son and the runt of the litter, really, was more annoyed about his sister's predicament than anyone. He was such a strange lad because, as short as he was, he had something inside him that transcended size or bulk; he was what Aiden always called a 'pocket rocket'. Porrick had a strength inside him that was far more dangerous than the others put together, including Aiden. Not that any of them had realised that, although *she* had known from when he was a baby. His father had been the same – 'little man syndrome' she called it. Porrick had something inside him that was frightening in its intensity. Like Aiden, he didn't possess a cut-off switch, but unlike Aiden, her youngest son didn't have the sense to use his anger for his own good. Porrick had never learned how to harness it; that was why the others gave him a wide berth at times like these.

Agnes was waiting patiently for Colin and his brother to arrive. She wanted this out in the open and sorted as soon as possible. There was a steeliness in her daughter that Reeva had never appreciated before. Looking at her now, with her thick black hair tumbling down her back, and her blue eyes, framed by thick lashes, she looked her usual demure self. But she was different – she was *alive* now. She had always been such a Holy Joe and here she was – her mother's daughter in more ways than one. Agnes was willing to fight for what she wanted and Reeva had a feeling that she would get it. Reeva was pleased for her girl, because if she ended marrying that fucker Colin she was going to need all the help she could get. He was a lot of things, but Mr Reliable wasn't one of them.

As she set the table and watched the clock, Reeva hoped that Colin Clark would be good to her daughter. He had grown on her, and she thought that her daughter could look further and fare a lot worse. Colin had money, he was known to the family and he was very easy on the eye. That he would shag anything that took his fancy was a given but, as Aiden would be on the case, she had a good idea he wouldn't rub her girl's face in it. Whatever happened this day, one thing was guaranteed – the child would be a beauty; they were a good-looking pair.

Jade and Aiden walked into the kitchen and Jade smiled at her nervously. Reeva knew that Aiden had to be watched, no one knew how he was going to react. That was the only worry, really – the boys' reactions.

'Something smells good, Reeva.'

Reeva gave one of her loud laughs. 'All my food smells good, Jade. I have a knack for cooking. It is the only thing I was ever good at. My mother can burn water as we all know. But, me, I can take the cheapest cut of meat and deliver a fucking feast!'

Aiden rolled his eyes in annoyance as he said without humour, 'Fuck me, Mum. Talk about "I love me, who do you fucking love"!'

It was the way he spoke to Reeva that set her off; he was being so disrespectful towards her. She knew he was upset and she understood that, but he was not going to talk to her like that and take his anger out on her. She had given birth to that lairy fucker, and she was not going to let him get away with it.

She turned on him, shouting angrily, 'Who do you think you are talking to? Eh? For all my faults, real and imagined, I fed you lot better than any of your fucking mates' mothers. So don't you *ever* forget that, Aiden. I brought you all up as best I could without a pot to piss in most of the time, and without any other fucker's help.'

That Reeva was genuinely offended was apparent, and even Aiden was shocked at the way she had retaliated.

'You know your trouble, Aiden? You forget how fucking hard it was for me with you lot. But I soldiered on, and I did my best! I was fourteen when I had you, mister. I was a child myself, remember. I never regretted any of you.'

Aiden could see how upset his mother was, and he did feel bad for what he had said.

Tony came into the kitchen then and, grabbing Reeva around the waist, he kissed her on her lips, saying calmly, 'Listen, woman, no fucking arguments today. Come on, darling, let's make this a good day, yeah? This is about building bridges, remember. This is about trying to make some good come out of this situation.'

Reeva pushed him away, but she shut up and that was what really mattered. Tony Brown meant what he said and Aiden wondered at a man who had stayed with Reeva for so long, knowing that she was a fucking walking nightmare. But that was Tony. He had always been there for them, especially for Reeva, no matter what she had done. Tony had somehow sorted it as best he could and Aiden admired him for that. He had stayed around longer than any of the men in Reeva's life and he had also always treated them well. Tony was one of the good guys, and his mother should really be reminded of that occasionally. Reeva was a lot of things but she wasn't what could be regarded as an easy woman. That Tony had stood by her for so long was something that Aiden could not help but admire. And, of course, without Tony Brown he would never have been given the chance with Eric Palmer. Aiden would never forget that, even though he knew that Tony didn't expect anything from him. That was Tony Brown's nature, and Aiden would always look after him. The mad thing was that Aiden knew that Tony didn't expect anything from him; he wasn't a man who expected payment for his actions. He had been over the moon for Aiden and his success with Eric Palmer. There had never been a hidden agenda.

Jade stepped in, trying to defuse the situation between Reeva and Aiden. They were far too alike.

'Come on, Reeva, get Aiden Junior down here. You are the only person who can get him off the computer.'

Reeva knew when she was being humoured but she chose to ignore that fact today. So, smiling cheerily and sarcastically at her eldest son, she left the kitchen. Tony followed her, smiling his usual apologetic smile.

Jade sighed before saying seriously, 'The Clark brothers will be here in a minute. Are you going to be able to contain yourself, Aiden?'

Aiden shrugged. He was not a happy man, and that was to

be expected as far as he was concerned. His friend, his good friend, who he had taken into his everyday life, who he had really liked, had fucked his little sister on the quiet. No one had ever made a cunt of him so spectacularly – no one else had ever dared. Now he was expected to swallow the insult, not just to him as a man but to his sister who he suspected had been seen as nothing more than a conquest by the man she was so in love with. Aiden had to box clever. But this was a complete piss-take, a personal insult. There was no way he could ever swallow something so heinous, especially when it involved his sister. But he would play the game tonight, there was nothing else he could do until the time to pay back the insult presented itself.

'Of course I will, Jade. As you keep reminding me, there is a child involved. He will marry her, and we will all forget the circumstances once the baby arrives. Except I will never forget that he went after my baby sister behind my fucking back. You and I both know that if she had not got pregnant that bastard would have never let on what he had done. He would have laughed up his fucking sleeve at me and I would never have been any the wiser. Really not impressed, OK?'

Jade couldn't argue because she knew he was telling the truth, but she had to try and calm down the situation, for all their sakes.

'That aside, he has stepped up, Aiden. She is mad about him, and he loves her. These things happen. Like you would have been encouraging him if you had known! You know that you wouldn't have let him near her!'

Aiden looked at Jade as if he could cheerfully punch her. 'No, you're right. I would have told him to keep as far away from her as possible because he is a romancer, a piece of shit. He loves the girls and he leaves them.'

Jade grinned sarcastically. 'Remind you of anyone, docs it, you fucking hypocrite?'

Just then there was a knock on the front door and, shaking her head in disgust, Jade walked out of the kitchen with Aiden following behind her. But she knew that her barb had hit home.

Chapter Eighty-Three

As Agnes sat beside Colin, she felt as if everything she had been dreaming of had come true – which it had, of course. Agnes O'Hara was getting exactly what she wanted. Aiden had been magnanimous. He had not lost his temper nor caused any kind of upset. Instead, he had been the epitome of common sense.

He had welcomed Colin to the family, had said that he was looking forward to the wedding. They had then all sat down to dinner and it had been almost a jolly affair. Eugene and Patsy had done their best at making it seem like it was just a normal night. Porrick, as she had expected, had behaved like the arse he was, acting like she should be shot at dawn, and Colin should be just shot. Murdered, removed from his sight. Porrick had taken it worse than any of her brothers. Like she cared what he thought!

Her mum, God love her, and Jade, had been marvellous, talking about the wedding and what she would wear, asking her what kind of flowers she wanted. They had made it seem almost normal. Jade proposed taking her to get a dress made and, after a while, everyone had seemed to get into the swing of things and it had actually been quite nice. Timmy had been wonderful; he had made a fuss of her and acted like he had known this was going to happen all along.

It had been a very stressful day for her, wondering what would happen, especially where Aiden was concerned. She understood how he felt. She knew that Colin and Aiden were such good friends and that Colin's behaviour could not be overlooked. It was her job to make Aiden see that they were meant to be together, that they were a perfect match. She knew that Aiden would never have allowed them to be together. Colin had explained that to her – as though she needed him to tell her anything about her brother! If it was left to him she would never have had a boyfriend. Between Aiden and Porrick she would have never had any kind of real life; they would have happily seen her alone for the rest of her days, going to Mass, looking after Aiden Junior, no man in her life. That was what the real problem was: her having sex with someone. Aiden had seen her as the eternal virgin, his baby sister who he loved but who he saw as without stain. The fact that she was so religious had really pleased her brother Aiden, because he could not bear to think of her as anything other than pure.

She was a different girl these days. She had been taken repeatedly by a man, a real man who had made sure that she had enjoyed it as much as he had. She was a different girl because of his treatment of her. It was unfortunate that Colin Clark had been the man who had pursued her and who she had fallen in love with, because Aiden was always going to see it as a direct attack on him personally. Aiden couldn't accept that anyone could ever do anything without his permission or his blessing. Now, thanks to Colin Clark, she had the courage to fight for what she wanted and not just do what everyone expected of her.

Taking a deep breath, she smiled at everyone around the table as she said lightly, 'I am so happy that we are all here tonight.

Colin and I didn't plan for this to happen, we couldn't help it.' She leaned across her eldest brother's lap and grabbed Colin's hand in hers tightly. 'I know you are disappointed in me, that I got pregnant. But I have never been happier than I am at this moment. Sharing my good fortune with the people I love more than anyone else in the world is just the icing on the cake.'

Colin got up then and, stationing himself behind her chair, he hugged her to him tightly and, kissing the top of her head tenderly, he said truthfully, 'Agnes, sweetheart, I can't tell you how happy you make me, darling.'

Looking at the two of them together, his sister, Agnes, so small and dainty and so fucking young, and Colin Clark so big and fucking heavy in comparison, did not endear either of them to Aiden or to Porrick for that matter. Even Aiden had been shocked at how deeply affected his little brother was about their sister's predicament. It pleased him that Porrick couldn't really see any kind of benefit from Colin Clark marrying their sister. Like himself, Porrick thought it was a fucking diabolical liberty – that Colin Clark slipping his little sister a secret portion on a regular basis was actually a fucking insult. It was not something that they should be congratulating him for. Colin Clark had snuck around behind their backs. He had broken bread with them at the table, while knowing that he was basically tipping them all bollocks. He was laughing at them because he had fucking had them over.

Agnes was as green as the fucking grass, she was a fucking innocent. Colin Clark, in contrast, knew *exactly* what he was about and therein lay the problem. He had done the one thing that Aiden would never be able to forgive: Colin Clark had used his baby sister and, no matter how they tried to dress it up, he would not have married her if she was not Aiden's flesh and blood. If they had not been such great friends, it would have been a completely different scenario. If it had been a young lad Aiden could have handled it. But a thirty-odd-year-old man, who everyone knew chased strange on a regular basis and bragged about his conquests, didn't sit well with Aiden.

Aiden himself had witnessed on more than one occasion Colin talk a bird out of her drawers and then brag about it afterwards, making them all laugh at his antics. His sister was worth much more, by Christ. But here he was, expected to swallow his knob and pretend that he was happy about the union that would bring the two families together. Well, that was not something he would ever be even remotely in favour of.

He would smile – and he would bide his time. And he would pray to the Good Lord above that he could somehow, eventually, get over these feelings of anger and dismay. But Colin Clark had stepped over a line and everyone, including the Clark brothers themselves, was more than aware of that fact. What really pissed him off was that he had really liked Colin Clark. He had finally found a kindred spirit, someone he could laugh and joke with, someone he felt a connection with. Somebody who wasn't a fucking blood relative but who he had really taken into his circle. Someone that he had really enjoyed working with, and who he had given his complete trust to. Someone who had eventually taken him for a complete cunt without one second thought and that was what really rankled.

Timmy Clark knew that Colin had to really up his game if he wanted to salvage his relationship with Aiden. The strange thing was, he could see Aiden O'Hara's point. But, unlike Aiden, he had always known that Colin could never be trusted completely; he was not capable of fidelity to anyone. Like Aiden, he didn't have any real conscience when it came to looking after number one.

Patsy and Timmy made eye contact across the table, and both of them were more than aware of how difficult the next few months were going to be.

Agnes, though, didn't care about anything. She wanted Colin Clark. She needed Colin Clark – he was now the be-all and end-all of her existence.

Chapter Eighty-Four

Joshie D was looking good, but that was to be expected. He prided himself on his look. He worked hard on it, and he spent a lot of money ensuring he had what he believed gave him the edge. Some of his outfits had been a cause for concern in the past but, given his reputation as a man who swung both ways, he had actually been allowed quite a lot of slack. He had his creds and that went a long way in this world.

While no one was relishing the atmosphere between Aiden and Colin, Joshie D had no knowledge of any bad blood between them. Nor would he find out – Eric Palmer had been clear on that. Though everyone involved in the coke deal knew that Aiden was the main man, the assumption had always been that Colin would be the distributor; that was what he had always done, and that was what he was expected to do here. He did his job well, and that was all anyone cared about outside the family. The real measure of a man was whether he could deliver. If he could then that was what counted. It was one of the perks of being in the criminal world – you could be the biggest cunt walking but, as long as you could provide what was required by the people you were dealing with, you would be tolerated, kept in the loop.

Joshie relaxed with a large Scotch. He looked around him at

the luxurious offices and gave himself a mental pat on the back. He was expecting great things from this alliance.

Eric Palmer sat in his chair and watched over the proceedings with his usual aplomb. He had deliberately decided not to go to Reeva's house for dinner, knowing instinctively that the best thing was to let Aiden and Colin sort it out between them. He had no interest in this kind of stupidity. He wouldn't offer an opinion unless asked, and he knew Aiden well enough to realise that he wouldn't ask unless he was desperate. He trusted Jade to smooth everything over although, if he was to be brutally honest, he didn't imagine that Aiden would ever exactly forgive and forget – it wasn't in his nature. He couldn't let things go, and that was why he had fucked up in the past. Aiden had a great mind – no one better – but he let his emotions dictate his actions. Never a good idea when you were working for someone else. Now, as they sat there in the expensively decorated offices – all chrome and leather – waiting for Aiden to arrive, Eric found he was hoping that his blue-eyed boy had not lost the plot. Because this deal was worth more money than any of them could ever imagine.

Chapter Eighty-Five

'Come on, guys, let's get this show on the fucking road!'

Aiden was laughing and joking but it wasn't natural, as everyone could tell. It was forced and it was almost challenging. He'd drunk a few glasses of wine with his dinner, and it was starting to show.

As Colin kissed Agnes goodbye, he made a point of not making it too obvious. He had hugged her quickly and kissed her lightly on the lips.

Outside the house they had all stood there embarrassed until Patsy had said loudly, 'Are we going to this fucking meeting or not?'

Colin had got into his car quickly, glad to be getting away from the whole O'Hara family for a while. His nerves were shot although it had gone much better than he could have hoped, considering the circumstances.

But then Aiden jumped into the passenger seat. Smiling nastily, he said, 'I thought me and you could have a little chat, Colin. I think you owe me that much, don't you?'

Porrick climbed into the back seat with Eugene and, as they pulled away, Patsy and Timmy looked at each other in despair.

'It looks like it's just us then, Timmy.'

The sarcasm wasn't lost on either of them.

Jade got into the driving seat and, as she started the car up, she waited until both men were seated before she said quietly, 'Whatever you both might think, he would not do anything to hurt Agnes until after the child arrives. So that gives us a good few months to sort this out.'

Timmy and Patsy didn't bother to answer her; it was going to be a battle, they knew that much.

Chapter Eighty-Six

Reeva was washing up, and chatting away to her daughter as if there was nothing amiss.

'I think it went better than expected, Aggs.'

Agnes was clearing the table, stacking the crockery and bringing it through to the sink.

As Reeva loaded everything carefully into the dishwasher she said through a yawn, 'Put the kettle on, girl, I need a cup of tea.'

Agnes did as she was asked and listened as her mother told Aiden Junior that he could have one more hour on his computer game before he had to have a bath and get his nightclothes on. When her mother finally came back into the kitchen, the dishwasher was on, and she had made a pot of tea. Reeva sat at the table and lit a cigarette, drawing the smoke into her lungs deeply and savouring the moment. Tony was rolling a joint and, when he had finished, Reeva took it from him and motioned for him to leave her alone with her daughter. He smiled easily and, as he left the room, he shut the door behind him.

Agnes poured the tea and, as she placed the cup and saucer in front of her mum, she said sadly, 'Aiden is bad enough, Mum, and I do get why he is upset. But Porrick! Who does he think he is?'

Reeva sipped her tea; it was perfect. Her Agnes was always the tea queen. She made everybody's tea just how they liked it – that was a big part of her daughter's nature. Remembering things, like who took one sugar and who liked ginger biscuits and who might prefer their toast heavily buttered. Her Agnes would be bothered enough to care about such trivial things. She was a people pleaser. Now she had brought the spotlight on herself over her relationship with Colin Clark and, for the first time ever, she had not done what everyone expected of her. It was a bigger shock than it should have been.

'Porrick is the nearest to you in age, Aggs. Of course he will feel that he should have looked out for you more, that he should have noticed that something was going on. I mean, be fair, darling – it wasn't like you and Colin were open and honest, was it? We all thought you were out with the church people as usual. Fuck me, you were always home by eleven, latest. So your brothers are fucking miffed because you had us all over. To be really honest, love, if it had been anyone else I don't think it would have caused such a stir. But with Colin Clark? Think about it, Agnes. If you didn't think it would cause any fucking drama why didn't you tell anyone that you were going out with him?'

Agnes sipped her tea and didn't say a word. Not that Reeva expected her to; she knew her daughter inside out. Agnes was what Trisha could refer to as a 'passive aggressive'. Reeva loved the morning talk shows, they really did help explain so much that she had never understood until now. Reeva adored Trisha Goddard, who she saw as an example of everything that was good about society. Until she had started watching her she had never understood herself, let alone the people around her. Clever bollocks Aiden called it 'pop psychology', whatever the fuck that meant. But Reeva saw it as an education, and she never missed a programme. It was a whole new world to her, and she embraced it wholeheartedly.

'Mum, if I had told any of you then it would have been nipped in the bud. And, to be honest, I didn't want anyone to know. I'm not a child and what I do is my business, surely?'

Reeva puffed on her joint and coughed her head off before saying jokily, 'I can see where you are coming from, Aggs. But, be fair, it's not like you have a lot of experience with blokes, is it? Colin Clark isn't exactly a fucking virgin and, in all seriousness, he isn't exactly reliable where women are concerned, you know? That will be your brother's worry. So, try and see it from that point of view. Colin loves them and leaves them. Your brothers wouldn't want that to happen to you, would they?'

Agnes didn't rise to the bait. She knew her mum was as always trying to justify her brothers' behaviour. She didn't blame her; she did the same thing herself. But trying to insinuate that Colin was only with her because they had been found out rankled. She knew that her mum was trying to warn her that sometimes things were not quite as you believed. But that was her mum's life, not hers. Agnes believed that Colin loved her and that she had changed him.

'Well, Mum, we are getting married. So all that is what I suppose you could say was a moot point.'

Reeva smiled sadly because, as much as she liked Colin Clark, she wouldn't trust him as far as she could throw him. She believed he would look after her daughter, and she believed he loved her in his own way. But she also knew that he would never be completely faithful, and that her daughter was the kind of girl who could never cope with that. But what could she do?

Instead, smiling, she got up and, hugging her daughter to

her tightly, she said honestly, 'I just want you to be happy, darling, that's all. You're my baby. My only girl. I want more for you than I ever had.'

Agnes hugged her mum back; she meant well, but she didn't know Colin like she did. He was everything to her. He was the love of her life, her first, and he would be her last – of that much she was determined.

Chapter Eighty-Seven

Aiden was watching his youngest brother with a mixture of pride and annoyance.

Pride that Porrick was looking out for his sister and annoyance because his brother didn't have the sense to keep his feelings private. That was something he had tried to instil in them all since day one of their educations: never let anyone outside of the family know what you are really thinking. It was not something he felt he should have even had to mention, but he did, because you never knew how much people were taking in.

Eugene was quiet and that pleased him, though he knew that Eugene was probably as upset as he was. Eugene had a natural reticence that was in his favour. Like himself and Patsy, he kept his own counsel until asked his opinion. Porrick, though, was like a fucking firework and he would go off at the slightest provocation. He could not control his emotions nor his actions and that could cause a lot of trouble.

Colin was nervous but he wasn't about to back down; he knew that he had to fight for not just himself, but for Agnes as well.

'Come on then! What have you got to say to me?'

It was bravado but the only way he could survive this was by making sure that these men believed that his attention towards their little sister had been for no other reason than he loved her. He had fallen in love with her in some ways but, truth be told, if she wasn't Aiden's sister he would have walked away as usual.

Aiden O'Hara was just watching him quietly; he was not even bothering to answer his question, and that told Colin he needed to work harder at convincing him.

'What do you want us to say, Colin? You fucked our sister. She is pregnant so now you have no choice but to hold your fucking hand up. After all the secrecy and the fucking clandestine meetings you really want us to believe that your intentions were honourable?' Eugene laughed, before adding, 'Hardly fucking Mills and Boon, is it?'

Aiden started to laugh as well. Eugene had hit the proverbial nail right on its proverbial fucking head and so he said as much.

'Come on, Colin, you can't pretend that my brother doesn't have a point. Because he fucking well does, as you well know. You went behind my back, and you took my little sister. You fucked her and now that she is pregnant you are going to marry her. Like that makes everything all right. Well, it doesn't.'

'Fuck him, Aiden. Let me sort the fucker out once and for all.'

Porrick was leaning forward in his seat. He was willing to murder Colin and they were all more than aware of that fact – no one more than Colin Clark. This was the make or the break of his life. He could not fight all of Agnes's brothers. They outnumbered him for a start. He knew that he had stepped over a line. Aiden would never forgive him for his actions and he couldn't blame him. He had really taken the fucking piss. They had gone out on the pull together and they had enjoyed each other's company. Now that it had all fallen apart he regretted his actions.

'Look, Aiden, I will hold my hand up. I was a cunt. But I couldn't help it. Agnes is a good girl. She is decent and loyal, especially to you lot. She is everything I ever dreamed of in a wife. How many times, Aiden, did I tell you that when I finally settled down it would be with a girl that I knew I could trust one hundred per cent? Who I knew would be beyond reproach? Who had not been out and about in every pub and club, who wasn't known to anyone but me?'

Aiden listened quietly; he had heard him say all of that and more. And he had understood him, even though his Jade was not exactly in the same league, of course. Everyone knew about her, and it had never bothered him as much as it could have. He had fallen in love with her and her alone. And her past had never been an issue unless he thought someone else was disrespecting her. Then, of course, he would defend her in any way he needed to.

'I fell for Agnes even though I knew that I shouldn't, Ade, because she is everything that I ever wanted in a girl. She is my dream. I will look after her and my baby, you know I will, Aiden.' He turned in his seat and, looking at Porrick, he said sadly, 'You wonder why I didn't fucking advertise our relationship? None of you would ever let her have a fucking boyfriend, that was part of the problem. She isn't a child any more, no matter how much you lot might try to deny that fact. She is well over the age of consent, and she knows what she wants. I never forced her into anything. All I ever did was love her.'

Aiden let Colin say his piece; then he held up his hand in a gesture that told his brothers to keep quiet. They were more than willing to do just that; after all, it was Aiden who would finally decide what was to be done about this situation.

'So what you are saying, Colin, *is*, that you and Agnes just fell in love? Our little Agnes, who was considering becoming a nun, who attends Mass twice a day whenever possible, and who was, without sounding crude, a natural virgin. She just fell for you in an instant?' He looked at his friend with scepticism as he carried on talking. 'You don't think that you might have had to, I don't know, cajole her or talk her into going out with you? You didn't have to assure her that what you were both doing was OK? That sneaking around behind her family's back was something that could be seen as perfectly fucking innocent? That together, you two lying and cheating and treating us all as complete and utter cunts was not really a problem? I mean, come on, Colin, tell me. I'm interested. Really, I want to know the truth.'

Colin Clark could understand where Aiden was coming from, but now he was starting to feel offended too. They had pulled up outside the offices for the meet – the meet that was so important, that was going to be the icing on the cake, and was going to bring them all untold riches. He wanted this sorted before they went inside.

Turning to Aiden, Colin said angrily, 'You fucking hypocrite, Aiden! How many times have we been out on the fucking nest and you have not even thought about Jade? How many times have we shared a pair of tarts, and laughed about it the next day? So, I fell for your little sister – at least I love her. I would never hurt her. I might not be the most faithful man on the fucking planet, but I would never let her know that. Can you say the same, Aiden? You rub it in Jade's face. You fuck the girls that work for her, you humiliate her, Aiden. So what the fuck does that make you, eh?'

Porrick couldn't listen any more. Grabbing Colin by the hair, he dragged his head backwards over his seat. 'Agnes isn't Jade, Colin. You better remember that – Agnes was never a fucking whore . . .'

Eugene and Colin were struck dumb by Porrick's statement. It was like he was on some kind of death wish. Aiden looked at his little brother; he could see that Porrick had regretted his words as soon as he had uttered them. But that wasn't the point – the fact he had said them was enough for Aiden. Colin Clark kept quiet; he knew that the best thing to do now was to keep as low a profile as possible.

Eugene was the first to move and he simply opened the car door, saying, 'Come on, we are late enough as it is. Eric Palmer won't be too thrilled if we keep him waiting any longer.'

But the damage had already been done.

Chapter Eighty-Eight

Joshie D was a breath of fresh air after the car journey and they were thankful to give him their full attention. The meet was intended to seal the terms of the deal – on Aiden's terms, of course. Joshie thought that his connections were all he needed and that pleased Aiden. It just meant that he could negotiate without too much fucking hassle. There was nothing he loved more than a flash cunt on his first real foray into the world of bastardy. So he sat there with everyone else and listened respectfully to Joshie D as he repeated what he had learned off by heart.

Eric Palmer was watching Aiden warily. After all these years he was more than aware of the man's moods and it had been obvious since he had walked through the door that he was not in a good one. Jade looked nervous too, which didn't help put his mind at ease. Eric Palmer was not happy; he didn't ask for much, but the one thing he insisted on was that the people who worked for him acted like professionals.

Aiden smiled pleasantly at Joshie and made him feel important – that was something that the Joshies of the world needed.

'I think that we can accommodate you, Joshie. It's a wonderful deal. But the one thing I will insist on is meeting the people you are dealing with, face to face.'

Everyone in the room knew that this was the one thing Joshie had not allowed for, and that was exactly why Aiden had requested it.

'I am willing to travel to Jamaica – wherever. After all, I have more than a few contacts out there, as I am sure you know. But I never deal with people I haven't met. That's the bottom line, Joshie: either they come to deal directly with me, or I travel out to see them. The former would suit me better, of course.'

Joshie D sensed that there was something going on here. And he was sensible enough to know that he should not try and get involved in any kind of dialogue. This was, after all, Aiden O'Hara, and he was not a man to suffer fools gladly. Instead of taking umbrage at Aiden's words, he said quite amicably, 'If that's what you want I am sure it can be arranged.'

Aiden grinned. 'You are agreed, Eric, I'm sure?' He didn't wait for Eric's answer. Instead, he turned his full attention once more to Joshie D saying, 'It's nothing personal, mate. I am sure you understand that.' Then, looking at Colin, he said innocently, 'The thing is, you have to know the people you are dealing with on a first-hand basis. After all, the one thing that we need is to be able to trust one another. Without trust, it's all a waste of fucking time.'

Joshie had no choice but to agree. When he left a little while later, they sat quietly waiting for the bomb to drop. They didn't have long to wait.

As soon as Joshie had been driven away, Eric Palmer looked around him at everyone in the room and shouted, 'What the fuck was all that about?'

Aiden went to the bar and, pouring himself a large Scotch, he turned to Eric Palmer. Shaking his head slowly, he looked at the man he had adored for years before bellowing, 'Are you fucking retiring or not? Only, if I remember rightly, Eric, you were supposed to be taking a back seat. I want to make sure that the people we are dealing with are on the up and up. That was something you taught me many years ago, Eric. You explained to me in graphic detail the folly of dealing with people you didn't actually know. If you couldn't put a face to a name you were a cunt, apparently. I mean, call me old-fashioned, Eric, but I am only doing what you told me years ago when you introduced me into this fucking life. Now suddenly it is OK to deal with people we have never clapped fucking eyes on. Is that what you are telling me?'

Eric Palmer was so angry he couldn't even talk. In all his days he had never been spoken to so disrespectfully, and he had never dreamed that Aiden, of all people, would have been the first one.

Aiden regretted his words as soon as he had said them, and he knew that he had to make amends as quickly as possible. Eric Palmer had always been good to him, and Eric Palmer deserved much more than he had ever given him.

Jade got up and started to clear the room, and Aiden knew that she was doing the right thing. He had been bang out of order in more ways than one, but he wanted to make amends in front of everyone who was there.

'Hang on, everyone. Before you go, I have something to say.'

They all stopped and looked at him in embarrassment; he wished that he had never allowed his anger to get the better of him. He wasn't even angry with Eric – it was Colin that he wanted to go for.

'I can't apologise enough, Eric. That was completely out of order. I am ashamed of myself. I know that there was no reason on earth for me to be so rude to you. I can only stand here and beg your forgiveness. The only explanation I can give you is it hasn't been a great day.'

His brothers were looking at him in amazement. Aiden admitting he was wrong was something none of them had ever seen before. They all knew that Aiden's personality did not allow for him to ever be seen as anything other than perfect.

Colin Clark sat quietly and watched everyone leave the room, knowing that Aiden expected him to leave with them. His brother, Timmy, had tried to catch his eye and, when he had not managed, he had sat back down beside him. Colin would always love him for his loyalty.

When Jade had escorted the others outside, and warned them to keep quiet, she pointed out that this was a really important deal and they needed to remember that.

She slipped back into the office. Like everyone else she was worried about Aiden and how he was going to react to the day's events. She was sick of having to always placate him, and be the sensible one. It was always left to her to sort out his messes – even the ones he got into himself with his girls on the side. As soon as the aggravation started, Jade stepped in and made sure that they disappeared from his orbit. Because, if it was left to Aiden, those girls would disappear off the face of the earth for ever. He was a fucking nutcase, she knew that. But he was her nutcase and she would defend him to the death.

Jade poured herself a stiff drink and, as she sipped it, she looked around her at these men who were held in such high esteem in the criminal world. Men who she knew, without her, would have sunk without trace a long time ago.

'Fuck me, isn't anyone going to speak? I mean, forgive me if I am out of order – not that I actually give a flying fuck – but are we going to address the elephant in the room or not? Only, personally, I am sick to death of you lot.'

They all looked at her wordlessly.

'Eric, I'm sorry, but in a way you asked for that tonight. You know and I know that the situation between Aiden and Colin is not exactly ideal. Colin has been sneaking around with Agnes, who is not exactly a fucking teenager, is she?' Jade finished her drink and, as she poured another, she carried on talking. 'Colin Clark is going to be your brother-in-law, Aiden, and I'm sure that will not curtail your evenings out together in any way. As for you, Timmy, I understand that you are shocked and outraged that your brother has got his mate's sister pregnant. But it could have been worse – he could have given her a fucking dose. What I am more annoyed about is you all put your personal feelings above the earn. And, like Eric, I find that very suspect. So my advice to you pair is to fucking grow up.'

Aiden was as aware as the other men that no one else could have said that to him and lived to tell the fucking tale. From any other person there would have been fucking ambulances arriving. That was what he had always loved about Jade: she had never sugar-coated anything – she just said it as she saw it.

Eric Palmer was still upset, and he voiced that anger. 'Jade is absolutely spot on, as usual. This is the last time any of you ever bring your personal problems into my businesses. The one thing you need to remember is that I can drop any of you if I decide that is what needs to be done. I might be on the edge of retirement, but I have not gone yet. And don't any of you lot forget that.'

Aiden and Colin were both aware that Eric Palmer was talking crap; he was well out of the game. Without Aiden and Jade he didn't have a fucking say in anything any more. Oh, he still had his creds – Jade made sure of that, as she always had done.

But it was a completely different world now. Not that any of them would ever have pointed that out, of course. Eric could still see a good earn when he was offered one. What Eric Palmer didn't have any more was the physical presence that was so important in this day and age. He was one of the old guard; he had known the Krays and the Richardsons. Eric had the stories and, more importantly, he had the life experience that was always something to be respected in the world he inhabited. But, at the end of the day, Eric was an old man. The people that they were dealing with were young and brash. In the drug-dealing world, many of their suppliers were lucky to get past thirty. It was a different world in more ways than Eric Palmer and his cronies could ever imagine.

Aiden didn't ever not give Eric his due. He was still a man to be reckoned with, Aiden would always ensure that. No one would ever be allowed to treat him like a fool. But the bottom line would always be that, for all of Eric's hands-on approach to his new businesses, and for all his big investments, he was still an old Moustache Pete. And, these days, without Aiden O'Hara and his brothers, Eric Palmer would not be taken as seriously as he was.

Aiden shrugged nonchalantly. 'What can I say, Eric? I can only hold my hands up, mate. You are right. I have been completely out of order.'

Colin Clark took his cue and, like Aiden, he stood up and apologised profusely. 'Eric, I knew I did a wrong one. Like Aiden, I can only hold my hands up. But all I can say in my favour is that I love Agnes. And I am heart sorry it had to come on top today of all days.'

Timmy Clark watched cynically as his brother, Colin, and Aiden O'Hara acted as if they were both ashamed and embarrassed over their actions; they were both so over the top. It was quite an act. But, like Jade, as much as he appreciated that they had put Eric Palmer's mind at rest – which of course was important, especially with this latest deal they had negotiated – he also knew that these two men were both devoid of anything even resembling decency or loyalty. They were as fucking selfish as each other. The pair of them were like little kids, and spoiled little kids at that.

Eric felt that he had made his point, and Jade and Timmy made sure that he believed that. But as they drank together, and acted like everything was OK, Jade wondered why she still protected the man that she knew could never be faithful to her or anyone else. But she had invested so much of her time and effort in him, and that was something she could never forget. The men around her were acting like nothing had happened and, instead of pleasing her, it just depressed her. Even Timmy Clark was playing the game. As always, Aiden got his own way. As always, he swerved anything that might show him in a bad light, show him up for what he really was. That she was instrumental in that, and always had been, was starting to irritate her.

But, as usual, she kept her own counsel, and made sure that everybody's drinks were replenished, and that everyone was happy and ready to move forward. She knew what was expected of her.

Chapter Eighty-Nine

'You don't look at all well, Nan.'

Annie was looking her age and she knew it. She was also feeling it. 'I'm just a bit tired. All this wedding stuff, I suppose.' She laughed as she said it and Agnes smiled gently. 'Fastest wedding I have ever known! I mean, it's not like having a baby out of wedlock is frowned on any more!'

Agnes sighed. She didn't care what anyone else thought – she was not going to have a baby without the benefit of marriage. That just wasn't her and, as far as she was concerned, this child she was carrying would thank her one day. Agnes Clark!

Even though she had her reservations about the love of her life, it was too late to do anything about them now. For better, for worse, as the saying went. She had seen a different side to her chosen mate lately, but she magnanimously put it down to the circumstances of their betrothal. She still loved him, but she wondered now if that was enough for either of them. Aiden had made his feelings plain, and she knew that her Colin was chary of the outcome of their union.

Annie held out her arms and her granddaughter went to her willingly. Annie wondered at how her girl, who was so intrinsically good and clever, had walked herself into what could only be described as a dilemma.

Reeva smashed into the room like the proverbial bull, laden down with a bottle of champagne, smoking her usual joint. 'Come on then, ladies, let's get this fucking show on the road! Tomorrow you are going to be a married woman!' As she poured the drinks, she said sadly: 'I would love to have got married, Aggs. It's the only sacrament I will never get. Better write to the fucking Pope, eh?'

They laughed with her, but Annie, in a rare display of affection, hugged her daughter to her tightly. 'Still time! You might get Tony up the aisle, you never know!'

Necking a whole glass of champagne in three gulps, Reeva said seriously, 'Mum! No one's that fucking optimistic!'

Suddenly Agnes saw just how much her single state had always bothered her mum and she found herself fighting back tears.

Reeva poured herself another large glass of champagne and, holding it up in a toast, she said with her usual bravado, 'Never say die, eh? More chance of this silly mare having a hen night!'

They all laughed, but it was laughter tinged with sadness.

Chapter Ninety

The lap-dancing club was closed for a private party, which was Colin Clark's stag do. This was Aiden's idea, and when Timmy and Colin arrived it was very quiet, with no one even on reception. They looked at each other warily and walked through into the actual club itself, where everything, including the stages, was in darkness. They turned to one another in confusion when suddenly all the lights went on and Aiden was walking towards them both, holding out his arms in a gesture of friendship. The music started up and the girls began to dance slowly around the poles. The club was packed with men from their world.

'Welcome, my son, my new brother from another mother!'

Timmy and Colin were both unsure how to react, which was exactly what Aiden wanted. Putting his arms around both their shoulders, he said earnestly, 'What can I say, Colin? I've behaved fucking atrociously. You know you were right. Agnes is a grown-up. But she is my baby sister, you know.'

Colin was so pleased at Aiden's change of heart he embraced him immediately. 'I would have been the same, mate. It's family. I understand.'

Timmy walked behind them as they went into the fray – because that was exactly what it felt like to him. The girls were dancing on their podiums, the men were getting drinks and the music and the sweat were just becoming noticeable. All he wanted was this night over with and the morrow as well – the wedding that Aiden had arranged – as quickly as humanly possible. None of this felt right.

Chapter Ninety-One

Jade walked in with a bottle of Bollinger and a fake smile. But no one except Reeva worked that much out.

'Beautiful dress, darling, you will look a million dollars tomorrow.'

Agnes smiled, but it was tinged with sadness. 'I hope everything is going to be all right, Jade. I'm still worried about Aiden, you know!'

She was on the verge of tears so Jade said as brightly as possible, 'Well, you can stop worrying, darling. Aiden has arranged Colin's stag for him, as you know, and he's determined to build some bridges.'

Reeva saw the pleasure in her daughter's face at this news and could have happily kissed Jade on the mouth.

Annie sipped her champagne and watched as her grand-daughter seemed to practically collapse with relief. But this was only to be expected; after all, Aiden had not exactly been discreet about his opinion of the situation.

'Thank you, Jade. I know this is because of you, darling.'

Jade hugged her but didn't comment. In all honesty, this change of heart had nothing to do with her at all. Instead she said, 'Come on then, let's get this party started, eh?'

Reeva chuckled, 'Yeah, party of the century. She can't drink because she's in the club, and in a minute we will be overrun with her Mass mates! Still, the stripper I ordered should sort it!'

Agnes squealed in dismay as Reeva said in mock sorrow, 'Don't worry. That was just a joke! Unfortunately!'

Chapter Ninety-Two

Colin Clark had been stripped, covered in baby oil and, as the men all laughed, he had been completely demolished by the drag queen who was supervising the night's entertainment. He was drunk, so was Aiden and, as they staggered around together with their arms around each other's shoulders, everyone breathed a sigh of relief. No one seemed to know how they were meant to react at the actual wedding itself. The workforce took their cue from the O'Haras – meaning, of course, Aiden. And there had been a lot of quiet speculation about what the upshot of the actual wedding day might be.

The big money was on Aiden causing ructions, but it seemed that had all been put to bed and he had had one of his lightning changes of heart. That wasn't anything unusual – as they all knew he blew hot and cold all the time; one minute he'd be smiling at you like he was your long-lost brother and the next time you saw him he could stare right through you as if he had never met you before in his life. But what could you do? No one was going to front him up, that much was guaranteed.

Colin and Aiden rolled through to the small back bar that was specifically used by the boys for business or their pleasure, depending. Inside, they fell on to a large leather Chesterfield and when Colin slipped off and fell on to the hardwood floor, they both laughed uncontrollably.

'Come on, my son, let's get you up.'

Aiden struggled to lift Colin and instead he ended up on the floor with him. They were still giggling like schoolboys.

In the end, they slumped on to the floor together, leaning back against the sofa to keep them upright.

'Fuck it, I don't think I can get up and go to the bar!'

They cracked up laughing again.

'I'm so glad you and me are mates again, Ade. I missed this, having a laugh and that.'

Aiden nodded his head in agreement. 'Same here, Col! But fuck me, I was annoyed.'

Colin nodded. Each time he put his head down, he belched, and soon they were off laughing again.

'Tomorrow will be a fucking great day, Colin. Wait till you see her dress. She will look splendid!'

Now the word 'splendid' set them off laughing again.

'Fucking splendid! And you will look top-hole, Colin!'

The rest of the O'Hara brothers all bundled noisily into the room. As Eugene went to the bar to make more drinks, Porrick and Patsy helped the two men up and dumped them unceremoniously on to the Chesterfield.

'What a fucking great night.'

Timmy Clark walked in and, even though he had had a few drinks, he wasn't half as wasted as everyone else.

Porrick was laughing his head off at something that Eugene had said and suddenly Aiden was up and off the sofa and confronting the two brothers.

'You taking the fucking piss?'

Patsy sighed and, putting down his drink, he went to where

his older brother was staring out Porrick as if he was his mortal enemy.

Porrick was shaking his head and, sighing heavily, he said, 'What the fuck are you on about, Ade?'

Aiden started to laugh, but he looked manic, from his red-rimmed eyes to his crumpled suit. 'You think I've forgotten, don't you, Porrick?'

Patsy put a restraining hand on Aiden's arm and was immediately shrugged off roughly.

'You called my Jade a whore. Or, more to the point, you said our sister wasn't a whore like Jade. Remember now, you red-headed prick?'

Patsy and Eugene instinctively stood between the two of them, and then Porrick said quietly, 'I'm fucking sorry, Aiden, but you know I spoke the truth.'

Patsy pushed his little brother away shouting, 'Are you on a fucking death wish? It's Aggs's *wedding* tomorrow and you two decide now that you want to have a fucking straightener?'

He grabbed Aiden around the shoulder and turned him round so he was facing the door. 'Eugene, you go now with Porrick. Timmy, you take Colin, and we will see you all tomorrow, OK?' He pushed and cajoled his brother back on to the Chesterfield. Once the room was cleared, he said angrily, 'You are off your nut again and you are supposed to be giving Agnes away tomorrow! Honestly, Ade, you are getting out of hand. Porrick didn't mean what he said and you know that. He was making an observation that day, and we were all out of sorts.'

Aiden closed his eyes and nodded imperceptibly.

Patsy sat down on the sofa and, putting his head into his hands, he said seriously, 'It's like you are on a self-destructive bent, Ade.

You are without any kind of fucking off switch. Jesus Christ, sometimes I wish I could take your fucking batteries out!'

His voice was so honest and so perplexed that Aiden burst into laughter.

'You are absolutely fucking right, Patsy. But you know me. I just don't think, I react.'

Patsy laughed ruefully, then said seriously, 'Well, let's react ourselves home. We have a long day tomorrow.'

'I hope our Agnes enjoys it while it lasts.'

Patsy didn't answer his brother, but couldn't shake the terrible feeling of dread.

Chapter Ninety-Three

Reeva had tears in her eyes as she watched her daughter walk down the aisle of St Peter's. It was an old-fashioned church and it seemed to fit into the whole theme of the wedding itself.

Agnes was dressed in a white gown with a high neckline that sparkled with small seed pearls. It fell to the floor in an almost Grecian look, and though there was hardly any of her actual body on display except her hands and face, she looked very sexy and very innocent at the same time.

Colin watched her walking towards him and felt his stomach flip. She looked amazing. Truthfully, he didn't want to be married to anyone really, but he was lumbered with this beautiful girl now – all he could do was make the best of it.

Timmy Clark, his best man, watched his brother's face and wished, not for the first time, that it was him Agnes was walking down the aisle to meet. Over the past weeks, he had fallen for her, and that was something he had never believed possible. He only hoped his brother looked after her, because he knew better than anyone that his brother, Colin, would rather be anywhere in the world right now than standing in this lovely old church.

Aiden walked beside his sister, looking suitably sombre. All the men were dressed in grey morning suits and they looked a handsome bunch. As they arrived at the altar, he pretended to grab his sister's arm and run. The whole church erupted in laughter and then he gently placed her hand in Colin's and patted him on the back in a brotherly fashion, which caused the congregation to give a collective sigh of happiness or relief, depending on their personal feelings.

The ceremony started and everyone relaxed into their seats.

But there was more laughter when Colin knelt down and, written in indelible ink on the bottom of his shoes, were the words 'HELP ME'.

Chapter Ninety-Four

The reception was at the Pont de la Tour restaurant near Tower Bridge. It was closed for the day and, as Aiden looked around him, he was well pleased with what he saw.

He loved this restaurant anyway, but seeing the extra touches, from the decorated tables to the seven-tier wedding cake in white and silver, pleased him.

Jade had excelled herself, and he smiled gratefully at her as he saw the reaction of Agnes and Colin. This wedding was his gift to her, and he had made sure that his mother had fuck-all to do with any of it. If it had been left to Reeva, it would have been a garish and over-the-top event. Reeva had wanted to give her daughter the wedding that she never had. As Jade remarked, the dress Reeva had liked would not have looked out of place on Miss Brazil at the Miss World competition. He could only imagine it.

He greeted the guests with his sister and her husband, while the boys kept their mother as far away from the drink as possible. Tony Brown had his work cut out because they had all asked him to try and keep her under control. But no one was really holding out much hope. She had started on the champagne early in the morning and was already louder than everyone else. She looked good, though, in a smart, well-tailored grey silk ensemble with high heels and a small fascinator on her crazy hair – Jade had seen to that. She had also arranged for a make-up artist, so Reeva didn't have her usual thick eyeliner and bright red lipstick. Silk purses and sows' ears came to mind, as he smiled at his mother brightly. The photos would look amazing, at least.

At the top table, Annie looked swamped, surrounded by all her grandchildren, and as Colin and Timmy both shook her hand and kissed her, Aiden nodded with pleasure. She deserved a fuss; she was a game old bird.

Eric Palmer, in pride of place at the top table, was positively beaming at everyone, and Aiden stopped to have a few words. It was a good atmosphere and everyone was on best behaviour.

'That young Peter Gunn is a fucking rascal, eh?'

'What are you talking about, Eric?'

Eric was still chuckling away as he said, 'The shoes! "HELP ME!" I laughed like a drain!'

Aiden had not found it the least bit amusing himself, but he knew better than to say anything churlish, so he answered jovially, 'He will fucking pay for that! Cheeky little fucker.'

They laughed together at the skulduggery of youth.

Chapter Ninety-Five

Agnes looked at her big handsome husband and felt herself finally relax. There had been a part of her that had worried he might do a runner before the big day. But now here they were together, surrounded by her family and friends, and she felt the urge to weep. She placed a hand on her belly and wondered if her child was as aware of her as she was of it. These were exciting times for her, and now she had to forget the past and get on with her future. It was the strangest feeling that she could begin to live outside of her brothers and her mother – it was heady stuff. All her life, she had been dictated to, smothered, and her only escape had been the Church. She had once seen herself accepting holy orders and entering a convent. She wondered now if that had been her way of rebelling against her mother's lifestyle and her brothers' constant surveillance; the more *good* she became, the less she had in common with any of them. And yet now she had met and married a man who was, to all intents and purposes, her brother Aiden's double. But there was something about him and, whatever it was, she was so attracted to him.

She was nervous, as any young bride would be, but she convinced herself that she would be happy with this handsome man of hers. She was desperate to be happy with him and she was determined. After all, she had fought for him, for this day, and she had got it. As he kissed her tenderly on the lips, she knew that, whatever happened, this really was the best day of her life.

Chapter Ninety-Six

'Honestly, Reeva, I despair of you at times!'

Reeva laughed loudly and pulled Tony into her arms, kissing him on the lips. 'Shut up, Tone! I'm just enjoying my daughter's wedding day, that's all! Fucking hell, can't I even do that?'

Tony kissed her back, but it was just to shut her up.

The meal had been perfect, the toasts had been drunk and the room had a festive atmosphere and, as the first few bars of Diana Ross singing 'You Are Everything' played, Colin Clark took his new wife's hand and swept her on to the dance floor. They made a handsome couple and, as he held her tightly to him, there was a small round of applause. Colin was loving all the attention and, as he twirled her around and enjoyed the reaction, he was as shocked as everyone else when Aiden walked on to the dance floor and cut in.

Unsure what to do, Colin stood there for a few seconds before handing his new bride over to her brother, who, giving a mock bow, continued the dance with Agnes as if it was the most normal thing in the world.

Everyone watching was uneasy, uncertain as to how to react. After all, this was the bride and groom's first dance together as man and wife! There were plenty of eager faces wondering what the upshot was going to be for this little escapade. It was evident to everyone in the room that Aiden O'Hara was making a point. Gradually other couples joined them on the floor, but no one could fail to notice that the bride was near to tears and the groom was drinking a large Scotch at the bar with a face like thunder. So much for Aiden's wonderful speech saying how he had gained a brother and how happy he was for his sister and her new husband. Aiden had just basically fucked him over in front of all the guests. It was a deep humiliation, and there was nothing Colin could do.

Timmy Clark's jaw was set, and he stood close to his brother in case he decided he wanted to reclaim his new wife. That was exactly what Aiden wanted, of course, and Timmy was not going to give him the satisfaction.

Jade sat and watched Aiden and wished that she had a large hammer, because at this moment in time she would happily fell that fucker of hers to the ground. He just had to ruin everything. It was like he enjoyed these displays of petulance, because that was all it was.

Even Reeva, as drunk as she was, noticed, and for a few seconds a terrible feeling of dread washed over her.

Tony said quietly, 'Fucking hell, he could not even give her that.'

Eric Palmer was shaking his head as if he could not believe what he was seeing, and all the brothers watched without even a small smile on any of their faces.

It had ruined the day, and everyone was aware of that. Especially Agnes Clark.

Chapter Ninety-Seven

Tony and Reeva were listening to Jade as she berated Aiden about his behaviour. They were back at Reeva's – it seemed that was where they always gravitated, no matter what the occasion.

Aiden Junior, who had loved the wedding, was now lying in his bed at his nanny's, listening fearfully to the argument going on below him. His new suit was hanging on the back of the bedroom door, and his excitement at wearing it was long gone. The wedding that had been so much fun had suddenly become full of undercurrents, and he knew that it was because of his dad dancing with his Auntie Aggs when he wasn't supposed to. He knew that his uncles were not happy, and neither was his nanny or his mum. He closed his eyes tightly because he was sick and tired of hearing it.

Downstairs, Jade was shouting at the top of her voice, her anger for once finally getting the better of her. 'You are a cunt, Aiden! And you of all people should have known better!'

Aiden shrugged nonchalantly, his arms open wide, saying, 'I gave her away. I was acting as any father would have done!' He had convinced himself of this now. That was a knack he had when it suited him; he could justify anything when he set his mind to it.

Reeva joined in. 'But you are not her father, are you?'

Aiden laughed sarcastically as he shouted, 'I am the *only* father she ever knew. She was a fucking *whodunnit* like the rest of us. I mean, be fair, Mum, if you don't know who the culprit was, how the fuck could anyone else, eh? Answer me that, clever bollocks.'

Patsy shook his head in disbelief. 'Don't you fucking take it out on Mum because you fucked up, Ade. *You* ruined her day and that is the end of it.'

'Fucking right and all, and you were all warning *me* to be good!'

Even Jade had to smile at that one. 'I think you owe your sister and Colin an apology, Aiden.'

Aiden stood up abruptly and poured himself another glass of Scotch. Taking a large swig, he said to Jade maliciously, 'Never *fucking* happening, lady.'

Porrick and Eugene banged out of the house then, and Patsy watched them go in despair, but he knew that, like himself, they couldn't listen to any more tonight.

The damage had been done, and there was nothing anybody could do to change that.

Annie walked into the lounge from the kitchen. She looked heartbroken and, looking at her grandson, she said sadly, 'I never thought I would ever say this to you, Aiden, especially after some of the stunts you have pulled over the years. But I was ashamed of you today. You showed yourself for the petty, vindictive fucker you really are. Now, if you will all excuse me, I am going home. I have had enough.'

Tony Brown used the opportunity to get away too. 'Come on, Annie, I will walk you home, darling.'

Without bothering to wish anyone a good night, Annie walked

from the room, and even Aiden O'Hara had the grace to look ashamed.

When they heard the front door close behind them, Reeva walked over to her eldest son and, looking him in the eye, she said loudly, 'She has cancer. Terminal. Dr Metcalf told me. He is not supposed to, but he was worried about her. She doesn't know I know. But the one thing that she wanted to see before she died was her only granddaughter get married. Well, you fucking naused that up for her, didn't you? Because it's always about you, isn't it?'

Aiden looked so devastated, even Patsy felt a sneaking pity for him, until he said nastily, 'Well, I had a good fucking teacher, didn't I?'

That was when Reeva slapped him and pandemonium broke out.

Chapter Ninety-Eight

Annie died five days later. She had advanced-stage bone cancer. She went peacefully in her sleep, and her passing was as unobtrusive as she had always been in life.

Reeva took it badly, and Agnes came back from her honeymoon in Marbella to attend the funeral with her new husband. Everyone was devastated, but no one more so than Aiden, who, as always with him, blamed someone else for his own bad behaviour.

It was another stick to beat Colin Clark with. Aiden's reasoning was that if Colin had never touched his little sister, if he had not encroached on his family's life, his nan would never have had reason to talk to him so harshly.

Annie's passing broke him in more ways than one. For the first time in his life, Aiden O'Hara was feeling an emotion called *guilt*, and he did not like it one bit.

Chapter Ninety-Nine

Aiden was feeling relaxed. He had just spent a few hours in the company of a young girl called Priscilla. She wasn't exactly a raving beauty, but she was all right; it wasn't like she needed a bag over her head. By the same token she would never win any competitions for her good looks. Her attraction for Aiden was that she possessed the body of a porn queen. And she was all natural. She had tits like fucking barrage balloons, heavy and full, not a hint of silicone. They were as natural as her blond snatch. She was built like women should be: nice knockers, a tiny waist and an arse that you could lose a puppy in. It had been a while since he had found himself such a little star.

The icing on the cake was that she was as thick as fucking shit. She couldn't count past fifty, and she had a problem reading *Hello!* magazine. She just looked at the pictures. She was perfect for him; she didn't question him or demand anything from him like his fucking phone number or his undying devotion. All he had to do was ring her up and arrange a meet. That was it, the extent of his involvement. She wasn't exactly a sparkling conversationist, but she suited him because of that. He didn't want a fucking candidate for Mensa. All he wanted was a fucking shag. And that was exactly what she provided.

When she wasn't with him she lap-danced at one of his clubs

344

and, once again, that suited him down to the fucking ground. He wasn't looking for a love job. Unlike Jade, who could hold forth on politics, current affairs and who was respected as an intelligent woman, Priscilla was like a pet: you stroked her regularly, fed her and made sure she was happy. And that was the height of her ambition. She was an uncomplicated person and, sometimes, that was all that any man really wanted. A completely brainless and purely physical fuck, devoid of the drama and mind games that most women expected.

As he walked into the club, he smiled sneakily. Joshie D was bringing his cousin's second in command to meet them tonight. Aiden really did want to know exactly who he was dealing with, even though they had already provided exactly what they had promised. The product that they had been given was top grade, there was no doubting that. But Aiden still wanted to meet the distributor face to face. He didn't have anything against Joshie D, but Aiden suspected that he was a front man who was more interested in getting himself famous. He had achieved that and all power to him. But, as Aiden had remarked on more than one occasion, Joshie D was bound to bring them to the notice of the powers-that-be. As he got more famous, his life would be scrutinised – especially a life that had everything the news-papers wanted. He was black, he swung both ways, and he courted publicity. That could only end in fucking tears. This wasn't a fucking Guy Ritchie film, this was real fucking life.

This was what he wanted to explain to the men he was meeting tonight. He already knew from his people on the ground that the men from Jamaica were suspicious of Joshie because of his sexuality anyway. It seemed that the Jamaicans were not as forgiving as the rest of the world. That they didn't really accept alternative lifestyles and he had heard that they were more than happy to bypass young Joshie if that was at all possible. Well, that suited Aiden; he wanted that preening cunt out of the way. He didn't trust him – and it wasn't because he was a fucking drama queen. He didn't trust him because he knew that his mind would never really be on the earn, it would always be on his DJing.

Aiden had arranged for him to DJ at his nightclubs, and he had made sure that it paid well. The clubs had benefited too, because people were queuing up to listen to him. He had to admit that the bloke had a fucking huge following. He had also invested in raves, and he had to admit once again that Joshie did pull the punters in. He was good at what he did, and he was on his way to bigger and better things. For Aiden, the sooner that Joshie did that, the better for everyone concerned. So, basically, it was a win–win for all of them.

He walked through the club slowly; he liked this place. Jade hated the lap-dancing clubs, and he could never understand that about her. She had no problem with the brothels, so he couldn't see what her problem was with girls dancing around a fucking pole. It was lucrative and fucking legal – that was the real attraction. Her problem really was with him, and his forays into the clubs and the ladies who worked in them. She loathed that he took up with these girls, and that everyone knew about it. A lot of the girls were more than happy to flaunt the relationship, and act like they were somehow suddenly special. That was what really bothered her, but he believed that she should not let it all get to her. It was one of life's fucking puzzles, because Jade knew that the woman had not been born yet who could ever replace her.

He stood for a few minutes and looked around him with pride. This place took thousands of pounds every day of the week. He had watched Jade as she had chosen everything, from the wallpaper to the carpets. She had designed it all and, as always, she had been spot on with what the punters wanted and what would work in the space she had been given. That was what she was so good at: she utilised everything and she made sure that every scrap of space was used to its best advantage. She even ensured that the girls they employed were given lessons in money management so they didn't piss it all up the wall. She reminded them that they had a very short shelf life, and that, within a few years, they would be replaced by younger, fitter girls, but that if they used their heads they could come out of this with enough money to either start a business, or even purchase a property of their own. Jade had always had her eye out for the girls that worked for them, which is why the girls wanted to work with them in the first place. Even though many of them were willing to do the dirty on her, they still knew that she, at least, had their best interests at heart.

He went to the bar and, walking behind it, he poured himself out a large Scotch. This club was really fabulous. The counter of the bar was black granite, and it had cost a small fortune. But it had been worth it. Jade had argued that with him and she had been right. She said that people got what they paid for and if you offered them a fabulous space they would happily pay through the nose for it. It was a private members' club, and the fees were not fucking cheap. But the men who frequented it, and the small female clientele, loved the look of it, and also the knowledge that they didn't have to worry about any of their antics being made public. It was all a big part of the club's success.

As he settled himself on a leather couch, he sipped his drink and waited patiently for his guests. He observed himself in the mirrored walls and was pleased with what he saw. He still looked good and he knew that was a big part of his charm. He was a lucky man in more ways than one. Women liked him for a variety of different reasons, and he used his looks, his position and his chat to get whatever he wanted from them. That was how Aiden O'Hara saw everything in his life – as no more than a means to an end. He was looking forward to this meeting, because he wanted to bring about a change in the hierarchy, and he would accomplish that no matter what.

Chapter One Hundred

Patsy was not sure what exactly was bugging him but something didn't feel right.

He had felt odd all day. He had gone to pick up the proceeds from one of the open houses, the new politically correct term for the brothels that were still a huge part of their empire. Another one of Jade's clever marketing techniques – even the girls who worked there felt good about being referred to as 'recreational workers'. As Jade had often argued, there was no reason not to give the people who worked for them a completely different take on the job they did. She reasoned it gave them the feeling of being part of something that wasn't seedy and made them feel that they were valued members of the team. When he had told Aiden that he thought that was all complete bollocks, Aiden had pointed out with a sarcastic laugh that, as Jade was also fond of saying, a happy workforce was also a productive workforce, and none of them could argue with that. They were coining it in, and that was not a fucking exaggeration either. They couldn't ever have foreseen such a huge turnover.

Jade had systematically eradicated the younger element that was once on the payroll, and now they ran adult brothels for an adult clientele. Except, of course, for when the Arabs arranged to take over the houses for a whole night to initiate their sons into the wonders of the European female. Those boys were normally about fifteen, but they were used to being given what they wanted and that was exactly what they provided. Jade charged the Arabs through the nose, and the girls were guaranteed an easy night with a good payment at the end of it. It was a different world now, and that was never more noticeable than when he went to the open houses. There was almost an atmosphere of gaiety and, as everyone concerned was earning a fucking fortune, that was to be expected. Fucking hell, Jade even made sure the girls were given tests every month, and she was adamant that they took precautions even though everyone knew some of the girls would still ride bareback for an extra few quid. That was only to be expected. But if they ever tested positive for any kind of STD they were politely shown the door.

In the first house Patsy had visited, all had seemed as usual, but there had been an undercurrent he just couldn't put his finger on. There was nothing blatantly wrong, but he had a bad feeling and it wouldn't leave him. It had been the same at the other houses and, even though he couldn't say what was exactly bothering him, he knew that there was something not right. In fact, Porrick had argued that he was imagining things, but for some reason he could not shake off the feeling. It had remained with him all day.

Now he was in the pub with Eugene and he didn't like what he was hearing.

'The thing was, Patsy, I arrived at the safe house and the money owed was paid without a murmur. But that was the strange thing, no chit-chat. Normally we all have a laugh, you know, the usual. I felt it the other week, and I just shrugged it off. But today it was like they couldn't wait for us to fuck off. Considering we pay their wages, I saw that as a bit of an insult.'

Patsy listened intently but he didn't offer an opinion; he knew better than to say anything until he knew what the score was. He needed to talk this over with Aiden and Jade. The last thing they needed was to cause a big drama when it wasn't warranted. But, if he was being honest, he believed that there was something iffy going on. But he couldn't even put a cause to it. What could possibly be occurring that they didn't have wind of? He shook his head and sighed.

'Come on, it's time to get to the meeting.'

They left the pub together quietly, but each of them had their own thoughts on the situation.

Chapter One Hundred and One

Marvin Hendry was born and raised in Jamaica. He was a Kingston boy who more than had his creds. He was known as a dangerous man, and that was not an epithet given lightly in the Jamaican underworld. There was an abundance of bad fuckers – the real knack was knowing how to be the biggest and baddest fucker of them all. That was something that came naturally to him; he had no conscience and he had no real interest in anything that did not pertain directly to him or his needs. He was known for his extreme viciousness and also for his astute business acumen. The men who worked with him were all known for doing exactly what Marvin requested or expected.

He had cherry-picked the entire workforce, personally requesting their services. They were mostly from the poorest townships and had each come to his attention because they were not only violent but were intelligent enough to use their brains when anything went wrong. Anyone could shoot their way out of trouble – that was the easiest fucking answer in the Caribbean; everyone had a gun. But if the people used their sense and their mouths, Marvin knew that they were just what he was looking for. Marvin appreciated the usefulness of these men and women; he understood that they were the real backbone of his business and also how expendable they were. That was nothing personal as far as he was concerned – that was just real life. He gave them a chance that they could never have had without him, and they knew that themselves. If you worked for Marvin, you were fucking rocking, he made sure of that. A great deal of his reputation was reliant on the people who worked for him. That was how the world worked. Young guns were falling over themselves to be a part of his organisation. He didn't need to do any recruitment drives. They were lining up to be taken on board. It was a fucking honour to work for him and he made sure that everyone knew that.

He had made a point of bringing these people on, of making sure that everyone knew exactly who they were and who they worked for. Marvin knew the importance of advertising. That was why he was so successful. Until him, the drugs trade had been hampered by feuding gangs, by complete morons who had thought it was enough just to muscle in on other people's fucking hard work. And it wasn't just in Jamaica that it was rife, it was *everywhere* that he supplied. He was a legend, he made sure of that. It was what he was good at and it was how he had made his brand so powerful.

The difference was that he had been born into money and privilege; he had been privately educated but he had known that, unlike his father – a successful businessman – he would always be attracted to the darker side of life. From his first tentative drug deal, selling third-grade grass to his school friends, he had loved the whole experience of being outside the law. It had been a revelation to him in that he had found his natural medium. His father's wealth and contacts had been what had kept him out of prison on more than one occasion, and he had learned every time by his mistakes. Now Marvin saw himself as untouchable. He made sure that no one in his organisation could ever get close enough to accuse him of anything even remotely sinister. He had legitimate businesses that accounted for his wealthy lifestyle, and he had enough people to put him anywhere at any time should that be required. In short, Marvin Hendry believed that he had covered his bases, and covered them well. He felt he had done the impossible and, in many ways, he had, because he was still at the top of his game after ten years and, in Jamaica, that was not an easy feat. It was a small island for a start and, worse still, there were far too many people after too few prizes. His family and his own intelligence had ensured that he could happily trade with the minimum of restraint. He had also made a point of paying off everyone in his orbit who might have the means of bringing him down. Even his own father had finally come round to his way of thinking.

As he walked into the premises that Aiden O'Hara owned with his crew in tow, Marvin was impressed. London wasn't Jamaica, and he was very aware of that fact. He was awed by the luxury of the reception area alone. This was what *he* wanted, what he saw as the next step for his workforce. Aiden O'Hara was what he ultimately wanted to be. Marvin's dream was to relocate to London and ply his different trades from here. He knew that, unlike Jamaica, London was an open door for anybody who could provide not just the product but, more importantly, the guarantee of an endless supply of it. The best product that these fuckers had *ever* had access to.

He had used Joshie because he was blood, he was family. But, as far as Marvin was concerned, Joshie would never be any real family of his. The boy was a fucking strutting queen – an embarrassment. Even his own father was suspicious of him. His saving grace was that he was doing so well as a DJ. Although Marvin could not help wondering just how well he would have done in Jamaica or any of the other islands, because while here he wore his Jamaican heritage like a badge, Joshie didn't have the presence needed to survive in the real Jamaican environment – yet. If Joshie made it here, he would automatically be welcomed back in Jamaica with open arms. Only then would he be one of their own.

Marvin knew in his gut that Aiden O'Hara would be more than agreeable about rowing that fucker out once and for all. Aiden had already given his cousin another fucking way of life – the way of life that he really wanted. Marvin appreciated that even though he couldn't stand the weirdo. He was family at the end of the day.

As he was shown through to the offices to see Aiden O'Hara, Marvin felt a great vibe, because he liked everything he had heard about this Aiden. He seemed to be a man after his own heart. They were of an age, and they were both men who knew exactly what they wanted, and made sure that they got it. That was how you controlled your workforce: you made sure that they felt they were earning enough for the time being. Eventually, if they were shrewd enough, you pushed them up the ladder and made them even richer. That was the main aim of everyone that you singled out. That way they either sank without a trace or they proved their worth.

Marvin had left his crew in the lap-dancing club – he knew that they would not be invited into the actual meet; they would be entertained, of course – he wasn't worried about that. He would have insisted on exactly the same terms. The job they did was never about advertising the meeting they attended, and never letting anyone know more than was deemed necessary;

his workers only ever knew enough to guarantee they did the job that he paid them for. Basically that meant he kept his meetings private – the people around him never knew more than was good for them.

Marvin Hendry had always made a point of guaranteeing to everyone who purchased his product that not one person in his organisation could ever bring any of them down. Once his people had completed what he had arranged for them to do, they were out of it, forgotten about. Marvin made sure that every step was a separate venture. No one person knew everything about who they were dealing with and, if anyone was a bit too inquisitive about the job in hand and what it entailed, they disappeared. Just disappeared without a fucking trace. They could never be linked back to him or anyone who worked for him. He knew better than to advertise his fucking villainy to the world; he didn't need to be a big man in a small pond. From the very beginning, he had just walked in and taken everything over without even one fucking person confronting him. His style of business was not the usual. He had slowly and quietly wiped out his opponents, while assuring certain other people of his friendship – meaning they now all worked for him.

As Marvin entered the VIP bar, Aiden O'Hara was standing there with his hand out to greet him and, as they shook hands, both recognised their similarities. Aiden looked at Marvin, and he instinctively liked him from his dreads to his handmade shoes. The man was class. Marvin looked at Aiden and knew that he could work with him. Marvin had taken in everything about him from his bespoke suit to his expensive dentistry. As they summed each other up, they both felt that they were going to get on like the proverbial house on fire.

Marvin Hendry looked around the empty bar; he recognised that this was Aiden's way of welcoming him, of making him feel at ease. The two of them were alone to discuss whatever needed to be spoken about, without either of them having to worry about what might be said. And, as they retired to a small table, he saw that there was every kind of whisky and rum there waiting to be poured.

As he sat down, Marvin looked at Aiden and said, 'Really? Cockspur rum. I'm impressed.'

Aiden laughed heartily. 'I know it's more Antiguan or Barbadian, but I think it's a fucking good drop of rum.'

Marvin poured himself a large glass. 'I was never a lover of the Appleton shit, you know. That is more for the tourists these days. So much is for tourism now. Not that I haven't jumped on that fucking bandwagon myself.'

Aiden grinned craftily. 'I think that me and you could broker a really good deal for everyone concerned, Marvin. I know I'm the only person you've dealt with so far. But I can tell you now that I am willing to offer you a wonderful opportunity. I can shift anything that you can bring into the country.'

Marvin stretched languidly; this was just what he wanted to hear. Smiling widely, he said confidently, 'That's what I came here for. I am here to tell you, Aiden, that I want an ally in London – a partner, if you like. I have achieved everything that I possibly can in Jamaica. But Jamaica is a small island, full of fucking wannabe gangsters. They can purchase a gun, but that doesn't make them a serious threat. They are amateurs, and that doesn't help when you're trying to build a proper business. I'm sure you understand what I am saying. I have had to remove young men who, if they had one ounce of sense, would have known from the off that they could *never* fucking defeat me.

It grieves me that so many young men died because they didn't have the sense to see that a gun could never guarantee them anything other than their own demise. Jamaica is still like the Wild West: too many young men thinking that they can just walk in with a brand-new gun, believing that would be enough for them to take what they wanted. It breaks my heart, Aiden, you know? But, eventually, I made them all aware of the fact that I was not going to suffer fools gladly.'

Aiden watched warily as Marvin took a large drink of his rum.

'I think that it's time for me to spread my wings and expand my enterprises. I think that between us we could accomplish a lot. *If* we could work together. You know I have the product, and it's the best fucking product you will ever get your hands on – I know that's a fact. What I'm offering *you* is the chance to distribute it to others alongside me. I can guarantee an unlimited supply, as you are already aware. I will also make sure that it arrives here as and when needed. I think that together we could really sew the market up.'

Aiden O'Hara sipped his whisky and, as he watched Marvin Hendry light up a huge joint, he saw a man after his own heart. Aiden could always suss out the people he should associate with. Those people were few and far between but Eric Palmer had always trusted what he called his gut instinct. He had already researched Marvin Hendry, and everything that he had learned about him had convinced him that he was a man to be reckoned with. Almost everyone he had spoken to had nothing but good things to say about Marvin. That had pleased Aiden because he really wanted to work with this man. It was more than enough that Marvin Hendry could provide such a pure product on a regular basis, but the added bonus that Marvin could also become his partner, and thereby give him the access to the product he needed, was the icing on the cake. Marvin needed him, and he needed Marvin. This was the perfect scenario.

Aiden O'Hara was delighted that he had not had to talk Marvin round; it had almost been too easy really. But they were of like minds; both knew they could each offer something to the other. That was how people like them could establish a new line of business. How long this mutual love affair would last only time could tell. But, until there was a problem, they were more than happy to play at grown-ups. That was the nature of the world they lived in, and that was why they were both well aware of what they were taking on.

'I think we could come to some arrangement, Marvin. I appreciate how candid you have been tonight. That was why I made sure there was only the two of us. I knew that together we might strike a good bargain.'

Aiden poured them both more drinks and, when they shook hands, they were both really pleased with themselves. Aiden had brokered a deal that could change the face of the British drug scene and also allow him to drop the people he had been dealing with so far, who were more than ready to be pensioned off in his opinion.

Chapter One Hundred and Two

Jade was tired, but she had to do what was expected of her and meet up with Aiden and Marvin Hendry as arranged. Aiden loved showing her off and telling people that they were together and had a child. He wasn't acting; she knew that he really did adore her and that he loved to introduce her to people. When they were out together she could not fault him; he gave her his undivided attention and treated her like a queen. It was ironic that he could then be unfaithful to her without a second fucking thought when she wasn't around.

The thing that had always worried her was Aiden's willingness to physically harm those girls he was so happy to use for his own fucking ends, especially if he thought they might cause discord between the two of them. His argument to her was always that he had only ever loved her. She knew that there wasn't another woman who could ever replace her; even if she left him, she believed that Aiden would never bring another woman permanently into his life. She would always be the only one for him and, in many ways, that was a hard cross for her to bear. Knowing that she was so important to him was not an easy way to live her life because, as much as she loved him, his love for her came with so much pressure. Aiden loved her with a frightening intensity and that was something he believed she reciprocated because she had always protected him – more so than he could ever deserve. She could not help herself, she did love him.

He knew everything about her past, that she had been used by men since being a young child, that she had overcome everything that had happened to her and had eventually risen up in a world that she loathed but was all she had ever known. The fact that he had never once questioned her, or used it against her, was something she could never forget. After all this time he still saw her as everything he had ever wanted. But every fucking tart he took up with broke her heart a little bit more.

As she walked into the lap-dancing club – a club that she had designed and watched over until it had been finished but a place that she vowed she would never again step inside once it was up and running unless she had to – she pulled her shoulders back and straightened herself. She walked through the place as if she owned it, which, of course, she did. But she avoided these places like the plague, because they were where her Aiden trawled for his newest fucks. She knew that these girls never lasted that long and they meant nothing to him – God knew *she* had stepped in to stop him harming them. But it still rankled. That he didn't try to hide it from her or from anyone was what really hurt her, but she had too much pride to let anyone think that she gave a flying fuck.

She walked into the bar with a big smile on her face, and no one would ever know just how hard it had been for her to meet here on one of Aiden's hunting grounds. Aiden, as ever, treated her with the utmost respect, and introduced her to Marvin Hendry as the love of his life. And Jade played along as always.

Chapter One Hundred and Three

Reeva was annoyed. Tony was on the missing list, and her daughter was acting like she was the bad bastard because she had had a few fucking drinks. Well, *she* wasn't fucking pregnant, so, as far as Reeva was concerned, she could do what she fucking liked. She didn't need Miss fucking Goody Two-Shoes telling her anything, thank you very much! Who the fuck did she think she was? Reeva was not in the mood for this shit. She was never in the mood when her kids decided it was a great moment to point out her fucking failings. Like she needed *anyone* to remind her, especially when she was feeling pleasantly drunk.

'Leave me the fuck alone, Agnes. So I am drunk! Let's be really honest here, it's not like it's the first time, is it? Love me or loathe me, darling, the one thing we know is that, for all my faults, I have always put my hand up when needed.'

Agnes could quite cheerfully clump her mum one, and she would not even regret it. Her mum was never going to change. Every now and then she would just disappear and, when she finally came home, she would be so drunk that she wouldn't even know who any of them were. In the past Aiden would take over. He would put her to bed, strip her off, make her drink a pint of water, even hold her head when she spewed up everywhere. Aiden had always argued that she was entitled to let rip every so often, that she was still a young woman and she needed to let off steam every now and again.

But Agnes didn't agree with Aiden's reasoning. Here she was – a married woman who didn't even live here any more and she was still expected to come over and sort it out. Reeva was a grandmother, and soon she would have another grand-child. The one thing Agnes was sure of was that she would never leave her child in Reeva's care.

'You are one mardy fucking mare, Aggs. Do you even realise that? A word of advice, lady: you have lumbered yourself with Colin Clark and, believe me, you will get the shock of your fucking life, I can guarantee that. Because, as fucking good as he is being now, it won't last, sweetheart. You should take a leaf out of Jade's book and deliberately look the other way. Because, darling, you have tied yourself to a man who couldn't be fucking faithful if his life depended on it. The only reason he is being so good now is because he knows that if Aiden heard even a *whisper* that he was doing the dirty on you he would kill that fucker stone dead.'

Agnes knew that her mother was speaking the truth and that was why it hurt so much. She wasn't a complete fool, no matter what everyone else might think. Trust Reeva to tell her everything she really didn't want to hear. But that was her mum all over, especially when she had had a few drinks. As Porrick had once proclaimed, if you can't hack the truth, keep as far away from Reeva as humanly possible. It didn't mean though that it was right to just allow her to say whatever she wanted to.

'Thanks a lot, Mum. I'm pregnant and you tell me that my baby's dad is a fucking womaniser.'

Reeva was too drunk to hear the hurt in her daughter's voice, and far too drunk to care. Reeva was at the stage where all she was interested in was saying her piece, which she was now even more determined to do. After all, as she reasoned with herself, if she didn't, then who would? That's what she'd like to know.

She liked Colin Clark, but her daughter needed a fucking wake-up call. Colin Clark was a man who didn't have a fucking loyal bone in his body. It was a truth, and one she felt that her girl deserved to know, sooner rather than later. Her daughter was a fool – a romantic who couldn't see that the fucker had played her. She could write the fucking script.

Suddenly she was all apologies. 'Look, Agnes, I would not hurt you for the world – you are my daughter, my fucking baby. I'm so sorry, sweetheart. Colin Clark is a handsome fuck but he will never be faithful. He is not capable of being with one woman. I'm not saying that he won't love you dearly, but he will always chase a bit of strange. Why do you think Aiden hates him being with you so fucking much? Because he knows that they are so fucking similar. A pair of fucking male slags. I'm telling you, darling, the sooner you accept that, the better off you will be.'

While Agnes accepted the truth of her mother's words she knew that her mum would never have said a fucking thing if she wasn't so drunk. Reeva would probably have no memory of this conversation after tonight. But Agnes would never ever forget. How could she? This was something that would stay with her all her life.

The real hurt was that her mother couldn't have said all this to her when she was sober. That would have carried more weight with her because she would have listened to her mother and what she had to say for herself.

Agnes had accepted that she couldn't ever trust her husband

and she felt guilty that her relationship with him had destroyed his with Aiden. Colin was terrified of Aiden and how he would react in the future and that was something she knew he was right to worry about. Aiden saw her as his little sister and also as his responsibility. She didn't think he would ever come to terms with the fact that she had let him down by getting pregnant.

The sad thing was that she really loved Colin but she had begun to see him for what he really was even before they got married.

She suddenly understood just how strong her mum had been when it had really mattered; she had kept all her children and loved them in her own way. It was only now, young and pregnant and finally understanding the enormity of what carrying a child really meant, that Agnes could finally appreciate her mother's determination to have her kids without any kind of help whatsoever.

She remembered once, on Aiden's birthday, Reeva had made him a wonderful cake. It had been a real work of art. And after they had all sung 'Happy Birthday', and he had blown out the candles, she remembered Aiden hugging a crying Reeva tightly and saying earnestly, so sadly, 'Come on, Mum. Stop fucking beating yourself up. You were only fourteen, Mum, and you fought to keep me, remember? And I love you for that. Mad fucking cow that you are, you always did your best for us all.'

And that was the truth; it was why they always forgave her when she caused murders. She would fight to the death for any of her kids.

As Agnes watched her mother lying on the sofa, ready to fall asleep, she wondered if she could ever be as strong as her. She was young, and she was nervous about what the future would bring. But, the strange thing was, she knew deep inside that, no matter what *did* happen, she could always depend on her mum and her brothers – and Tony, of course. She still wasn't sure if that was a good thing or a bad thing – only time would tell.

She knew that Aiden wasn't enamoured of Colin any more and that was because of her – Aiden and her other brothers had lost a lot of respect for him. He had taken her without the permission of any of them, and that would always be a fucking problem because it was something they saw as underhand and sneaky. Which, of course, had been the real excitement for her. The sneaking around and the stolen moments together were like nothing she had ever experienced before in her life. It had never occurred to her until it was too late that there might be consequences to her actions. But now they were married and she had to make the best of it. She covered her mum up with a blanket and, as she tucked it in, Reeva opened her eyes and, smiling gently, she whispered, 'You will always be my beautiful girl, Agnes. Never forget that, my darling.'

Agnes kissed her mother softly on the forehead and she left her to sleep.

Chapter One Hundred and Four

Jade liked Marvin Hendry and the feeling was mutual. Now that the meeting was over, and the business was sorted, the bar was packed out with men from both sides. She was pleased that she was the only woman there, because she knew that Aiden had arranged it to be so, understanding that she could always hold her own, and that she could be trusted to make him look good. She sat between him and Marvin as requested, and made sure that the conversation was serious but also witty. She could feel Marvin's interest in her; she could tell that he admired her. Her reputation always preceded her, but the days of caring about that were long gone. The one thing she had learned many moons ago was that there was nothing that anyone could do about gossip; the best thing was to embrace it and make it work in your favour.

Aiden was giving her his undivided attention, and Marvin was impressed about that. She looked amazing, but then she knew how to dress to impress.

Looking around the bar, she watched as Patsy and his brothers made sure that the men who were with Marvin were being looked after. The music was loud enough to be heard, but not so loud that it intruded on private conversations. The bar staff had been handpicked and were all males and, although not subservient, they were very discreet and they made sure that no one's glass was empty for any length of time. Jade had also arranged for Marvin and his posse to have exclusive use of the VIP room if they wanted it. She had a feeling that Marvin might offer it to his workforce but she sensed that he would not avail himself of it. He was a man who didn't need to pay for a woman, that much was obvious to her. He wouldn't take one for free either; as he smiled at her, she knew that the only woman he wanted was *her*. She understood that it wasn't because she was Aiden's woman – it was because he liked grown-ups.

She could sense immediately that Marvin had no interest in the club at all. Most men spent their time asking about the girls, how old they were, how much they had to spend to get them interested. It was embarrassing, really, just how fucking scummy most men were, if given the opportunity. It didn't matter how many fucking laws were brought in, there would always be certain men who would want to pay for women they didn't have to be nice to. If they paid enough, they could conveniently forget that they were someone else's daughter or niece, or some kind of female relative. That was why the girls could make so much money and that was why prostitution was the oldest profession in the world.

Aiden was smiling at her; he was as aware of Marvin's interest in her as she was, and just took it as a compliment. He never ceased to amaze her. He was either up for committing murder, or delighted that someone else saw her as he saw her. There was never a happy medium with him; everything depended on how he felt at the time. She continued to play the game, exactly as was expected of her. But she couldn't shake the feeling that there was something off, she just didn't know what that might be. She knew she wasn't the only person to feel that there was something wrong. Until Aiden saw fit to tell them what was occurring, they had no choice except to wait and see.

Chapter One Hundred and Five

Colin Clark and his brother, Timmy, were quiet. Colin was well aware that his brother was very annoyed with him, and he couldn't blame him. As Timmy had pointed out frequently during the course of the day, he had been the cause of all this fucking upset. Colin couldn't deny it – Timmy was absolutely fucking spot on. Talk about stating the fucking obvious! But, by the same token, what could he do about it now? This was his only chance to make some kind of sense out of what had happened.

'Do you know what really fucks me off, Colin? That you honestly couldn't see something like this coming. Did you really think that Aiden was just going to let you walk away without a fucking mark on you? Are you really that big a fool?'

Colin Clark pulled into the parking space and switched off the engine. Turning in his seat he looked at his brother and, taking a deep breath, he said, 'Do you really think I need you to keep reminding me of what I have done? Do you not think that I already know what a complete fuck-up I have made? It's hardly like I haven't worked it out for myself.'

Timmy Clark could see that his brother was regretting his actions and trying his hardest to make amends. But it just didn't make him feel any better. Colin had ruined everything they had worked for. Even his brother's relationship with Aiden, and that had been a true friendship, was now in tatters. There was no way he could claw his way back into his good books. Timmy Clark thought that Colin had gone too far and he was his own brother, so where did that leave Aiden?

'Look, Timmy, I get it, all right? I fucking did a serious wrong one. But it doesn't matter how many times you point that out to me, it won't change anything, will it?'

Colin got out of the car and took a few deep breaths. Timmy watched his brother sadly, broken-hearted because he had basically ruined them overnight. He couldn't let him off easily; he had to make him understand just how badly he had fucked up.

Timmy stepped out of the car. 'You just fucking didn't take the time to think of what your actions might cause, Colin. Now look where we are! Look what we have to do to try and make everything all right again. And this is all because of *you*!'

Colin Clark didn't answer because he honestly didn't know how to apologise to his brother. He had really put them in a terrible position. And now Aiden had given them this 'errand', as he insisted on calling it, for tonight. Neither of them wanted anything to do with it – but they had no choice.

Timmy looked at his brother for a long moment. 'Come on, let's get this done and dusted, eh?'

Colin laughed with relief and, hugging his brother tightly, he said happily, 'Finally, bruv, you are seeing it from my point of view! Now me and Agnes are married it will settle down. Aiden knows that I will look after her and I will. I promised her that.'

Timmy smiled sadly. 'I hope so, Colin, I really do, mate.'

They walked to the house together. Timmy rang the doorbell; he was still so annoyed because he hated that it had come to this because of Colin and his fucking rank stupidity. Eric Palmer answered the door and ushered them inside. They followed him into his kitchen where he poured them large whiskies.

'Aiden said you would be coming by. Sit down, lads. I have everything you need here. I think you'll find everything in order.'

He was smiling at them happily, the books they were to pick up placed neatly on the table next to him.

'Sit down, for fuck's sake!'

Timmy looked around him at Eric's home. It was luxurious, if a bit old-fashioned. But that was to be expected – he was not a young man and his surroundings were not of great interest to him any more. He already had his credentials and he didn't feel the need to prove himself to anyone. Eric Palmer was respected by everyone who knew him, and especially by those who had ever had dealings with him. He had never felt the need to trade his wife in for a younger model who would insist on everything being as expensive as humanly possible and all put into her name. Eric Palmer was the last of the old school; a one-off these days. He was a dinosaur who had still managed to keep himself in the frame, thanks to his association with Aiden O'Hara, of course.

Eric was suddenly aware that there was something amiss. There was a bad feeling rising up inside him. Colin and Timmy Clark were both just standing in his kitchen, staring at him. He realised in a flash what the score was going to be tonight, but he didn't want to admit it. There was a part of him that had expected something like this – he was nothing if not a realist, after all. He knew Aiden O'Hara better than anyone else. He had given that boy everything he could give him, loved him like a son. He had just not wanted to believe this day would ever come.

As Colin removed the gun from the back of his trousers and walked towards him, Eric Palmer knew exactly what was going to happen – he would have done the same if it had been his call. He had gone soft in his old age; there was a time when he would have pre-empted this and struck first. Sometimes you had to speculate to accumulate, how many times had he said that same thing to Aiden? Sometimes you had to do things that were not always easy, but that might be the only option open to a person. It was about saving your own life, making sure that you got what *you* wanted – and sometimes that meant sacrificing people in your life who you cared about.

There was a bit of Eric that was impressed at Aiden's acumen; he had really thought this through. He was as great a man as Eric had always believed him to be, and this had only proved to him that he had been right about Aiden all along. This was such a fucking audacious move. He had taught the fucker well. Probably too well, but there wasn't anything he could do about that now. He smiled at Colin and said easily, 'Tell Aiden, Timmy, that I would have done exactly the same.'

The first shot hit Eric in the chest, and he dropped to his knees. The second shot hit him in the groin. He was writhing around on the floor in agony, and the third shot Colin put through his head. There was blood everywhere; it had sprayed all over the kitchen cupboards and the ceiling, and now it was making a huge, red stain on the black-and-white tiles on the kitchen floor.

Colin Clark turned and looked at his brother; he was devastated at what he had been forced to do. 'Oh, Christ, Timmy. What the fuck have we done?'

Timmy Clark took the gun off him, and sat his brother down at the kitchen table. He gave him his whisky. 'Drink that up, mate, it will do you good.'

Colin Clark downed the drink in one swallow, and then he coughed heartily because it was far too strong for him.

Behind him, Timmy Clark quickly put one bullet into the back of his brother's head.

As Colin dropped forward and slid on to the floor, Timmy wondered at a world where this could be classed as even remotely normal. But what choice did he have? Aiden O'Hara had made it very plain that this was exactly what he had to do if *he* wanted to live for any length of time. It was either one dead or both of them gone, for ever.

But, as a result of his choice, Aiden's sister had lost the father of her child, Timmy had lost a brother, and it would look like Colin was the bad bastard, caught out while trying to kill Eric Palmer. The worst of it all was that Timmy would be seen as a hero, as a man who had murdered his own flesh rather than stand by a man who would take out someone like Eric Palmer in cold blood. Aiden had even made sure that he was given some of Eric's businesses to run, and that would give the truth to the lie. It was a lie Timmy would have to live with till the day he died. There was no way Aiden was ever going to let Colin get away with sleeping with his sister and getting her pregnant. Colin should have worked that much out for himself and just once in his life thought about what the fuck he was doing. But that was a moot point now. It was over, and there was nothing anyone could do about it.

Timmy looked at his brother's body and then, picking up the ledgers, he walked away from the carnage. As angry as he was with Aiden, he knew in his heart of hearts that he couldn't fault the fucker's logic. Tonight Aiden had taken out two people and no one would ever suspect that he had a hand in any of it.

Chapter One Hundred and Six

Aiden O'Hara was holding his sister to him as tightly as possible. She was crying so loudly and shrieking as if she was in such pain that the police were more than willing to leave him to it. She was frightening *them*.

Aiden had already been on the blower and arranged things to his satisfaction. He'd made sure that the police involved were more than compensated for their troubles, and that his sister would be left in peace long enough for him to work his magic.

Reeva had sobered up in no time, and Tony and the boys had made sure that Agnes was not allowed within two feet of anyone outside of the family.

Sitting with her in her bedroom, Aiden held her until her crying stopped. Aiden was sorry for his sister – something like this was a big shock to the system. No one could deny that. It was outrageous! Who could ever have thought it possible? But, as he would explain to her when the opportunity presented itself, Colin had not been as trustworthy as they had all thought – even Colin's own brother could tell her that. After all, it was his own brother who had been forced to take him out, that was how out of control the fucker had become. Colin had murdered Eric Palmer, a man they had all loved and who had been like their own flesh and blood. Colin Clark had already been given a good earn, a serious amount of scratch, but he had wanted more. The man was a fucking disgrace; all he had needed to do was to wait and he would have been given everything he had ever dreamed of. Why would anyone want to hurt Eric Palmer? That was what Aiden would never understand, as he told anyone who came within two feet of him, especially Agnes, who could not disagree with him. She had loved Eric too.

As Agnes finally calmed down, Aiden helped her into her bed gently and he sat beside her as she tried to bring her breathing under control. She could feel her baby inside her, and she cradled her belly in her arms, wondering what the future held for them both.

'Look, Aggs, this is a very unfortunate situation, darling. I mean, who would ever have believed that Colin could have been so fucking unpredictable? But, from what Timmy says, Colin didn't seem to think that Eric was giving him his due. You can see all of the paperwork, sweetheart. That was why they had gone to Eric's in the first place. I had discussed with Eric about giving him a really lucrative business, you know, to welcome him to the family. I don't know what possessed him, darling. You would have to ask Timmy about that. He was there. At the moment, all we can do is to try and minimise the damage, you know?'

Agnes looked up at her brother; he saw the hurt and the pain in her eyes, and he wondered why that didn't really bother him. He knew it should, but he genuinely believed that he had done her a big favour, saved her from future heartache, because Colin Clark would never have been a faithful husband to her. And she wasn't like his Jade; his sister would have been destroyed by Colin's outside interests. Colin Clark could never have been good enough for his sister; he was a fucking nothing, a no one, a piece of fucking *shit*. He was supposed to have been his mate. Aiden had genuinely liked the man, and how had he repaid him? He had fucked his sister. Colin Clark had honestly believed that he could further himself by aligning himself with his wife's family? He had been determined to make sure that it would never happen.

At the same time, Aiden felt that Eric Palmer had outlived his usefulness so it was just good business practice, really. He had killed two birds with one stone, getting rid of Colin Clark and Eric Palmer. Eric, bless him, was nothing more than collateral damage, but he would have a send-off that would be talked about for years; Aiden knew that he owed him that much. No expense would be spared.

Now Aiden didn't have to answer to anyone, and that was exactly what he had wanted and what he had been working towards for a long time.

Agnes watched her brother for several minutes. As upset as he was with Colin, she believed he had always had her best interests at heart. But she had loved Colin so much, and she knew that he had loved her. What she couldn't understand was why he would have wanted to hurt Eric Palmer.

'Look, Agnes. We are all here for you and your baby. Your baby will be the most loved child on the planet. Don't ever forget that, darling.'

She began to cry once more and he held her tenderly and told her everything that she wanted to hear. Everything that she needed to hear.

Chapter One Hundred and Seven

Reeva and Jade were in the kitchen drinking tea laced with whisky and smoking cigarettes. The boys were standing around silently wondering what they were supposed to be doing. Patsy motioned to Eugene to come with him. Eugene followed his elder brother out of the house and together they walked slowly down the road. Anyone watching them would have thought they were just taking a short stroll, trying to clear their heads.

Both were quiet until they were well away from their mum's house. Then Eugene said to his older brother, 'That bastard planned this, didn't he? I felt there was something wrong on the streets all day. There was a fucking atmosphere but I just couldn't work out what it meant. They must have thought it was all over for Aiden.'

Patsy sighed heavily. He really could do without this. But he understood where his brother was coming from. The fact that Aiden had used outside people to set this up was going to rankle. But it was a clever move – there was no disputing that. It made his brother look innocent, because they genuinely didn't have any idea what he was planning. The masterstroke was that Aiden had used Colin Clark's own brother against him. Timmy Clark had been forced to use the people that Aiden had recommended to him and, because of that, everyone in their world was now convinced that the O'Haras had nothing to do with any of it. Certain people had known that something big was going down, except, of course, they were not aware that the gun they had supplied so readily would be used against someone like Eric Palmer. They had assumed the firearm was to be used on Aiden O'Hara. After all, the situation with Agnes and Aiden's opinion about it wasn't exactly a secret.

They had been well and truly fucking had over. The people who had supplied the gun were in Aiden's firing line because they would all be aware that he would already know everything he needed to about the latest events. The way they had treated his brothers this day would now be a big fucking worry. Patsy had to give it to his brother, Aiden had played them all – his own brothers included. In one fell swoop Aiden had taken out the two people he had really wanted gone, and he had also found out who in his circle would be willing to work against him if the need ever arose. Patsy didn't hold out much hope for any of those fuckers in the next few weeks. It was a brilliant strategy. Even though Aiden could fuck up quickly, when he really put his mind to something the clever bastard could outsmart anyone. This just proved it.

Patsy started to laugh, he couldn't help himself. He looked at Eugene and he could see the complete wonderment on his face and that just made him laugh more.

'You really don't get it, do you, Eugene?'

Eugene shook his head and, as expected, he was getting angry because he felt that he was being left out of the loop.

'No, Patsy, I don't fucking get it.'

Patsy explained everything to him and he could see the shock and awe on his brother's face as it finally dawned on him just what Aiden had done. Eugene lit a joint and, after he had pulled in a few deep tokes, he passed it to Patsy.

'Fucking hell, Patsy, that's fucking cold, man.'

Patsy shrugged. 'That's Aiden, Eugene. *Never* underestimate him. And *never* let him think that he can't trust you. He deliberately kept us out of this drama today. Remember that, always. He kept us all as safe as houses.'

Eugene nodded. He understood exactly what had gone down. If they didn't know, then they couldn't ever discuss it. It was brilliant.

'But he fucking killed Colin and Eric.'

Patsy held up his hand as if he was stopping traffic. 'And you want to call him on that, do you, Eugene? He took out not just the father of our sister's child, a man he was best friends with, but also arranged the murder of the man who treated him as a fucking son. Fucking hell, use your loaf, Eugene. You better do what I'm going to be doing – acting as fucking shocked as the next man. For all his lunacy, remember that he kept us out of the frame. He's going to want to know who you think might have been in on it, and my advice to you is to tell him. He knows anyway, believe me.'

Eugene nodded in agreement. 'Of course I will. I get it, Patsy.'

Patsy smiled and hugged his brother tightly to him. 'Listen, mate. Aiden is a law unto himself. But never forget that he loves us. He has always been there for us. Especially for our mum. He has been looking out for us all our lives.'

Patsy knew that bringing Reeva into the equation would help Eugene to, if not understand, then at least accept the latest developments. The one thing they had in common was that they loved Reeva, no matter what she might do, say or cause.

He only hoped that he could convince himself of Aiden's good intentions, because, lately, Patsy was finding it harder and harder to justify his actions.

Back in the house Aiden had already started on his spiel about looking after Agnes's child, and how they all needed to be there for her. He was walking away without anyone looking in his direction, and that was exactly what Aiden was so good at. He had achieved everything he wanted, and come out as the hero of the hour.

Chapter One Hundred and Eight

'Push, darling. Honestly, it's as easy as pie, I promise you!'

The midwife, Miss Maudell, was clearly getting more and more exasperated at the bleached-blonde, megaphone-voiced woman who had insisted on being present to help her daughter give birth. Miss Maudell was a large woman, a spinster of the parish, as Reeva had so rudely called her, and quite unable to control Reeva in any way.

Agnes was watching the interplay between her mother and the poor midwife – she would have smiled if she had had one in her. As another wave of pain washed over her, she took a deep breath and tried to roll with it. She wished so much that Colin was here with her; it was a daunting prospect to be bringing up this child on her own. Oh, she knew she had her mum and her brothers – especially Aiden, who had been amazing since Colin had passed. Timmy too had promised her that he would look out for his brother's child as if it was his own, but it was Aiden, who had really stepped up to support her; he could not do enough. She knew that he was outside even now, waiting for this to be over so he could come in and meet the latest addition to the family.

After the trouble at the wedding he had apologised, which had meant the world to her at the time. He had once more treated Colin like his best friend, and she had really believed he had come to terms with their relationship. Afterwards she had heard whispers that her husband had not exactly died in the best of circumstances so, all in all, she felt now that Aiden was being very magnanimous in his generosity towards her and her unborn child.

'Right, I'm going for a fag, darling. You keep pushing away! And don't have it till I get back, OK?'

Like Miss Maudell, Agnes was relieved when Reeva finally left the room. Even the air seemed clearer without her mother's overwhelming perfume wafting in her face constantly.

Miss Maudell was pleased with how things were progressing. 'I can see the head, Mrs Clark, not long now. When I tell you, I want you to give a nice big push!'

Chapter One Hundred and Nine

Aiden was waiting outside the delivery suite, practically in more of a state of anticipation than he had been for the birth of his own child. Everything was playing out just as he wanted. He knew that he had hurt his sister in taking out her husband but he had faith she would get over it. He intended to make sure she would never want for anything and neither would her child. He hoped it was a girl; that would make life much easier for him.

He had seen his mother off for her fag gratefully; there was nothing more annoying than Reeva when she was excited. Her voice went up by twenty decibels and she insisted on airing every thought that popped into her head. Even in the lift she had been regaling everyone and anyone about her new grand-child's imminent arrival. He smiled. She was a card, really, was his mum. She meant well, but when God was handing out brains Reeva must have been having a day off.

Aiden looked at his watch and wondered why his brothers weren't here already. He had told them that Agnes was in labour. Where the fuck were they? Come to that, where the fuck was Jade?

He heard his sister scream and, without thinking, he burst into the room, just as his nephew pushed his way into the world in all his bloodied glory. Aiden stood there open-mouthed as the midwife laid the child across its mother's belly and, when he gave out an almighty wail, Aiden said, laughing, 'Fucking right pair of lungs on him, girl!' Agnes looked tired, but when she was handed her son it was as if she had suddenly been lit up from inside. Still her voice was tinged with sadness as she kissed her boy's head and said, 'Oh, I wish your daddy could see you, son. He would have been so proud.'

Even the midwife felt choked at the emotion in Agnes's words. The moment was ruined, though, when Reeva burst into the room shouting, 'About bleeding time! I'm fucking starving!'

Without a second thought, Agnes handed the child to Aiden and, taking him into his arms expertly, he sat on the chair provided and looked down in wonderment at this brand-new human being. No doubt about it, each one was a miracle. The child's eyes were looking into his and, when he grabbed at his finger, Aiden was amazed at the strength in the little bugger. He was going to make sure that he was a good father figure to his nephew. It would be like Colin Clark had never existed.

'Well, give me a fucking hold then, Ade!'

He passed the child reluctantly to his mother and then, reaching over, he hugged his sister tightly, saying honestly, 'He's beautiful, Aggs. And I swear to you now that I will look after him like my own. I will look after both of you, darling.'

Agnes nodded happily because she believed him. In this moment, she trusted that he meant every word he said.

Book Five

And his unkindness may defeat my life,
But never taint my love.

Othello, William Shakespeare (1564–1616)

Chapter One Hundred and Ten

2010

'Are you trying to fucking annoy me, Porrick?'

Everyone was laughing at Agnes and her pretend anger. Porrick was laughing harder than any of them; he knew that his sister was just joking with him. But, if he was honest, he could do without it. He hated being the centre of attention – he always had. But he loved his sister and liked to see her like this, relaxed and having fun. She was so serious most of the time.

'Why would I bother to annoy you, Aggs? Tell me. I'm interested.'

Agnes hugged her brother quickly. 'All I asked you to do was to pick up my friend Juliet, who I think you like!'

Porrick wasn't laughing now but he wasn't about to cause any kind of upset – her friend Juliet was as embarrassed as he was. Agnes was of the opinion that Porrick needed a kick-start, and she was determined to see that he got it.

Reeva was laughing with pleasure; she liked the girl, and she had been wondering for a long time when her youngest son was going to finally bag himself a decent bird. Eugene and Patsy were both smirking good-naturedly; they were both aware that Porrick was *not* going to be taking Juliet out on a regular basis.

As they walked out into the garden they both began to laugh loudly. Aiden came up behind them and, sticking his head between them, he said jovially, 'If Juliet was called John, I could see the fucking attraction! I just can't believe that our mum and Agnes still haven't cottoned on!'

'Come on, Ade, you know our Aggs. Religious Lil from Harold Hill! She doesn't want to believe he's gay. Nor does Mum, and that really shocks me. I mean, I thought she would be all over that one!'

They laughed together. Agnes had been given this house by Aiden as a birthday present a few years earlier, and it was a really fabulous property. A beautiful detached house, early Georgian, set within an acre of landscaped gardens. Agnes loved it, and she was so grateful to her brother because he was so very good to her and her son. He was like a surrogate father to her boy, and he had made sure that they had never wanted for anything.

The night her son had been brought into the world her brother had been there for both of them and he had been there ever since. Now it was her boy's eighth birthday, and they were having a huge party to celebrate. Her son looked nothing like his father which had always saddened her – he was *her* double. As Porrick said, he looked like her in drag. He was dark haired, and dark skinned – he looked more Mediterranean than she did. It was ironic, really, considering all her mum could tell her about her father was that he was a Turk. And, as Jade had once pointed out to her, knowing Reeva like they did, that might not even be the truth. Men had always bullshitted poor Reeva and most of them had never stayed around long enough for her to actually get any kind of address or plausible story from them, so it was all a bit sketchy, to say the least. Jade had always believed that

Agnes looked far more Kuwaiti than Turkish, and she had to admit herself that she was very dark, although Reeva had always insisted that her father was a handsome Turkish guy – with a great body and not much else going for him. That had always caused a big laugh but didn't give her any kind of information that could help her to find him. But, as Aiden had once pointed out, none of them could ever point a finger at a father so what did it matter? They had each other and that should be enough.

She walked through to her kitchen and saw her mum and Jade in deep conversation. As the years had gone on they had just seemed to get closer and closer. Eugene said they were like a witches' convention and sometimes Agnes could see his point. They were definitely in league somehow and, like her brothers, she had never been invited into their little world. Reeva held her arms out and said drunkenly, 'Come and give me a fucking hug, Agnes. My only daughter!'

Agnes knew better than to refuse so she hugged her mum tightly, and she waited until Reeva let her go. When Reeva had a few drinks, it was much better to give her whatever she wanted. If she hugged you, then you made sure you waited till she pushed you away, otherwise it could cause upsets. Reeva was still as unpredictable as ever. And she still took offence easily when the drink was on her. Jade winked at Agnes, knowing exactly what was going down.

Aiden Junior came into the kitchen. He'd been outside with the other young men, and Agnes watched as he poured himself another drink. He had inherited the best of Aiden and Jade's looks and he was a real head-turner. Well over six feet tall, he had thick black hair and piercing blue eyes. He was a big man, broad-shouldered with a natural grace. But what really set him apart was his personality: nobody could ever say they did not like him. He was such a terrific guy, really friendly and open, respectful of everyone he came into contact with. Funny, genuine and kind, he was a favourite of everyone in his orbit. Coupled with his intelligence, he was the real deal.

Jade was so proud of him, as was Aiden. Reeva adored him because he had spent so much time with her. He also adored Reeva; he never went one day without talking to her on the phone or visiting her. He was her boy, and always would be – Reeva and her grandson had a real bond. Aiden Junior had infinite patience with his grandmother, no matter how outrageous she might act, or how much trouble she might be the cause of. Smiling at them, he went back out into the garden to join his friends.

Agnes sat at the kitchen table with her mum and Jade and poured herself a large glass of wine. Taking a gulp of chilled Sauvignon, she looked around her, satisfied that she had done a good job. The house was looking fantastic, and she had filled it with wonderful food and friends and family. The atmosphere was great, and the DJ was playing music that suited every age group. Her son, Colin, was a nice lad. He was growing up fast and she knew that she could not stop that, even though she would love to. She would quite happily keep him a baby all his life. She could see him in the garden with his uncles and his cousin, being made a fuss of because it was his birthday, his party. He loved being a part of the men's world, and they spoiled him. He was like the family mascot.

'Look at my Colin, Mum. He is eight! I really can't believe how fast the time has gone.'

Reeva laughed her loud, deep laugh, the very same laugh that told everyone who loved her that she was already as drunk as a fucking lord. Porrick always said his mum was like *Stingray*, and then he would say seriously in an American accent, 'Anything can happen in the next half-hour!' They always laughed, but it wasn't really a joke. Where Reeva was concerned it was a true statement.

'How the fucking hell do you think I feel, Agnes? You lot have grown up so quickly, darling. One minute you were my babies. Now you are all fucking adults. Take my advice and you enjoy your boy while you still can.'

Jade laughed with her. 'She has a point, Aggs. Believe me, the time goes so fast.'

Agnes smiled, and drank her wine. She knew as well as Jade did that Jade's son had spent most of his childhood with her and her mother. Not that she would say that, of course, but it was the truth nonetheless. Jade had always been a hard worker and Agnes would never say anything in the least detrimental about that, but she had to admit her nephew had spent more time with her than he ever had with his parents.

'I think you are both right. But he is eight already!'

Reeva was already pouring them all more wine. 'Well, believe me, Agnes, you have done a marvellous job. He is a credit to you, darling. A really nice lad.'

Agnes knew that was the truth; she had been there for him since the day he was born – she had made sure of that. He saw a lot of her mother but she wasn't his surrogate parent like she had been with Aiden Junior.

Timmy Clark walked into the kitchen and Agnes jumped out of her chair to greet him. She was always pleased to see him.

'Oh, Timmy, I was worried you wouldn't make it!'

Timmy Clark smiled. He was a very handsome man, with an easy way about him. That he looked like Colin was also a big part of his attraction for Agnes, and he had always kept in close contact with her and her son.

'Sit down, Agnes, and relax, darling. I'm just going outside to see our young Colin.'

He kissed Reeva hello and spoke a few pleasantries to Jade before he walked out into the garden to see his nephew. He knew that Aiden and his brothers were out there, and he was quite happy to touch base with them all. It was hard for him to even look at Aiden O'Hara but he knew that he had no choice in the matter. He would never get over what had happened, but he had to put it behind him so he could be a part of his nephew's life, if for no other reason. The fact that Aiden acted like there was nothing amiss had been difficult at first but now Timmy knew to just play the game.

Aiden saw him and shouted happily, 'Hello there, Timmy, me old mucker! Come over here and have a drink with us blokes.'

Timmy walked over to join them. He shook hands with everyone, and when his nephew ran to him and hugged him he said gently, 'Happy birthday, Colin.'

Colin was thrilled to see his uncle and Timmy looked at his brother's child wondering how Aiden could stand there year after year as if nothing had ever happened. That he loved this boy was blatantly obvious – Aiden had been a surrogate father to him from day one. But Timmy could not help but question Aiden's motives. The child adored him, and he really did put himself out to see that this lad had everything that he needed, as he did for his sister. This house alone was proof enough of that. It had to be worth a million and that was a conservative estimate but, knowing Aiden, it was all in his name – another asset to liquidate should the need arise. He didn't trust this fucker as far as he could have thrown him. Everything he did was part of his own fucking agenda.

Timmy Clark loathed Aiden O'Hara and would never forgive him for what he had made him do. He had had no choice – Aiden O'Hara had made sure of that – but to do what he had been asked just to save his own arse. How could he ever live with what he had done? Even worse was the fact that the circumstances had assured him of a notoriety that he had enjoyed for so many years, thanks to Aiden's forward planning, of course. Timmy was revered because he had apparently murdered his own fucking brother in cold blood because he could not allow the death of such a wonderful man as Eric Palmer to go unchallenged. He hated that Aiden had been sure enough of him to know that he would do what was asked. It had been the hardest thing he would ever do but, as Aiden had pointed out, he had still done it. That was what Aiden was so good at: making people do what he wanted, and at the same time holding that over them. They were now in a devil's alliance.

They worked together, and acted as if they were friends, but they were just playing a part. Over the years they had both managed to fool everyone around them. Timmy Clark had made sure that he would never give Aiden any reason to doubt him so he could stay in his nephew's life and carry on with his businesses unhindered. The strange thing was, he could tell that Aiden actually did like him and he was willing to leave the past in the past. That was one of the kinks in that fucking nutter's personality: he could just put what had happened out of his mind. He sent work his way, socialised with him. It was surreal. Timmy knew that as long as he never rocked the boat, Aiden was quite happy to deal with him as an equal in every way.

'Our Colin is more like his mum, admittedly, but I have to

say, there are times when he smiles and he looks just like his old man. Don't you think so, Timmy?'

Timmy smiled easily. The scary thing was that Aiden was being absolutely sincere. 'Occasionally, I have to admit he has a look of his dad. But I think he's the spit of Agnes.'

He knew that was what Aiden liked to hear. And it was the truth; he didn't have anything of his father in him really except his size. But then his uncles were mostly big men, except for Porrick, but he more than made up for his lack of inches with his psychotic personality. No one ever picked a fight with him twice. He was a legend in his own lunchtime for his uncontrollable temper. But young Colin walked like his father; he had the same gait as him. It could just be wishful thinking, of course. His nephew was the nearest thing Timmy had to family, and he felt an obligation to make sure that this boy had every chance available to him.

Porrick and Eugene were walking towards them with a tray of expensive beers and Patsy was already handing them out to everyone.

'Come on, guys, let's toast the latest deal with Marvin Hendry and his posse.'

Aiden Junior leaned over his uncle's shoulder and, grabbing a beer, he said jovially, 'I will drink to that! I had the best fucking time in Jamaica with him. It was amazing! It's a really dangerous place, mind. Like Marvin said, it's still like the Wild West! But he looked after me well.'

Timmy could see that the boy was embracing his introduction to the real business, and Aiden was clearly proud of him – and so he should be. He was a great kid. Unlike his father, Aiden Junior had an innate sense of fair play and that was obvious to anyone who had any dealings with him. Patsy was laughing with him; there was a real closeness between them that anyone could see. Aiden Junior and his uncles were a tight band. For all Reeva's faults, she had instilled a loyalty in her kids that would be hard to infiltrate.

'I heard that you were out there on the pull every night!'

Aiden Junior was grinning happily. He had told everyone that he had already met the love of his life. Marvin's youngest daughter had really bowled him over. She was eighteen and absolutely gorgeous. But he was quite happy to play the game. He had already worked out that his dad wasn't too enamoured of his choice of girlfriend. He couldn't really understand why. After all, his own brothers were black – one was Jamaican and the other one was African – so it was a bit weird that his dad was against it. But he knew that he was still a young man as far as his dad was concerned, and he could only assume it was because of that. Patsy and Eugene were trying to smooth things over for him and he really did appreciate that; his uncles were so good to him.

He could feel his father watching him and, as always lately, his father's scrutiny made him feel irritated. He knew that his dad was a hard fuck, but that didn't mean he had the right to dictate everything in his life. He was an adult, and he could do what the fuck he wanted to. But he knew better than to say anything in public, so he kept his own counsel and waited for what he knew was going to be a big event in not just his life, but also his father's.

A few minutes later he was pleased to see Marvin Hendry, with his closest kin and his stunning daughter, Loretta, arriving. He watched as his Aunt Agnes and his mum welcomed them with open arms. Marvin liked Reeva and always made a big fuss of her, which, of course, she loved. He was aware that everyone around him was suddenly speechless and waiting for his father's reaction; he didn't give a flying fuck what he thought.

Waving at Loretta and her father, he motioned them to join them in the garden.

He knew what he wanted and he was determined to get it. He looked at his father and he saw him settling his face into a mask of ambiguity; no one on the outside would know that his dad was not pleased with this turn of events. In fact, his father was the first one to greet the newcomers, which he did with the carefully manufactured excitement that Aiden Junior had witnessed many times in his life before. He acted as if he had been waiting all night for them to arrive so they could finally be together. It was a real learning curve to see at first hand just how easily his father could fake any emotion he felt was needed. Marvin and his crew really believed that they *were* welcome, that they were honoured guests – which they would have been, of course, except for the fact that his father had such a problem with Loretta.

Loretta came straight to him, and he automatically opened his arms. As she settled herself into his embrace he had no doubt that she was the girl for him. She was beautiful, of course, with coffee-coloured skin and her mother's thick dark hair. Her eyes were almond shaped and a deep hazel colour. She was tiny, just five feet tall, and slim as a wand; she wasn't voluptuous, she didn't have huge breasts or a big booty. But Loretta was just perfect for him, and he loved that he was so much bigger than her, that she was so tiny and so feminine. She was so lady-like.

He kissed her quickly on her lips, and was relieved to see his mum and his grandmother come out to the garden to join them all. Reeva loved Loretta and so did his mum. Agnes followed them out and made a big fuss of getting them all drinks, and encouraging them to feel free to enjoy the buffet.

Marvin Hendry was happy to see his youngest daughter looking so enamoured of Aiden Junior. He liked the boy, and saw in him a real decency and goodness that he knew was more than just his demeanour. Marvin Hendry couldn't ask for a better mate for his Loretta. She was never going to win any prizes, she wasn't an academic. She had no interest in university like his elder kids, and she didn't want to train for anything except being a beautician. She was a good-looking girl who needed to be looked after. He believed that Aiden Junior could take care of her. As young as they both were, Marvin really did believe that these two had a genuine connection. He hoped he was right, because he wanted more for his girl than wanting to be with a fucking Yardie, with his slick talk and the hope that his association with his daughter would guarantee the ponce a place in his world. That was his biggest worry – that his daughter would succumb to a plastic Rasta with a cheap gun, and dreams of the big time. He could only hope that he was right about this lad.

Aiden O'Hara watched as his son and Loretta enjoyed each other's company. He was well aware that Jade wasn't impressed with him or his opinion of young Loretta.

She couldn't see it from his point of view. He didn't want his only son to tie himself down at such an early age. He was twenty, for fuck's sake. The girl was eighteen years old, and ripe to trap him. She had the personality of a fucking mannequin. She was pretty – he could not dispute that – but she wasn't exactly a fucking news reader. She would be hard pushed to fill in a job application without help. Even Marvin had said as much – not that he would remind him of that.

Marvin Hendry still held all the cards, because it was his fucking contacts who were in Colombia and calling the shots. That was something Aiden could not change to his advantage. He needed Marvin Hendry, and Marvin knew that.

Although, in fairness to him, Marvin had never used that in any way that could be construed as disrespectful. He had always given Aiden his due. That was what made this situation so fucking awkward. Unlike Marvin, he didn't see his son tying himself to Marvin's daughter as a fucking result. He just couldn't get his head around it. Why his only son, who had the world at his feet, would think that tying himself down at such a young age was even fucking remotely sensible, he didn't know. She was a nice girl, but she was not what he wanted for his son. No, he saw his boy as marrying class. And he could – they had more than enough money to do that for him. His boy could have his pick; his grandchildren could be fucking part of the real moneyed class. That was what he had always envisaged for his son. Not a fucking half-caste girl from Jamaica whose only fucking asset was her father's fucking relationship with Colombian drug barons. But he knew that he had to play along, and hope that he could talk his son into using his fucking brain, and not selling himself cheap.

Jade was watching Aiden; she knew exactly what was going through his head, and she actually felt a terrible sorrow for him. He never allowed for real life – it never occurred to him that his dreams could only ever be fulfilled if the people involved were as interested as he was. She liked Loretta, and she knew that her son was already on a love job. Unlike his father, her son didn't see what was in his best interests. He didn't plan every step of his life, wondering what would bring him the most money, or kudos. Her son just wanted to be happy. He had not inherited his father's belief that *everyone* in the world was only there to be used by him. Her son was a nice guy, and she loved that about him. She loved that he was a nice person who didn't have hardly any of his father in him except for his good looks. They were chalk and fucking cheese.

Marvin Hendry was holding court, which he did often and well. He could tell a story, and he could make people laugh. That was a big part of his attraction; he was a man who had the creds needed, but he didn't feel the need to ram that knowledge down people's throats. He was quite comfortable in his own skin, and he laughed at situations where people didn't realise who he was at first. He was a man who didn't need to be constantly feted.

He was also a man that Jade could not help admiring. He was handsome as fuck, but that was nothing unusual in her world. Handsome men were ten a penny; what she liked was Marvin's outlook on life. He was a man to be reckoned with, in more ways than one. But what Jade liked about him was that he was an interesting and basically gentle man – at least where women were concerned. All his baby mothers were looked after and given the utmost respect. He had always taken responsibility for his children and made sure they were a big part of his life. So he was handsome *and* dependable.

That was a dangerous combination because she was attracted to him – she had been since they had first been introduced.

Reeva was drunk as a skunk and Tony, bless him, was trying to keep her in line. The music had been turned up, and the DJ was now playing old-school reggae. That was Reeva's cue to dance and just forget that she was the mother of five children, and a grandmother to boot.

The garden was lit up with lanterns, and it looked really

beautiful. The gardens were landscaped, and it bothered Agnes that she didn't know anything about the plants, or the trees. Aiden had engaged a gardener who arrived three times a week and who she made tea for. That was her only involvement in the garden! Looking at it tonight, she was aware of how big it was, and how gorgeous it looked. The French windows were open, and everyone was outside. The DJ was very good; he had them all up dancing and, for the first time in years, she was sorry that she didn't have a man of her own. Couples were dancing in the lamplight together. Her nephew, Aiden Junior, and his girl were hanging on to each other for dear life, just happy being there together. Her son was standing with his uncles. Porrick had given him a sneaky sip of lager and she knew that he didn't like the taste, but he loved acting grown up with everyone. It was his night, his birthday party, and she wanted him to enjoy it and remember it all his life.

The DJ put on Desmond Dekker's 'Israelites' and Agnes laughed as she saw her mother dragging poor Marvin over to dance with her. She got herself another glass of wine and walked over to her brothers and Aiden, putting his arm around her, hugged her to him tightly.

'Look at your Colin, drinking his uncle's beer. This is what life is all about, Aggs. Making new memories, and remembering the good old times.'

Agnes was watching her mum and Marvin Hendry when she felt a hand on her arm. It was Timmy and, pulling her away from her brother, he led her to the patio dance floor and she happily started to dance with him. Agnes was really feeling good for once. She still relied on the Church and she went to Mass at least once a day. It had always been her solace, the place where she felt she belonged. Her faith was very important to her. But tonight she had drunk a few glasses of wine, and she was feeling young and attractive. She knew she was a beautiful woman – men had always given her attention, from a very young age, often attention that she had not wanted to receive. Suddenly, tonight, she wanted to be young, to enjoy herself. Her mum was always telling her that she was a fool to spend the best years of her life mourning a man who could never come back to her. That she should be out there enjoying her life while she still could. But tonight, she didn't know if it was the wine, or the moonlight, but for the first time in years she felt the urge to let herself go. In Timmy's arms she felt safe and she also felt like she was young again; inside she had always felt so old, like she had to always be the adult. But that was because her mother had never quite mastered the grown-up bit for herself.

Timmy was pleased to see Agnes enjoying herself. He always felt conflicted around her because he was as much in love with her as ever but couldn't forget that he had murdered her husband. But he couldn't stay away from her.

'You look beautiful, Agnes, do you know that?'

Agnes laughed delightedly and said quickly, 'Well, Timmy, it is very dark!'

Timmy looked at her and said seriously, 'Agnes, you are a very beautiful girl. My brother would have wanted you to build another life for yourself and for your son. Look at you, lady!'

Agnes was so embarrassed she turned her head away from Timmy's gaze, and sighing heavily she said nervously, 'Oh, stop it, Timmy. Please! You know I don't know how to react to that kind of talk.'

Timmy could quite happily have shouted at her; she was such a fool. She was so determined to stay on her own, and honour the memory of his brother.

'Listen to me, Agnes. You need to get a life of your own. All I am saying is, there is a big world out there. For fuck's sake, go and join it before it's too late.'

She didn't answer him; she didn't know what to say.

Reeva was still holding on to Marvin Hendry and he was quite happy to dance with her. He liked Reeva and he admired her. As Patsy pulled her away from him, and danced her over to Tony, they were all laughing good-naturedly. Tony was quite happy to dance with his Reeva. After all the years they had been together it was quite plain to see that he actually did love her.

Aiden and Jade were dancing to 'Kingston Town', the original version – it was their record in a way. And, as they danced, she saw him watching their son and his young girlfriend.

'I think they are a lovely couple, Aiden. What's your problem? They are young, and the chances are this won't even last.'

Aiden snorted at her with complete disrespect and, shaking his head slowly, he said angrily, 'I might have known you would think this was fucking love's young dream! Are you stupid, Jade? I had you down as a lot of things, but not a fucking idiot. If he ties himself to her, it's all over for him. Look at her, a fucking Jamaican drug dealer's daughter!'

Jade pushed him away from her violently. She was furious at his complete disregard for his son's feelings and his first foray into the world of relationships and love. How could he be such a hypocrite and still keep a straight face?

'Who the fuck do you think you are, Aiden? Look around you. You think that you can just want something and it will happen. Well, it doesn't work like that, mate. Our son is a grown man, and the sooner you fucking remember that the better it will be for all of us.'

Aiden was aware that their little contretemps had been noticed, and he was not happy about that. But he was more annoyed that Jade couldn't see what he was trying to tell her. He had really believed that she would see where he was coming from. Surely she wanted the best for their son? That was all he wanted for him, all he had ever wanted for him. Unlike his mother, of course, who it seemed didn't care if he threw his fucking life away at twenty. Women were cunts. His mother had been used by men all her life, from fourteen years old. His attraction to Jade had been because she had the nous to use the men – she wasn't a fucking silly girl with dreams of fucking romance and weddings. Now it turned out that she was as fucking deranged as every other fucking idiot woman he had known. Why did everyone seem to think that he was the bad bastard because he wanted the best for his boy?

He looked around him as he walked back to his brothers, and seeing his sister still dancing with that fucking Timmy Clark did not do anything to help with his bad mood. But he plastered a smile on his face, and he played the part of the happy uncle.

But he wasn't happy at all. In fact, he was fucking fuming.

Chapter One Hundred and Eleven

'Jade, will you just stop for one moment and talk to me.'

Jade had no intention of talking to Aiden because she believed it was a complete waste of time. As she walked past him to leave their bedroom, he grabbed her arm roughly and threw her back on to the bed. Jade was shocked because, as threatening as she knew Aiden's behaviour could be when thwarted, he had never once used violence against her. She jumped back up immediately – she wasn't going to let him get away with this.

'You would fucking *dare* to think that you could ever lay a hand on me? I don't think so, Aiden. The man ain't been fucking born yet who could get away with that.'

Aiden was trying his hardest to keep his cool but Jade was not making it easy for him and she was more than capable of giving him a run for his money if it came to a physical fight. He didn't want to have to fight with her but she was really winding him up. He was surprised; she was generally sensible enough to know that the best way to deal with him when he was aggravated was not to fucking push her luck too far.

'I am telling you again, Aiden – our son can do what he likes. You can't fucking stop him caring about someone. You cannot even really believe that you have that much power over him, surely? He loves us, Aiden, but he loves Loretta too. She is a terrific girl. It might all fall out of bed next week, but that is up to *them*, not you! Who the fucking hell do you think you are?'

Aiden was on the verge of losing his temper big time. He couldn't even breathe properly. He was so angry and disappointed with Jade's stupidity.

'He ain't you, Aiden. He doesn't see everything and everyone as a fucking opportunity. I have had to stand in for you and stop you physically harming the girls you were *fucking*. I have had to make sure that you didn't get the poor mares murdered. Because you are *more* than capable of that kind of hatred, especially when they think they might be in with a chance. You are such a fucking lunatic, Aiden. You only ever see what you want to see. You just never let other people be, do you?'

She could see that she had really got his temper up and, for once, she didn't care. Her days of pussyfooting round this fucker were over.

'I am warning you, Aiden: don't fucking push this. If you are not careful you will push that boy away. He's a grown man and he doesn't have to listen to you!'

Aiden could see that she was talking sense on one level, but he could not allow his son to throw himself away on a girl like Loretta. He could do so much better for himself – why couldn't he see that? What really bothered him was the way that Aiden Junior looked at that girl; he was absolutely besotted with her.

Jade was watching him, she could see the different expressions on his face and she could read him like a book. Placing her hand gently on his arm, she said sadly, 'Leave him be, Aiden.

For Christ's sake, just leave our boy alone. He won't thank you for your interference.'

He pulled her into his arms and held her tightly. When he held Jade like this it was the only time that he felt safe. Jade gave him a stability that he desperately needed. The fact that she still loved him, knowing him as she did, was something he would always be awed by. Because he knew that he wasn't like other people; his take on the world wasn't fucking perfect and he saw a lot of things from a very different perspective to most of the people around him. Well, that was why he was so successful, and why he had created a world for everyone he cared about.

He followed her down to the kitchen and watched her as she made them their morning coffee. She was still a very attractive woman; as old as she was, she could still give a lot of younger women a run for their money. He realised he was lucky to have her – if only he was capable of sitting back and enjoying the life he had built. But it wasn't in his nature. He'd always had control of everything around him. It had been the bane of his life; from the time he was a young kid, he had always had to think about all the people in his life, from his mother, Reeva, to his brothers and his sister. That had just been his lot and he accepted that. He had been the man of the house – he had had to be, no one else was going to look out for them, were they? So he had done it. He had taken on that load and he didn't regret a second of it.

But to see his handsome son tying himself to a girl whose only conversation was about fucking celebrities, and who spent more time looking at her social media accounts than she did actually talking to the people around her, distressed him. She was a fucking moron, a very pretty moron but a first-grade one, nevertheless. From her expensive shoes to her false nails, she was everything that he loathed. He employed girls like her in his houses and his clubs, but they were for no more than a dalliance. You didn't fucking marry them.

Jade placed a mug of coffee in front of him, breaking his train of thought. 'You really can't see what you are doing wrong, can you, Aiden? It scares me that you can't see what the real problem is here. Something so simple even your fucking mother could suss out while on one of her massive benders, is beyond your comprehension. Be honest, Aiden. It's not *Loretta* you object to. Your fucking problem is that your son is striking out on his own, doing something that you had no hand in, something that you can't control. Don't try and bullshit yourself that this is about anything else – because we both know that it's not.'

Aiden shrugged. She made a good argument – and she was absolutely right. But that didn't change the fact that he still believed his son was making a big mistake.

Jade lit herself a cigarette. He clearly wasn't going to admit anything so she tried another tack. 'Is it because she's black, Aiden?'

Shaking his head slowly, he looked into her eyes as he said, 'In all honesty, Jade? I just don't know. I really can't answer that, darling.'

Jade looked at him for a long moment before saying sadly, 'You *never* fucking cease to amaze me, Aiden.'

She was so disappointed in him, and he understood why she would feel like it.

'I could have lied to you, Jade, but I didn't, did I?'

She didn't know what to say to him any more. They were a strange pair, but they had been through so much together. She knew everything about him – the good as well as the bad, and there was a lot of bad in him. He was ruthless and vicious and he could be very petty when the fancy took him. Yet somehow they worked together; they were both broken people. But she had been broken by circumstances – Aiden had been born broken.

'Promise me one thing, Aiden. Please leave Aiden Junior alone. Let him follow his own road because there is a lot of you in our boy and he won't take kindly to you interfering in his life.'

Aiden couldn't deny she was right about that.

'It's his first real love job, Aiden, and that's a big thing at his age. You remember how it felt, don't you? I concede that she isn't exactly a fucking bluestocking, but that doesn't bother him. And Marvin – he thinks the sun shines out of our Aiden's arse. You know what the real irony is? That Marvin isn't bothered about his precious daughter with our son. Unlike you, he thinks that they are entitled to love whoever the fuck they want.'

She walked over to him and, slipping her arm around his shoulder, she sat on his lap. He immediately held her to him as she knew he would.

'This is a *good* thing. It will cement our relationship with Marvin, and that alone will gain for us untold benefits. Marvin wants to take Aiden out to Colombia and, let's face it, that is something he has never offered anyone else. Whether Aiden and Loretta stay together or not this is a good alliance for the boy. Surely even you can see that?'

The best thing to do with Aiden was to appeal to his logical side, to his business side. That was always the most important thing where he was concerned. He was smiling now, and she kissed him gently on his mouth.

'You're right, Jade. I can see where you are coming from. If

Marvin does decide to take our Aiden into the actual supply chain as a buyer then that can only benefit us as a business, as a family.'

'Exactly.'

She hugged him to her and hoped that she had talked him down, even though she knew that Aiden was as unpredictable as a menopausal Russian weightlifter.

Chapter One Hundred and Twelve

Marvin Hendry had recently purchased a building in Brixton; as it was being gentrified it was becoming a great place for investment opportunities. He had always felt at home in Brixton – he had even met one of his baby mothers at The Fridge many moons ago. She was a good-looking girl from Essex who had produced a son for him and, more to the point, had always understood the situation of being involved with him. She was a realist. She was married now to a nice guy who wasn't short of a few quid and who his son really had a great relationship with. The boy had finished university and was training to be a doctor. He was interested in surgery, and Marvin was quite happy to bankroll his education. He planned to gift him one of the flats in this block that he had purchased and was now being renovated. Marvin liked to see his blood achieving. He had always partied away from home, and that would never change, but he also prided himself on never shirking his responsibilities. It grieved him that so many men in his world produced a child and would often abandon that child along with its mother. Marvin was a staunch believer in taking responsibility for your actions.

He was pleased that his adored daughter, his Loretta, and Aiden O'Hara Junior were so enamoured of each other. He really liked the boy and he was quite happy to bring him into the operational side of the business if he became family. Marvin was well aware that it bothered Aiden O'Hara that *he* had never been able to get a foot into the actual Colombian distribution. But as much as he liked and respected Aiden, Marvin could never allow him to become too involved in that side of it. He knew Aiden O'Hara too well; the man had a natural greed and that, coupled with a personality that would never let him be anything other than the top earner, automatically disqualified him from ever getting anywhere *near* the people concerned. This, along with the knowledge that Aiden would always try to infiltrate the organisation so he could further his own agenda, pretty much guaranteed that Marvin would never let the fucker get too close.

But his son was a different entity entirely. He was young and he was hungry, but the boy's real talent was his ability to get along with everyone around him; in this particular game that was a real bonus.

Marvin's connections were real Colombians. Fanatical Catholics, they were passionate about family. It was a given that the only people you could ever really trust were your own family – that was how they had survived in the world they inhabited for so long. Family also included the people who had married into the clan; unless they were deemed weak or fake they would be welcomed with open arms. Marvin believed that he could quite easily take Aiden Junior under his wing and teach him everything he needed to know. Marvin didn't have any of his own children this high up in his business; the sons he had working for him were good boys but they would never have the brain capacity to do anything more than run whatever side businesses he provided for them. It broke his heart to admit

411

their limitations, but in his world you couldn't ever put the wrong people into positions of power. That was a mistake too many others had made, and he knew exactly how it tended to turn out – he was normally the person who had to go in and pick up the pieces.

Instead, he was quite happy to bring Aiden Junior into his business on a really good footing. The boy was an up-and-coming young Face, already talked about as a diamond geezer, as the cockneys would describe him. And then there was the fact that Loretta was pregnant; she had already confided in her mother, who had immediately confided in *him*. But he would wait for his daughter to tell him in her own time. He was also very interested to see how Aiden O'Hara Junior handled the situation. Marvin had worked out for himself that Aiden's father wasn't exactly a big fan of the youngsters' relationship. That had irritated him. He really didn't like to contemplate that a headcase like Aiden O'Hara could actually think that his daughter wasn't good enough to align herself with *his* son. That was a real melon scratcher, all right. The plus was that Marvin had great hopes for Aiden Junior, and he believed that the boy would step up to the plate where his daughter was concerned. He liked the kid and he trusted him.

So Marvin was doing what he always did: keeping quiet about what he already knew and waiting. That was something he had learned at an early age: never let anyone know what you knew. The chances were that most people were very rarely scrupulously honest about the part they played in whatever drama you were suddenly involved with. He had learned to always find out everything he could about everyone around him, and that way he could never be surprised at what they might be capable of. That meant that he was already aware of how they were going to react before they even crossed his threshold. It was called covering your own arse, and he was the fucking king of it.

He looked around his new apartment, pleased with what he saw. It was very luxurious and it was also soundproofed. Marvin never left anything to fate.

That was why he was so successful.

Chapter One Hundred and Thirteen

'I can't believe it, can you, Aiden?'

Aiden Junior was still on cloud nine. He didn't see Loretta's condition as something to worry about. He was just excited to know that he was going to be a father. It wasn't planned and she was only eighteen, but he would stand by her, of course.

'I'm over the moon, Loretta, darling. But you are only young and if you don't think this is the right time for you to have a baby, I would understand.'

Loretta appreciated that he was trying to be fair and how hard it had been for him to say that to her. That he would stand by her decision meant a lot to her.

'What did your mum say again?'

Loretta snuggled into him. She loved everything about him – his smell and the feel of his body beside hers.

'She said that it's up to me. Well, us. That we had to decide what we thought was the right thing to do.'

Aiden kicked the covers off the bed and, as Loretta squealed at her nakedness, he started laughing. She was already trying to pull the blankets back over them and, grabbing her gently, he pinned her down on the bed.

'You are beautiful, Loretta. I don't understand why you are

always so body-shy with me. You know I think you are fucking amazing. I adore you, darling. I fucking love you.'

He kissed her hungrily and she responded as he knew she would. He pulled away from her and stared into her eyes; he could look into her eyes all day and all night long. She was such a revelation to him. From the moment he had clapped eyes on her he had been smitten. It had never happened to him before. He had had his fair share of girls, but they had been no more than conquests. Working at his family's business, the one thing he had always had access to was females, and willing females at that. But it wasn't until he had seen Loretta standing there in that nightclub in Ocho Rios in Jamaica, with her wide smile and her trim little figure, that he had ever felt such a strong attraction to anyone before. She had walked over to Marvin and he had kissed her and hugged her and, when Marvin had *finally* introduced her to him as his daughter, Aiden had felt such a rush of relief as he had never felt before in his life. They had been inseparable ever since. That she had been a virgin when they had eventually come together had only added to her appeal. She was everything that he had ever wanted and dreamed of.

'If you want this baby, Loretta, I'm willing to stand by you. We can get married, darling. I would marry you with or without this child. But I don't want you to feel that you have to have it. I would understand if you didn't think you were ready or old enough for something this important.'

Loretta had tears in her eyes. He was such a lovely man – so tender and so caring, and she knew that he was being truthful with her. That must be why she felt so emotional; it didn't occur to her that it might have anything to do with her being pregnant.

'I want this baby, Aiden. I want *our* baby. I know it wasn't planned, but it has happened and we made it together. I conceived in Jamaica and, going by the dates, I think that it was probably the first night we spent together.'

Aiden remembered that they had not used any contraception that first time. Both full of alcohol and grass, they had walked along the beach together and talked for hours under the stars. They had eventually gone back to his suite and, as his Nanny Reeva would say, nature had taken its course. Well, now they had to face the consequences of their actions.

'I am glad you don't want to get rid of it, Loretta. I don't think I would have really been as easy about it as I let on. But I would have respected your decision – after all, you are the one who has got to have it.'

Loretta finally pulled the blankets back over them both, laughing as they tried to tidy the bed around them. She was so happy to be with this man, who she had fallen in love with the second that she had laid eyes on him. The fact that he said he had felt the same thing was something she would always remember and cherish, especially as the night they had met, her friend Leona had been beside her, and there was no way anyone could compete with her. She was the whole package: tall, high-breasted, firm booty and she looked like a movie star. But Aiden had not even given Leona a second glance, it was like fate – they were meant to be together.

'What do you think your dad will say about it, Loretta?'

She snuggled into him, enjoying the smell of him and the softness of his skin against hers. She looked up at him and kissed him gently on his lips.

'He already knows, Aiden.'

She saw the incredulity on his face and, giggling, she pulled away from him and lay on her back as he leaned on his elbow and gazed down at her in consternation as she said flippantly, 'I told my mum, as you know, and she tells my dad *everything*. The truth is, Aiden, if you had not wanted to be a part of this, I would have let you walk away. I already knew that I was going to have the baby anyway. I don't think I could actually have an abortion. You know, I think that once I knew that there was a child inside me I felt that I would have to keep it, but I didn't want you to think that I had trapped you.'

Aiden kissed her deeply. Then, jumping out of bed, he started to pull his clothes on.

'Where are you going?'

He sat beside her on the bed and took her hand in his.

'I am going to buy an engagement ring and then I am going to see your dad and explain the situation properly. I owe him that much, Loretta. He has always been good to me and I want to assure him that, even though this baby wasn't planned, we are both happy with the situation. I'll tell him that we will be marrying sooner than we had anticipated, but that it isn't a problem, because we had already discussed our future together. I will also assure him that I will look after you and my child to the best of my ability.'

Loretta knew why she had been so attracted to this man; he was such a good person. He was by no means a pushover – she knew that from listening to her father and his cronies. On the contrary, Aiden was a rising star, as her father had referred to him on more than one occasion. She loved that he wanted to do the right thing by everyone, not just by her and the baby, but also by her father, who she knew he liked and also respected.

'My dad thinks you are a great guy, Aiden.'

He grinned cheekily, but she could tell that he was already

sorting everything out in his head. That was one of things she admired about him – he thought things through, and tried to ensure that he did the best for everyone concerned. She knew that she wasn't as intelligent as he was, but he didn't mind that about her. She was confident that her dad would not be averse to their predicament – she just wished she could be as sure of his father's reaction. Because, although she had never said it to Aiden, she could tell that his dad didn't really like her at all. The comfort was, of course, that she also knew that *her* father wasn't a man that people crossed if they had an ounce of common sense.

Chapter One Hundred and Fourteen

Aiden O'Hara was looking at his son as if he had suddenly grown a set of antlers and a long, grey beard. He saw Reeva jump out of her seat and scream with excitement, and saw his brothers smiling and shaking his son's hand as they offered their congratulations. And he saw his sister sitting there with her hand covering her mouth and trying not to cry at the wonderful news. Yet all *he* wanted to do was fell that stupid fucker of a son of his to the floor. Just take him down with a huge punch to try and knock some fucking sense into him.

His son had really used his loaf; he had made sure that they were all at Reeva's house before he dropped this fucking bombshell. She had been in on it, of course, and she had cooked them an excellent meal and provided plenty of alcohol. Jade was clearly also in on the big news – she and his mother were closer than a nun's fart these days. He had to keep calm and pretend that he was on board with everything. But as Aiden Junior's father, he was surely entitled to say a few words of caution as well. That was the fatherly thing to do, after all. He plastered a smile on his face and, standing up, he went to his only son and after shaking his hand he pulled him into a manly embrace.

Aiden Junior held on to his father for a long moment. He

was so pleased that he had finally told everyone the good news. He had taken his mother's advice and waited till the whole family was there before letting his father know what had happened. Reeva had agreed with his mother, and he had done as they had advised and tried to sweeten the pill for his father as best as he could. This wasn't something his father was going to embrace and Aiden Junior wasn't happy about that. After all, his father had no real say in his life now – he was a grown man. He earned his own wage and he had proved himself more than capable in his chosen profession. It was his dad who had introduced him to this business, and he had embraced it as his father had desired.

He would love his father to, just once in his life, accept his decision about what he wanted to do, especially as this was such a momentous occasion for him. He was going to be married, and he was going to become a father. There was nothing that his dad could do to stop any of it, no matter what he might think.

'So, Ade, I assume that you have already spoken to Marvin?'

Aiden stepped away from his son and, as he walked back to his seat at the table, he was aware of the atmosphere that he had caused. Everyone in the room was suddenly struck dumb. That should have told his boy what was really going on. Aiden was pleased with the effect his words had had on the merry-makers in the room. He watched as his son sat back in his seat, and picked up his glass of wine.

'Of course Marvin knows, Dad. Loretta told her parents as soon as she found out she was pregnant.' He smiled at his mum as he said, 'I think that is a daughter thing, don't you?'

Jade nodded. 'I think you are right, mate. It's natural, really. Girls are more inclined to tell their mum first, I suppose.'

Porrick stood up and started to pour more wine into everyone's glasses. He was determined to make sure that his nephew had a good night, no matter what his brother might want. He couldn't understand how his oldest brother could try and ruin his own boy's day. He could cope with the fact that Aiden often really pissed him off, but he was fucked if he was going to sit back and see him piss all over his lad's dreams. What was wrong with the man? It was like he deliberately set out to destroy his own son's future happiness.

'I think this calls for a toast! What wonderful news, Aiden. Congratulations.' Porrick stood up then and, as he held his glass up in the air, he snapped, 'Hello, people, it's a fucking toast!'

Reeva and Jade stood up and Agnes watched as her brothers rose too. Then she looked at her brother Aiden and saw his scowling face. She wondered how this lovely day had suddenly become so frightening. She saw Patsy and Eugene raise their glasses, along with her mum and Jade, and she knew that she had to get up and join them, even though she really didn't like that she always had to take someone's side. She just wanted to keep out of it. But when Tony stood up and shouted loudly, 'Congratulations, mate! I wish you both all the best,' she stood up and toasted Aiden Junior along with everyone else. By doing so she was going against her eldest brother, which made her nervous because she depended on Aiden for everything these days – from the roof over her head to the food she cooked, which he provided.

Reeva and Jade were congratulating Aiden Junior, and the boys were all asking him questions. He was standing there, thrilled to bits, and there was her oldest brother just sitting at the table as if his son's news meant nothing to him.

Aiden Junior went over to his father and, looking into his

eyes, he said earnestly, 'Come on, Dad. Tell me you are happy for us. This is one of the best days of my life. I love Loretta, and I know that we will have a good life together.'

Aiden saw the naked longing in his son's eyes. Getting up from his seat, he opened his arms out in a gesture of supplication, as he said brokenly, 'Of course I am pleased for you, son. I want you to be happy, of course I do. But you are both so young to be having a baby.'

Reeva snorted in annoyance as she shouted, 'Oi, mister. I was only fucking fourteen when I had you, remember! And you were only twenty-one when you got Jade pregnant. Of course, as we all know, Jade was *well* over the age of consent.'

Jade was laughing as she cried, 'That's right, Reeva, rub it in, why don't you!'

Everyone joined in the laughter, and Aiden knew that he had lost the opportunity to say what he had wanted to say to his son.

'Marvin was all right then, Ade?'

They had sat back down around the table, and the atmosphere was light again. Aiden looked at his Aunt Agnes and he smiled as he answered her question.

'Marvin has been amazing considering it's his daughter, but he knows that we are serious about each other. I even asked him for her hand in marriage. He was quite chuffed, I think. He's talking about me going out to Colombia to learn the business from the supply end. He thinks that I have the temperament to deal with people, and also the acumen to work out the figures in my head. As we know, nothing is ever written down – there's never a paper trail of any kind.'

Patsy was well impressed and he said as much. 'Fucking hell, Ade! That's a real fucking compliment to you, mate. None of us lot has ever got within a donkey's roar of any of the main people involved.'

Eugene and Porrick were thrilled for him – they both got up and shook his hand with delight.

Patsy looked at his nephew with genuine respect as he added, 'You have fallen on your feet there, boy! Marvin Hendry is a good fucking bloke to have on your side. He will look after you. I know he has always liked you, but who wouldn't like you, eh? You were always a likeable kid, even when you were getting on our nerves!'

They were laughing and joking again, and Reeva motioned to Tony to open more wine. Aiden watched his son as he chatted with his uncles, and he couldn't help but wonder at why his boy, a young man, was suddenly being given the opportunity to go to Colombia to learn the supply business, when he had never once been invited out there for even a meeting.

Jade came and sat beside him and, as she sipped her wine, she said quietly, 'You all right?' When he didn't bother to answer her she leaned towards him and, putting her lips close to his ear, she whispered, 'You ruin this for our son and I swear to God that I will never forgive you.'

Agnes couldn't hear what had been said but she knew from her brother Aiden's face that, whatever it was, it wasn't anything good. She listened to the talk and the banter around the table for the rest of the evening, but her eldest brother's silence frightened her.

Chapter One Hundred and Fifteen

'There's definitely something not right, Jade. I'm sorry, darling, but he needs to get a fucking reality check.'

Jade knew that Reeva was as aware as she was of what was really ailing Aiden, but she was too shrewd to say it out loud. No one was willing to say it out loud, that was the trouble. Aiden was like the Antichrist because his son, who he should be pleased for, had been given a serious in with Marvin. Aiden couldn't see that it was something that would benefit them all. He could really be so fucking stupid at times. Any other man in their world would be over the moon to think that his son was being given such a lucrative and important position. But not her Aiden – he took it as a personal insult. To make matters worse, Jade knew that her son's refusal to listen to his father's advice was now being seen by Aiden as a declaration of war. He believed that his only son was being poisoned by Marvin Hendry and was turning into the enemy.

Usually Aiden took against people that she didn't care about enough to even bother interfering. But this time it was different – this was their *son*. And this was the one time that she couldn't help him to justify his mind-set. She knew she was guilty of making Aiden feel better about his actions when it suited her. She feigned agreement with his more suspect decisions. Take the time he'd nailed poor Peter Gunn to a door, all because he thought he had been disrespectful to him, when the lad had only been making a joke in his usual way. Turned out it was the last joke he would ever make.

That had been a really low point. With the help of Eric Palmer she had eventually straightened it out. Aiden had recognised, in the aftermath, that it wasn't exactly his finest hour, and he had been grateful for her interference. If only she had been straight with him at the time. But she hadn't called him out on his actions because, as usual, she was trying to protect him from himself, from his own anger and lunacy. She still felt sick when she remembered seeing the boy nailed to the door. After over twelve hours of hanging there he had still been alive – barely – and she had been forced to oversee not only his removal from a lock-up in Canning Town, but also his burial on the salt marshes in Essex when he died shortly after they had found him. As hard as she could be, Jade had never really got over that. His only crime had been to make one fucking joke at Aiden's expense. From what Patsy had told her, it had been a really funny joke, and on any other day Aiden would have laughed. But obviously he had not found anything even remotely amusing on *that* particular day. Aiden's weakness was his quick temper and his need to prove himself when that wasn't even really necessary. He harmed certain people because he wanted to hurt them: the men were either too good-looking, or he perceived them as some kind of a threat – if not at that particular moment in time, then he would argue that they would be dangerous in the future. Her Aiden could justify anything that pertained to his bad behaviour and she was guilty of making sure that he was proved to be right. She had always cleaned up behind him; along with Patsy and his brothers she had always been the one they called when Aiden lost his cool and fucked up.

But this time it was about their son. That Aiden could believe for one minute that his boy would ever even *think* of doing anything detrimental to his own father was fucking mental. He adored his father but, for the first time in his life, he was not doing what his father wanted him to do. She was pleased that he was taking the initiative for once. This was exactly what Aiden Junior needed. He was being given the opportunity to make his own way and make his own mark. Why his own father couldn't see that this was a fabulous opportunity was beyond her.

'Look, Reeva, I am sorting it, all right? So can we just drop the subject please?'

Reeva was annoyed but she chose not to take the conversation any further. All she had really wanted was for Jade to know that her son Aiden was on his own as far as she was concerned. He was being a prize fool and everyone in the family was aware of that. But, as usual, they were depending on Jade to sort it out. Reeva was confident that Jade would not let Aiden harm their son; at least that was what she was counting on because she was more than aware of what her eldest son was capable of. That was why she was so worried.

Chapter One Hundred and Sixteen

Eugene and Porrick were waiting for Patsy in a spieler that Patsy had purchased a few years earlier. The previous owner had owed Patsy a big favour, and he had happily signed the place over. In all honesty he had been glad to get shot of it as he was finding it harder and harder to police the fucking place. A particularly audacious murder on the premises – a bloody shooting late one night over a game of fucking cards – had been the final straw.

Patsy had hushed it up, and the man had given over the ownership without a backward glance. It was a different world these days, and he knew that he was too old to be arsed with any of it. It was an illegal drinking club in Romford and, even though the powers-that-be were aware of its existence, they knew better than to cause any aggravation. It was a lucrative little earner and, since Patsy had taken over the ownership, the clientele had suddenly found their manners.

But today, in the early afternoon, it was empty except for a barmaid and the manager. The manager was a young black guy from Mile End who was quick with figures and even quicker with his fists. Garry Coleman was a much-respected man, married to his childhood sweetheart, and the father of three young sons under five. Not exactly a conversationalist but, as Patsy always pointed out, you couldn't have everything. He did what was required, and he did it with the minimum of fuss. Even when he ejected people, he always did it in such a way that they could come back after a proper apology and the gift of a drink to soothe his anger.

The barmaid was a transsexual called Martine. She looked better than most page-three girls when in full drag – and could take down a drunken rugby player with one punch, as had been proved on more than one occasion. No one with an ounce of intelligence would ever deliberately set out to upset her; even in high heels, she was still more agile than her more masculine opponents. Basically the fucker could fight and, if pushed, fought to the death.

Porrick and Martine got on like the proverbial house on fire as they often saw each other socially. Eugene liked everyone because that was his nature so, as they sat together having a drink while they waited for Patsy, the talk was about local gossip. Martine, as always, was full of mirth; she had a seriously funny sense of humour and, as she regaled them with the story of the previous night's excitement, they were laughing so much that they didn't notice Aiden walk inside the bar area.

The doorman was an old bruiser who had really had his day but, as a daytime doorman, he was more than sufficient. He was a big lump with what Reeva always referred to as six hairs and a nit – meaning he was almost bald – and a smile like a mouthful of dog ends. He had never managed the oral-hygiene thing; it was always best when discussing anything with him to stand downwind. But he had his creds and Patsy was quite happy to let the man get himself an earn and also a bit of respect. He deserved it; he had been a bare-knuckle boxer in his youth and he had acquitted himself well, but his serious fighting days were long over.

'Something fucking funny, I assume?'

Aiden looked and sounded menacing. This was Aiden on a bad day. Looking around him at the tattered old club, Aiden wondered if they'd still bring in any punters if it wasn't for the fact that it was safe place to do a deal and lay low. And, of course, if you got drunk there was always someone to help you get home.

Martine shrugged and, standing up, said in her high voice, which she knew annoyed the likes of Aiden, 'Can I get you a drink, darling? Your usual Scotch and water?'

Aiden nodded and took a seat beside his brothers. 'This is a fucking shithole during the daytime. It needs a fucking make-over. A roof on a skip would look better!'

Eugene shook his head in denial. 'That's part of the charm. Not everyone wants a fucking state-of-the-art drinking hole, Aiden, with inflated prices for a fucking show-off clientele. I think Patsy was right to keep this as it is.'

Aiden knew that somewhere in that sentence he had just been put in his place. He decided to overlook the insult. He needed everyone onside at this moment in time. There was definite skulduggery afoot, and he wanted it all sorted quick sharp.

Garry excused himself politely and made himself busy stocking up the bar, all the while keeping a beady eye on the proceedings going on at the table. He had never entirely trusted Aiden O'Hara – not that he would ever say that, of course. He wasn't about to cause himself any unnecessary aggravation. But he had observed him over the years and he had come to the conclusion that he was more than a few fucking cakes short of a birthday party. He was a nutbag, and Garry didn't care how hard or how clever he might be, he didn't trust him and he never would. He was never rude, but he made a point of avoiding him if possible. Aiden O'Hara had too short a fuse for his liking.

Porrick had to admire Martine, she was a feisty fucker. Martine placed a large drink in front of Aiden and said, as camp as possible, 'Your drink, Aiden, just as you like it!'

Aiden looked at Martine, who was consequently fluttering her eyelashes, and he actually did laugh at the humour. He took a deep draught of his whisky and nodded happily as he said, 'You might be a poof, Martine, but you do pour a decent drink, love.'

Martine took that as her cue to leave and she smiled as she went behind the bar and automatically started to help get it ready for the evening's punters. Like Garry, she had no interest in being in Aiden O'Hara's company.

Aiden O'Hara might be respected, revered even in some circles. He was a hard man and he earned a great deal not just for himself but for everyone on his payroll – no one would ever dispute that. But the one thing that Aiden had never been and never would be was liked. He was tolerated by most people as a necessary evil and he wasn't a man that the majority of people would cross without a fucking army of some kind behind them. He was a violent fucker, who didn't need that much encouragement to find fault or take umbrage when the mood was on him.

From his position behind the bar, Garry could see that Porrick and Eugene were both uncomfortable, and he wondered at a family who were so close, and yet so far apart.

Chapter One Hundred and Seventeen

Marvin Hendry was in a serious quandary. He was in a position that he would not wish on his worst enemy – it was a fucking problem for him and the people close to him. He had been left with one final chance to try and make everything right – not just for his daughter but for everyone else concerned in this fucking stupidity.

Clearly Aiden O'Hara was not thrilled about his son's upcoming nuptials. Well, that was too fucking bad. Marvin could swallow that, though he would never forget the insult. Where business was concerned, it wasn't unusual to have to deal with people that you would not necessarily choose as your bosom buddies. Business was a different thing altogether. You might socialise with these people as part of the process when making a deal, but that was part of the game. The business they were involved in meant that you often had to accept some very strange bedfellows. It was the nature of that particular beast. What Marvin could not overlook was the fact that Aiden O'Hara, who he had always had such a good relationship with, could be so fucking cold at a time like this. He had known that Aiden O'Hara was not the most stable-minded person on the planet but that he actually had the nerve to voice his disapproval of his only son's relationship with his daughter, Loretta, well, it just confounded him. The man had to know that, if push ever came to shove, he didn't stand a fucking chance against Marvin. He might think he had London by the balls, but he wasn't dealing with London Faces now. He was now dealing with people who were known to terrify the American judicial system, who lived in a country that was devoid of anything even resembling laws if you didn't choose to obey them. He would be dealing with Colombians, as well as Jamaicans. No one could oppose them if they didn't want them to.

Loretta was his favourite child out of all his offspring; as the only girl, she needed his protection far more than his sons ever would. She was a loving and trusting girl who he had adored from the moment he had looked into her eyes. His fear had always been that she would be swept off her feet by a Bob Marley lookalike. But she had impressed him with her choice of mate; Aiden Junior was shrewd and he was respectful – and nothing like the fucking psychopath that had sired him. He was ready to learn and, unlike his father, would happily admit his failings and ask the relevant questions needed so he could learn the business properly, thereby ensuring that he would eventually go into said business with a good working knowledge behind him. It was what any intelligent man would do – he would make sure that he learned from the best so *he* could deliver his best when the time came. Marvin would trust the O'Hara boy with his Loretta. The man was exemplary in every way that mattered. He had only ever heard good things about him, and he had never had cause to question the boy's intentions where his girl was concerned.

Yet now he was hearing from all different sources that the boy's father, Aiden, the fucking strangest Face in London, was against the match and had given his boy an ultimatum. How could he dare to even insinuate that his daughter wasn't good enough for his son? It couldn't be her colour, surely, as his own brothers were black: one was Jamaican and one was an African. It was like the man had lost his mind or, as he had been told this day, it was because he didn't like his son getting the offer of being a part of the Colombian cartel. Because that is what his new son-in-law would become, of course: a valued member of that cartel, treated as an important member of the family. If what Marvin had been told was true, then Aiden's father's real problem was with the fact that his only son would eventually become far more powerful than him. Knowing the man as he did, Marvin realised that it would be Aiden's greatest fear, something he would never allow to happen. And Marvin suspected if there wasn't a plan in play already, Aiden would soon be up to skulduggery. Marvin had to think long and hard about his next steps. Whatever happened, though, he would only do what he believed was in the best interests of everybody concerned, please or offend as the case may be.

Chapter One Hundred and Eighteen

Patsy knew there was no chance his nephew was going to give her up. He wondered how he could sweeten the pill for his older brother, even though there was no way he could make this sound any fucking easier than it was.

Aiden was drunk. They were still in Patsy's bar in Romford and he had made sure that none of the usual punters gained access. Porrick and Eugene were on standby to disabuse any who felt the urge to be vocal about not being given admittance. The whole family were coming in support of Aiden Junior, well aware of the choice Aiden had given his son to leave Loretta and his unborn child.

Aiden Junior turned up early with his mum. He sat down beside his father and it was clear he knew that his dad was over the moon he was there with him, believing his decision made. Aiden was grabbing his son by his neck, and roughhousing with him, ostensibly play fighting even though everyone watching could see that he was deliberately using his strength against his son, and was physically hurting him. It was a warning and everyone, including Aiden Junior, was aware of that.

'I've always believed, my son, that when it comes down to it, you choose your family. You are one of us and don't you ever fucking forget that.'

Aiden was acting like his boy's appearance in the bar at tonight's family gathering was enough to prove to everyone that his boy would *never* dare to go against his wishes. That his only son would always follow his father's advice and his opinions, no matter what he might think himself.

Aiden Junior had turned up in the hope he could reason with his father and prove to him that marrying Loretta and working with Marvin was not a betrayal of his own family. If anything, he was doing it to make things better for them all – just as his father had done for so many years. It hurt more than he thought possible that his father didn't know him at all. How could his father believe that he would be willing to desert the mother of his child without a thought?

He had always been aware that his parents were not like his friends' parents, but he had never really cared because he had spent the greatest part of his childhood with his Nanny Reeva and his Aunt Agnes. He had worked out from a young age that his mum, as much as she loved him, needed to spend most of her time looking after his dad. He had never resented it because he had been in a house full of people who cared about him and, as he had grown up, he had preferred being with his uncles and his nanny to being with his parents. Things were so complicated and there was always drama around them when they were together. He loved them, but his mother had always made it clear that his dad was number one in the household. He had understood the importance of that all his life. His dad was a loose cannon – he had seen his father when he had one of his fucking tantrums on many occasions, and watched as his mother had talked him down. There was drama at Reeva's house too but it was a different kind of drama – and after it was over, Reeva would always feel remorse. His father, on the other hand, could never admit that he was wrong.

Now, as he listened to him pontificating to everyone around him, Aiden Junior wondered how his own father could expect him to just roll over. He was never going to do that, and the fact that his dad thought that he might really did offend him. His father seemed convinced he was betraying the family. Well, Aiden Junior felt exactly the same about his father's actions. And he didn't know how much more he could take.

Patsy made sure that there was another round of drinks delivered to the table. He squeezed his mum's shoulder and Reeva put her hand over his and squeezed it back. Porrick and Eugene were both on edge, Jade was doing her best to talk everyone down, especially Aiden, who was not only drunk but also happened to have a good bit of Charlie up his nose into the bargain, and Reeva and Tony were both trying to keep the mood light. Everyone around the table was doing the very best that they could to help them.

Even through his drunken and drugged haze, it dawned on Aiden that his son was trying to tell him that he didn't want to walk away from that fucking leech Loretta who had deliberately set out to fucking trap him. He wasn't unsympathetic; he knew that love could hurt so much more than a fucking good hiding, but he had been confident that his boy was intelligent enough to see the error of his ways. He couldn't be expected to just stand back and watch his son being fucking manipulated by a fucking half chat, with nothing of any real value to offer him. She was about as fucking useful as a nun at a bikers' gang bang.

Jade was quiet, watching what was going on, and she appreciated that the boys were making sure that the atmosphere in the club was good. Aiden stood up unsteadily and Jade immediately jumped up to help him. She motioned to Patsy, who reluctantly got up to join her, and together they held him upright. He was slurring his words and his eyes were like piss holes in the snow. Aiden was completely out of his nut, but he was absolutely determined to make his son do what he expected – what he demanded of him.

'I want to make a toast to my handsome son, my namesake, who tonight is making an important decision about his life, as you all know. And I am pleased to report that he will make the right one.'

Porrick stood up and walked away from the table with Eugene close behind him. Reeva looked at Tony and he shrugged; lighting a joint, he passed it to her quickly. Patsy grabbed his older brother by the arm and, with Jade's help, they dragged him through to the small office behind the kitchen.

Aiden sat down in the chair offered to him with relief. He knew that he was not the full ten bob tonight. But he had every reason to celebrate: his son had seen the logic of his argument. His son had seen that he was right – that family was what really mattered. Your *real* family.

He looked at Jade and Patsy and felt anger bubbling inside him. Who the fuck did these two think they were? They were both looking down on him for some reason, like they thought that he was a fucking cunt of some sort.

'Jade, is there a reason you've brought me in here? Am I about to be fucking given a line of good cocaine, or are you two just trying to annoy me?'

Jade knelt in front of him and, taking his hands in hers, she said brokenly, 'Listen to me, Aiden. You *have* to listen to me, my darling. You can't really believe that our boy would ever walk away from his girl. We brought him up better than that. He loves her and they have a baby on the way. If you don't try to get your head around this, if you don't even pretend that you can somehow accept what is going to happen, I can't help you any more. I can't make this go away, Aiden. Not this time. Marvin Hendry is not a mug. He won't sit back and let you get away with it like anyone else would. This is about more than money or business. This is about his daughter and *our* son. Why the fuck can't you see that? What is wrong with you, Aiden? How can you be jealous of your own fucking child?'

Aiden was having none of it. He understood now that they were all in league with his son. That they were all against him. 'I cannot believe that you and my brother could have the fucking front to treat me like a complete cunt, Jade. You think that I should bow my knee to Marvin fucking Hendry? That fucker should be bowing to *me*! He has poisoned my own son against me. And none of you can see it, can you?'

Patsy wondered how his brother got through the day; he could convince himself of literally anything, believe his own bollocks and then he would pass it on to them. He couldn't stay silent any longer.

'Have you never once ever listened to the people around you, Aiden? Do you really think that we are all so fucking *stupid* that we just believe every word that you tell us? Well, I have a big shock for you. We sussed you out years ago, mate. We know everything about you – the good *and* the bad, you mad bastard. Christ knows you have really pushed the fucking line at times. You are our brother and we never forget that you looked after us. But we have paid you back one hundredfold. You treat everyone around you like shit. You never once think about how the people in your life might feel about your fucking actions.

You have deliberately treated every one of us like we never meant nothing to you. You made us feel that we had to prove ourselves, and we have.'

Aiden looked at Jade and his brother and all he could see was that they were trying to put him down. They were trying to make him feel that his son's defection to Marvin Hendry and his family was something that he should just allow – and be pleased about. He was the head of this fucking family and he always had been, and he was not going to allow any of them to make him feel that he was doing something wrong. He had been taking care of everyone in his family since he was a fucking kid – how could they act like he was the enemy? He had tried to explain that he didn't trust Marvin Hendry and that should have been enough for them. He had been the only person that had made sure they were safe and looked after. They should trust his instincts and not question his motives. But now, here he was being treated like a fucking complete moron by the two people he trusted more than anybody else.

'Do you think I could really give a flying fuck about what you lot think of me? And that includes you too, Jade. I know that you would rather sit back on your fat fucking arse and watch our son throw his life away. I always knew that I would have to deal with people who didn't have the fucking brains they were born with, but I was quite happy to look after my family, and I fucking did, Patsy – don't you ever forget that. While you are all busy sucking Marvin's cock you remember that *I* was the only one there for you from day one. I think that I deserve some kind of fucking respect for doing that, don't you? A bit of fucking loyalty wouldn't go amiss.'

Patsy poured himself a large whisky. He was going to need it – his brother was evidently determined to make his point.

'This isn't about loyalty, Aiden, and you know that. This is about your only son and his first fucking chance of happiness. Why can't you admit that you are jealous of him? That your biggest problem is that your son is man enough to follow his own star. Any other man would be so fucking proud of him, but not you. That says more about *you*, Aiden, than it will ever say about your son. He has tried his hardest to bring you on board, to make you a part of his life. He was depending on you looking after him and standing beside him. We have all been witness to your fucking juvenile pettiness and we are disgusted with you. There are no other children, are there? Just your Aiden and Colin Junior. We all feel that they deserve the fucking best that we can offer them and, if that means we have to go against you and your fucking lunacy, then that is exactly what we will do, Aiden. You need a fucking wake-up call. We know that you murdered Colin Clark, and that you made sure that his brother did your dirty work for you. Believe me when I say, Aiden, that no one holds that against *him*. *You* are the bad bastard. But you are also our brother, so we were willing to overlook your fucking mentalness. But not any more. If push comes to shove, we will all be behind your son. Remember that.'

Jade could see that Aiden was able to take in the enormity of what he was being told even though he was out of his head on drink and cocaine. He would never have believed that his own family would ever go against him and, until all of this had happened, she wouldn't have either. But tonight changed everything.

Chapter One Hundred and Nineteen

Jade couldn't sleep. Aiden's showdown with Patsy was playing over and over in her head. There was a chance that there would be a fight of some description and she was determined to avoid that at all costs. She had immediately made the arrangements to bring Aiden home and he had not even attempted to stop her. That alone had told her that, paranoid as he was from the drink and the drugs, he had understood that his brothers were not willing to stand behind him this time. For so long, like her, they had made a point of pretending that they believed that his latest fucking argument was valid and that he was absolutely in the right, even when Aiden had just taken umbrage for no real reason and decided to pick a fight with someone because he felt like it.

Aiden was a bully and a fucking Looney Tunes. Jade knew that she should not be trying to protect him because he was quite willing to harm their son. It was clear now that he saw his boy as a fucking threat to him, as someone who could never again be trusted. She should not be trying to defend him. He deserved everything that was coming to him. But he was the only man that she had ever loved. She still held out hope that if she could just talk to him when he was sober and explain to him that his only son was all that they would ever have, she could make him see sense. There was still enough time for them to make sure that they were a part of his life and the life of their grandchild. If Aiden could only see that his actions were going to push him away from his closest family.

She couldn't come to terms with the way that Aiden had turned on their son – it was something she really couldn't fathom. What's more, if he went up against Marvin, as she feared he would, it would jeopardise everything they had worked for all these years. But it was their boy who was the most important thing in their lives. How could Aiden turn against their only child overnight? He had always had a really strange take on the world, but she had never believed that he would use that against his only son. It broke her heart to think that her Aiden had done this. It was an unforgivable betrayal of their family.

Chapter One Hundred and Twenty

Reeva was upset – having her sons at odds with each other was something she found difficult to cope with. The usual arguments she could deal with – that was an everyday thing with four boys who would always have their spats. But this time it was really serious.

Agnes made a pot of tea and, as she poured them both a cup, Reeva worried about what was going to happen with the family. There had been a few bust-ups over the years but never anything on this scale. It seemed the whole family were against Aiden, and that was never going to end well. She looked at her daughter and she could see the concern mirrored in her eyes. Everyone was on edge. It was like they were all waiting for the axe to drop. But just what the outcome of all this angst was going to be none of them was sure.

Chapter One Hundred
and Twenty-One

Aiden O'Hara was in a phone box in South London. Like his brothers, he never made work calls from a mobile. He believed that those phones were too intrusive for their kind of conversations. They kept times, numbers, dates – everything people in their position could well do without. Far too many of their ilk had been stitched up through what Aiden saw as complete stupidity. He didn't even trust the burner cells as he knew that if the Filth could trace it back to where it was purchased, the chances were there was CCTV. That was the problem with the modern world – everyone was being fucking monitored without even realising it. He saw himself as much shrewder than that. He was old school and he prided himself on that. He had never once sent even a text that pertained to his earn, and he was not about to start now. He made a call, and walked back to his car.

Porrick was driving him and Aiden wasn't too happy about being in the company of any of his brothers at the moment. He couldn't believe that he was getting so much fucking grief from everyone about his son's foolishness. But the call that he had just made would prove him right, and it would ensure that they all saw it from his point of view even at this late date. Oh, he had his fucking sources, and he was pulling in more than a few favours. Once he had arranged this meeting he would show his brothers just what the fuck they had to deal with. *They* were the ones who needed the fucking wake-up call, and he was going to make sure that they got just that.

Grinning pleasantly, he said to Porrick cheerily, 'Get everyone rounded up. We have a meet with an old mucker of mine, Johnny Denton. He has a story to tell that I think everyone might be interested in. We're meeting at his licensed premises in New Cross. It will be open just for us lot. Tell them I want everyone there as soon as.'

Porrick didn't answer his brother; he just did what was asked. He had been expecting something like this. They all had.

Chapter One Hundred
and Twenty-Two

Loretta was very upset, although she was trying her hardest to pretend otherwise. Aiden was being put into an impossible situation because of her and, knowing how much he thought of his dad, she could understand that the situation was really difficult for him and his family. But she was having his child, and she just couldn't understand why his dad was so against them being together. Her father was thrilled at the prospect, while Aiden's father thought it was a terrible situation.

For the first time in her life she had come up against somebody who did not like her. Even though she could see why his father might think they were far too young to be starting a family, she had not expected such harsh criticism. And, even though her Aiden had assured her that his father's opinion meant nothing to him, she still could not help being sad that she was the reason for them to be at odds. She could never remember a time in her life when she had been on the receiving end of someone else's utter dislike. This kind of reaction had really knocked her confidence. She had never before felt unwanted or not good enough.

Of course her dad wasn't happy about Aiden O'Hara's behaviour and, knowing what she did about her father, she was frightened of how he might react. She was well aware of her father's reputation; she always had been. Her father wasn't a man who suffered fools gladly; he was dangerous even by Jamaican standards – and that meant he was capable of real fucking bastardy. That was her mother's description of her father, not hers, though she knew now that her mother had just been trying to prepare her for the day when she would find out the truth about her family. Most people were terrified of him – of his temper along with his refusal to ever accept what he saw as an insult, which was something that he seemed to have in common with Aiden's father. Loretta knew exactly what her father was capable of but it suited them both if she pretended that she had no real idea of his businesses. She was grateful that he liked her Aiden, and she trusted him to do whatever was needed to see that they would stay together. He was ruthless and, even though she wasn't as savvy or as clever as everyone else in her family, she was shrewd enough to know that much. What's more, she didn't care what happened to Aiden's dad. There was a part of her that was as ruthless as her father. The strangest thing of all was she had not really known that until now.

Chapter One Hundred
and Twenty-Three

'I wish you weren't so fucking hard-headed, Aiden. That Loretta is lovely, and Aiden Junior is crazy about her. All the family are against you on this. Doesn't that tell you anything?'

Aiden sighed heavily. His brother was really pissing him off because while there was a big part of him that knew he was being unreasonable, he couldn't backtrack now after everything he had said. It was too late. Anyway, he didn't want to. He didn't *want* to see his only son tie himself to that little fucking Jamaican booty. Because that was all she was – he didn't care what anyone said. She wasn't good enough for his lad.

'Fuck off, Porrick. You will not understand my problem until it's *your* son tying himself to a fucking leech like her.'

Porrick started laughing then. 'Oh, Aiden! Listen to yourself for five minutes. That girl will be the making of him. She's a really nice lass. What is going on in your fucking brain? Please, tell me. You are supposed to be the clever bastard, remember?'

Aiden was fuming. Wasn't it enough that he had voiced his disapproval already? What did they want? A fucking government White Paper on it?

'Look, Porrick, just shut the fuck up. I guarantee that after tonight you will understand my logic. Until then, give me a fucking break.'

Porrick pulled the car off the road and braked quickly. Then, turning to his oldest brother, he looked at him for a long moment. Aiden knew that his little brother was trying to talk to him sensibly, but it was too late for that. He was sad that his brothers could not see that he was just doing what he had always done – looking out for his family. To think that they were willing to turn against him was something he would never have believed possible. But that is exactly what had happened.

'You can still make this right, mate. Honestly, bruv, just remember that your son is the father of Loretta's baby. He is fucking mental on her, and she is mental about him. Why can't you see that this is a good thing? Why are you so determined to cause murders when there is no logical reason to do so? It's like you are on a fucking death wish. Like you are so out of touch with everyone around you that you can't see what is really going on. Please, Aiden, listen to me. *No one* wants this situation – least of all your boy, your own son. He is in fucking bits. All he wants is for you to respect his choice of partner.'

Aiden O'Hara was looking at his youngest brother with scepticism and anger. Who the fuck did they all think they were? It was like everything that he had ever done for them had been forgotten overnight. Like he was suddenly this bad bastard, when all he wanted was the best for his boy – that was all he had ever wanted.

'I know that you all think that I have a problem with Marvin, and I do. Because he has never once offered any of us an in on the Colombian end of our deals. I was always suspicious about that. Now it seems that he suddenly wants to groom my boy. Suddenly he thinks that there is a place for my son to become a part of it. Well, I have good reason not to buy that and we're going to do something about it.'

Porrick was shaking his head in abject consternation. He couldn't believe what he was hearing. It was like his older brother, who he had revered all his life, had feet of clay. He knew that his brother had to know on some level that there was no way in the world anyone was going to even give this shite houseroom.

'Again, Aiden, can you fucking hear yourself? You sound just like one of our dealers trying to talk their way out of trouble. No one is buying your bullshit. This is all about you having a problem with your only son getting a big push into the upper echelons of the Colombian cartel. He is a clever lad, Ade, he deserves everything that he gets. Think about this: do you honestly think that someone like Marvin would bother to push him forward if he didn't think that he could be an asset? Marvin has sons that he has never bothered to bring into his businesses. He knows their limitations. Marvin Hendry would not even dream about bringing our Aiden into the fold if he didn't think that he could acquit himself well. That stands to reason, Aiden. Your son is being given a fucking golden opportunity. And into the bargain he is going to get the love of his life, the girl of his dreams, and what have you done for him? You have made his fucking life a misery, because no matter how you try to dress it up everyone knows that you just can't hack your boy achieving more than you. It's fucking laughable, Aiden. None of us could believe that you could actually be so fucking petty, and so fucking childish.'

'Why don't you just shut the fuck up, and drive us to our destination, eh? I am going to overlook your fucking stupidity because you are my baby brother.'

Aiden was so furious he was having trouble controlling himself but he was trying to keep a lid on his anger until his brothers had listened to what Johnny Denton had to say. He was completely confident that, once they had heard his story, they would understand exactly what he needed to do. That fucker Marvin deserved everything that was coming to him. He was looking forward to it and hearing everyone's apologies for ever questioning Aiden O'Hara.

Chapter One Hundred
and Twenty-Four

Jade and Agnes were sitting with Reeva in the local pub. It was busy and Reeva was on top form, ordering drinks and keeping them entertained with jokes and outlandish stories. It never ceased to amaze Agnes how many of the local people actually did like her mum, considering some of her outrageous escapades. She couldn't help being impressed with how easily her mother managed to slip back into people's good books. But that was her mum's forte. She could be having a stand-up fight with someone on the Monday and swearing undying friendship to them by the Wednesday.

Agnes knew that people's willingness to forgive had a lot to do with her mum's sense of fair play. On more than one occasion her mother had helped other women out financially, even if she was not talking to them at that particular moment in time. Her mum had always had a soft spot for women like herself – women alone and trying to bring up families without a man behind them. Even if Reeva had engaged in an all-out punch-up with another woman – and that wasn't exactly a rare occurrence – if she heard that the same woman needed help she would be the first one to go around to her house and offer them whatever they might need. There were more than a few women on the estate who could thank Reeva for making sure that they didn't lose their homes, get their electric cut off or that their kids didn't go hungry. The funny thing was, she was quite happy to be seen as the bad bastard, the argumentative fuck, but she could never handle when she was being offered thanks or gratitude. As Agnes has pointed out, that was a good thing because it proved that Reeva was doing her good turns for the right reasons. Reeva had never forgotten where she came from – she refused to leave the house she had brought up her kids in, even though Aiden could have bought her a mansion. It wasn't her style, she said.

Jade was drinking her wine steadily, and that wasn't like her. Agnes sensed that there was something going on – there was a reason that her mum was drawing so much attention to them all. Agnes was frightened, but she wasn't sure what she was frightened of.

She saw Timmy Clark walk into the pub with her son, and she felt a sudden relief inside her chest. She stood up quickly and beckoned them both over. Colin Junior ran to her side and she hugged him tightly to her.

'Did you have a lovely time, Col?'

He pulled away from her and said loudly, 'Yes, Mum! Come on, Uncle Timmy. Show Mummy what you bought me.'

Jade stood up and hugged Timmy hello, and he squeezed her tightly. Then he bent down and pecked Reeva on her cheek. They were both making sure that people remembered them, though Reeva and Agnes didn't realise any of that yet. Timmy could feel Jade's body trembling, and his heart went out to her. But, unlike her, he wasn't upset about what was happening tonight.

Chapter One Hundred
and Twenty-Five

'I need a piss, Aiden.'

Porrick had pulled into a lay-by and shut off the engine. It was a quiet lane and, without the headlights on, it was dark and menacing.

'Well, fucking hurry up, Porrick. I ain't got all night.'

Porrick quickly lit a joint and, taking a couple of deep tokes, he handed it over to his brother, saying jokily, 'Take a fucking chill pill, will you! Honestly, Aiden, it's like you deliberately get up in the mornings determined to fucking irritate everyone around you. Jesus wept. I just need a piss. Relax, will you?'

Aiden took a deep puff on the joint and, grabbing his brother by the arm, he stopped him from exiting the car. 'Look, Porrick, I know you are all fucked off with me over this business with Marvin and my boy. But, honestly, I can't in all conscience allow my boy to get himself involved with that cunt. He is deliberately trying to row me out. I can tell what's going on. Marvin sees this situation as an opportunity to not only take my fucking son away from me but also to turn all of my own brothers against me. But you lot just don't see it.'

Porrick sighed heavily. 'We don't *see* it though, Aiden, because it's a load of old fucking fanny. You really can't tell that all you have done with your usual determination is make us turn against you?'

Aiden O'Hara looked at his youngest brother. Porrick would always be the baby boy, the smallest of them all. But his size had never mattered, because Porrick could have a fucking fight, a real punch-up.

'Do you remember, Porrick, when I had to go up the school about you, that first time? You had hammered the fuck out of a kid twice your size and two years older. I remember taking you home and thinking that you would be all right. I knew that you could look after yourself. It was a weight off my mind, if I'm honest.'

Porrick laughed his deep, husky laugh. 'I remember that, of course I do. Dafydd Jones, a Welsh bastard who thought that he was the dog's fucking gonads.'

They were both laughing together now. Porrick got out of the car and Aiden could hear him pissing into the bushes.

'Here, Aiden, come and look at this, mate.'

Aiden got out of the car and stretched lazily. He walked to his brother's side saying, 'This is a lovely puff, Porrick. I am feeling very mellow! What am I supposed to be looking at, bruv?'

Porrick zipped up his flies slowly and, smiling genially, he turned to his older brother and, shaking his head sadly, he said, 'I'm so sorry, Aiden. But it is better this way, mate.'

Aiden O'Hara felt the sharp pain as his little brother stabbed him in his groin and watched in shock as he felt Porrick drag the knife up through his stomach and up to his heart. His brother, his youngest brother who he loved, had just gutted him like a fish. He had taught him well. That was all he could think of. He had taught the fucker well.

He dropped on to his knees and Porrick held him gently as he laid him on to the grass verge. As Porrick removed the knife, Aiden felt the pain as his insides tumbled out of his belly and on to the dirt. He tried to hold them in with his hands, but it was already far too late.

Porrick knelt down beside Aiden and pulled his brother's head on to his lap. He held him in his arms and waited patiently for him to bleed out. He had tears running down his face as he said brokenly, 'You just couldn't listen to fucking reason, could you?'

Aiden was unable to talk, he could feel his throat filling up with blood. There was so much blood. Porrick was cradling him still, and Aiden could see the devastation in his eyes. He could feel all the love that his brother had for him.

'I'm so sorry, Aiden. But this is for the best, mate. Believe me, this is the lesser of two evils. You always had to push everything to the limit. Well, this time you really did push everyone too far – especially Aiden Junior. I couldn't let your son do this to you. I promised Jade that I wouldn't let that happen. You were never going to leave Johnny Denton's alive. You had to have known that. So I decided to sort this out by myself. I owed you that much, Aiden.'

Aiden O'Hara passed away in his youngest brother's arms quietly and without saying a word. Porrick held him tightly and prayed for the repose of his brother's soul. He had a feeling that Aiden O'Hara was going to need as many prayers as he could get.

Getting up, he went to the car, opened the boot and took out a can of petrol. He soaked his brother's body, and the surrounding area, then he set fire to him.

He drove away slowly, knowing that he had done the best

thing for everyone concerned. He had promised Jade that he would personally make sure that his brother died with dignity and he felt that he had, at least, kept his side of the bargain. He had been determined to ensure that his nephew would not have to live with the knowledge that he had murdered his own father, even though Aiden Junior had been more than willing to do that and had been angry enough to do what he thought was right. Porrick could see the boy's logic but he couldn't in all conscience allow that lad to do something he would have to live with for the rest of his days. Jade felt the same way and that was why she had asked him to be the go-between. And why he had promised her that he would make sure that her Aiden would not die surrounded by hatred.

He drove to the meet covered in his brother's blood, but certain that he had done the right thing. He put the radio on and the record playing at that moment was The Hollies, 'He Ain't Heavy, He's My Brother'. Porrick O'Hara felt that it was a fitting tribute to the man that he had just left behind him burning into the dirt and completely unrecognisable. He was a man none of them would ever forget, but who none of them would ever really mourn, either.

Aiden had forced his family to make a choice, and that is exactly what they had done. There was an old Irish saying of his nan's that used to make them laugh when they were kids: 'May God forgive you, because I won't.' Porrick could not help but think it was more than apt this night.

Epilogue

My son, may you be happier than your father,

Sophocles (c. 496–406 BC)

2016

Reeva was very drunk, but she was not so drunk she couldn't work out what was going on around her. Tony Brown thought she was the funniest thing that he had ever seen and Reeva couldn't help but see the funny side of it herself, even though she knew that she was the butt of the big joke.

Tony grabbed her hand and squeezed it tightly. 'You're a fucking girl, Reeva, do you know that?'

She laughed with him. 'That is part of my fatal charm, darling!'

Agnes shook her head in despair; her mother was never going to change and it was pointless to think otherwise. Reeva and Tony had more fights in a week than Sky Sports could boast in a year. They fought with every ounce of their being, and then they would make up as if nothing had really occurred. They wore her out at times with their antics. But, for all that, Tony had been the only man to ever stay with her mum, stand beside her, and offer her his strength. He was also the only man, other than her sons, who had ever defended her when she needed it, and Tony was seen by Reeva's kids as a saint. He did really care about her and, knowing her like they all did, they could not help but think the best of him.

Agnes looked around her garden and felt really happy at how

this party was progressing. She was thrilled to be hosting this event for her nephew and his lovely wife. She was now the party queen, and she loved it. Aiden and Loretta were five years married, and they had two gorgeous sons. They were a wonderful couple and Jade loved that they were living near to her, as she had told Agnes on more than one occasion. She felt she could enjoy her grandchildren in a way she had never been able to enjoy her own son, since she had spent most of her time policing Aiden. Loretta was a really nice girl, and they were all mad about her. She had fitted into the family immediately. She didn't want anything other than to be a mum and to be Aiden's wife; that was all she aspired to and Aiden Junior was more than happy with that.

Agnes watched as Marvin Hendry made a big fuss of her son, and that pleased her. As he had got older, she could see more and more of his father in Colin. He had her colouring, but he had his father's features. Her Colin was never going to win any awards – he wasn't an academic – but he was savvy enough in his own way. He was already destined for the family business, and there was nothing she could do about that. She loved that he had that easy way with him that his father had possessed – he was charming, as her mum had always said.

Eugene was standing by the bar with a beautiful young woman called Christine Mayer. He was smitten, as Reeva had informed them. It was not before time either. Patsy was with them too, and his new wife, Hannelore, was five months pregnant. Patsy was as pleased as punch. He had met and married Hannelore within six months, and they were a really good couple. Hannelore was a woman who had met the man of her dreams, but who had the sense to know that the man of her dreams needed taking in hand. She had done just that and no one could fault her. Reeva thought she was the greatest thing since sliced bread. She had been convinced that her sons would never settle down. Now there was a definite future for them on the cards, and that was all that Reeva could ask for. Even her Porrick, God love him, was living with a lovely black guy called Ernest. He was absolutely gorgeous, and he adored Reeva. They even took her on holiday with them, which she loved. She didn't care that her boy was gay – she embraced it. She loved that he had someone to care for and who cared for him.

Her sons had really blossomed in the last few years. It was as if, after Aiden had been murdered, the whole family had somehow changed, and they had changed for the better. Aiden's death had somehow shifted the dynamics of her family.

Reeva had taken her eldest son's murder really badly. She had grieved for him with such pain, it had been hard for her kids to witness, but they had all been there for her, and she loved them for that. Jade had taken his death even worse than Reeva. She had been devastated. It was as if she had aged dramatically overnight, ravaged by grief and guilt. It was only the birth of her first grandson that had pulled her through and helped her accept the decision she'd made.

The newspapers had made such a big story out of his death, about how he had been murdered and his body burned. They had not skimped on any of the details, glorifying the violence of Reeva's son's death at every available opportunity. The truth was never uncovered, of course, and it was still dragged up every now and again when a gangland murder hit the news. But, eventually, Reeva and Jade had both come to terms with the truth of Aiden's demise, and they were closer than ever.

Agnes knew how hard her brother's death had hit Jade. She had loved that man much more than he had ever deserved – not that she would ever say that, of course. Like so much in her family, the less said the better for all concerned. Agnes sighed sadly. Whatever her brother Aiden might have been guilty of, he had always been very good to her and her son, even though as time had gone on, she had begun to form her own opinion on what had really happened to her Colin. She was enough of an O'Hara to know that nothing was ever as it seemed and it was likely Aiden had had a hand in it. There were some things you were better off not knowing about though. All this fucking talk these days about facing up to the truth and owning the truth! The truth will set you free! It was such complete and utter bollocks. Whoever had coined that phrase had never lived in a family like hers. Well, one thing she had learned over the years was the truth was often not as fucking spectacular as it was made out to be. Sometimes, as Jade had said to her on more than one occasion, the truth was the last thing you needed in your life. The truth could be brutal, and the truth could open up old wounds that were best left alone. The truth was not all it was cracked up to be.

Agnes looked around her at the people she loved, and she knew that if some truths were ever blurted out in her family it would cause fucking ructions. She couldn't help smiling to herself, because despite everything she had done to step as far away from her family as possible, she was more like them than even they could know.

Jade was in the kitchen pouring herself a drink when Porrick joined her.

'All right, darling?'

Jade smiled sadly. 'I'm good, Porrick. How's that lovely man of yours?'

He pointed out to the patio where Reeva was the centre of attention. 'Dancing with me mother. Honestly, Jade, they are like fucking yin and yang. He loves her!'

Jade couldn't help laughing. She saw her two grandsons as they danced with Reeva, and she saw Marvin Hendry join them on the dance floor. Her handsome son pulled his wife into his arms and danced her over to join the party. Marvin and Reeva were going at it with everything they had. Porrick grabbed Jade around her waist and hugged her to him.

'You all right, Jade?'

She smiled sadly. ''Course I'm all right, Porrick. Why wouldn't I be?'

They stood together watching the party going on outside. They were alone in the kitchen and that suited them. There was a bar outside, but they both knew that the decent drinks were in the kitchen or, as Agnes called it, 'the family self-service bar'. They watched as Timmy Clark walked over to Agnes and start chatting to her. He had just arrived and they both knew that Agnes had been looking out for him for most of the evening.

'I wish those two would just fucking come out and admit they are together. He has been knocking her off for years!'

Jade nodded in agreement. 'I know but it's up to them, Porrick. Sufficient to the time thereof. Fucking hark at me!'

Porrick laughed with her. 'Jade Dixon, quoting the fucking Bible! Will wonders never cease!'

They both cracked up with laughter before Porrick said seriously, 'Look at your grandsons, Jade. Such handsome little fuckers. Your Aiden really fell on his feet with Loretta.'

Jade nodded sadly. 'I know that, Porrick. I have always known that.'

She turned to face him and, looking into his eyes, she said softly, 'Let it go, Porrick, please. You did the right thing. You did something that I will always love you for. Because of you no one will ever know for sure what might have happened that day.'

Porrick swallowed down his whisky and Coke. Jade was as aware as he had been that Aiden Junior would have ended up having to murder his own father if Porrick had not taken things into his own hands. Who could have blamed him? It wasn't as if Aiden had not asked for it – he had pushed everyone around him to the limit of their endurance. That was what he had always been so fucking good at. Aiden had never been happier than when he thought that he had the upper hand; even when he was dealing with people who, by rights, should have been so far below his radar, he was still petty enough to enjoy bullying them. That was one of the main reasons why Porrick had lost all respect for him.

But that didn't mean he didn't feel bad about taking his oldest brother out, even though he knew that he would do it all again if he had to. He had taken it upon himself to remove his brother Aiden from this earth, because he had known that it was a foregone conclusion anyway. The only question had been who was going to be guilty of his brother's murder. He had decided that it would have to be him. He knew that he had to protect his nephew and his brothers. Marvin Hendry couldn't be a part of it either because, at the end of the day, this was still Aiden Junior's father. Porrick had wanted to do it by the end – he had actually wanted to kill his own brother, and he had gutted him like a fucking fish. He should have shot him, but he didn't want to shoot him. He wanted it to be up close and personal.

'I still feel guilty, Jade, but not about Aiden. I would do it again in a heartbeat. He asked for everything that he fucking got. But I feel guilty about you, Jade, and my mum. Because, whatever he was, I know that you both loved him.'

Jade sighed sadly. 'We all loved him, Porrick – that will never be in dispute. But, truthfully? Both me and your mum were so fucking relieved to finally be free of him in the end. He was like a cancer – he was toxic and he was dangerous. It took us both a while before we could actually admit that to each other. But really, Porrick, never doubt that you did us a favour.'

Porrick was really taken aback at Jade's words.

She laughed then, a real throaty, dirty laugh. 'We both knew what he really was. We just didn't want to admit it.' She poured them both large whiskies. 'Come on, Porrick, one last toast.'

He picked up his glass and held it up. 'OK, then.'

Jade gently touched her glass to his, as she said loudly, 'To Reeva's boys.'

Porrick said quickly, 'Or what's left of them, anyway!'

Jade laughed with him. Porrick swallowed his drink down in one and immediately refilled the glasses.

Agnes and Reeva walked into the kitchen together and Reeva put her hands on her ample hips as she said drunkenly, 'I heard that!'

Reeva was as pleased as punch to hear them saying 'Reeva's boys'. She liked hearing that. What she didn't like hearing was the 'what's left of them' jibe. That really hurt. But she wasn't going to cause any upset about it. It was over, it was in the past. It was something that had broken her heart and it was also something that she had learned to live with.

Reeva grabbed them both and started to pull them towards the door. 'Come on, you pair, we want you all outside.'

Agnes was already opening the door wide and, as they trooped out together to join in with the dancing, Jade and Porrick started laughing together again. Between them, they started to round everyone up.

Reeva O'Hara looked around her and she saw all her family and she knew that, no matter what had happened, and no matter what she had done, her children had always loved her and they had always forgiven her. She saw Tony Brown smiling as her children and grandchildren surrounded her, and he saw his Reeva beaming with happiness. The DJ was playing The Pointer Sisters, and Reeva's kids were singing along to 'We Are Family'. Reeva knew that was the truth. It broke her heart that it had taken the violent death of her firstborn son to bring them all together like this, and to admit that, as much as she had loved him, he had been willing to smash the family apart to achieve his own ends. She knew that his demise had been manufactured by someone in her immediate family. She wasn't a fool – she had just not wanted to know the details. Her Aiden was dead and gone, and now she had all of her remaining family around her and there would be no more upsets and no more heartbreak. She wouldn't have it any other way.